A PLUME BOOK

ALL THE STARS CAME OUT THAT NIGHT

KEVIN KING is a published poet whose work has appeared in *Ploughshares*, the *Threepenny Review*, and the *Prairie Schooner*. This is his first novel.

Praise for *All the Stars Came Out That Night*

"King's set pieces capture the era, and his droll cast of characters, fictional and historical, provide the entertainment of a World Series skybox seat."
—*Publishers Weekly* (starred review)

"Fans of W. P. Kinsella, sports history nuts, and anyone drawn to prewar popular culture should sprint for this book. It's a bracing, bottom-of-the-ninth grand slam." —*Kirkus* (starred review)

"King's fantasy for seamheads is in a league of its own."
—*Entertainment Weekly*

"You don't have to be an expert in baseball history to enjoy the novel. King brings names you may only recognize from the record book to life and taps into the imagination of baseball fans in a way that isn't done much since the national pastime turned into just another sport." —*SI.com*

"[A] home run of a first novel." —*USA Today Sports Weekly*

"King's debut novel is a wonderful portrait of the culture of Depression-era America—in all its glory and its ugliness. The excitement of what would have been the greatest game ever played is an extra treat." —*Charlotte Observer*

"King's play-by-play description of the greatest game never played is alone worth the price of admission." —*Pittsburgh Tribune-Review*

"[You don't] have to like baseball to like *All the Stars Came Out That Night*. Limiting its readers to baseball fans is roughly the equivalent of telling people they'll like *Ragtime* only if they like the music of Scott Joplin."
—*Richmond Times-Dispatch*

"Baseball fans will find much to love in this novel; casual readers will find in it a great story with lots of laughs, a few tears, a sharp sense of history—and the tickle of 'what if.'" —*Wichita Eagle*

ALL THE STARS
CAME OUT
THAT NIGHT

A NOVEL

KEVIN KING

A PLUME BOOK

PLUME
Published by Penguin Group
Penguin Group (USA) Inc., 375 Hudson Street, New York, New York 10014, U.S.A.
Penguin Group (Canada), 90 Eglinton Avenue East, Suite 700, Toronto, Ontario, Canada M4P 2Y3
(a division of Pearson Penguin Canada Inc.)
Penguin Books Ltd., 80 Strand, London WC2R 0RL, England
Penguin Ireland, 25 St. Stephen's Green, Dublin 2, Ireland (a division of Penguin Books Ltd.)
Penguin Group (Australia), 250 Camberwell Road, Camberwell, Victoria 3124, Australia
(a division of Pearson Australia Group Pty. Ltd.)
Penguin Books India Pvt. Ltd., 11 Community Centre, Panchsheel Park, New Delhi – 110 017, India
Penguin Group (NZ), 67 Apollo Drive, Mairangi Bay, Auckland 1311, New Zealand
(a division of Pearson New Zealand Ltd.)
Penguin Books (South Africa) (Pty.) Ltd., 24 Sturdee Avenue, Rosebank, Johannesburg 2196,
South Africa

Penguin Books Ltd., Registered Offices: 80 Strand, London WC2R 0RL, England

Published by Plume, a member of Penguin Group (USA) Inc. Previously published in a Dutton
edition.

First Plume Printing, March 2007
10 9 8 7 6 5 4 3 2 1

Copyright © Kevin B. King, 2006
All rights reserved

Ⓟ REGISTERED TRADEMARK—MARCA REGISTRADA

The Library of Congress has catalogued the Dutton edition as follows:

King, Kevin.
All the stars came out that night : a novel / Kevin King.
p. cm.
ISBN 0-525-94905-4 (hc.)
ISBN 978-0-452-28762-4 (pbk.)
1. World Series (Baseball)—Fiction.   2. St. Louis Cardinals (Baseball team)—Fiction.   3 Detroit
Tigers (Baseball team)—Fiction.   4. Baseball players—Fiction.   5. Baseball teams—Fiction.   I.
Title.

PS3611.I5833A79   2005
813'.6—dc22   2005006514

Printed in the United States of America
Original hardcover design by Daniel Lagin

PUBLISHER'S NOTE
This is a work of fiction. Names, characters, places, and incidents are either the product of the author's
imagination or are used fictitiously, and any resemblance to actual persons, living or dead, business es-
tablishments, events, or locales is entirely coincidental.

"I did it for my father, who was an exalted man."

—Ty Cobb

This novel is dedicated to the memory of my father, Jack King

CONTENTS

PART TWO: CHOOSING SIDES

PART THREE: THE GREATEST GAME EVER PLAYED

THE GREATEST TEAM
OF ALL TIME

Well, one could quibble with this selection, because it's timeless. Center field is Mercury. What could he not run down? Catcher, I'd choose Zeus. On a passed ball he could easily produce another from his thigh, and who would challenge him on the rules? At third I'd have Charon. Try to get past him, especially with those hounds that make pit bulls look like toy poodles. Venus—on the mound, of course. When she goes into the stretch, who could keep his eye on the ball? First base would be a mortal, Frank Chance, the anchor of the double play trio—Tinker to Evers to Chance. Let me explain the choice, with reference to short and second, neither mortal nor immortal—Scylla and Charybdis: I just love the sound of the double play combination—Scylla to Charybdis to Chance, and the human injects some degree of fallibility, which makes it more interesting. And obviously nothing is getting through up the middle, between those peaks of perception. Left field, Paul Bunyan. I like his stick. In right field, Homer. Someone has to write about it, epically.

—Walter Winchell

PREFACE

This is Walter Winchell and this is my last story. It's coming to you from the grave, because I swore I would never write about the greatest game ever played. Wherever I am now, baseball doesn't really matter. That promise was my ticket to the game. You might have heard rumors about it—I'm talking about the last great barnstorming game between All-Star teams from the Negro Leagues and the Major Leagues, in October of 1934, in Fenway Park, in Boston.

The white players didn't talk because Kenesaw Mountain Landis, quondam commissioner of baseball, threatened to ban from the Major Leagues anyone who talked, the way he banned Shoeless Joe Jackson. The Negro players didn't talk because Landis promised them that colored players would be playing in the Major Leagues within ten years. As it turned out, that was a lie, but it was understood among them that Landis was trying. Branch Rickey was already scouting Negro players eight years later, in '42. By '44 he was in Cuba, talking directly to Jackie Robinson, so everybody knew the wheels were in motion. It was too late for Josh Gibson, though, and it killed him that they were scouting Robinson, who literally couldn't swing Gibson's fifty-six-ounce bat and metaphorically couldn't carry it, period. And Jackie, when he came up, was far from an All-Star fielder.

Who else at the game might talk? Darrow? He died about a year later, as did Knowledge Clapp. Shoeless Joe? Who would believe a man banned from baseball? George Raft? He was a baseball fanatic and honor-bound to his best friend, Leo Durocher. Henry Ford? He did everything he could to distance himself from it. And those guys working the lights were executed for kidnapping, a few years later. That leaves Carole Lombard, my favorite actress from the thirties, after Dietrich. For her it was either a promise to Raft, or my threat to tell my colleague-in-ink, Louella Parsons, the real color of her hair.

The thirties was the decade of Prohibition and the Depression and lawlessness—Capone, Dillinger, Bonnie and Clyde, Pretty Boy Floyd, Bugsy Siegel, Owney Madden. There were the stars that played the gangsters—Cagney, Raft, Bogart, Robinson. It was the golden era of Hollywood and baseball. It was Lindbergh, the flights and the kidnapping. And that's how our story starts, with a couple of kidnappings. Not to mention the kidnapping of baseball by white players and owners. I say "players," because it's hard to underestimate the impact of redneck stars like Ty Cobb, Rogers Hornsby, and Cap Anson. Anson devoted much of his life to keeping Negroes out of baseball. The last person of color to play in the Major Leagues was Moses Fleetwood Walker, in 1889. After that a few did play, but not as blacks. They were snuck in as Indians. Everyone had a "Chief" something-or-other, for a while. Of the great players in the Negro Leagues in 1934, only Satchel Paige made it to the Majors—he pitched for Cleveland in '48 and '49 and for the St. Louis Browns from '51 to '53, and was *Sporting News* rookie of the year at age forty-two. I remember Casey Stengel saying, "We've got to get ahead by the sixth, 'cause if we don't, the Browns bring in that damned old man and we're sunk."

In 1934, Dizzy Dean went 30-7, arguably one of the best seasons of any Major League pitcher. Dean was no model for social reform in race issues in general, but baseball was different. On the field what mattered was how you played the game. Dean and Satchel Paige played against each other in barnstorming games often enough to earn the other's respect, even friendship. Those barnstorming games were played in the post-season by thrown-together teams, sometimes literally behind someone's barn, anywhere they could draw a crowd that paid admission. In 1934 Diz made almost as much money barnstorming as he did in salary from the Cardinals. His toughest opponent, the black fellow with a strong arm was just that, a fellow. That year Paige had probably his best season, at 13-3, with a 1.99 TRA—*total* runs allowed, not just earned. Biz Mackey, the second-best catcher of the Negro Leagues, after Gibson, said Paige's fastball would "hop a little at the end of the line. Beyond that, it tends to disappear. Yes, disappear. I've heard about Satchel throwing pitches that weren't hit but that never showed up in the catcher's mitt either. They say the catcher, the umpire, and the bat boys looked all over for that ball, but it was gone. Now, how do you account for that?"

How do you? That October night in Fenway a ball did disappear, but it wasn't a *throwed* ball, it was a hit ball, the legend of which is finally being told.

PART ONE
KIDNAPPERS

1

MUMBLETY-PEG

You make a pool hall the same way you make a schoolhouse. First you lay the planks you're going to walk on. Then you lay out two longitudinal logs and notch them for the cross-logs. And so forth, making allowances for a front door, a back door, and windows on all but the north side. You want a door big enough to accommodate a full-sized pool table. Then you saw yourself shingles for the roof. Once it's constructed, there's not much difference what goes on inside. In the schoolhouse you learn the three Rs and how you're supposed to behave in good company. In the pool hall you learn the geometry of angles in a hands-on way, learn to read the lie of the table, learn to chalk up a won game, and you learn *not* to interact with your peers, similarly piped out of the schoolhouse by a game. Like James Atwood Gray, who had no peer at mumblety-peg and was at least a cut above anyone in Ossage, Kansas, at pool in 1933.

In school James Atwood Gray was average in every way except his mouth, which ultimately got him expelled. He felt sorry for *the sine, the cosine, the tangent*—the suffocating compatibility of three peas in a mathematical pod, their every function predictable or provable, the perfectly wrapped present, the perfectly made bed, no corner untucked, and inside was everything that could be predicated of regular shapes, their mouths sewed shut by those *Three Fates*, and revealed by Mrs. Pearly, his geometry teacher. Unable to fathom any of the nebulous world in which Euclid worked his fabulous propositions, James Atwood became the Clarence Darrow of the merely numerate, docked for their insufficient or shabby proofs. Ultimately, it was his defense of his sweetheart Hanna Dunwoody that got him expelled. "So what if the 'e' done gallivanted from Hanna's 'sin_,' " he announced to Mrs. Pearly. It was obvious to James Atwood that Hanna was being docked for the axiomaticity of her chest. "You're just jealous cuz her tits are bigger than yers."

"You open your mouth again, James Atwood, and I'll kick you upside the head."

"You're as flat as Kansas. That's why you teach *plane* geometry, ain't it?"

What James Atwood learned instead was patience. He learned to wait his turn, playing mumblety-peg by himself while some stranger beat regulars Malachy Grimes and Spottswood Love out of their stakes. His thumb grew callous where the awl-point of his jackknife began its series of flips before striking the dirt or a pine board. He learned to let a stranger challenge, coax, blandish, even spot him before folding up the jackknife and picking up a cue stick. He learned not to lose the wet-behind-the-ears look, the aw-shucks voice, augmented by a naturally slow, monotone delivery. But every hustler has a run of bad luck. James Atwood Gray's came on an early December night. After two days of snow a warm front moved in, alternating the snow with freezing rain. Not many folks ventured out. At the pool hall that went by his first name, Eddie Moss opened cans of pork and beans and heated them in a battered, dented tin pan for the hungry. Duane Brown stopped in twice, on his rounds of saloons. Once to see what was going on, and once because he mistook the pool hall for a tavern. Each time that he left, he had to walk up the street to find his horse-pulled wagon, because his horse was tired of being beaten and just took off. When Duane's grandfather's slaves ran off, the old man would whip them with a cat-o'-nine-tails, then rub salt and red pepper into the wounds. The horse's delinquency was punished in equally cruel but less imaginative ways.

Duane was nearly hit by a toboggan sliding down the small hill that terminated at Eddie's Pool Hall because he was too drunk to hear the warnings while listening to the peculiar music that played between his ears, a jumble of ballads he'd heard at the tavern he'd just left, adjusted to the tempo of the freezing rain pelting his face, never once thinking about mortality, which stalked him as he fumbled for the right lyrics, the right notes, to get it all right just once.

He stumbled into Eddie's and shook his long, tangled, unkempt hair like a dog, which caused him to lose his balance and have to sidestep to regain it. He was thinking that the kids on the toboggan were, albeit sober, more out of control than he, that they had no cause to curse him as they flew past, that he might see fit to roust the snot-noses from the toboggan for one final joyride.

Duane warmed his hands over the stove and inhaled the aroma of pork and beans burned to the bottom of the long-handled tin pan whose bottom was out-of-flat and that spun and tipped at the slightest touch, which Duane too provided. He picked up the noisy pan and set it back on the stove.

"Jesus, Duane, get a haircut. Your head looks like a patch of tumble-weed and cockleburs."

The stranger sized up Duane and told himself to forget it. James Atwood didn't look much more promising, but a hustler is a variation of suitor—the hustler has to ask.

"How 'bout you, kid? Want a game?"

James Atwood didn't need to do much to make himself look like a mark. He was in that respect a natural. His straw-like hair formed an indomitable cowlick. He looked even younger than his eighteen years, with deep-set blue eyes and a slight outward bend to the nose. The curve was a perfect complement, a miniature mirror image, to the hunch of his back as he leaned against a pool table.

"Mumblety-peg?" James Atwood responded. He had an indeterminate mien that could be taken for a scowl or a smile at any one time. Speaking with his mouth half-closed only accentuated the ambiguity.

The stranger laughed. "Pool, son. Name your game."

"Ain't much of a pool player."

"Eight-ball, for a dollar. I'll spot you three balls."

"Make it four."

"You hustling me?"

"Go play by yourself."

"Okay. Four balls."

James Atwood broke and sank a striped ball. Duane took advantage of the distraction, sticking his finger in a half-full can of pork and beans, then licking it.

"Duane, get your finger out of those beans. And get your mangy ass out of here. You're falling-down drunk."

The still life that presented itself to the five other men in Eddie's Pool Hall might be entitled *Coitus Interruptus with Finger and Beans*. The offending finger remained involuntarily erect, the brown-caked digit a black sheep to the closed fist, as if Duane felt obliged to air his dirty laundry. The small token of guilt, in Duane's mind, did not warrant expulsion. But Duane was too potted to argue. He turned, exited, and missed James Atwood's last two games of pool in Kansas. He won the first, thrown by the hustler, who skulked and ordered a beer.

"Remind me of the name of this town."

"Osage, Kansas."

"I didn't ask the state. I know that."

"Betcha don't know who's from here."

"Ulysses S. Grant?"

"Nope. Pepper Martin. He wasn't 'Pepper' then. Just Johnny. Pepper's better." Martin grew up in Oklahoma, but since he was known as the wild horse of the Osage, James Atwood claimed him for a hometown neighbor. It gave Osage, Kansas, some panache, and truth never stampeded the wide open plains of James Atwood's consciousness.

The stranger sat onstool, put a foot on a rung, and slugged down his beer. "Pepper Martin ain't nothin'. What did he hit, .300?"

".316. Made the National League All-Star team. He was the Associated Press athlete of the year in '31."

The stranger scoffed. "Now, you take Gehringer. There's a hitter. Every ball, he knows exactly where it's going, like Willie Keeler. I figure

I'm the Charlie Gehringer of pool. Make my living with a suitcase and a stick."

"You a Tiger fan?"

"From Detroit."

"We're St. Louis here. Everybody's for the Cardinals."

" 'Cuz of Pepper Martin."

"Yup. Like the way he plays, too. Leo Durocher's quite a pool player, they say. Better than anyone the Tigers got."

"You think you could take Durocher?"

"At wrasslin', no problem."

At 5'7", James Atwood was about Durocher's height, but he was built more like Pepper Martin. Not as big as Pepper in the chest, but his arms were well developed.

The stranger looked at Malachy Grimes. "Where'd you get this sass-ass?"

Malachy lit up a cigarette and didn't look at the stranger, who smiled at James Atwood. "At pool, knucklehead. That's what we're talking about."

"Pool? Heck, no. I need a four-ball spot and luck to beat a small-time slicker like you."

Eddie Moss didn't like the tone of the conversation, and he was fa-miliar with James Atwood's temper. He changed the subject. "Dizzy Dean's holding out again. Did you hear?"

"Yeah," said the stranger, laughing. "About a month ago. I guess news travels slow in Kansas."

"You don't like Kansas much, do you?"

"What I see, all you got is corn and snow."

"Got Kansas City. Got a Negro team there, the Monarchs. They'd kick the ass of your Tigers."

The stranger laughed derisively.

"I seen 'em do it," said Spottswood Love. "Those black guys beat a bunch of Tigers, barnstorming down in Texas in the winter. Charlie Gehringer put that team together, so you know it was good. Beat the House of David team, too."

"I've heard those Negroes beat Dizzy Dean's team, too," said Malachy Grimes. "Got a guy named Paige that throws a ball out of hell. Guys say you can't see it. You know what Paige and Dean make for one of those barnstorming games? Five hundred dollars. And that sonofabitch Dean is still holding out."

James Atwood shook his head. "Five hundred clams for just playing. I don't understand it. You get all that money for playing. You don't work a lick. Then you ask for more. Soon as I get a proper stake together I'm going to St. Louis and have a talk with Dizzy Dean. Talk some sense into him."

"You're going to St. Louis to talk sense into Dizzy Dean?" The stranger laughed.

"Don't pay no attention to what he says. He's a megalomaniac," said Spottswood. "That's what they called him at the high school, when they kicked him out. Got a mouth, too."

"You know what a megalomaniac is?" asked Malachy.

The stranger got up and picked up his cue. He threw a few balls on the table and began to practice. "Don't reckon I do. Megalo-what?"

"Megalomaniac."

"Is that what's on his face? Or did someone play mumblety-peg on it?"

"I got some blemishes, I admit. They'll disappear in the course of time."

"See what I mean?"

James Atwood grew self-conscious. He smoothed down the hair that was the color and texture of straw, hair that was to "coiffure" what the "Gashouse Gang" was to baseball.

The stranger imitated James Atwood patting down his hair. "What's that roosting on your head, boy?"

James Atwood resented being called "boy" by someone just four or five years older. "Why don't we make this game fifty dollars? You give me a two-ball spot."

"You got fifty dollars?"

James Atwood pulled an indeterminate wad of bills from his pocket, then shoved it back in. "Satisfied?"

"Rack 'em up."

Inside, James Atwood was grinning. The hustle couldn't have gone better. The would-be hustler thought he'd gotten his goat, to where taking the hustler's money was his only way to save face. He could beat the man three out of five, he figured, straight up. And now he had a two-ball spot.

Maybe so, maybe not. Maybe the hustler was holding something back. Or maybe all the skill in the world doesn't matter when your opponent hits a streak of good luck, or you hit a streak of bad.

Suppose you went back a few years. You're James Atwood Gray. You're ten years old and the best mumblety-peg player in Ossage since Pepper Martin. Suppose some kid beats you and wants to take your knife, and your identity. Not a hustler, but a local kid named Sammy Colt, who's eleven and likes to gloat and talk about what he's going to do with your knife. But you're only ten and not yet fully cold-blooded. Your options are the bottle opener, the can opener, or the awl—the additional blades on your jackknife—because the long blade you play with is both scary and, you think, unwarranted in this case, and some proto-notion of justice is gurgling up through your blood. If you were James Atwood, you'd go for the *awl* 'cuz you liked the sound of the word—the way the vowel got caught like a needle in the groove of a Victrola and dragged out. And what a surprise it would be that the awl would not penetrate the skin through the belt loop to Sammy's belly but could cause so much pain anyhow.

In the years of miscreancy and crime that followed James Atwood Gray's departure from Ossage with nothing but a cue stick and a small suitcase, any sharp-eyed detective could have discerned the agency of James Atwood in the small slits in the floors where he entertained himself with the same very sharp mumblety-peg knife he'd withheld from the future mayor of Ossage, Sammy Colt.

Such are the dangers of seeing identity as fixed, not evolving, not subject to catastrophe, of not believing that something out of your hands might be in someone else's.

Now suppose you're the best pool player is Ossage, Kansas, even though you're only eighteen. Then some hustler from Detroit comes into town, takes your crown and all your money. Such a man, though he's only twenty-two himself, has stolen your identity. Who in his right mind would permit such a thing? Especially in a small town where hustlers are not loved. If, for every thing there was a season, then for James Atwood Gray the long cold winter of Ossage fit like old galoshes, or the tip of a cue stick in the eye of a shameless hustler. James Atwood, who would have graduated high school if they hadn't expelled him, was smart enough to know that the blunt end of a cue stick would land a stinging but not incapacitating blow and that the slim, chalked end was not sharp enough to puncture a man's skin, especially if he was wearing a shirt and jacket. He knew his best bet was to go for the face, and the most vulnerable part of the face was the eyes. And so he left the hustler with a short list of new nicknames. He liked "dead-eye" best, because of the multiplicity of meanings, and because something like irony, which he was barely aware of and had no name for, stirred in his head. It was kind of thrilling, in itself.

James Atwood left the pool hall with his fifty dollars and stepped into freezing rain, which was more uncomfortable than the driving snow he'd entered the pool hall with. He had no idea where he was going except that he had to get out of town. If not tonight, then tomorrow. He headed down what he thought was the road, covering his face from the freezing rain with his arm. "Shit," he said, stumbling over something and nearly falling in the snow. He looked down and saw a body, face-down in the snow. He kicked the body again in the leg and was unsure whether the sound he heard was a groan. "You alive?"

Duane Brown groaned. "I think so."

"Too bad."

"It's me, Duane."

"I know."

James Atwood noticed a toboggan to one side of Duane and guessed that he had crashed into something. Duane tried to get up but couldn't. "Hey, shit, I'm stuck."

James Atwood started to walk off.

"Hey, help me! My hair's stuck. Frozen to the ice."

James Atwood chuckled and kept walking.

"Hey, come on! I'm serious! My hair's frozen. You gotta help me!"

"You got any money?"

"No."

"That's what I figured. I can get five dollars for you at the medical college if you're dead by morning. You ain't worth nothin' to nobody alive. You're just a piece of shit, Duane. And now you're dead."

"Come on, James Atwood. I'm gonna freeze to death here."

"I reckon so. Here lies Duane Brown. Too cheap to get a haircut. Spent every penny on booze. Even the great must fall."

"Real funny, James Atwood. I know you got that mumblety-peg knife. Give it here, so's I can cut my hair."

James Atwood continued in the tone of eulogy. "Duane froze to death on account of his long hair. And his drinking. And because he was such a prick to his horses that folks were glad to see him go."

"Fuck you, James Atwood!"

" 'Fuck you' were the last words anyone ever heard Duane Brown speak."

"Fuck you, James Atwood."

The wind picked up, and the frozen rain stung James Atwood's face. He dimly heard Duane mutter, "Let go of me, dumb-ass ice."

Duane could see the toboggan. He reached out for it, though it could do him no good. He just had an urge to reach out, as if dying with a toboggan were better than dying alone. A line drawn in the snow connecting Duane's feet to the toboggan's end would describe an oblique triangle, James Atwood reflected, and was astonished at how curiously the lessons of the schoolhouse could come back in times of extremity.

2

SAWDUST

Flush with $25,000 from his first kidnapping, John Henry Seadlund headed east to Chicago. He bet heavily at the track, and spent summer afternoons at Comiskey Park whenever the White Sox were at home, getting drunk on cheap beer and losing large sums on the home team, who finished thirty-one games behind the pennant-winning Washington Senators. He almost caught the home run that Ruth hit in the 1933 All-Star Game. He considered hammering the kid who picked the ball up after it had stung and bounced off his hands, but then realized he could buy it from the kid for a buck. That made him feel good, feel like a big shot. By September he was broke, and decided to try his luck in St. Louis. It would be thirteen months before he got there. On October 1 he stole a car in Memphis and sold it in Tuscaloosa, which put the FBI on his trail for violating the National Motor Vehicle Theft Act, the same one that put the G-men on Dillinger's trail.

Nearly broke, John Henry held up the State Bank of Centuria in Milltown, Wisconsin, and got away with $1,039. He hadn't made the Chicago Crime Commission's Public Enemies List. That wouldn't happen till '37, with the kidnapping of Charles Ross. In December he drifted to Brainerd, Minnesota, where he robbed the Van Restaurant and got away with $48. Remembering something from a Cagney movie or something he'd read about Dillinger, he went back to the restaurant three hours later, talked with the locals about the robbery, and paid $1.85 for a fish fry and corn on the cob. He grabbed a toothpick and re-called a column he'd just read in the paper by Damon Runyon compar-ing the bat of the Cardinals' Leo Durocher to a toothpick, which reaffirmed his desire to get to St. Louis. He hitched a ride outside the restaurant to Mille Lacs Lake, and caught another to just south of St. Paul. It was snowing lightly. He had to wait two hours before a car stopped.

"Get in. Where are you headed?"

"St. Louis. What about you?"

"Just down the road," said the girl. "What's in St. Louis? Got a sweetheart?"

"Nope. Just like the Cardinals. Think this could be their year. You heard of Dizzy Dean?" The girl glanced at him and nodded. "That boy can pitch."

"So, that's the reason you're going to St. Louis? To watch baseball?"

"Can you think of a better one?"

"Work. Gotta have the do-re-mi." She held out her hand. "My name's Ginger. What's yours?"

"John Henry."

"I thought I might pick up a John."

Ginger stepped on the gas. "Dillinger's a John, too," said John Henry.

She laughed. "They say he's strapped."

"Beg pardon?"

"Has to put it in a holster."

John Henry was in denial of the innuendo he thought he was pick-ing up. "You talking about his gun?"

Ginger looked at John Henry and rolled her eyes up, smiling. "Dillinger is tops on J. Edgar Hoover's list of wanted men. And from what they say about Hoover, I can understand why."

"What do they say about Hoover?"

Ginger took a deep breath and let it out audibly, grasping the steering wheel a bit higher. John Henry stared at her, thinking of how he might make that list.

Her hair was too blond not to be dyed, but it curled up cutely in back. He could tell that her bust was full and her waist small, even with a jacket on. Her legs, partly covered by a plaid wool skirt, were perfect. She was just a schoolgirl, but a beautiful one, creating dreams as fast as the mint presses out a shiny new penny. Dreams occupied a higher rung than thoughts in John Henry's mental ladder. And Ginger was the embodiment of his minimalist, scantily fleshed out dreams. He left his dreams in that state because he had long been smart enough to know that only God could fulfill those dreams, that the sketchier his dreams were, the less time God would need to fill in the details, and the more modest his dreams, the more virtuous he would appear in the eyes of God, and all of this upped the chances of his getting what he spent a very immodest amount of time contemplating. He had faith in his ability to pull himself up by any dame's garter straps, up to where he wanted to be. He had a vision of Ginger's barely clothed body, as he stared at her, while she stared unabashedly back. "Barely clothed" rather than "naked" for reasons akin to the parsimony of grace he expected from a God who rewarded a parsimony of desires.

Ginger blew a pink bubble large enough to obstruct her vision, then let it collapse.

"That's a mighty big bubble."

"Thanks."

"I never could get the knack of a really big bubble."

"Want some gum?"

"No thanks."

"I get a lot of practice." She winked at him, smiling.

"You know, you kind of look like Jean Harlow. I saw her in a movie, once."

"Thanks. You're kind of cute yourself, John Henry, in a Wallace Beery kind of way."

John Henry saw himself as a rougher-edged Bogart, handsome, tough, with an undercoating of tenderness, which he was reserving for the right girl. His nose was on the prepossessing side. It was somewhat noble, he thought, perfectly symmetrical in spite of the many fights it had been party to, and the slope was perfectly straight, at a not-ostentatious angle, a minor-league Ernie Lombardi nose. Beneath it was the tough-guy smile, the close-lipped Bogart look, presiding over a cute knob of a chin that invited tweaking, reminding the Hollywood historical buffs that Bogart started out a happy, chowing-down toddler, advertising baby food.

His eyes looked drawn, in charcoal, long brown rectangular smudges under full, gallant eyebrows, above which the flesh of his forehead swelled slightly, which he referred to publicly as "too much brains," but which privately he worried might be his conscience fleeing, being chased by something unspeakable.

It created a dramatic vertical furrow that led to the slope of his nose, a kind of drainage ditch for the sweat on his forehead. Peculiar, he thought, that nothing grew here. Hair, whiteheads, pimples—all made themselves scarce. Unlike John Henry's skull, which produced a great curly mop that he plastered down with Vaseline to look like George Raft. But it always sprang back up, in matted curls, and made him look pretty silly, he thought.

John Henry felt good, cozy. He felt saved. Felt like sticking his head out the window and catching a random snowflake with his tongue. Elements of the divine, he thought, were ubiquitous. Why didn't everybody see? In the arc of a Dizzy Dean curveball. In the teardrop wheel covers of a '34 Cord. In the line cut by the profile of the girl's cheek, turned so that the nose was just out of sight, from the eye socket over the cheekbone to the first cut under the chin. When she turned a fraction so that her lips were just visible, John Henry's heart jumped. The lines were so exquisite. A short mapping of perfection.

"This is a pretty nice car."

"Paid for it myself."

"My favorite car's a Cord."

"Never seen one."

"Got wheel covers that kind of swoop down and around." John Henry carved the lines in the air. "Kind of like running your hand down a cat's back. That smoothness."

"Men . . ." Ginger shook her head. "Everything comes down to pussy."

John Henry was offended. "That's not what I mean. I'm talking about an automobile."

Ginger shrugged. "Have it your way."

"What do you mean, 'Have it your way'?"

"Some guys don't go for pussy."

"I go for it all right. I'm just talking about an automobile is all." Ginger put a stick of gum in her mouth.

"You couldn't chew gum in school, where I'm from," said John Henry.

"Where's that?"

"Ironton, Minnesota."

"They got iron there?"

"Yeah. But no jobs. Laid me off a good while back. Laid everybody off, almost."

"I wouldn't want to work in a mine anyway. Down in a tunnel?" Ginger shook her head and looked at John Henry for confirmation.

"Me neither. I worked in the blacksmith shop and the machine shop. Miners need tools."

"Everybody needs something. What do you need, John Henry?" Ginger smiled and looked at him, then blew a bubble.

"Need a job, I guess."

She laughed. "What do you like doing?"

"Nothing. Been an automobile mechanic. Delivery boy for a grocery store. None of them particularly suits me, though. I'm looking for something else. I could always go back up to Ironton and play hockey. Got some offers."

"Professional?"

"Semipro. Got offers from colleges, too. Teachers' colleges. But I'm not cut out to be a teacher."

John Henry watched the snow slant through the headlights' beams.

It was beautiful. It reminded him of machine-gun bullets in a Cagney movie, while Ginger reminded him of Harlow. He fantasized her becoming his moll.

"When I was growing up I always wanted to be a G-man."

Ginger laughed. "I always wanted to be Bonnie Parker. You got a cigarette?"

"You smoke?" John Henry said, incredulously. "You're chewing gum, for criminy's sake."

"I'd take it out, if I had a cigarette." Ginger showed some impatience in her voice.

"Well, you can keep it in. I don't have any." John Henry had a ten-pack, but he didn't feel like sharing.

"You don't smoke?"

"Sure. I smoke. Sometimes. Just not now."

"Don't have the swag for some cigs?"

"Where'd you learn to talk like that?"

"The movies. You really think I look like Jean Harlow?"

"Only you're prettier," John Henry said with a smile and a blush that was imperceptible in the darkness of the car.

"You kind of remind me of Cagney, a little bit."

"I do?"

"The forehead, a little bit."

That made John Henry Seadlund feel good.

"Wanna know why I got kicked out of school?" she asked. "Was on account of spelling. I spelled 'penis' with two 'e's, like, 'cause you pee with it, right? Got into an argument with Mr. Arnold *Big-ass* B. Holmberg and told him what his middle initial stood for."

John Henry shook his curly head, feeling like James Cagney. "First time I got kicked out—I was just feeling up Patty Graves in the auditorium. They woulda kicked her out too, 'cept she quit."

Ginger felt the Ford skidding a bit in the accumulating snow. She slowed down a trifle and looked at him. He thought it was a kind of seductive look, despite the high-school banner and pompoms on the seat between them. Then she looked at the gas gauge. "I'm gonna have to get some gas soon."

John Henry leaned forward for better depth perception. "There'll be a filling station before long, I reckon."

"You could fill up my tank right now, if you had the dough." Ginger let the Ford coast to a stop, just off the road. She took her gum out and pressed it to the wheel. She smiled at him. "Just five dollars."

John Henry recoiled. "What the hell are you, a whore? I thought you were a schoolgirl."

"Well, I used to be. We got a Depression going, case you hadn't noticed. A girl's gotta pay her way, even up in Irontown."

"*Ironton*. I liked you. I thought you were really something."

Ginger pushed her skirt back down over her knees. "Well, maybe it's time for you to catch another ride. I don't have time for nickel-and-dime chumps like you." Ginger reached past him and opened his door.

John Henry realized that this was the middle of fucking nowhere, and it was snowing and goddamn cold out. "How am I gonna get a ride out here? I coulda liked you. But you're nothing but a five-dollar whore. Get your own ass out." John Henry pulled her on top of him, then threw her half out his door.

She clung to his jacket. "This is *my* car, asshole!"

John Henry tore out of her grip, put his foot in her rump and shoved. "Yeah? Who's the asshole now, huh?" He threw her banner and pom-poms at her.

"You are! Asshole! And you always will be. You look more like Robinson than Cagney! Stupid furrow on your forehead!"

John Henry slammed the door. Ginger got up and grabbed the handle. John Henry pushed the lock down.

"That's my car!"

"Yeah. I bet you worked hard for it." He slid over to the driver's seat. "So long, doll." John Henry pulled back onto the road, looked for a mirror to look back, but there wasn't any.

"Cheap-ass car."

John Henry hadn't planned on stealing a car, but this didn't seem like stealing. Not that he had reformed. It was just that stealing a car never really crossed his mind. But as he thought on it, it was the logical thing to do. Why stand in the cold waiting for benevolence? Benevolence was like a currency without a gold standard—it could not be counted on, he thought, craning his neck for one more look at the golden-haired girl. Bogart would know how to handle her, how to handle the whole situation, while John Henry felt betrayed and at the same time somewhat adolescent and small. He didn't think of Ginger freezing her tush off back there. When he thought of her tush his thoughts were warm, cozy. Such a thing could never freeze.

He hadn't gotten fifty feet when he heard a thunk, and he knew, even before checking his coat pocket, that it was the ball. It must have fallen out when he and Ginger were struggling. He stopped the car and ran back to where he thought the car was when the thunk occurred. He looked around in the whiteout, distraught.

"Where's the ball?" he hollered.

"Who the fuck cares?"

"Me. That's who. Babe Ruth hit that ball for a homer at Comiskey Park. I caught it. Babe Ruth is the greatest hitter that ever lived. A ball like that is special."

"So is my car. If I find that ball, I'm gonna stick it up your ass." Ginger made a run for the car. John Henry realized the futility of his search at the same time that he made a mental calculation of the present value of the car as opposed to that of the ball. He lit out for the car and left Ginger trudging helplessly behind.

Driving away in a stolen car, John Henry regretted giving her his real name. Then he regretted not giving her five bucks for a blowjob, pretending she was everything he thought she was. He slowed down, contemplating turning around, going back to pick her up. He felt the car decelerating. He thought of her standing there with her pompoms, freezing, pleading with him. Then he thought, *Ah, go melt some snow with it*. He gritted his teeth, made a *gr-r-r-r* sound.

Snow came down from Canada, settled in Minnesota. Snow followed by cold and colder. Followed by Seadlund in a Ford Victoria that didn't have a mirror and had a gas gauge that lied, never indicating less than full. He filled the tank five miles down the road, then drove through the night, through the snow. When dawn came, the snow had stopped, and he worried that the cops might now be looking for a stolen car, maybe even the Feds. He remembered he'd told Ginger that he was headed to St. Louis, and decided to detour slightly to the east, by way of Chicago, on smaller roads, with less chance of being caught. He'd been falling asleep for half an hour. Keeping the window open no longer helped. He started slapping himself, which worked for a while. He came to an intersection after falling asleep and nearly heading off the road. Opening his eyes, he saw a kid at the intersection with a small suitcase and a pool cue. *Hustler*, he thought. He rolled down the passenger-side window.

"Can you drive?"

"Yup."

"Where you headed?"

"St. Louis, I guess."

"What do you mean, 'you guess'?"

"Well, I'll go as far as you're goin', if you're not goin' all the way to St. Louis."

"I'm headed to St. Louis, but I'm turning left here. You in a hurry?"

"Nope. What's up there?"

"Just the country. Beautiful country, ain't it? Kinda like to see all of it. Hit the back roads for a while. That okay with you?"

"Sure. Long as you're headed to St. Louis eventually."

"Well, I am. Gonna see them Redbirds play."

"They won't play till spring. You fixin' to take that long?"

John Henry laughed and shook his curly head. "Don't think I could take being in a car with anyone that long, 'less I was married to her."

John Henry slid over to the passenger side of the Ford Victoria. "Go on, take a turn. I've been driving all night." He held out his hand. "John Henry Seadlund."

The hitchhiker shook it. "James Atwood Gray. Pleased to meet you."

James Atwood had done precious little driving in his life, and all of it joyriding stolen cars, but this was not the time to admit it, and there didn't seem to be much to it. He'd done a lot of tractor driving, and you could fall off of a tractor. You couldn't fall off of something you were inside to begin with.

"Pepper Martin's from my hometown. That's why I'm goin' to St. Louis. I also plan to have a talk with Dizzy Dean about holding out."

John Henry barely heard the grinding of the gears, barely felt the bolts that accompanied a shift. He was asleep before they were in third gear. Once he reached thirty miles an hour, James Atwood just let 'er steam ahead, driving down what he thought was the middle of the road but was not demarcated. The snow covered everything, leaving a vague depression where the road had once been plowed. Never would be plowed. He let the depressions or hills on the sides of the road guide him. For thirty miles they hadn't met a car coming the other way.

The thought of mugging John Henry never crossed his mind until he noticed a pistol on the seat, partly under John Henry's leg. He didn't figure on John Henry having much cash, but the car would be worth at least five hundred.

He was unsure how to dislodge the gun from under John Henry's leg. Ease it out slowly, like a pickpocket, or grab it fast? James Atwood's hand seemed to decide for itself on the second option, just as John Henry readjusted his position, covering more of the gun with his butt. Something inside John Henry seemed to be keeping watch. The God-loves-a-drunk gremlin. The gangster's guardian angel who could be as fickle as any gangster, as fickle as James Atwood himself, who was innocent of all intention to mug John Henry until opportunity knocked.

For those first few seconds after James Atwood's probing hand roused him, John Henry was like a cat in a bag when it first hits the river, struggling most to get his bearings out of sleep, conscious of the hand-not-his sliding between his leg and the cold steel. He instinctively rolled toward the interloping hand. Handicapped by having to steer the car with one hand, James Atwood nevertheless grasped the gun, while John Henry pulled himself up on James Atwood's arm, up to where he could bite him on the ear, which hurt so much that James Atwood pulled the trigger, sending a bullet through the upholstery and John Henry's butt bouncing in fright. James Atwood braked the car, which skidded off to the right as he let go with his left arm to push John Henry's head away. He got his fingers in John Henry's eyes, convincing

John Henry to let go of the ear with his teeth, but John Henry now had two hands on the gun, which he twisted out of James Atwood's hand. But the Ford's momentum threw James Atwood's body on top of him. When the car came nearly to a halt, John Henry pulled on the door handle and rolled out from under James Atwood. An accidental somersault and he was on his feet with the gun pointed at his adversary.

"Okay. You got me. I didn't mean you no harm."

John Henry doubted he could get the Ford back on the road without help. And in spite of the incident, he was still pretty tired and could use more sleep.

"You're a pretty low-down character. I ought to shoot ya, but maybe I'll give you a second chance."

"If you don't shoot me, you won't regret it." James Atwood realized he ought to come up with a reason why. "We can be partners. You must be an outlaw. And I'm pretty much an outlaw myself."

"All right. I'm gonna steer, and you push. And no funny stuff."

"You're not gonna leave me here, are you?"

"No. I still need you to drive. When we get on the road, I'm gonna sleep in back. If this car stops for any reason, I'll plug ya. Y'understand?"

"You can count on me. I'll drive all night."

"Just keep heading east, till we get to Milwaukee."

James Atwood got out and assumed a pushing stance. John Henry steered. After a lot of sidewinding, they got back on the road. John Henry climbed in the back, and lay down. As he was falling asleep, he was thinking about the first time he woke up next to someone beautiful. He was maybe thirteen and she was Princess, a chestnut-haired spaniel who licked his face into consciousness. The next time it was a girl who woke him with her tongue all over his cock, so that that time he fell into a deep sleep from which he awoke next to no one, and though his pants were still hanging loosely over the chair, his wallet wasn't in his pocket. The next time he woke up next to someone beautiful he already had one eye open.

James Atwood was good to his word, but shortly after dawn the Ford started bucking, then stopped.

"Don't shoot me. I ain't done nothin'."

John Henry checked the liquid in the gas-gauge tube. It registered "full," but he hadn't gotten gas since he stole the car, more than twelve hours earlier. "We're out of gas. Those hydrostatic gauges never work."

James Atwood got out, walked around the Ford Victoria, then kicked it. "Asshole car!"

John Henry felt a halfhearted need to defend his newly acquired car. "Dillinger said a Ford was the best get-away car. Clyde Barrow, too."

"We're not trying to get *away*. We're trying to get *to*."

James Atwood impressed John Henry with his cogency in a time of stress. James Atwood continued, "Clyde's car had a hundred and seven bullet holes and they drove it away. This piece of shit's never even been shot and it ain't goin' nowhere. We should have stayed on the main road. Seeing the fucking countryside! I should have knowed better than to hitch a ride with a nutcake like you."

"Hey, you watch your mouth or I'll change my mind about shootin' you. Let's walk down the road a piece and see if anything's there."

Their feet sank completely into the new snow as they walked east on the country road. James Atwood complained again, "We're like Lewis and Clark out here. They won't find us till fucking spring."

John Henry blew some snowflakes off the hair on his unshaven upper lip and looked down, feeling suddenly contrite and guilty. "Maybe this is what we deserve. I stole the car."

James Atwood was not surprised at the larceny. These were desperate times, but desperate times didn't need the aggravation of contrition. "It's *day*time and it's fucking freezing. What are we gonna do at fucking night? We're gonna die out here. I ain't eaten in two days."

John Henry was an optimist. He had an inchoate understanding of regression to the mean, and applied it to situations like this. He called it "the law of averages." When Durocher was 0 for 4, John Henry didn't think that Leo was having a bad day. He thought that Leo was due. Now he and James Atwood were due to see a farmhouse or a town.

"Roads just don't go out and stop. They connect things," said John Henry. After a couple of miles, it started snowing again, and they were walking into the wind. A quarter of a mile later they gave up and went back to the car.

John Henry said, "You know what day it is?"

"Sunday?"

"It's my half-birthday. January 27th. I was born on July 27th. It's my half-birthday. And I'm half dead."

James Atwood chuckled while resenting John Henry for his predicament. Adversity seemed to be bringing them together. They hung around the car till late afternoon. The only thing that passed was a rabbit, and John Henry said no more about the law of averages and about being due. It was getting colder and more blustery. John Henry could look directly at the sun behind the clouds without squinting. That eerie orange color recalled for him his first intimation of Armageddon. In the woods, preparing the safekeeping hole for his first kidnapping victim, Wallace Riggs, the sky cracked open and for a stunning millisecond turned a dull flame-orange, a conflagration seen through isinglass. Then the sky seemed to break vertically, emitting a flash of jet-black, jagged lightning that radiated to form something like a bat's skeleton, over which the orange sky hung like curtains. The first earthly thing he saw after his vision was a three-foot stick lying on the ground, which brought to mind a bat of another kind. He knew then that Armageddon and baseball were engraved in his future. Which meant that he could not die here in the snow, a fact that, given the cold, was even more regrettable. He cursed the day he met Ginger. He thanked God for his overcoat and the suitcase of clothes, all of which he would put on to stay alive through the near-zero cold of the January night. James Atwood had less in his suitcase—one pair of trousers, two pairs of socks, some underwear and one shirt. He had gloves and John Henry didn't. John Henry considered killing James Atwood for his gloves, but decided that his body warmth was more valuable. He could put a pair of socks on his hands and pull them up into his sleeves.

"I can barely feel my toes," said John Henry.

"I can feel all of mine, and they're freezing." James Atwood heard a noise and surveyed the woods. He jumped up, pointing at a rabbit. "Look! He's gettin' away. Give me the gun!"

John Henry worried that his partner would shoot him for his clothes instead of shooting the rabbit. James Atwood seemed to read his mind. "I ain't gonna shoot ya."

"How do I know you ain't?"

"Same reason you ain't shot me. We're partners. Like Bonnie and Clyde."

"Don't even mention broads right now, okay?"

"He's getting away!"

"You think I'd trust you with my gun after you tried to hold me up?"

"We weren't partners then."

John Henry shook his head in exasperation. "I must have the dumbest partner in creation."

James Atwood held out his hand. John Henry's desire to fill his stomach compelled him to fill James Atwood's hand with the pistol. The certainty of starving outweighed the risk of taking a bullet. "I'm so hungry I don't care if you do shoot me. One bullet is all you get."

"One's all I need."

John Henry stomped his feet in the snow to keep them warm. He adjusted the collar on his overcoat, then stuffed his hands deeper into his pockets, as if to access some secret recess of warmth.

Beneath two inches of powdery snow was a thin crust of melted and refrozen snow. It was just thick enough to break beneath the rabbit's hind feet, which had to sink in several more inches before the snow compacted enough to allow it to spring forward. The rabbit was easy prey for a fox in these snow conditions, but James Atwood, who pursued it with the single-mindedness of hunger, was still no match for it. He remembered the anecdote about Dizzy Dean doing sixty in the desert in Texas. First he's passed by a jackrabbit, then he looks out the window and there's Pepper Martin chasing the jackrabbit.

John Henry was not entirely relieved that his partner hadn't shot him. He was hungrier and colder than he ever remembered being, and the cold seemed to reinforce the hunger.

The rabbit was easy to track, and James Atwood with his one bullet was relentless. When he saw the rabbit's flanks expanding and contracting about twenty feet away, he figured he'd never get closer. It looked at him with one eye. He looked back with one eye down the sight of the pistol and fired. John Henry hoped James Atwood was due, or that the rabbit was due. His heart jumped when he saw James Atwood holding his prey by the ears. He raised it and smiled, and John Henry almost expected him to spank it next. Instead, he handed the gun back to him.

"Got any matches?"

"Nope. Got some cigarettes, though."

"What are you doing with cigarettes and no matches?"

"A guy owed me. Didn't have any dough."

"For the love of Pete! What are we gonna do? How are we gonna make a fire?"

"Gotta find some matches. Turn this car upside down if we have to. Stupid whore that owned it smoked. Ought to be matches somewhere."

"This a whore's car?"

"Regular cat-mobile."

The search took two hours. They pulled out the back seat, emptied the trunk and glove compartment, combed the crevices of the front seat, and looked under the seat.

"Another fucking used rubber," said James Atwood. I never seen so many rubbers in my entire life."

"She was a whore. I told you." John Henry shook his head. "You wouldn't have believed it, though. Looked just like a schoolgirl."

James Atwood picked up another used rubber. "My brother says cum burns. He lit it once." He shrugged. "I don't know. Kind of makes sense, though."

John Henry slammed his fist on the roof of the Ford. "James Atwood, forget about whether it burns, and think about how we're gonna spark it."

"I'm plumb out of ideas on that, John Henry."

"Well, I guess we're gonna have to eat it raw, fur and all. I ain't got a knife, and Ginger don't either."

James Atwood took out his mumblety-peg knife. "I can skin and dress her, but I ain't so sure about eating raw rabbit."

"Foxes do."

Foxes, thought James Atwood, *did not know how to cook.* He bowed his head.

"What're you doin'?" asked John Henry.

"Saying grace."

"It's a fucking rabbit. Save your praying for a fucking fire."

"Well, I ain't happy about it, neither."

He also found out that animal teeth were much better suited to tearing off flesh than human teeth. He and John Henry shared the knife, stripping small pieces off the thigh. A few bites were all that John Henry could stomach.

"The trick is imagining it's something else," said James Atwood.

John Henry didn't want to think or talk about food. He stepped out of the car. "Tell me when you're done."

"I reckon I'm done now. Can't eat when you're not. Feel like a cannibal, all by myself." With a disgusted look, James Atwood threw the rabbit onto the hubcap that served as a platter, then stuffed it under the passenger seat of the car.

The two men huddled in the back seat as night fell, taking turns staying awake, in case a car came by. None did. In the morning James Atwood awoke with an almost visionary sense of what it meant to be frozen stiff. Fingers and toes he had virtually given up on, but his neck and trunk had nearly seized up as well. What got him fully up was an idea for fire. He did not relish essaying the leftovers that would now have to be thawed by chewing. He budged his partner. "Wake up. I've got an idea."

John Henry was too cold to respond. He walked to the closest bush and had considerable difficulty peeing with his hands gloved in socks and his widdler inside two pairs of trousers and three pairs of boxer shorts. He ended up kneeling and contorting himself, and felt none of the usual relief a morning piss could afford.

"How many bullets you got?" asked James Atwood.

John Henry wasn't sure. He fumbled in his pocket. "Four."

"All right. We put one in the chamber, empty the powder from the others, put it in a pile and shoot it."

"You think that'll make a fire?"

James Atwood didn't want to be quizzed on it. It was the only idea he had, and it seemed like a good one.

"Might explode," said John Henry.

James Atwood got angry. "Yeah, I reckon it might. But I don't want no more raw rabbit. So, unless you've got a better idea, I say we give it a try."

That clinched the argument. James Atwood insisted on doing it inside the car, since the wind was so strong outside it could blow the powder away. He found a large, flat stone under a group of small pines and put it on the back seat. He took a rag from the trunk, disconnected the fuel line from the fuel tank and let the last few drops of gas soak into the rag. He got another ounce from the gas can in the trunk. John Henry opened three shells with the help of James Atwood's knife and tools from the trunk. He put the rag on the rock and the powder on the rag, meticulously building a fortification of pine twigs and bark shavings around it. On the top he placed an old bird's nest. He had a pile of sticks on the seat to add to it, and another pile of sticks outside, inside a packed-snow campfire place, to which they would transfer the stone and the burning kindling.

Both men hunkered down in the front seats, leery of a ricochet. James Atwood aimed, closed his eyes for fear of a ricochet, and fired. John Henry looked over the seat just after the shot ran out. "You missed! How the fuck could you miss?"

"I don't know. My hand was cold."

"You shot a rabbit for chrissake! How could you miss?"

Looking over the seat, James Atwood was at the point of sobbing. John Henry punched him on the shoulder, holding between his forefinger and thumb one more bullet.

"That's the last one."

James Atwood felt betrayed that John Henry had held back one bullet, but he didn't say so.

"Don't miss this time. Put the barrel right up close."

He didn't miss. The powder exploded and lit the rag that lit the twigs. John Henry whooped and threw on a handful more kindling, while James Atwood bounced up and down, as much to keep warm as for joy. Flames crackled through the bird's nest while the partners made the joyous noises of cavemen. Until they realized that the upholstery was on fire, and there was nothing to put it out with. Dense smoke and a noxious smell forced them away from the car. The back seat was in flames. Pretty soon the front seat too was burning, and that was it for the car. They stood as close as they could, upwind of the smoke, warming themselves until the fire was out. James Atwood joked, "Don't know if the rabbit's cooked, but we sure as hell are."

The partners simultaneously began walking down the road. After a couple of hours, James Atwood started shaking.

"What are you doing?" said a perturbed John Henry.

"I think I'm dying."

John Henry shook him, as if one kind of shaking were an antidote for another. But John Henry's shaking was more violent, a kind of reverse homeopathy.

"You were okay a minute ago."

"I was holding it in."

"Just keep walking."

James Atwood took a few steps, then stopped and announced, "I'm freezing, John Henry! I can't feel my toes. I'm freezing!"

"Shut up and stop freezing. You're hurting my ears."

"I think I'm dying."

"Well, don't die so loud."

"John Henry, I think I'm gonna shit my pants. That's how I know I'm dying."

"You shit your pants and I'll fucking kill you myself. I can use them pants when you do die."

James Atwood began to shake more violently. He sat down in the snow and struggled to get his shoes off with frozen fingers, then his socks. John Henry was too stunned, too annoyed, and too frozen himself to say anything till James Atwood had his socks off.

"What the hell are you doing?"

"Johnny Appleseed would walk in the snow with bare feet and he wouldn't freeze his toes."

John Henry bent over to look James Atwood in the eye. "You ain't Johnny Appleseed. If you were, we might have something to eat. Put your damned socks back on."

James Atwood just stared at his toes. John Henry slapped him. "If you wore a decent pair of brogans instead of those pointy-toed pimp shoes, your toes might not be frozen." John Henry picked up the green socks and dropped them in James Atwood's lap. "Put them on. You hear me?"

James Atwood sat mesmerized by his toes, thinking of Duane Brown lying in the snow with his hair frozen to the ground, unable to move. John Henry pulled out his gun and cocked it, then put it in James Atwood's face. "Put 'em on now or by God I'll shoot you."

"Go ahead. I'm gonna die on account of something I did. There ain't no reprieve from divine retribution."

"What are you talking about?"

"Duane Brown couldn't move, and now I can't neither. I would have taken his shoes, 'cept they weren't no better than mine." James Atwood looked him in the eyes, and John Henry saw the same incomprehension of a pig staring down a rifle barrel. He put the gun away.

"No. If I kill you, you'll be warm for maybe an hour. Then you'll be useless. If you die slow I might get something out of you yet."

John Henry kneeled down and picked up a sock. He felt James Atwood's toes. "Jesus Christ. They're as cold as ice."

"I told you. Can't feel nothing. Don't even hurt no more."

So this was it. The end. How did I come to this? James Atwood asked himself. What came to mind was a day like this, December 1923. Trimming the tree. James Atwood looked up the skirt of the Christmas-tree angel and saw nothing. And wasn't satisfied. And didn't stop there. He put a finger, then his whole fist up the cardboard skirt of the Christmas angel.

"James Atwood, what are you doing?" his mother said.

"Nothing."

"That was the angel of the Lord you just put your finger in." James Atwood's father carried him on his hip, like a small balsam, to the cast-iron woodstove.

"Put your hand there."

"It'll hurt."

"The one that offended thee."

"It'll hurt."

Johnny Appleseed, it was said, could put a pin through his hand and feel no pain. He had the same initials as James Atwood, who felt pain his whole life. Now he felt nothing, where his toes should be.

John Henry rubbed one foot, then put a sock on it and dangled a shoe over it. Then he took the frozen great toe and part of the other toes of the bare foot into his mouth and felt their cold. James Atwood said nothing but began to cry softly. After five minutes, John Henry put a sock and shoe on that foot and went to work on the other one. The silence inside his head was broken by the voice that said, *Holy Hanna, I'm sucking James Atwood's toes.* At that moment John Henry's appreciation for the complications of life soared, as did his appreciation of irony, feeling that he was unlikely to live long enough to fully savor it.

"I think you saved my toes, John Henry. I can feel a tingle."

John Henry's head was spinning. Was he saving a man's life, or at least his toes, just for the warmth that, dead, he could not provide? Or was it something else? It was too much for him to chew on. Even minor epiphanies were better left in the realm of emotive response, with no interference from the red ants of rationality. Ants in the snow-dusted pants of John Henry Seadlund.

They walked without speaking for what John Henry thought was an hour, but it could have been three. He reflected on the silence. Silence was all the animals of the forest with their mouths shut, a plug that you put in noise. Silence was the nippled breast thrust into the mouth of a Minnesota kid who first said "Mom" in German and cried in the universal language of noise. They walked without hope, without snow-boots, without even the kind of shoes that would make sense off the dance floor. This was the time for John Henry's guardian angel to cut in and waltz him over fields of icy hexagonal crystals. Walking for walking's sake because it beat sitting, walking to where curiosity ended and kindness began; a beat-up Model T could sputter and stop and a man looking too stubbly to be an angel might lean his head out the window, or it could all be a cold-induced mirage.

Conversation, when it happened, would become two-sided only when polite convention thawed out. Rules didn't cover frozen jaws. No one expects gratitude from a man whose lips had gone the color of raw rabbit flesh. Gratitude comes later, when the lips are no longer numb and feelings have thawed. Winter was for waiting. Then an oh-pshaw wave of the hand would be the Kansas farmer's response to John Henry's and James Atwood's coming in from the cold, from the cold province of gratitude.

"I saw some smoke, thought maybe I heard some shots. You two fellers look near dead."

The next morning, when John Henry awoke and had a lukewarm bath that felt hot, he reversed a two-decade habit of putting on his drawers left-foot first. He wasn't sure why, but the compulsion to do so was overwhelming. He stretched the somewhat crusty, checkered drawers, stared at the two-holed choice, and deliberately inserted his right foot, knowing it had something to do with luck, which was associated in his mind with a rabbit's foot shot at midnight on Halloween that he'd carried on a belt loop throughout his childhood, and with the Ruth home-run ball he always carried. He knew something had to change, that he had to live more deliberately. By putting his right foot through first, he thought he'd start to turn his life around, or at least his luck. He should have set about his maiden-drawer voyage sitting down, for the left foot, unused to the new batting order, struck out into the fabric he clenched with both hands and sent him sprawling onto the hardwood floor. *The only thing that turned around,* thought John Henry, *was my ass.*

His trousers on and trussed with red, white, and blue suspenders, John Henry made his way to the woodshed, on the farmer's behest, and began chopping with an earnestness he hadn't felt in years. He was giving thanks in the only way he knew how, the violence of cold steel biting off bits of wood.

The snow was half a leg deep that day in February 1934, on the other side of the country, in Sudbury, Massachusetts. Spring training was two months away. Babe Ruth too was chopping wood, working on his swing. When all you do for a living is play, what stand out are the precious moments that feel and sound like work. He also liked sledding and playing hockey on Willis Pond, or just watching the kids play. The shack he rented was near the one he lived in with his first wife, Helen, back in his days with Boston. It was his favorite trysting place, out of the orbit of his second wife, Claire. He contemplated retiring here, buying back the one-hundred-and-eighty-acre farm on Dutton Road where he had lived with Helen. The thought of retirement immediately set his arms in motion. Babe split logs with a semi-vertical version of his immortal swing, and he'd swing harder the next time if the blade of the axe came down anywhere but square on the spot where he was aiming. He stopped to wipe the sweat from his forehead and asked himself what the difference was between swinging the axe and the forty-four-ounce bat. He reveled for a while in the coziness of philosophical quandary, where the formulation of the question was in itself a revelation, the answer to which was always a comedown, but a pleasant one, like standing on a sunny, windless summit, then skiing down. The answer came to him—competition. Pitchers trying to get one by you, trying to beat you—all of them emissaries of the guy with the dark, pointy hood and the scythe, the ultimate Sultan of Swat, the guy who never missed.

Inside the shed was a full cord of wood, and Babe swung from the heels, sweat soaking his white woolen sweater, as if the pile could come to an end now, as if this were the last at-bat. For a moment, he was a kid at St. Mary's in Baltimore, stumbling wide-eyed into a body he realized could do amazing things.

For a while there was nothing but the comforting rhythm of his swing. But the rhythm begat words, out of the only doubt left in his mind. *What about Gibson?* were the lyrics his mind generated as he chopped and the snow silently accumulated. Annoying, because the line was synchronous with his stroke, no matter now hard he swung: *What*—the upswing; *a-bout*—the apex and downswing; *Gib*—the blade striking the log; *-son*—the log falling in two.

At the Sudbury hardware store and at the filling station they'd be staring at him, the Negroes, and Babe knew they were sizing him up, comparing him to Josh Gibson, the great slugger for the Pittsburgh Crawfords in the Negro Leagues, wondering who was the top dog. Babe and Josh were similarly built, but their styles at the plate could hardly be more different. Babe had a huge uppercut swing that sent him sometimes whirling when he missed. Josh's swing was compact, more wristy, and his home runs had much less arc, but when he did uppercut one it flew as far as the Babe's. Babe had heard the rumor that Josh had launched one out of Yankee Stadium, the house Babe had built. He heard the Negroes whispering the same, and it gnawed on him. *Did he really do it?* he wondered. *How much easier it was,* Babe thought, *in antiquity.* Two men would simply pick up their axes or clubs and have at it. There would be no question, no doubt. One man standing, the whole bloody world his home plate.

The Sudbury finale was always the same—a total of thirty two-foot logs on end on the slate-lined patio outside the woodshed. Babe spat on his hands and rubbed them together, then gripped the axe-handle. A minute later, he wiped the arm of his sweater across his forehead and inspected the carnage, smiling. Thirty logs cleaved in two, the magical sixty of the '27 season. Retirement seemed further away. *Let Gibson try that,* he said to himself.

Babe looked at the woodpile, diminished by two-thirds. He was confident it would get him through the week, and the good feeling it inspired would get him through one more winter. He wasn't one of those who couldn't wait till spring. Spring always brought with it training, which he dreaded. Babe sat down to a plate of six eggs over easy, as many pieces of bacon, and a one-pound steak, the woman who had cooked it all in the background, always in the background. He looked out the window and urged the snow on, then smiled, thinking that if he couldn't out-hit Gibson he could sure as hell out-eat him. Babe's output had declined in '33, but he was still second in home runs and seventeenth in batting. He homered in the All-Star Game and pitched a complete game, beating the Red Sox 6–5. He knew he was on the downside of the slope, but he felt he was still good enough to go head to head with Gibson. The cord of wood put up in October would soon be reduced to splinters and sawdust, which made Babe think of scattering sawdust on the floor of his father's Baltimore saloon. The sawdust was kept in a barrel in the cellar with the beer kegs and the booze. Babe remembered how once he'd thrown a match in the barrel on a dare and stood back to see if it would explode. It did. The memory was a nugget he closed his fist on when one reporter wrote him off after the '33 season. He was the Babe, the Sultan of Swat. If from dust we come, this was the dust to which he would return.

Babe slit three eggs and doused the liberated yolk with salt. Putting down the antique shaker, he looked out over the pond. He chuckled over the rumor that one night in 1918 he'd gotten drunk and carried his piano to the pond's edge and smashed it on the ice. The truth was less Ruthian, but impressive nevertheless. He'd pushed the piano out the door, down a hill, then to the middle of the pond, where Helen entertained the local kids with a surreal performance. Getting the piano back into the house would have been Herculean, but Babe knew as he pushed it out that it was not coming back. It was like those stories of an Eskimo knowing his time had come, floating off on a mini-iceberg.

The piano finally sank, just days before he took off for spring training. Babe remembered the piano now, on its last legs, tilted comically before its final slide, all four feet in the bucket.

3

SCALLIONS

After the Yankees failed to win the pennant in 1934, owner Colonel Ruppert offered Babe Ruth a chump-change contract. Babe called his bluff, officially retiring and taking a job covering the Series for a national newspaper syndicate. Babe hoped that the St. Louis Cardinals would take it to the Detroit Tigers. In his column, he had predicted that Dizzy Dean and Leo Durocher would be the stars in the Series. But as if to spite him, Diz lost game five and Leo was two-for-eighteen in the first five games. The pitcher who went 30-7 should not lose to Tommy Bridges, thought Babe, and no one should be allowed to hit as bad as Leo had. Babe took it upon himself to end Leo's slump and Diz's woes. Even though he suspected Leo of stealing his watch years before when Leo was playing with the Yankees, he liked Leo's style. The watch theft still irked him. Someday he'd turn Leo upside down and shake him till the watch dropped out of his pocket, but not till after the Cards had won the Series.

As a spectator instead of a player in this Series, Babe had the feeling that his own baseball clock was running down, as if Leo had stolen not just a watch from him, but time itself. Ironically, it was as if Babe had chosen as his successor an ex-teammate who was as unreliable a friend as he was a husband or a batter. After the Cardinals lost game five in Sportsman's Park, Babe called Leo back into the nearly empty stadium and sat down with him behind the dugout. There he revealed to Leo the secret of ending a slump—scallions. Leo, more than Diz, believed in magic, but then he almost had to. He couldn't hit the way Diz could pitch, and he only hit .014 higher than Diz in '34. It was as if the power that Babe was magically relegating worked only if you believed in it.

Babe then made his way to the Cardinals' dressing room, stopping at the concession stand for a hot dog. Sportsman's was the only ballpark where you could get hot dogs grilled instead of steamed. He covered it in onions and mustard, the way everyone did in St. Louis, and ate it in three bites.

Frankie was commiserating with Dizzy Dean, who had lost the game and was making no excuses for his performance. Babe congratulated the players individually for giving it their all and approached Diz at his locker after Frankie went to his own locker. Babe put a large hand on his shoulder. "I picked you as a star in this Series. You pitched like shit today. I'm not going to let you make a chump out of me. I'm going to take you and Pat to dinner tonight and straighten you out so you'll win the day after tomorrow."

Diz was confident that he would win, if Frankie would let him pitch, but no one said "no" to the Babe. They met at a new restaurant in Bush's Grove called Hono-Lulu's and ate in little screened-in huts. Babe ordered a bottle of wine for himself and one for Diz and Pat. "You're throwing like a Humpty Dumpty, and I don't have time to pick another star, so tonight I'm going to put you on stride. You ever had scallions?"

"Horse meat?"

"No. S-c-allions, dummy. If you weren't across the table, I'd slap some sense into you." Babe turned to Diz's wife. "Excuse me, Pat, but this is my old teammate here."

"This is my husband here."

"Okay, so I'll only smack him a little." Babe looked back at Diz. "Scallions are the greatest cure for a slump ever invented. Doesn't matter if it's a pitching slump or a batting slump. I've had both kinds. They've never failed me yet."

"A hitting slump for you is a streak for me. That goes for pitching, too," Diz said self-effacingly. "Hell, you beat the Red Sox last year, and you hadn't pitched in ten years."

Babe laughed. "Ten? Hell, it was more than that, except for one game in 1930."

Pat enjoyed Diz's self-deprecation. But what else to do, Diz thought, in the presence of Babe Ruth?

"Chin up, Diz. And bottoms up. Here's to the star of the Series."

Diz raised his glass, then took a sip of wine, rinsed his mouth with it and swallowed. "This is good. Frankie would sure like it."

Frankie Frisch was the Cardinals's connoisseur.

"Scallions, Diz. Forget about the wine. We're talking scallions."

Diz shrugged. "Can't hurt. I'll give 'em a try."

"I clued Leo in last night. He was one-for-sixteen going into the game today, and he hit one square."

Babe ordered a three-pound steak with mushrooms and scallions and another bottle of red wine. Diz wanted pork chops, but Babe ordered calf brains and scallions for him.

"I never had brains," Diz said, unaware of the ambiguity.

Babe laughed. "Maybe so, but you need 'em."

"Never had scallions, either. Don't think I want them. I'm gonna change that order to pork chops with Lea & Perrins sauce."

Babe put the glass down with such force that it thudded, even on the thick linen tablecloth. "You're gonna eat those scallions, if I have to sit on you the way Leo sits on guys coming into second."

Chastised, Diz got brains and finished all of his scallions. Six long, bitter pills that wrinkled his face as he forced them down. The green parts were the worst. He cut the scallions in half and ate both top and bottom halves together. Babe smiled. "That's good. You'll mow 'em down in game seven. Just remember—lay off the scallions while you're smoking it."

Diz would not mind swearing off the miniature, oniony baseball bats that turned green at the handle. A clump of them would serve as a whisk broom for Brick Owens to sweep home plate off with. Diz started to wonder what else it was about Babe's diet that produced the prodigious home runs. As if there was some version of the law of conservation of energy by which the amount consumed had to be equal in some respect to what came out.

Then Babe farted.

"Aw-oh! Trouble in the bullpen."

Docile Pat came to life. "Is that all you can say? There's a lady present."

"What am I supposed to say? I farted." Babe lit up a cigar.

"Excuse me."

"What—d'you fart, too?"

"Jay!"

"This is Babe Ruth, honey. What did you expect?"

"A little more couth. A little more respect would be nice."

"Couth, schmooth, lady. How many did you fan?"

Pat looked at her husband, bewildered as well as belittled. Diz shrugged.

"When you strike out a dozen, you get respect. That's what your hubby's after. And if you can't strike out a dozen, you give the ball to somebody else and go powder your nose."

"Jay!"

Pat pushed her husband petulantly on the arm, upset that he had in no way come to her defense.

"What?"

"That man is drunk. And he's insulting me."

"Aw, I ain't insulting you. Just ribbing you a little. Don't let it bother you. It's when a man is *not* drunk and he insults you, that's when you get your dander up." Babe staggered forward in his chair with a wine glass in one hand and pointing at Diz with the other. "Besides, what do you expect him to do about it? He bats ninth. Though with Durocher going two-for-eighteen, I wouldn't be surprised if they bump him up to eighth."

"Jay, I'm not going to take this anymore. And you shouldn't, either. I'm leaving."

Pat got up. Standing, she was just a head taller than her husband, but the petite brunette was no pushover. She handled all the Dean family's finances.

"You're getting a taxi, right?" Diz asked, pushing his chair back and standing.

"Yes. What did you think?"

"Nothing. I'll catch up with you later. He might be rude, but he's still my buddy, and he's getting me out of my slump."

"You lost one crummy game. That's not a slump."

Diz kissed Pat on the forehead and sat down. Babe felt the blind, tentative expansiveness of gas making its way south from his stomach. He lifted himself onto one cheek and raised his foot as if striding into a pitch. Then he let it go, loudly.

"Farting is a lot like hitting. You just let it go. Don't think about it. Just let it out. When you're hitting, just let your hands go."

Diz took a slug of wine and recalled that Babe never wore drawers. "Do you ever fart so bad sometimes it gums up your drawers?"

Babe laughed and slapped his knee. "The old squeeze play."

Diz laughed. "Suicide squeeze."

Babe turned serious. "Like I said, you just let it go. Same thing with pitching. When you're on, you don't throw high or low, you just let it rip right down the middle. Let the ball decide where it wants to go. Sometimes I fall down swinging. It's embarrassing—don't let anybody kid you. But I get the sonofabitch the next time."

Why was it Babe never changed his drawers after a game, those seven years in Boston? Did the Bambino love the game so much he couldn't bear to part with any drop of sweat that bore witness to a particular moment of greatness that blended into the whole cloth of the game? Could the ill-schooled, unsophisticated Bambino have been that romantic? *Nonsense,* Damon Runyon would reply. He was just crude. *Nonsense,* Westbrook Pegler would reply. He was just a beer-swilling, overeating Sancho Ruth, not a curveball-tilting Quixote, lacking the *education sentimentale* to articulate, even to himself, *I wear those drawers because I want those moments to last as long as the smell does.* There never was a

Dalai Lama of baseball. There was just the sultan of sweat, looking for a broad who would love those drawers the way a prince might search for the damsel whose foot fit a certain slipper.

Diz's mind rumbled like Babe's belly. "So what if Leo is two-for-eighteen—that's a lot of numbers crap. I mean, two-for-eighteen is three-for-nineteen, right? Or they would have said, 'two-for-nineteen.' Statistics are crap. Maybe I'm not in a slump and Leo's not either."

Babe shook his head and put his napkin on the table. "I've got to take a piss." He got up, appeared distracted and sat back down. "That reminds me of something I want to tell you before I forget. I had a dream that somebody stole our toilet bowl. Then I thought, 'Who the fuck would do a thing like that?' And I thought—'Leo! He's the only fucker I know who'd steal a toilet bowl.' Then I was fucking an Upper East Side broad—not in the dream—this was for real. Didn't mean to. Her car just broke down and I stopped to help her and she says, 'Aren't you Babe Ruth?' And I say, 'Honey, I ain't Kris Kringle.' So I fixed her fuel line, went back to her penthouse and straightened out a couple other pipes for her, and I went to take a piss and the bathroom's so big and I'm so drunk I couldn't find the bowl. Then she's got this other bowl next to it with no water in it, and I'm confused. Which makes me think of the dream. So I go back and I tell her about the dream, and it turns out she's a psychiatrist, and she says, 'That ain't a toilet bowl somebody stole. That's your career.' Like it's in the toilet and it's gone.

"Then some time later, I'm reading that Leo is one-for-sixteen, and I'm thinking, 'Leo's in a slump. Right now *he's* in the toilet.' So I figured I had to tell him how to get out. And it's working. Today he ripped one like Medwick." Babe nodded and shook a finger at Diz as he got up. "Scallions." He kept his eyes fixed on the pitcher as he retreated, as if that were part of the casting of the spell. When he got back, Diz said, "There's luck to it, too—hitting."

"Lady Luck's got the stick. No doubt about it. One at-bat, one game. But over the long haul there's no luck in it. The numbers don't lie, kid." Babe took a big slug of wine and wiped his mouth with a linen napkin patterned with an extraordinary set of stains.

Diz pouted. "You've got the same horseshoe up your ass that you cork your bat with. Stop to fix some broad's car, and she turns out to be a real tomato." Diz shook his head.

"Tomato? She was a female tomcat. There's a lesson in that for you—you can't trust a broad, any broad. That wife of yours," Babe shook his head, "I heard a thing or two about her."

Diz sipped his wine and waited for the besotted Babe to continue. He hesitated only for a moment. "I heard she screwed half the team in Houston."

Diz laughed. "Well, hell, yeah. I was one of them. That's why I married her."

Babe's brow wrinkled. He thought maybe he had Diz figured out, but he realized that Diz was in a different orbit altogether. He had one hell of an arm, thought Babe, but his head was not on quite right.

The lit-up TAXI emblem in front of the sunroof of the white Checker reminded Pat Dean of a pagoda. She recalled that Babe and a group of All-Stars were going to Japan in a month, but her husband was not chosen for the squad. Before she slunk into the taxi, with her skirt rising well above the knees, exacting a mumble from the taxi-man, Pat's next thought had already materialized. The thought deepened as he clunked the door closed and as she inhaled the cigar aroma inside the cab, the thought that there was nothing to fault the Babe for in any significant way. She saw instead something brave in the Bambino being himself and in so doing rising above the arbitrary norms of behavior. Why apologize for a fart? The word itself was funny. As if to spite herself, she began laughing, alone, in the back of the cab, saying to herself, over and over, "fart, fart, fart."

The mannequins at the store where she worked selling hosiery were the only lifelike forms that didn't fart. She had half a mind to wolf down a chili dog, saunter back to Hono-Lulu's, straddle a chair, light up a Camel, tilt onto one cheek and blow her panty hose right off. If Diz didn't like it, fuck him. The Babe, she realized, with a perceptible chuckle of irony, was a breath of fresh air.

At the hotel, the taxi door was opened for her by a bellhop. The revolving door revolved without her having to lift a hand. The elevator door opened and the operator punched the button for the sixth floor, then swung down the lever and pulled back the clacking lattice gate. She walked down the corridor, Mrs. Pat Dean, lonely as a doorstop, the kind of doorstop that seldom got the chance even to bunt, a rubber knob cracked with age, protecting a wall from a door that seldom swung from the heels. And when Pat opened, by herself, the door to room 619, it sailed into its stop like a two-bagger off the wall in Fenway, where Babe put ball after ball after ball.

4

TICKETS TO THE WORLD SERIES

It was a time for marriages, partnerships. Dizzy Dean had insisted on Bill DeLancey as his battery mate. Terry and the Pirates mixed it up in the funny pages. Satchel Paige married Janet Howard in October. Lynwood "Schoolboy" Rowe postponed his marriage to Edna May Skinner till right after the Series to placate his mother. By game six of the 1934 World Series, fans had already given him shotguns, bird dogs, fishing poles, a couple of sacks of cornmeal, a house full of furniture, and a fur coat for Edna. There was also the partnership of Schoolboy and the ball: "I eat a lot of vittles, climb that mound, wrap my fingers around the old apple and say to it, 'Edna, honey, let's go.' "

And in September, just before the World Series between the St. Louis Cardinals and the Detroit Tigers, Leo Durocher asked Cardinals general manager Branch Rickey for permission to marry Grace Dozier.

"Mr. Rickey, I want to get married."

"Sure, son."

"You sure you won't regret this?"

"Yes. And I hope you won't, either. Marriages are never a terrible mistake. They're always something more banal."

* * *

In Hollywood it was Clark Gable and Carole Lombard, and somewhere north of St. Louis it was the partnership in crime of John Henry Seadlund and James Atwood Gray.

The old man in a salt-and-pepper suit and wide yellow tie slouched against the green hood of a '34 Rolls-Royce Phantom II. Shaggy, rumpled, slightly corpulent, his belly slanted out from his chest at the same angle that sand creates naturally when falling from a bucket onto the beach. He also looked like he had car trouble. The seventy-six-year-old man who had once said that "inside the wreck of every lawyer is a poet" watched at the periphery of his vision the approach of two young men on foot who would rewrite his life. The first drifter chuckled, thinking of the old man's belly as a busted spare tire with the inner tube protruding. "Nice car. Got a problem?"

Indeed he did. He was stuck. Stuck on a country road with no one in sight. So stuck he couldn't bring himself to walk a quarter mile to a filling station for help. Not only could he not walk, he couldn't even turn his head or pull his hat down to keep the sun off his face. He was frozen. It had happened to him before. At a diner. He'd ordered a cup of coffee and just stared at it. Couldn't pick it up. Only after he realized that the waitresses were giggling at the frozen man did he notice the reflection of his mouth in the black coffee and pick up the cup, breaking the spell. This time it was fear of the drifters that snapped him out of it. To forestall further conversation he looked straight ahead and answered in French, *"En panne."*

"On what?"

"I reckon that's his way of saying he's out of gas," said James Atwood Gray.

The old man held back a smile. "Metaphorically, yes," he answered, realizing that the drifters were determined to help. "More to the point, I'm broken down. Brakes are shot."

"I could take a look if you want," John Henry Seadlund offered.

"You know something about a Rolls-Royce?" said the old man derisively.

John Henry scratched his head. "Let me get the hayseeds out of my hair and think about it . . . Far as I can tell," he said, craning his neck and bending to look over the hood, "a Rolls has got four wheels and mechanical brakes."

The old man felt apologetic about his attitude. "You think you could fix this buggy?"

"You got a tool box?"

The old man showed John Henry the set of tools under the front seat, including valve springs and spark plugs, and another set of tools under the hood. John Henry picked up a spanner engraved with ROLLS-ROYCE that looked like it had never been used. "Hell, you could eat with one of these."

James Atwood poked about the front of the car. The vertical bars of the grille reminded him too much of cell bars for him to be comfortable. John Henry finished a quick inspection of the Phantom, got off his knees, and said, "Got servo-assisted brakes. Front and rear drums. Whole mess of cables and rods attached to the brakes. At least one of them is busted."

James Atwood smiled. He looked at the old man, pointed to the Spirit of Ecstasy radiator ornament and said, "Looks like you got the flying lady, too. I kind of like her." James Atwood spoke at times like a ventriloquist, hardly opening his mouth.

"Tell you what," said John Henry. "Looks like you're headed to St. Louis. We are, too. I'll fix your buggy if you give us a ride."

"Sounds fair to me," said the old man, a populist who trusted the hoi polloi more than he trusted the drivers of luxury automobiles, though he didn't have much use for either. He regretted not trusting his misanthropy when they were finally a mile down the road and John Henry introduced himself and his partner as outlaws.

"Actually, I'm an outlaw. He's a kidnapper," James Atwood revised.

John Henry slapped James Atwood on the shoulder. "Right now we're nothing. All depends what opportunity turns up. Could be mending our ways, but James Atwood is pretty determined to get his feet wet in the kidnapping business."

The driver fidgeted, breathed quickly, and gripped the steering wheel more tightly. John Henry leaned forward. "Ah, don't worry none.

We ain't gonna kidnap you. Or rob you neither. We're beholden to folks who give a poor man a ride, especially in a nice car like this."

James Atwood rubbed his hand on the red leather upholstery. "Sure wish I had one of these. When I get my hands on some dough, the first thing I'm gonna do is buy me one. They say that crime does not pay, but sometimes it pays a whole lot."

The driver coughed nervously. "I can see how you might think that, but you need to take a long-term view."

"What do you mean?"

"Look, I've had my share of trouble with the law, too. I'm $50,000 in debt because of it, but I'm not about to kidnap anybody. The FBI catches them all eventually. Say you make fifty G's kidnapping. Divide that by twenty years in the slammer and it comes to $2,500 a year." The driver shrugged. "You can make that in Detroit," he said, swerving to avoid a dog. James Atwood pushed the wheel back at the mutt and laughed.

John Henry shook his head and lit up a Chesterfield. "Friend of mine had a job in Detroit. Depression came along and they fired him. Kept the niggers on, though. My friend was making more money, see?"

James Atwood, who had a hard time processing two arguments at once, was just digesting what the driver had said. "Maybe the man's got a point—what's the man's name, John Henry?"

"On-Pon," said John Henry, mimicking the driver's French.

"Darrow," the driver corrected him, awkwardly extending his hand.

"Not Clarence Darrow?" said James Atwood, smiling and shaking his hand.

"You can just call me 'Darrow.' "

"Hell, that's what they called me back in Ossage, on account of my big mouth."

Darrow laughed. John Henry took a half-full pint of Four Roses from his jacket pocket. He unscrewed the top and swigged, then handed Darrow the bottle. "Have a slug."

Darrow waved his hand in front of the bottle. "I gave up drinking, ever since I had callus mastoiditis."

Callus mastoiditis. It sounded perfectly Neanderthal, prehistoric. Sounded like what ailed a mastodon, some ingrown tusk. It reminded Darrow of Gaul, of a bellicose Caesar swinging the jawbone of a mastodon and whacking him upside the head. The same pain. Callus mastoiditis.

Darrow pushed back a loose throw of hair that was hanging over his right eye like a washrag in tatters. Hair, for Darrow, was an afterthought. Even a two-dollar cut looked like an act of vengeance. His head was completely balkanized.

Wrinkles seemed to have fallen faster than the rest of his face flesh, accumulating on his jowls, chin, and around his mouth, as if a harrow had run amok, as if facial treatments included applications of "Essence of Prune." The newly pressed salt-and-pepper suit jacket on his shoulders immediately sagged. His eyes were tired and baggy, as if every morning he emerged not from a bedroom but from a closet where the clothes he wore were his bedding. Darrow had stopped drinking, a wise decision for a man with a straight razor in his hand, trying to cut down what grew in the fissures and folds left by a retreating glacier.

"You know what the problem with you is, Darrow?" John Henry asked both rhetorically and presciently. "You're more than half dead already. If we hadn't come along, you'd still be leaning against the side of this car feeling sorry for yourself. Now, take a slug." John Henry jabbed Darrow just hard enough with the bottle to intimidate him into sipping the whiskey.

At the next red light John Henry stared at a dopey-looking young man with a Cardinals hat on backward and his thumb out. He stuck his head out the window.

"Where you going?" asked John Henry.

"St. Louis."

"You're in East St. Louis now."

"That's right. That's why I'm going to *Saint* Saint Louis."

"You don't mind if we give him a ride, do you, Darrow?"

Darrow shook his head. He was relieved to have another passenger, a kind of buffer, though John Henry and James Atwood were both in the front seat.

"Thank you very much, mister. Sure is a nice car. What kind is it?"

"Rolls-Royce," said James Atwood.

The young man sat suddenly back. "Never heard of it."

"What's your name, son?"

"Name's Elmer. And your'n?"

"I'm Darrow. This is John Henry and James Atwood."

"They got two names and you got one."

"I've got two, too, but I only use one."

It was clear that the kid was not all there, mentally. James Atwood looked over his shoulder. "We're kidnappers, John Henry and me." Elmer's face registered no emotion. He leaned forward. "I was kidnapped once. My big brothers, Jay and Paul, they looked for me but they couldn't find me. I was gone four years. But I'm back now."

"What are you doing in St. Louis?" James Atwood managed to ask with no apparent movement of his jaw.

Elmer sat back and spoke dispassionately. "Going to see my brother Paul pitch. Sixth game of the World Series."

"The game's in Detroit," said James Atwood, quick with a fact, but still trying to get his head around the bizarre suggestion that the kid's brother was pitching.

"Paul didn't tell me that. How far's Detroit?"

"Take a day to get there."

John Henry and James Atwood turned and studied the kid's face. John Henry laughed. "I'll be damned. You could be a Dean."

"I am. Elmer Dean, the youngest of the three Dean brothers." Elmer unfolded the jacket he was carrying and showed John Henry and James Atwood a piece of cloth sewn vertically into the inside of the right lapel with his name written on it. "My daddy put that there. I can pitch, too. They just might bring me up. Back in Hot Springs, the House of David team gave me a tryout, and some say I'm the best Dean of 'em all. I can throw a peanut in a cup at twenty feet. I'm the peanut man at the stadium in Houston. Folks watch me all the time."

James Atwood didn't believe the kid. "If there's Dizzy and Daffy, what do they call you—Dopey?"

Elmer leaned forward, as he seemed to do every time he spoke. "No, sir. They already got a Dopey. He's a cousin, I reckon. From Texas, too.

His 'Texas Twister' levels everything in sight. Hitters down there re-member him more than the Alamo. Specially the ones he hits, and there's a lot of 'em. That's why the House of David brought me up in-stead of him. I got control, like my brothers. The House of David is Jewish fellas. They all got beards, and they don't play on Saturday. You know who else played with the House of David? Grover Cleveland Alexander. He used to put a pint of whiskey under the rosin bag and take a slug now and then. Hell, I could throw as hard as Old Pete. Could have been better, but my brothers stopped me. Yessir. When I was twelve I tried to cut off these two fingers so I could pitch like Three Finger Brown. But it wasn't so easy. Hurt too much. Shoulda used a sharper knife. My brothers heard me screaming, so they ran into the kitchen and took the knife away. But I throw pretty good for a guy with five fingers, and my brothers think so, too."

James Atwood put his hands over his ears. "Elmer Dean, you can shut up now, okay?"

"Okay."

Crazy as it was, James Atwood was beginning to believe Elmer's story. He studied Elmer's face for some sign of lying but couldn't find any. He turned back and looked at the road in front. "I don't know about playing with Jews, what with them killing Christ and all."

Darrow, feeling the Four Roses, suddenly came to life with the same defense he made for Leopold and Loeb in the trial of the century. "Christians are much better at killing than the Jews. The characteristic crime of Jews is swindling. They're not brave enough to kill."

"I don't know about that," said James Atwood. "I was in jail once with a Jew. Said he'd killed ten men. He worked for a Jew called Dopey Benny, on account of a sleepy eye."

"There's Samson, too," said John Henry, who was well versed in the Bible. "He was a mass-murderer and he was a Jew."

Darrow smiled at being contradicted by a couple of men who proba-bly never finished high school. John Henry, meanwhile, scratched his curly head. As he cogitated, a long, deep furrow appeared on his fore-head. "Why do you think God ordained that, killing all those innocent people?"

Darrow smirked. John Henry had unearthed his deep-seated pessimism. "What I think is that the whole thing is a game. When your turn at bat comes, God throws you the sinker, and it's Tinker to Evers to Charon for you, sucker. You're out. Then it's the next guy's turn. And if you manage to get around third, He still gets the last laugh, 'cause there is no 'home.' You never score and you're never safe. God is the master of the force-out. That's life, son."

"You ever kill anyone, Darrow?" John Henry asked, running a finger down the barrel of his pistol.

"No, but I've read a lot of obituaries with great pleasure." Darrow avoided a squirrel on the road, its insides out, flattened enough to be pressed into service as a shirt cardboard. A trophy of the road, thought Darrow, courtesy of Ford, the organs indistinguishable on the 1934 democratic highway.

Elmer looked out the rear window. "We're on the trail of my brother Jay, all right. We never called him Dizzy. Every time I see a flat squirrel I say to myself, 'Jay's throwin' right-handed.' "

"He always throwed righty," said James Atwood.

"No, sir. When we was kids, Jay always threw at squirrels left-handed. If he'd a throwed at 'em righty, he woulda squished 'em, like that one. When we was kids and we saw a squished squirrel, we always knowed Jay was feeling mean."

"That's all right," said Darrow. "The squirrel will come back as something else."

"That ain't Christian," said John Henry, whose theology blended attenuated morality with apocalyptic Fundamentalism.

"No, it's reincarnation," said Darrow. "And I can prove it. Back before you were born, when the automobile was new, a chicken would run straight for home when a Model T came down the road, and it would usually get killed. But today when a car comes along, a chicken will run for the nearest side of the road. That chicken has been hit in the ass in a previous life."

John Henry felt self-conscious about leaning forward to see how broad Darrow's grin was, to see whether he was being put on or if Darrow was serious about his belief. He would never know for sure. Darrow changed the subject. "You're a lucky young man, Elmer. World Series tickets are hard to come by."

" 'S'matter of fact, I've got four tickets to the game. Jay gave me two and Paul gave me two. Say, why don't y'all come with me?"

Elmer produced the tickets. James Atwood snatched them from his outstretched hand and examined them.

"Sonofabitch, they look legit. Maybe the kid's who he says he is."

Darrow held out his hand and James Atwood crossed his palm with a ticket. Darrow examined it at nearly arm's length, his close-vision ability diminished. "This is real, all right." He gave the ticket back to James Atwood.

"What do you say, Darrow?" asked James Atwood. "Want to see the World Series?"

"I'm tempted, boys, but I've got work to do."

"You're a lawyer, right?" said James Atwood.

"I'm retired from law. Right now I'm Chairman of the National Recovery Review Board. We go around making sure that monopolies behave themselves. That's the New Deal. But if I have my way, it'll be the Dead Deal."

"FDR has been a friend of the workingman," said John Henry.

"He'd rather be his friend than be one. Don't kid yourself. When I was a boy I was told that anybody could become President. With Roosevelt, I'm beginning to believe it. Grover Cleveland was better, in my book."

"Old Pete?" said Elmer.

"No. Old Grover."

"He throws some heat, too?"

"I'd say he took it," said Darrow.

"You know," said John Henry, who like Elmer did not get the play on the name of pitcher Grover Cleveland Alexander, "you're an odd bird, Darrow." John Henry took out his pistol. "When James Atwood asked about the World Series, he was just being polite. We're kidnappers, remember?"

Darrow raised his hand deferentially. "Maybe we can work some kind of compromise."

John Henry pointed at Darrow the pistol that had no bullets in it. "Here's the compromise. You put your foot on that accelerator and I won't blow your brains out."

They drove through the night. Mid-morning found them in Paradise Valley, Detroit. The sidewalk bustled. John Henry had his head out the window, taking it all in—the hustlers, gamblers, sharpies, monte artists, street-corner preachers, ladies of the night, snake-oil salesmen, swells, would-be swells, dandies and dollies. The centerpiece seemed to be a septuagenarian black Baptist deacon proselytizing with the Good Book in one hand and a cane in the other. The diminutive, scrawny deacon had a torso like a warped door and shoulders like a broken hanger, so that the perfectly tailored and pressed suit looked comical. He had a big, bristly white mustache, a neck like a very old turtle, and veins that bulged like ropes over his wrists and hands.

"Slow down," ordered John Henry, with his head out the window and his hand on his gun. He was surprised at how women looked back at men cruising in a Rolls. John Henry was now in his own world, which included a plaza and sidewalk that he had arrogated as personal space and leased out to his libido. "Are you kidding me with those tits!"

Darrow shook his head. At the same time, John Henry's vulgarities had an almost innocent, prelapsarian quality to them.

"And what the hell are we—a bunch of one-eyed dicks just watching. Does that make any sense?" John Henry pointed at two women on the sidewalk. "Look at that. Broad is sticking 'em in our goddamn eyes."

"Damn right," seconded James Atwood.

"I can't stand it. It ought to be a crime."

"Damn right."

"I'm gonna get me one of those tonight. And when I'm done, I'm gonna get me another one. What kind of fucked-up world is this?"

Darrow sped up a bit.

"Slow down!" John Henry pointed the gun at him, then turned his gaze back to the sidewalk. "You married, Darrow?"

"Yes."

"Ever get a whore?"

"No. I'm self-employed."

James Atwood Gray tittered. "I don't get it. But it's funny anyway."

John Henry's attention was diverted to the moving bust of a tall woman in a high-necked calico dress. "Stick 'em out and see who salutes. You fucking kidding me?"

"I really am getting tired of that, John."

" 'John Henry.' "

"John Henry."

"Now, what is it you're tired of, Darrow?"

"Your saying that."

"Why don't you say it?"

"This is getting really infantile." Darrow lifted his hands from the wheel and slapped them on it again with a sigh of exasperation.

"Pull over there."

"What for?"

"Just do as I say."

Darrow pulled to the curb.

"Wait . . . wait . . . Okay. Here's one coming. See the broad in the red dress and the hat? Get out and say it to her."

"Say what?"

"Say, 'You fucking kidding me with those tits?' "

"I'm not going to . . ."

John Henry poked Darrow in the ribs with his pistol. "Get out. Now. It'll do you some good, you crusty old codger. Get your juices moving again."

Back aching from driving so long, Darrow got out, thinking again of the monkey-gland operation that was the rage in Chicago and Los Angeles. John Henry followed him. Darrow stopped in front of the lady. "Excuse me . . ."

"No fucking 'scuze me.' Just say it."

The woman in the red dress looked puzzled and a little scared. Darrow felt his voice rise from a conversational tone to the stentorian bellow he employed in closing arguments in a courtroom, as if his voice had a mind of its own. "You fucking kidding me, with those tits?"

Darrow felt his body buzz with something other than arthritis for the first time in more years than he could remember. He understood for the first time in a career of defending outlaws what it meant to be an outlaw, the thrill of it. The visages of Leopold and Loeb came to him, then Mont Tennes, the kingpin of Hawthorne Race Track, whom Darrow had advised to take the Fifth, infuriating Judge Landis, eighteen years earlier. His spine tingled with adrenaline. John Henry slapped him on the back and stepped aside to let the red-faced dame pass. For his part, John Henry got a thrill from forcing Darrow to act out his own fantasies. They got back in the car. Darrow could not express his feelings of guilt, infantility, and exhilaration. He sat motionless and silent in the driver's seat for a few moments, with the dumb look of a just-unstuck dog. "What are you thinking about?" asked John Henry. "Pooty?"

"I was thinking about Charles Bovary and about a madeleine."

"She hot?"

Darrow spoke slowly, as if in reverie, looking straight ahead. "Madeleine? No. That's a cookie. You eat it and you're flooded with memories. Then I was thinking about poor Charles Bovary, and how much like him I am, and I didn't even know it. Charles—he had a wife but couldn't keep her. And I was wondering—if that had been Emma Bovary back there, what would she have done?"

"She live near here?" asked James Atwood.

"No . . . No. She's . . . far away. France."

"I'd like to get a French broad," James Atwood piped.

"Emma Bovary was the creation of the novelist Gustave Flaubert. When he was a kid, he wanted literally to send his heart to a girl on a bed of straw in a hamper full of oysters."

"Sounds crazy to me," said James Atwood.

"Yes, but the point is the whole world wants to die for love. You, John Henry, even Elmer."

"I don't want to die," said Elmer.

John Henry smiled. "You know, Darrow, I only understand half of what you say, but you sure got a sweet way with words."

John Henry lifted the pint of Four Roses, toasting Darrow, then took a healthy swig and let out a sigh from a burning throat, and as if he inchoately understood Flaubert's symbolism, said, "I could go for some oysters right now."

* * *

Collision. Collusion. Coitus. Darrow's ruminations on the clouds moved from tortious interference to sex. A white *mouton* tupped by a *dramatis persona* in dark gray. The miscegenation of clouds turned Darrow's rumination to his defense ten years earlier of Ossian Sweet, a black doctor who stirred up trouble by moving into a white neighborhood when the black population of Detroit had increased nearly two thousand percent in seven years and a KKK write-in candidate would have won the election for mayor if his name hadn't been misspelled on a few thousand ballots. When Sweet was acquitted he asked Darrow to help Negroes obtain the right to play in the Major Leagues. Darrow considered it, but turned it down because there was no money in it. Headed now to a World Series game composed of all white players, Darrow felt bad about turning down the opportunity to do something fundamentally good for financial reasons.

Now the rain. Mind-numbing relief. Nature throwing a wet one. Darrow turned on the wipers.

"I always liked walking in the rain," said John Henry.

"I liked baseball," said Elmer.

"Not me," said John Henry. "My father used to hit my mother with a bat. After he'd hit her, I'd go walking in the rain. Used to think that when the last raindrop fell I'd die. The time I had to live was when it was raining. That was it."

"You know," said Darrow, "for a psychopath you're a pretty romantic guy."

"What's that—psychopath?"

"That means no matter what you do you'll never be hanged, 's long as you've got a good lawyer."

"Am I a *cyclo*path too?" asked James Atwood, eagerly.

"You, James, I don't know. Maybe. You're at least a sociopath."

"What's a sociopath?"

"That means they might hang you and they might not. Depends how heinous the crime is."

"I'm pretty heinous most of the time. Wouldn't you say so, John Henry?"

"Yeah. I'd say so." John Henry's attention was captured by a blonde struggling with some urgency in high heels. "That's one drenched chicken. What do you think, Darrow?"

Darrow was moved by the blonde who had resigned herself to being soaked, who walked with a different kind of urgency, the kind that he had always been attracted to, the urgency that seemed embedded in the thighs themselves. He missed the urgency of attention that well-made women used to demand of his consciousness, an urgency that had gone underground and was being brought back to the surface by his hooliganistic, psychopathic passengers. He recalled hearing that Yeats had had the monkey-gland procedure and that the absinthe crowd was crowing about its restorative powers, not only for sexual function but for the ebbing life force itself. He parked the car and the foursome walked a quarter mile to Navin Field, for game six of the World Series.

Thank you, John Henry, Darrow said silently.

5

CALLED OUT

God said to Gus, "Bring me a son."
Gus said to God, "Hey, which one?"

On the afternoon of the sixth game, October 8, 1934, William Augustus Greenlee looked out the window of his office on the third floor of the Crawford Grill in Pittsburgh's Hill District and saw a corpse float by. A very particular corpse, and one that haunted him. Amos S. His first. A cherry that bled more than Gus imagined a man could. More than the pigs he had slaughtered as a kid. The cloud resembling Amos S. had come back with a message, Amos himself as a postcard, a reservation.

Gus had been listening halfheartedly to the game Darrow and his crew were watching, reading the obituaries, half-expecting to see his own. He'd become obsessed with death, as one of Pittsburgh's main purveyors thereof. He had a certain intimacy with it not available to the average Joe. How stunning and final it was. How reluctantly it came to strong, young men. How a *stove-in* head could look back at him as if from a convex mirror and not be dead, how it would need a little touch-up with brick, would call out for brick to be more liberally applied.

How dog-like a man could become in extremis, his own belt applied as a collar, his tongue hanging out, unto one complete revolution in the hay before lying down for good.

Gus ran numbers in the Hill District. He was also involved in bootlegging and a Whitman Sampler of racketeering. He was the discreet, gentle, Pooh-bear of the rackets, St. Patrick of the Hill, sweeping the strong-arm protection guys out and building a ballpark for his Negro League team, the Pittsburgh Crawfords. Numbers bankrolled the team, enabling him to steal players from rival Cum Posey's Homestead Grays and put together one of the greatest teams in baseball history, white or black. The second floor of the Grille was occupied twenty-four hours a day by whores and penny-counters and -stackers. A million pennies were routed through the Crawford Grill, the biggest piggy bank in town.

The same innate ability to remember scores of numbers enabled a photographic memory of all the bodies that were *his*, sowed in the grounds of the Entress Brick Company. The bodies were labeled, in Gus's cranium, by first name and initial, for anonymity's sake, and maybe the victim's memory would diminish along with his surname, blend in like the corpse and the dirt that surrounded it, a gradual, ineluctable loss of identity and with it whatever guilt that may have weighed on Gus, which he feared was responsible for the puffing out of his nose, the way lies elongated Pinocchio's. Gus had a broad, protuberant honker that looked like a deformed legume, a squashed squash. You kind of wished that Gus had been born a girl in one of those Middle Eastern harems where they have to wear veils. It was that pudgy. When he gave away hundreds of turkeys at Thanksgiving on the Hill, you couldn't help but think of a miniature oven-basted roaster's self-portrait in a convex mirror.

As for the rest of the bodies, some of which had been disinterred when the ball field was put in, Gus just smiled, thinking of the banners in Cum Posey's office on Frankstown Avenue, the same street Gus lived on, where Cum managed the affairs of the Homestead Grays, who had no home field of their own, a fact that Gus impressed on Cum every time he saw him. Gus resented Cum because he was an "OP," an Old

Pittsburgh Black. Cum's banners were from a private East Coast boarding school where he sent his kids. It read, NON SIBI, or "Not For Self." And Gus imagined himself waving the banner in the cops' faces as the bulldozers uprooted the bones of all the corpses *non-sibi,* while all of his victims had been prudently reinterred elsewhere.

In Gus's dreams, which were always a gray area between sweet and nightmare, Willie and Crabs were stone coachboys-with-lanterns on either side of the sidewalk leading to his house, while Rabbit stood naked on a rock in the shallow, natural pool in his garden. His arms were clasped behind his head, his elbows spread like wings, and from his long, erect penis shot a stream of water in a ten-foot arc. And Gus wondered if he himself, as a corpse, might someday appear as a coachboy in someone else's dream, lighting some small area of Pittsburgh sidewalk, allowing lesser creatures to play their version of baseball all night.

Greenlee magic. Abra cadavera.

It was laughed at—how superstitious Gus was, never coaching from the third-base box, but the superstition went ironically deeper. About four feet deeper than anyone but Woogie Harris understood. Woogie was Gus's cut-buddy, sharing equally in profits and losses on numbers. It struck Gus as horribly ironic that Amos S., who played third base for numerous semipro clubs that played against Gus's team, had been potted directly under what was now the Greenlee Field's third-base coaching box. And in years to come, when Ruth's body lay in state at Yankee Stadium, the ironic nexus of baseball and death weighed unbearably on him, as much from guilt as from the irony that his garrulous, raconteurish nature felt compelled to give words to, but couldn't. If only the grass could speak, Gus idylled.

Gus imagined Amos, Rabbit, and the whole ghastly crew rising and standing at the end of the line when the National Anthem was played at Greenlee Field before a game, as if the dead had a sense of patriotism unknown to them while living. When Cool Papa Bell was called out on a close play at first, Gus would yank his head twenty degrees to the right, expecting Willie N. to overturn the call, or at least confirm that he was right, as if the dead did not believe that *no one was safe,* as if they had a predilection for truth over lying, as if they knew if the runner was safe or out, as if truth somehow inhered in death, to compensate for its scarcity in life.

The cloud moved slowly and diverted Gus's attention from the Tigers tying the score at 1–1 at Navin Field in Detroit. The forty-five thousand on hand were on their feet when Jo-Jo White stole second and took out Frankie Frisch. While the ball rolled toward the outfield, White went to third. Mickey Cochrane was next up against Paul "Daffy" Dean, who was pitching on two days' rest, which was common for the Dean brothers. Second fiddle and then some—Paul Dean already had a win in the Series. He threw a heavy ball, nearly as fast as his brother's, but without the hop. He never got out of Diz's shadow and didn't crave the limelight. All folks knew about Paul was that he hated being called "Daffy."

Cochrane fouled off six straight, then hit a slow bouncer to Rip Collins at first. Ripper had no play on White, who scored the tying run, and Daffy was late covering first. Cochrane slid in headfirst and pulled a ligament in his leg. Beans Reardon called him safe as Daffy stepped on his leg and opened a one-inch gash.

"I told you the Tigers are gonna wrap it up," said Woogie Harris.

"Don't be so sure," said Knowledge Clapp. "Greenberg's been shitting the bed at the plate since he sat out on Yom Kippur. But it all comes round. Regression to the mean."

"What's that?"

"He's due. Watch out when he starts hitting."

"Woogie's right," said Gus. "The Cardinals are going to take it. And you know why? They're playing black-ball." Gus nodded in agreement with himself. "Hm-hm. The way Daffy spiked Cochrane."

"The Tigers ain't no cream puffs neither," said Woogie. "Cochrane could have come out, but he didn't."

Outside the Crawford Grill, a half-block down Wylie Avenue, Satchel Paige sat with Josh Gibson in Satch's Packard, listening to the game on a new wooden radio that two guys had brought out onto the stoop. The radio was streamlined and hot, but brazenly displayed. The corners of the radio were rounded, like a bus's. Even the knobs were positioned so as to simulate wheels. The speaker was wheel-shaped, with slits of wood over fabric that looked like the speed lines left from the radio waves traveling from Detroit to Pittsburgh.

"That's a righteous radio. Mind if we listen?"

"Fine-looking piece of machinery. I'll trade you."

"Radio's hot. Car's not," Satch said with a smile.

The man turned the volume up on the radio, which had grooves in the walnut veneer, like the worried forehead of the other Dutchman, Frankie Frisch. The Fordham Flash was flashing signs to catcher Bill DeLancey, and Cochrane was watching him, hawk-like, and Frankie didn't know if Cochrane knew that he was actually calling the game, not DeLancey. He knew that Cochrane didn't know how exhausted he was, on thirty-six-year-old legs, lumbago-stricken back, and the stress of calling the pitches and positioning his whole club, then dealing with Ducky Medwick when he wouldn't shade over toward center and threatened to bust Frankie's beezer if he kept up his McGravian harangue. Frankie was tired of fining the Hunky fuck, tired of arguing, tired of teaching Pepper Martin the rudiments of fielding, and of dealing with the wackiness of Dizzy Dean, tired of the game he loved to be tired of. And maybe most of all he was tired of arguing with the competitive Leo Durocher, the Cardinal yannigan who thought he already knew more than the skipper.

"Who's winning?" Satch asked Josh.

"One, one. Top of the fifth."

"Who's up?"

"Durocher."

"This is it. I can feel it. Rally coming on."

Josh looked at Satch with disbelief. "Durocher? He's the all-American out."

"Seven games. It's in the bag."

Tiger ace Schoolboy Rowe didn't have his fastball. He claimed that comedian Joe E. Brown hurt his hand shaking it—unlikely, since Brown weighed a hundred and fifty pounds and the only muscles he had were in his mouth. A hotel door was the most likely culprit. "It's painin' me, but I'm gonna take those Cardinals," Rowe said. It must have been paining him, for he gave up a single to the light-hitting Durocher, and Babe

Ruth stood and cheered, "Scallions, Leo!" Daffy sacrificed him to second, and he scored on Pepper Martin's shot to left. Goose Goslin's throw was wild and Martin went to third, then scored on Rothrock's infield out.

"I still think the Tigers are gonna take it. Those G-men are too good." Josh was referring to Gehringer, Greenberg, and Goslin. Gehringer hit .356. Greenberg .339, with twenty-six home runs. And Goslin .305, with a hundred RBIs.

"I like the G-men too, but Schoolboy don't have it. Gonna go seven." Satch punched his companion on his oak-like arm. "You a G-man yourself. If you was playin' for the Tigers . . ." Satch shook his head. "Think about that lineup. Nobody wanna face that."

Josh gave a melancholy, fatalistic smile. "Don't think so, Leroy. Niggers ain't gonna get a shot. Not in your lifetime." Josh's mood turned foul just thinking about it. He changed the subject. "You gonna talk to Gus, or we gonna sit here all day? I could do with a couple of Ballantines."

Satchel was trying to screw up the courage to demand a raise from Gus, who also owned the Pittsburgh Crawfords and had stacked it with some of the best players in the Negro Leagues—Satchel, Josh, Oscar Charleston, and Cool Papa Bell. Barnstorming against white teams, Josh hit .426, facing the likes of Dizzy Dean, Paul Dean, and Lefty Grove. Oscar was a complete ballplayer, with a lifetime batting average of .357. Cool Papa Bell was arguably the fastest man ever to play professional baseball.

Gus was inside, waiting for Satch, drinking the Crawford Grill's famous daiquiris, reputedly the best north of Havana's *La Florida*, with Woogie and Teeny Harris, Jap Washington, and Jew McPherson. Knowledge Clapp emptied the ashtrays and kept the glasses filled. As he lit Gus's Havana, Gus whispered to him, "How many men on third?"

Knowledge straightened up and looked at Gus's eyes, which were between wistful and glassy. "Nobody's on third."

Gus uncrossed his shrapnel-filled leg and stamped his foot on the floor. "Not in that game, you idiot. All over."

"I don't understand."

"All over the world."

Knowledge nodded acknowledgment of his idiocy and went back to the bar. He picked up a pencil and began to figure how many baseball games might be being played and the odds that at any given moment a man might be on third. Knowledge was the only black college kid who hung around the Crawford Grill. He was also a mathematics whiz whose talents Gus used in his numbers business. Knowledge had a near-photographic memory and encyclopedic knowledge that was dulled by a cocaine addiction that Gus enabled.

Knowledge eliminated Japan and other countries where it would be nighttime. He included Cuba and the Dominican Republic in his calculations, and made allowance for the odd game in Haiti or on military bases elsewhere, minus the audience expected to be occupied with the sixth game between the Cardinals and the Tigers. He knew his answer would be far from accurate, but he was proud that, given limited resources and time, there were few men in the world who could calculate a more accurate answer.

"Three hundred and twelve."

Gus's mind was as tickled by the answer as his lungs were by the sucked-in cloud of Havana tobacco smoke that was blown out in rings the diameter of which, before dissipating, Gus also wanted to know, but could put off to another time. Now, as the last of three rings exited his mouth he asked, "How many under?"

"Under what?"

"Third base."

"You mean, how many bodies?"

Gus smirked at the obvious and blew the last bit of smoke from his mouth. Knowledge gave a weak grin and went to work. He was an oddsmaker. More comfortable with odds than with straight numbers. He did not need a pencil and paper to figure that the odds of anyone being buried under third base were between small and infinitesimal. Then he realized that Japan and China, with their large populations, had to be taken into consideration, since burial admitted no limitation to day and night cycles. Then he added to the calculation the fact that the question itself indicated that Gus knew of at least one. As he let the thought linger, he upped it to two.

To extract credibility from fear, Knowledge retreated to the bar, played with his pencil while rolling an old numbers slip into a cylinder through which he inhaled a line of cocaine the way the Japanese read, and let inspiration flow through him. He walked back to Gus on lighter feet and said, "Three point five."

That sounded right to Gus, who pulled a double sawbuck from a wad and held it like a leaf to the October wind and felt it slide through his first two fingers. Gus had a personal bet with Cum Posey of a thousand dollars on game six. Gus bet on the Cardinals, and it wasn't so much the money as beating Posey that motivated Gus. As much as anything else, it was personal animosity toward the light-skinned black man who had everything, especially women, that motivated Gus to start his own team and stock it with the best colored players money could buy. At the root of it all was women, Posey's possession of them and his smug confidence in his own good looks.

"We been sittin' here an hour at least," said Josh. "You goin' in or not?"

Part of Josh's anxiousness was due to the fact that the six-pack they'd bought from the guys on the stoop was drained. Satch shook his head. "It's not just Gus. That Knowledge, he give me the heebie-jeebies."

"Never bothered me none."

"Can't even talk baseball without he turn it into numbers. Supernatural shit like three strikes and three outs, four bases—four balls for a walk, nine innings—nine guys on a side. But so the fuck what? Just coincidence."

Josh Gibson, the Crawfords' catcher, listened intently as Mickey Cochrane blocked the plate and Ernie Orsatti insanely tried to score, coming at Cochrane like a freight train in the top of the ninth. He was out, but so was Cochrane, knocked out, with probably a concussion. There is no school for catchers, where they learn to tag a freight train and get out of the way. Training was completely on the job, and it was the toughest job in baseball. Cochrane did it better than anyone in the Majors, and if there was ever an immovable object in front of home plate, it was Gibson.

The Cardinals were back to playing Gashouse baseball. Gus Greenlee's kind of baseball. Gus beamed, stamped his feet and smiled broadly, with the Havana gripped between his teeth. He saw clouds go by, none of which had any resemblance to a human form, but as the Cardinals finished with a win, Gus slipped into a dark reverie. Each of his "hits" had a special place in Gus's memory, the way a singles-hitter like Durocher remembered his home runs. Circumstances could bring them back, circumstances like the digging up of a property to turn it into a baseball field. Autumn held a disproportionate share of life-ending events. Leaves falling from trees triggered the hit on Amos S. Frost on the pumpkin brought back Willy N., on whose head Gus had smashed a pumpkin before turning the skull into a dropped pie with a shovel. Snow resurrected Freddy F., the backbreaking work of digging Freddy's grave, which took all night and was Gus's last winter hit. He had nightmares the whole winter of 1929, whenever frost heaves levered the head or the feet of Freddy out of his shallow grave behind the Entress Brick Company building.

Gus was dozing in his chair. Satch knocked on the open door. Slumped in his lounge chair, Gus awoke and simultaneously saw Satch and his cigar burning a hole in his silk tie.

"Holy shit, I'm on fire!"

He sat up rapidly, grabbed his drink, and tossed it on himself. Behind the bar, on the floor, was a cachinnating Knowledge Clapp, who knew that Gus's cigar had fallen from his fingers onto his tie. He knew that if his soundless laughter turned audible he was in big trouble. He was laughing so hard his stomach hurt.

"Looks like I saved your ass," said Satch.

"What do *you* want?"

"Little talk."

"Cardinals in seven," said Gus, lighting up another Havana. "Wanna bet?"

Satch waved at the smoke blown in his direction. "Have to see. Maybe Dean will pull one of his holdouts when he's got their ass to the wall."

"He ain't pitchin' anyway. Hallahan's up."

Satch shook his head. "Forget what you read in the papers. It'll be the money-man—Dizzy Dean."

"They just said it on the radio. Hallahan."

"They don't know shit, either. Dean'll pitch. You can bet the farm on it. Anyway, I come here for a reason, Red. We've got to renegotiate our contract, or I'm going to Bismarck. I'm a married man now. Expenses is a lot more than I expected. I got two mouths to feed now."

"I've got a few myself. Got the whole Hill."

Satch gripped the back of the chair Woogie had been sitting in and looked Gus in the eye. "I need five hundred."

Gus looked out the window. "Every time you come in here I feel a powerful lightness in my pockets."

"Like I said, I got a family now. Got bills to pay."

"Why not try *not* buying every suit you pass? Maybe trade in that car of yours—thing's so big you got to walk three blocks just to check the tires."

"Dizzy Dean's gonna hold out for fifty thousand if the Cardinals win. I'm just asking for a modest five hundred a month."

Gus spat a piece of tobacco on the floor. "He'll be lucky to get ten. Ruth's only making thirty-five."

"That's why he's retiring. Meanwhile, you makin' a million off of me. Fans come to see me pitch. They don't come to see you. I'm the one filling the seats at Greenlee Field."

"Right—*Greenlee* Field, and don't you forget it. Ain't *Paige* Field. It's Greenlee Field. I put up the cash. I took the risk."

"Wasn't no cash, Gus. Was a million pennies you stole from all the niggers on the Hill. And risk—don't talk to me about risk. Every day I pitch I'm riskin' my right arm. That goes, and I've got nothin'. That's what risk is."

Gus would have leaned farther forward if his belly hadn't lodged up against his broad mahogany desk. He slammed his large fist on the "shine" he'd been reading so hard that the chartreuse ceramic ashtray with gold-painted butt-holders jumped. His arm jerked back up to vertical and he shook his forefinger at Satch. "The champ of today is the chump of tomorrow. You thinkin' of jumpin' on me, you riskin' more than just your arm, nigger. Five thousand is a lot of money. The average player's salary is a thousand, and you're makin' four times that. And for what? For playin'. I've got to work for my money. All you do is play. Ain't a workingman in America wouldn't trade his job for yours. Those guys are makin' twenty-two cent per hour. That's less than five hundred a year. You makin' eight times that off me alone. You hold out, and the fans be throwin' shit at you like they do to Dizzy Dean. Ain't no sympathy for a man makin' your kind of money holding out."

"I don't want no sympathy." Satch glared down at Gus. "And I don't want to argufy. All I want is fairness. Do the math, Red. Every time someone plunks his ass in a seat you're makin' a dollar. When I'm pitchin', there's lots of asses in those seats, and when I ain't, ain't no asses in a lot of 'em."

Gus got up and poured himself a shot of whiskey from an unlabeled bottle. He slugged it down and wiped his mouth with the back of his hand. "Fuck fairness. Ain't nothin' fair about life. You ought to know that. If life was fair, how come you ain't got Knowledge's brains? How come all those niggers be linin' up for free turkeys when Satchel Paige be drivin' by in his big Packard with nothin' for 'em but that big-ass smile? How come you ain't invited to Japan with Ruth and Berg and those guys? You want fairness, you go to Russia. But if you want to play baseball, you stay right here in Pittsburgh. Ain't nothin' fair here, and nothin' free."

Satch knew when to fold. He ambled slowly toward the door, then turned. "Greenlee Field ain't nothin' but a dump anyway. Dilapidated from the day it was built. Got no clubhouse, no protection anywhere from the sun, got chicken wire in the outfield. Don't nobody want to play there."

Satch had been prepared to argue fairness with Gus and was flummoxed by his outright dismissal of the principle. His mind started wandering to the other things Gus had said. He had images of past barnstorming against Dizzy Dean and other white clubs, and images of him and Josh showing the Japs how to play baseball the way it was played in the Negro Leagues. Against this backdrop Satch decided that God could not be all-knowing. Wasn't the whole purpose of inventing baseball the excitement of letting it all unfold in a way He could not foresee? Satch tried to envisage the earthly baseball game God would like to watch above all others. Hearing the play-by-play of a scallion-scarfing Durocher scoring the winning run on a hit by Paul Dean, it came to Satch—the game God would want to see would be the white champs against the guys who never got a chance to play, a team of Satchel Paige All-Stars. It would be the greatest game ever played.

God's emissary was speeding down Wylie Avenue, to get to a phone to talk to Dizzy Dean, before he got kidnapped or something.

Still in his uniform, Diz was in the room the Tigers let Sam Breadon use for an office. Diz was arguing about his contract for next year, when the call came in. Diz said he was busy, and Pat Dean offered to take the call.

She listened, mumbled something, and said, "Jay, it's someone named Satchel. He says it's very important." Then she whispered, "I think it's a Negro."

"I'll be right there."

Pat moved the receiver a little farther from her mouth. Safer. "If this is about his uniform, I've already mended it."

"No, ma'am. Not about his uniform. It's about some stars coming out at night."

Diz took the phone. Pat twirled her right hand twice, finger pointing at her ear, silently mouthing, "cuckoo." Diz walked as far as the cord extended, turning his back on Sam Breadon and Branch Rickey, who moved to the far corner of the room to give Diz some privacy.

"Hello, Satch."

"Mr. Dizzy Dean?" Satch said with an Alabama twang.

"You looking for tickets?"

"For what?"

"World Series. Where you been?"

"Pittsburgh."

"I reckon they've got newspapers in Pittsburgh. Paul just evened it up with the Tigers, three games to three, and I'm gonna fix their wagon tomorrow. Detroit ain't far from Pittsburgh. I'll get you a box seat, long as I can get one back from my brother Elmer. I gave him two."

Diz had asked for a Falstaff, but Breadon frowned and gave him a glass of water. Diz took a slug and put the glass down on the Bible Rickey had left on Breadon's desk.

"I've seen you pitch plenty. Beat you the last time we played," Satch said with a laughing but taunting tone.

"I've got to hand it to you, *podner*, you threw a beaut. But we'll get you next time."

"That's just why I'm calling, Diz. You're gonna whup those Detroit pussies and have a big parade and call yourselves world *champs*, but you Cards ain't no *world* champs. You *white* champs. Ain't nothin' *world* about it. I got nine boys can whup you any day of the week."

"You birds give me three days to rest this wing and you won't get a tick off me."

"Me, Josh, Cool, and the boys, we'll whup you sure."

Diz paced as far as the telephone cord would allow. "Satchel Paige, you got my rabbit up, and there's nothing I'd like to do more than give you birds a licking, but Landis wouldn't allow it."

"We can do it on the sly. Night game. The Monarchs got portable lights. We can rent 'em."

"Who's paying for the lights? And the Cards? Those boys won't play for fish cakes."

"You've got to find a patron. A Negro-hating cracker with deep pockets. Shouldn't be too hard to find."

No, it shouldn't. Diz's mind was already working on it. He knew that Satch could put together one hell of a team. Josh Gibson, Cool Papa Bell, Oscar Charleston. They could all play in the Majors. Some of them might be All-Stars. Diz had no doubt Satch would be. Some of the pitchers the Cardinals faced in the regular season couldn't hit the red door on Pa Dean's barn. But Satchel Paige—that boy would blow it down. Paige was a gunslinger.

"You calling me out, Satch? I mean, personally. Dizzy Dean versus Satchel Paige?"

"I'm calling you out."

"That's all I needed to hear."

6

NICE WORK IF YOU CAN GET IT

In game six, Leo went three-for-four. When Babe came into the dressing room to congratulate the Cardinals, Leo's eyes widened. He hugged Babe like he was a giant teddy bear. "It's like it wasn't even me, Babe. I came up on the ball as it was dropping and it just lifted off the bat."

"Right."

"Right? It felt all wrong. Felt like I'd got dressed up in women's clothes."

Babe laughed. "Leo, if you were a broad, you'd be turning tricks under the bleachers. You're laying off those scallions now, aren't you?"

"Yeah."

"They're only for a slump. When you're ripping it, you lay off, or it could have the opposite effect."

Leo rolled back the cuffs of his starched white shirt and inserted fourteen-carat cuff links. "Sure. I'm laying off."

"Game seven tomorrow."

"I don't know?"

Babe chewed on a cigar as they talked. Leo looked at his watch.

"Hey, let me see that," said Babe.

"Let go, you big ape." Leo pulled his arm free. He tried unsuccessfully to put his hand in his pocket, forgetting that he'd had his pockets sewn shut, like George Raft, to keep the line of the trousers smooth.

"You ain't got no pockets?" Babe laughed.

"Grace sewed 'em for me." Leo burped.

"Get her to sew up that hole in your glove."

"I like it that way. Rabbit Maranville gave me that glove."

Babe nudged Leo. "Don't forget. Lay off the scallions."

"Yeah."

"I mean it."

"Yeah."

"When you burped, I smelled scallions."

"That was onions."

"You sure?"

"Sure I'm sure. Scallions turn my stomach. Too bitter."

"Big game tomorrow."

"Yeah."

"Let me see that watch."

Playing minor-league ball with George Raft, Leo picked up his buddy's penchant for silk suits, in his favorite color, green. In the pool halls of Springfield, Massachusetts—Winterborn's and Smith's—he became known as the Green Phantom. His suit this day was not quite scallion green. Still, in a field of scallions with his green suit and white shirt he would be nearly camouflaged from Babe's view, were he to lie in the green and watch the white that lies just beneath the surface. The essence of scallions—white lies. *It ain't your watch, Babe.*

That night Leo would dine on prophylactic scallions, in spite of Babe's warning not to. His rationale was that throughout his Major- and minor-league careers, every time on deck he felt he was on the verge of a slump. If scallions worked once, they would work again. It might have been cheating, but so were the cut-balls that he and Frankie handed Cardinals pitchers. Honest guys might win ballgames, some of the time, but when you're born with a short stick you look for an angle, especially when you've got six grand riding on it. If there was a counterpart to scallions, Leo would find it to keep Wild Bill Hallahan down tomorrow. He would finagle a Dean start in the seventh game.

Diz sulked back to the dressing room where he showered and changed, then left in need of some chocolate bars, as he always did after a game. In the Trumbull Avenue gutter he saw a brown Hershey's wrapper, and he imposed the eight letters on the license plates of the cars that passed, filled mainly with depressed Detroiters after their team had lost. They needed a Hershey bar more than he did, but Diz was obsessed in a way Detroiters were not. He could taste it. He imagined two squares at a time in his fingers, his postgame indulgence. He wasn't thinking of Cardinals owner Sam Breadon's warning about kidnapping. After game three, Diz was about to accept a lift to the Forest Park Hotel from some louche-looking guys in pin-striped suits and a black car with New York plates when Breadon happened to look out the window. Diz was practically yanked out of the car by Breadon's staff and hauled back to the owner's office.

"Didn't your mother tell you not to get into a car with strangers? They could be kidnappers, for chrissake," said Breadon.

"Shit-fire, Sam," Diz replied, "it wouldn't do 'em no good to get me 'less they got my brother, too. Paul'd be madder than a snake with a plugged asshole, and he'd mow them Tigers down two games in a row."

As he walked down the wide Trumbull Avenue sidewalk now, Diz's thoughts moved to a call he'd gotten from an old friend, an admirer, a rival, doppelgänger: He was wondering why Satchel Paige couldn't play in the Major Leagues, and he decided to press the issue with 'the Mahatma'—Cardinals general manager Branch Rickey—at dinner that night at Henry Ford's. Ford had already hosted the Tigers, and it was good public relations to invite the Cardinals as well.

Tiger loyalists were retreating to their domiciles to gear up for tomorrow's seventh game, as the wind kicked up diverse paper trash from the wide sidewalk and the Tin Lizzies that kept Detroit going kept a slow pace on the wide avenue. Diz walked past a doubled, black steel utility pole and recalled how his brother Elmer insisted on walking between the poles, the way a kid would. Elmer would stand out, too, for wearing a baseball cap backward while every other man wore a respectable emblem of masculinity—a bowler, stovepipe, or snap-brim.

For no particular reason, Diz turned. He found it curious that the four thuggish guys would keep their fedoras on inside the Model A, whose New York license plate brought to mind Breadon's warning after game three. Curiosity turned to suspicion when the Model A was still behind him a half minute later, obviously trailing him at his foot-speed. The two beefy guys in the front seat, Diz reflected, did not have the sad miens of fans whose team had gone down. He thought about running but decided not to show his hand, decided to trust the same dumb luck he had on the mound. Plus, he really wanted those Hershey bars.

Through the corner of his eye, he noticed another car pulling up abreast of him, then a gun in the hand of the man in the passenger seat pointing at the roof. The back door sprang open.

"Hey, Jay! Come on in."

Diz saw his brother Elmer smiling at him, then glanced at the Ford pulling up behind them. He got in fast. Elmer himself had been kidnapped in 1927 when the Dean's Ford truck was stopped with a flat and a cotton picker gave Elmer a ride to the grocery store. The next time the Deans saw Elmer was in 1931.

"I knew you'd be heading for the candy store. I told my friends here. They're kidnappers. And this one's Darrow. He's retired."

"Kidnapper?" asked Diz.

Darrow shook his head "no," then looked the tall man in the eye for just a moment and extended his hand. "So you're Dizzy Dean. This is an honor. Pleased to meet you."

"Likewise," said Diz. "Those bolagulas in back of us were aiming to kidnap me, too."

Darrow and James Atwood nearly knocked heads looking in the rearview mirror, while John Henry stuck his head out the window to check out the thugs.

"New York guys," Diz continued. "Mr. Breadon warned me about 'em. I'm sure glad my own brother kidnapped me instead." Darrow could not decide whether to take Diz seriously or not. Diz slid forward on his seat, looking at the pistol, and spoke to John Henry Seadlund. "Say, where'd you get that? Can I see?"

"Never mind where I got it. I got it, and I can use it."

James Atwood turned and spoke to Diz. "Your brother's telling the truth. We've been thinking about holding you for ransom. But the reason we came down here in the first place was to talk some sense into you about holding out for more money. Then we got to thinking we could make some ourselves, and maybe be famous."

Darrow looked through the back window. "I suggest we get out of here fast and talk about it later."

John Henry craned in front of James Atwood and looked in the mirror. He saw a beefy man in a pin-striped suit opening the passenger-side front door of the Ford. He fumbled for the bullets in his pocket and quickly loaded his gun, stuck his head out the window, followed by his arm, but he didn't shoot. The angle was bad for a right-hander. He pulled his torso back into the car and the man behind them quickly got back in his car.

"Drive!" John Henry ordered.

Darrow pulled out.

"Where are we going?" asked James Atwood.

"Shit! I've got to think," said John Henry.

James Atwood pointed at a police car at the end of the block. "Look! There's cops. Pull over."

"No. Keep going." said John Henry. "We can't call in cops if we're kidnapping Dizzy Dean."

"Oh, hell. I won't say nothin'. Just pull over."

Darrow was approaching the cops. He looked at John Henry. "What do I do?"

John Henry's mind was freewheeling. He just stared straight ahead. James Atwood looked back and forth between the cops and John Henry.

"Look," said Darrow, "you've got a peashooter. Those guys probably have four Thompsons. We're seriously outgunned. I'm going to pull over."

John Henry was still dumbstruck. Darrow pulled over, and the Ford stopped right on their bumper. James Atwood waved out the window and shouted to the cops. "Hey!"

The two cops were already approaching the Rolls-Royce with guns drawn. Darrow figured the pursuers would keep going rather than shoot it out with cops. He figured wrong. When the cops got close, Darrow blanched and his myopic eyes widened. "They're not cops!"

James Atwood looked over his shoulder at Darrow, as did John Henry. No flies on Darrow's foot. The black cop dived out of the way of the accelerating Rolls.

"How do you know?" shouted Diz.

" 'Cause I defended him ten years ago in the Sweet trial. Mingo Drumgoole has done more time in jail than you've done in baseball, and his record's a lot worse than yours. He's a psychopath with an IQ of about ten."

Diz shook his head and smiled. "Shit, that was a good plan—having phony cops stop us."

"Jesus, this thing flies," said James Atwood.

Darrow turned to John Henry. "Where to now, if you don't mind my asking?"

"Just keep driving," said John Henry.

Diz slid forward on the leather seat. "Let me tell you how to get rid of these hound dogs. We got a dinner in a couple of hours with Henry Ford, and I been to Henry's place once before. It's like Fort Knox there. We'll just head on to Henry's a little early, and if these goons want to take on Harry Bennett's army, we can watch the carnage."

James Atwood and John Henry looked at each other. John Henry looked out the window at the pursuing Ford.

"Head that way. Let me think about it."

Diz directed Darrow to Michigan Avenue. The Ford Estate in Dearborn was twenty minutes away by car.

"Say, how'd y'all like to be in a parade?" said Diz.

"What kind of parade?" asked James Atwood, who loved parades as much as John Henry did.

"When we get back to St. Louis, tomorrow. Gonna have a great big parade after game seven. The whole city'll be out. After today, when Rickey hears about the two guys who saved me from kidnapping, you'll all be celebrities. Heroes. The both of you. You'll be my personal body-guards. Go everywhere I go. Ride in the parade with me and Paul, Leo, Pepper, Ducky, the whole Gashouse Gang."

James Atwood scratched the straw that passed for hair and glanced at John Henry. "What do you say?"

John Henry could see that his partner in crime had gone south on him. Diz slapped John Henry on the back and preempted him. "All right, then. It's a deal."

"Not so fast. I'm still thinking. The Cardinals will pay good money to get Dizzy Dean back. I figure he's worth a hundred grand, easy."

Darrow scoffed. "Breadon? Rickey? Those guys want to make money, not give it to you. Besides, where are you going to hide him? Not to mention Elmer and me. You'll have the whole country looking for you. If folks were angry about Lindbergh's baby, how do you think they're going to feel about Dizzy Dean?"

James Atwood glanced at John Henry. "Maybe he's right, John Henry. We ain't thought it through the way we said we would."

"We ain't been invited to Ford's," John Henry protested meekly.

Darrow shook his head in disbelief at the kidnapper worried about the etiquette of crashing a dinner party.

"And don't forget about the parade," said Diz.

"I'd like that," said Elmer. It was the first thing he'd said in minutes, and it seemed to have just the right weight.

"All right, then," said John Henry. "Henry Ford's place. Step on it."

Parade. The word itself cast a spell that captivated John Henry. There was an inherent innocence to it that felt to him like the road to re-demption. Riding through the streets of St. Louis with the Gashouse Gang was irresistible. Girls as beautiful as Ginger twirling batons, fa-thers with bats that swatted nothing but balls. Dizzy Dean tossing base-balls into the crowd. Flags, balloons, balls, confetti, shouts, and the sounds of shining brass, the thunder-simulating rolls of drums, all soaked up by the insatiable air of a parade.

John Henry's rumination halted abruptly, along with the Rolls, at the gate of Henry Ford's residence, where an armed guard looked down from a tower. The Model A slowed and two mustachioed men posed, puzzled, heads out the windows. Diz got out and motioned to the guard who recognized him and waved the Rolls on in.

"How are me and John Henry gonna get into the party?" James Atwood grumbled. "We ain't ballplayers, and we ain't famous, like Darrow."

Diz slapped him on the shoulder. "Bodyguards, like I said. After game three, Breadon had four of them following me everywhere. Two ought to be easy to get in."

Harry Bennett, Ford's chief of security, greeted them and had no problem believing that John Henry and James Atwood were bodyguards. He had a problem with their attire, but he had a closet full of extra suits for occasions like this. John Henry and James Atwood ended up looking like the hundred thousand they were going to demand for Dizzy Dean's return. None of Bennett's suits quite fit Diz, who was 6'2", and Diz insisted on keeping on his western leather string tie and his cowhide belt with a buckle the size of a longhorn's head.

Henry Ford's chef, Wagner, was unmistakable for the high white hat, if not the arrogance. He carried a stack of menus, which he distributed to the quintet of Diz, Elmer, Darrow, John Henry, and James Atwood.

"What's pheasant?" said Diz.

"A game bird, *monsieur*."

"Got feathers?"

"Yes."

"I don't eat feathers."

"We dress it."

"Red meat?"

"No."

"I don't eat red meat unless it's well done."

"Then it's not red."

"Oh, shit-fire, mister, spare me the pheasant and all the rest. I'll tell you what I want and you make it, okay?"

"We should be able to manage that."

"And make it the same for my brother Elmer."

"Pheasant's good," said Darrow.

"Then you eat mine, and Elmer's." Diz turned to the chef. "So, your honor, I'd like scrambled eggs, bacon, biscuits, gravy, Johnny bread, crackling bread, beans, milk, and Lea & Perrins sauce. Okay?"

The chef scribbled it all on the back of a menu, looked up at Diz, and nodded. He started back to the kitchen. Diz called after him, "Better make that three helpings. My other brother don't like squirrel, either."

The first thing that James Atwood stuffed into his pants pockets was a small silver gizmo used to pick up sugar cubes. It looked like something he'd seen Garbo pluck her eyebrows with in a movie, and he thought it would be a swell present for the girlfriend he was bound to find sooner or later.

Ducky Medwick was the first of the other players into the Ford mansion. "Wow! Ain't it grand?"

It was grand, all right, but its grandiosity made Diz uncomfortable. The dimensions of everything were all wrong. The windows were too tall and went down too low. A window should not start at the strike zone, in Diz's estimation. And the ceiling was too high. The room went on too far. Posts turned into ornamental columns that were all Betsy Ross and George Washington. It had nothing to do with the Deans of Arkansas. Even if he could afford it, this house would flaunt its class at him, would put him in his place, would keep him in the kitchen eight hours a day, as the army had done.

Diz had the feeling of being watched, but not in the good sense of thirty-eight thousand people at Sportsman's Park watching him fog it in. These were not fans. These folks looked at him from pedestals, from paintings. They had strange hairdos and their faces were as stern as his father's. These guys were watching for your mistakes, making sure that you ate your soup as if you were feeding it to somebody else then changed your mind. These guys were making sure no one stuck a piece of bread in his pocket, a roll down his pants, the silverware inside his shirt.

"This is what they call opulence," said Frankie Frisch, which made Diz think "opossums"—all these guys on the walls whose eyes probably

glowed in the dark. They'd all been struck by something moving, perhaps a Ford. They'd been stuffed and mounted. A family of animals.
Predators.

"They can call it anything they want," said Diz, "and they can keep it."

They were not keeping a good eye on James Atwood. He'd pocketed
an antique gold letter-opener with a beautifully carved whale-bone handle. The only letters he ever got were from court. He smiled at the
thought of opening a summons with a purloined gold letter-opener.

In old khaki pants, torn sweater, and beat-up loafers, Branch Rickey
was sitting in a leather chair reading his Bible, glasses on the end of his
nose, thinking about the importance of piety. Piety was the fence between the neighbors that made them good. Piety was what brought us
to put people in the ground for as long as they could be remembered,
making good neighbors of the dead as well as the living.

The short and stocky general manager of the Cardinals looked like a
cross between a preacher and a turtle. The distance between his nose
and his upper lip was vast enough to disconcert the interlocutor. His
smile was pleasant, without showing any teeth. Behind the gold-rimmed
glasses were kind eyes, which disarmed all those who negotiated with
him as he snapped. He was both ruthless and ingenious at finding ways
to convince a player of the rightness, even righteousness, of a pay cut.
Rickey invented the farm system in baseball and was responsible for the
great St. Louis teams of the thirties. He was notorious for getting rid of
an aging player who was still good but would command a high salary.
Every time he unloaded a Dizzy Dean or a Rogers Hornsby, he came up
with a Rip Collins, who would have a fabulous year or two.

Darrow excused himself and went to the bathroom, which was as big
as most folks' dining room, and cleaner. Everything that wasn't marble
was brass or plated gold. He looked in the mirror and smoothed down
his hair with some water. The hair objected. Had always rebelled. But
today the overrule came with a thunderous finality, from somewhere
Darrow didn't know was in him. The mane of his hair would lie down
ungreased beneath the earpieces of his sheepish spectacles, or by God he
would shear it himself. He pulled a hanky from his pocket, wiped off
the grease, and discarded the hanky that held, he reflected, a king's ran-

som for Bobo Newsome, who put similar quantities on his curveball. Darrow opened a drawer and took out an ironed hanky. He blew his nose, let the wild phlegm flow. Did the Huns have summer colds? Goths a flu? Did the Visigoths suffer croup? Ague? *My nose,* thought Darrow, *isn't running. It's galloping.*

Henry Ford spotted him as he left the bathroom and asked, "Aren't you the lawyer from that Scopes trial?"

Darrow nodded.

"Darrow got a lot of publicity from that trial," said Will Rogers, who spent most of the evening at Ford's coattails. "But I don't know if it was worth it. He's had to spend the last fifteen years proving he's not descended from a socialist."

Ford risked a smile. "You beat the pants off William Jennings Bryan. He had it coming to him. Never heard a man so full of himself and determined to spew it out."

Diz walked over with a glass of sherry in his hand and the best cigar he'd ever had in his mouth. He slapped Ford on the back. "Mr. Ford, I want to tell you how to get this country out of the depression it's in. You take Burgess Whitehead, Frankie Frisch, and Moe Berg and put 'em in charge, and we'll be out of the hole in no time. Those are the three smartest sons of bitches you ever met. Burgess is a Phi Beta Kappa, and you know what that is. Also has the biggest hands in baseball."

Ford gave a smile of recognition. "Now I know who you're talking about. One player I shook hands with—it was like something out of Barnum & Bailey. He must be one heck of a hitter."

"Runner, actually. Not much with the stick. But I can see why you might think that. If we had to play the series over again, I'd have him give Schoolboy Rowe's hand a better shake than Joe E. Brown did."

Diz put a playful squeeze on Ford's hand, then looked back at Ford. "Yes, sir, those three guys—can't get nothin' by them. It's a surer thing than Tinker to Evers to Chance."

Ford smiled. Steeped in Emerson, he was more impressed by Diz's individual effort than by any notion of proletarian infielders.

"To tell you the truth, Mr. Ford, Frankie and I are in kind of a jam, and we were wondering if we could speak somewhere in private."

"There's still some light left. Let's take a walk."

"Darrow, too. You never know when you might need a lawyer."

Diz had tried to enlist Darrow in the cause of persuading Ford to pony up for the black versus white All-Star game. Though he loved the idea, Darrow was too busy with the NRA to get involved. He agreed to intervene only if Diz and Frankie failed. Ford signaled Harry Bennett from across the lawn. Harry was Ford's confidant, as well as his bodyguard and jack-of-all-trades—the unspeakable ones, the ones that he could get away with because he was Henry Ford.

Ford loved the daylilies he had planted around the house, something about their boldness yet plainness. They were the Model T of the flower world. Lunch-bucket flowers. Still, it bothered him that they were encumbered with banality by accident of a name—*daylilies*. There was none of their vibrancy, energy, robustness in the given name—"day." He wanted to know their Indian names—their names in Nipmuc, Shoshone, Iroquois, Huron—the right sound for them.

This kind of sentiment he would only communicate to Harry Bennett. Harry would just hop to it. He'd get it done. He'd dig up the last dead Huron if he had to and beat it out of him. Someone would know. Someone, thought Ford, must be in charge of not letting things die— the counterpart of Harry, who let things die. Unionists, anarchists— things like that.

Henry Ford should have posed the question to Dizzy Dean's trio of knowledge, but he was not a baseball man. Unlike Darrow, Ford had no childhood memories of clouting one over the dry goods store, then dropping the *club* and running around the *ring*—what they called the "bat" and "base path" in Ohio in the late nineteenth century. When Ford moved to Detroit, the principal sport was still cricket. Baseball and the motorized engine came to Detroit at about the same time and took off at the same breakneck pace. Ford had his epiphanic encounter with a steam engine at the same time that Frank Woodman Eddy replaced the cricket pitch of the Detroit Athletic Club with a baseball field. He grew up in the era of populism in the late nineteenth century, when teetotaling hoedowns were popular and the *McGuffey's Eclectic Readers* were the limits of literacy. The gilded age grew up on these moral tales, which were big on rags to riches but left empathy out of the pantheon of Christian virtues. Hard work would make Raggedy Dick a Rockefeller. Remaining in your rags was evidence that you lacked virtue. About the time of Ford's epiphany came Darwin's. The populist Detroiters were not quick to accept the theory of evolution, but when they did, it was an evolution that did not take into account natural disasters or simple bad luck. If your bootstraps broke, don't come crying to society. Ford didn't. In fact, he cut his own bootstraps twice. The first two automobile companies he founded foundered because he was off doing something else. He was a talented tinkerer with a vision and a passion, a man whose heart was in a rural America he largely destroyed. He did not believe immediately in evolution but did believe in reincarnation, and the soldier whose soul Ford believed he inherited from Gettysburg must have been a quondam bicyclist who expired shouting, "Wheels! Wheels! My kingdom for some wheels!"

Ford eventually grew out of McGuffey and into Emerson's transcendental vision, which he translated as meaning that we should ignore the limitations of reason and embrace the erratic and creative impulses of our rugged individual genius, which was why he warmed up so much to Dizzy Dean. Ford loved Emerson, who loved impulsive and spontaneous action. Emerson was the key to Dizzy, who didn't know it, and wouldn't understand Ford's explanations but would bask in his encomiums. When Jay Hanna Dean decided he didn't like his name, he just changed it to Jerome, an Emersonian creative impulse. Now only his brothers and his wife called him Jay. Emerson believed that an intelligently designed machine was in harmony with nature. Dean's right arm was such a machine. The curveball was one of God's finest creations. The batting order was an assembly line in which each out was a part to be affixed in the most efficient manner possible.

"God moves in you, Jerome, in your right arm."

"Gol," said Diz. "My right arm's kind of sore now. I sure hope God's not sore at me."

The quintet walked silently for a moment into the warm front that was blowing the sweet smells of autumn leaves and dying things across a landscape lit up by the fading sun in a cloudless sky. A perfect evening, thought Darrow, for a cabal. He whispered to Diz and Frankie, "Can I give you some advice? Just tell Ford the Jews are behind the Negroes and you can write your own ticket. He doesn't have much use for Negroes, but he doesn't hate them, like he hates the Jews."

They came across two kids tossing a ball, one white, the other black. Both were sons of caretakers on the estate. Ford didn't know them, and they didn't know him. But he was comfortable with them, the kind of lower-class kids he'd grown up with.

"What's your name?" Ford asked the black kid.

"Hank Greenberg."

Ford straightened up and put his hands on his hips. "You can't be Hank Greenberg, son."

"Why not?"

"Well, you're Negro. And Greenberg's Jewish. You're not Jewish, are you?" Ford bent toward the kid, smiling.

"I'm six."

Ford patted him on the head and looked at the other kid. "And who are you?"

"Schoolboy Rowe."

"That's a good choice."

"Mister, if he can't be Greenberg, can he be Babe Ruth?"

"I don't see why not. In America, you can be whoever you want to be."

"I don't want to be Babe Ruth. I want to be Josh Gibson."

"Oh? And who is he?"

"He's the Negro Babe Ruth," said Diz. "Hits the ball a mile. Hit one off of me once. I think that ball is still traveling. They say he hit one out of Yankee Stadium. I know he hit one out of Griffith, straightaway center field. That's four hundred twenty-one feet just to clear the fence, never mind out of the park. DeLancey's a fine catcher, but I'd sure like to have that Gibson playing for us."

"I tell you what, boys," said Ford, "you tag along with us and we'll get you a couple of nice apples."

The boys nodded. Schoolboy asked him, "Are apples better for you than grapes?"

"I don't know."

"Will you know when you're bigger?"

Ford smiled wryly. "Why don't you just ask your mom?"

Schoolboy hung his head and looked sad. After a few steps he asked, "Is your mother dead?"

"Yes," said Ford.

"Oh." The sound of authentic understanding, like the closing of the hood latch on a Model T after it had been fixed. Just enough gap in the plug to create the spark with which it all explodes into movement. All's forgotten. The kids were running ahead and laughing. One picked up a stick and aimed it like a gun at the other, who stumbled as if shot.

"He shoots them. They're dead. And then . . ." Schoolboy hesitated, pensive, while the elderly mortals—Henry, Harry, Frankie, Diz, and Darrow—hung on his words.

"And then . . . they die."

Thoughts were coming to Diz like wildfire. When he was alone, they came from around every corner. Sometimes, he thought, he was in a virtual ambush. His mind was a great grab bag of thinking. *I don't want no regular, rectangular grave. I want a big circle, and I want it dirt with grass around it, raised up like a mound. But no headstone. I want me a rubber with my name on it, and I want an inscription to let folks know that if I'm in heaven they can be sure I'm foggin' 'em in up there.*

Frankie broke Diz's reverie with an elbow to the ribs, and momentarily Diz broke the silence. "Mr. Ford, I just got a call this afternoon from Satchel Paige. You might not know about him, but some say he's the greatest pitcher of all time. Trouble is, he's black. Can't play in the Major Leagues, and neither can a bunch of other guys who ought to. Satchel thinks his boys could beat the Gashouse Gang, and Frankie and I are fixing to show them colored fellas who really is the World Champs, after we beat your Tigers tomorrow."

"What's the commissioner going to say when he finds out about this?" asked Ford.

"We're not telling him," said Frankie. "Landis is filled with just two things that aren't brown—himself and God. And so is Rickey. I never understood why those two didn't get along like two peas in a pod."

Ford smiled. "The pod's not big enough for their egos. It's like two kids fighting over a toy. They both want unlimited power, and neither one of them wants to share."

Darrow nodded. "If there's pie in the sky, those two will be in a food fight when they die."

"Let's come back down to earth for a minute," said Ford. "Why are you telling me this?"

" 'Cuz the only way I can keep the Gashouse boys together for this game is to pay them. Five hundred apiece ought to do it. Ten men. That makes five thousand dollars, roughly. We figured that would be a drop in the bucket for you. What do you say?"

Ford never missed an opportunity to instill the virtue of thrift in younger men. He shook a finger at Diz. "Five thousand dollars will buy a Model A for everyone on your team, with trumpet horns and chrome headlamp shells. But what I'm more worried about is the commissioner. He banned interracial play. If word leaks out about this, he might point the finger in my direction."

"Maybe we should be taking a longer view," Darrow interjected. "Maybe we should put our efforts into getting those colored boys into the Major Leagues. They have a right to play."

Ford laughed cynically. "There are no rights. Every advantage in the world goes with power. Think of a fastball pitcher, like Jerome, at twilight. The batter doesn't have a chance. It's just a case of what you can put over, and for the foreseeable future, Negroes don't have the power to secure the right to play in the Major Leagues. Besides, I have no interest in advancing the cause of Negro players. 'Souls are not saved in bundles,' Emerson said. 'The spirit asks every man—how is it with thee?' "

The soul had bootstraps, too. And a jock, which it put on one leg at a time. Back in Pittsburgh, Satch's soul might reply, *How is it with me? Me? You talkin' to me, Ralphy? It's kind of crowded here, at the soul-bus's rear end. I'd kind of like to move up to the front, with Ty Cobb's soul. See that down there? That's Cooperstown, just a place I go fishin' in. Mostly I be hangin' out at the Crawford Grill. . . . So, how is it with me? When I'm playing the Monarchs at Greenlee Field with those portable dim lights and they can't see my be-ball, it is very well with me indeed. But I'm wondering about what it's like in the soul locker room of the white boys. I suppose they gets hot water and towels, and if souls got jocks, I wonder if any one of the white souls is big enough to hold mine. But then I hear my soul sayin', 'The big leagues? Satch, you got as much business there as a mule in a garage.'"*

"To tell the truth, Mr. Ford, my soul would be a lot better if we could make this game happen," Diz replied.

Ford looked at Harry Bennett, whose body and facial language Ford read as a go signal. "Are you sure you can beat these colored fellows?"

Diz laughed. "As sure as I am we'll beat the Tigers. So, I'll tell you what. If we don't beat the Tigers tomorrow, you can forget about the whole deal. If we do, you back us."

It was hard to say no to the ingenuous smile of Dizzy Dean, especially when he was filling it with one of your own cigars like a kid who'd just found what the tooth fairy had left him. And Ford loved a wager. He shook Diz's hand, and they walked back to the house. He put an avuncular hand on Frankie's shoulder and spoke softly. "Harry will take care of you. Anything you need. You'll like Harry. No tomfoolery there. He won't piddle in your ear. He's solid. I like a man with three double consonants in his name. That's rare. And solid. He's got balls."

Frankie was surprised at Ford's vulgarity. Double consonants. Two balls. They kind of went together.

When Wagner saw Ford approaching, he hit a brass gong. *"À table."*

Everyone stood behind a chair. Will Rogers raised his glass. "A toast, please. To Henry Ford. Great educators try to teach people, great preachers try to change people, but no man—produced through ordinary channels—has moved the world like Henry Ford. He put wheels on a man's home, and a castle in his sedan. So now life's greatest catastrophe is a blowout. Everybody's rushing to go somewhere they don't have no business, so they can hurry back to the place they never should have left."

"Hear! Hear!"

"And here's to the end of the Depression. The Republicans have been saying they don't want to rock the boat. But I say, turn 'er over and maybe the bottom side has some barnacles we can eat."

Burgess Whitehead cheered loudly. Frankie Frisch, a Republican with some sympathy for FDR, was smiling.

"And one more. To the St. Louis Cardinals. Talk about World Series timber . . . we got a whole lumberyard here."

In a starched white shirt and shiny borrowed wingtips, Diz still looked like a New Deal official in charge of plowing under crops in the Ozarks. He stared at the puzzling array of glasses and silverware, and said to Rogers, "I like breakfast best 'cuz they only give you one fork."

The waiter appeared between Diz and Paul. "Your Johnny bread and crackling bread."

Diz took a piece of Johnny bread, opened the bottle of Lea & Perrins Worcestershire sauce, and poured half of it on his eggs. He looked disparagingly at Rogers's plate. "That bird's got less fat on it than a Branch Rickey contract."

Even Rickey chuckled.

"Forgive me if I ask," said Mrs. Ford, "but what is Johnny bread and crackling bread?"

Diz waited till his mouth was only half full. "Johnny bread's a kind of cornmeal soaked in grease. Crackling bread is just corn bread with bits of pork rind mixed in the batter. Good, ain't it?"

"I didn't know you could make such things, Wagner," said Mrs. Ford to her chef, who laughed. "I can't. One of the caretakers' wives made it. She made me promise to bring her any leftovers."

"Ain't gonna be none, if I can help it," said Diz, who had an appetite.

Rogers shook his head as Diz chowed down. "The only folks I've seen eat as much as Jerome are cotton-pickers and opera singers."

A sparrow caught Diz's eye on the balcony ledge outside the tall white window. Not that it wanted to come in. It was content with the crumbs. Then with an almost haughty flick of the tail it took a white shit on Ford's white balcony.

Will Rogers finished his consommé and said to Ford, seated across the table, "I think it's great that you put $100 million into practical education. Right now, baseball is about the only practical education in America's schools."

"There's a lot to be learned from baseball," said Branch Rickey, who had the ability to find moralism everywhere.

"Stealing," said Joe E. Brown, deadpan, without looking up from his soup.

"Look who's talking," said Rogers. "Joe was born with a silver spoon in his mouth—sideways."

They all laughed. Rogers continued, "Henry, you'd better count the silverware, and if there's anything missing, check Joe's mouth."

Joe had even Westbrook Pegler cracking up by eating two hotdogs at the same time at the Navin Field press conference. James Atwood slapped his thigh, ostensibly out of laughter, but checking his own stash. It was still there. When the laughter at Ford's table subsided, Rogers deadpanned, "Take my friend Diz, what good did baseball ever do him?"

"He can count to four," Frankie chortled, referring to a base on balls.

"But I'll bet he doesn't know the capital of Michigan," said Rogers.

"Aw, hellfire, I ain't no capitalist."

"A little practical knowledge is a dangerous thing," said Mrs. Ford.

Ford chuckled. "But he's learned to turn his liability into an asset, like Joe—with his mouth. Jimmy Durante, with his nose."

"Whitehead, with his dick," said Leo Durocher, sotto voce, so that only the players around him could hear. Rookie Burgess Whitehead also had the biggest hands in baseball. Pepper Martin bent forward and tried to contain the laughter-spat soup in his bowl. Ducky slapped Pepper on the back. "Hey, mind your manners." He turned to Mrs. Ford and said, "We call him the 'Wild Horse of the Osage.' "

Frankie mock-frowned. "You can dress 'em up . . ." Pepper wiped his mouth, excused himself, then covered half of his face with his napkin as he kept laughing.

"Why is he turning into a beet?" said Mrs. Ford.

"He's thinking about Whitehead, who's got what it takes to play in the Negro Leagues," said Leo. "I mean—he's that fast. Fastest man on the team." The rest of the team, including Burgess, broke up.

When the waiters had cleared the table of the main course, Rogers tapped his glass with a fork. "Another toast, to our distinguished guests Jerome Hanna Dean and Clarence Darrow. Jerome can throw a baseball ninety-five miles an hour over a gum wrapper, and Darrow could write the whole NRA plan on one. Maybe Moses should have gotten into that act, too. Woulda been easier to carry than those tablets, and we could have omitted the less necessary commandments."

The diners raised their glasses and drank to Diz and Darrow.

"Speech," said Frankie, elbowing Diz.

Diz stood up in his ill-fitting suit and raised his glass. "I'm sure glad to be here 'cause I heard so much about you, Mr. Ford, but I'm sorry I'm a-gonna have to make pussycats of your Tigers. They've got as much chance of winning as a bowlegged white girl's got of getting into the chorus line at the Cotton Club. If Frankie lets me pitch tomorrow, I'll have 'em swinging like a ham on a hook. And one more thing—I know y'all don't like Jews, but you let them play in the Majors. The Negroes get treated the way Hitler treats the Jews. So I just want to say it's time to let those boys have a shot. You know, the press guys, like Mr. Rogers here, have been writing a lot about Dizzy Dean, saying what a great pitcher he is. But a bunch of the fellows get in a barber session the other day and they start to argufy about the best pitcher they ever see. Some says Lefty Grove and Lefty Gomez and Walter Johnson and old Pete Alexander and Dazzy Vance. And they mention Lonnie Warneke and Van Mungo and Carl Hubbell, and Johnny Corriden tells us about Matty and he sure must have been great, and some of the boys even say Old Diz is the best they ever see. But I see all them fellows but Matty and Johnson, and I know who's the best pitcher I ever see and it's old Satchel Paige, that big lanky colored boy. Finally, I just want to thank the Lord for giving me a good right arm, a strong back, and a weak mind. And I want to thank Mr. Ford for this here dinner. Paul, Elmer, and I never ate no special vittles or nothing to put the speed in our soup-bones. God just made us long and loose, like houn' dogs. So I thank you for not makin' us eat pheasant, and for givin' us this corn bread that ain't made to be exalted by knife and fork." Diz picked up a piece of corn bread from the plate surrounded by knife and fork and stuffed it into his mouth, then sat down.

"Don't you love him? Such a droll realist. Under the mud language you'll find the most profound truths," said Mrs. Ford.

"From the mouths of babes." Henry patted his wife on the hand.

"Is there something y'all don't like about the way my friend talks?" blurted James Atwood, with his fork gripped in his fist, not out of menace but because he always held it that way.

Darrow leaned toward James Atwood and spoke softly, "You're his bodyguard, not his lawyer."

John Henry swallowed a bit of pheasant. "They called him the Darrow of Ossage, on account of his mouth. Don't pay him no mind."

Mrs. Ford changed the subject. "Speaking of babes, I heard someone recently say that something was 'Ruthian.' Something gargantuan. Can you believe that that fat man has permeated even our language? Imagine, a booze-hound, a serial adulterer, bequeathing his name to the English language, perhaps for centuries?"

"Wait till someone hits more home runs. They'll forget about Ruth," said Henry.

Mrs. Ford seemed to suck in her cheeks as she formulated her thought. "It's so ironic that 'Fordian' just doesn't sound right. Nor does 'Fordish.' But 'Ruthian,' it's like 'ruffian.' It has a homonymic cousin. It fits right in." She looked at the chandelier at which her fork was pointed, drawing inspiration from flickering crystal. "But then 'Ford' does have a sturdy sound."

Diz noticed her gazing at the chandelier and her brow wrinkling in thought. He smiled. "Henry, you didn't get no crate of lemons when you married Mrs. Ford."

Henry thought for a moment before returning the smile. "Yes, Mrs. Ford is . . ." but the complement eluded him. Realizing that Ford was at a loss for words, Branch Rickey, who never was, finished the sentence for him. "Mrs. Ford is right, about Ruth. That man is very unsavory."

"What do you mean, unsavory?" asked Diz.

"He means he's got a few dames stashed around," said Durocher.

"You misunderstand me, Leo," said Rickey. "It's not the company he keeps. That's a man's private business. It's that he does it on the Sabbath. That's what riles me."

"I've got to hand it to old Branch," said Diz. "He keeps the Sabbath. I ain't never seen him at a game on a Sunday."

"Yeah, but if Mammon could hit .300, Branch would sign him," said Leo.

Whitehead and Frisch laughed at Leo's gaffe, and Rickey corrected him, "Mammon is riches, not a person."

"Heck, I thought he was one of those fallen angels," said James Atwood.

"Baseball, however, does point the way to our salvation," said Rickey.

Henry Ford didn't share Rickey's vision of baseball. Branch might as well have been preaching to eight cylinders.

"You know what they say down at the Rouge?" said Joe E. Brown, curling his wide mouth into a smile. "You cut the top off a cross and you've got a 'T.' That's the religion in Detroit—the Model T." Brown laughed, contorting his mouth wide enough to drop a melon in there without hitting an incisor.

Henry was stuck in time, stuck in the first decade of the twentieth century, when cars were owned by white people, professional baseball was played by white people, and William Jamesian pragmatism was the reigning philosophy. The Model T represented the triumph of pragmatism over style. It looked like the box a Grosse Pointe maven would put her Sunday bonnet in. It looked like the bust of Branch Rickey in a Sunday suit, with the same turn-of-the-century Protestant preachiness. The Model T proselytized. It said, *Forget about the frills of Bugatti, Royce, and Cadillac. The stairway to heaven is straight and narrow, black macadam lined with humble servants in black with four wheels, a million strong in the procession to the funeral of style.*

"The Model T was made by hard work," said Rickey. "That's the ticket out of the Depression. We could do with more hard work and less bellyaching. The only place we're callused is on the underside of the driving toe."

John Henry Seadlund scowled. He wasn't one for talking politics, but he could smell a red herring. "Back in Minnesota I saw a rat eating an onion and crying. Times are rough when a rat's got to eat an onion."

Ford glared at John Henry, wary of a socialist in the woodpile.

"Branch loves his Bible," said Whitehead, baseball's only Phi Beta Kappa. "But the payroll's a more important document."

"The payroll's the Magna Carta, all right," echoed Frankie.

Diz spoke with a mouth half-full of apple pie. "Y'all's frugal when it comes to payin' a man. But when it comes to paying yourselves, y'all's prodigal sons-a-guns."

"What baseball needs is a union," said Frankie.

Ford looked like he was choking on a bite of pie. "Organized labor is tyranny. What unions do is nothing more than blackmail."

Darrow had held his tongue as long as he could. "Two years ago there was a hunger march at your Rouge Plant. Four men were machine-gunned to death. The workers who went to the funeral were fired. You've got spotters who mark how much time a man spends in the toilet, marked 'stolen minutes.' "

Henry took a little jump in his seat. "Dadblast it, that's just what they are."

Will Rogers saw the conversation taking a bad turn. He jumped in to defuse the situation. "They used to say Henry Ford had one foot on the land, the other on industry. But it looks like he's got a third leg on the potty."

It worked. Even Henry forced a smile. Rogers continued, "And since most folks don't have enough land for a garden, Mr. Ford is going to put out a car with a garden in it. A kind of rumble seat for roses and peonies. You hoe as you go."

Darrow leaned to his right and whispered to Joe E. Brown. "They used to say, when the first Model T came out, that it could be any color, so long as it was black. Now the workers are saying the Model A can be any color so long as it's red, for blood."

The gong-servant hit the instrument that gave notice that dinner was formally over and the gang could retire to cigars and brandy in the sitting room, where the heads of dozens of large game animals, most with horns, kept watch through the thickening Havana haze. Mrs. Ford retired to the bedroom, and Joe E. Brown entertained the men lounging in the plush leather seats, while at the other end of the room a quartet played jazz. Frankie Frisch, who was soused, tried to explain it to Paul Dean.

"Jazz . . . see, jazz is it. Jazz can be anything, see. You take classical music, take a piece by Bach, jazz it, and you've got 'Air on a G-string.' See?"

Paul wrinkled his brow and moved a little farther from Frankie.

In his study, Henry Ford couldn't help thinking of Frankie Frisch's nose. It was bent worse than some fighters' noses. And it jolted him to recollect his recent dream that his own nose had inverted. It went in instead of out, creating a peculiar hole on his face, a sconce in the architecture of his face, a convenient place to store small objects—paper slips or a key he might otherwise forget, but the isosceles foyer of the hole was prone to collect cobwebs, and it was unpleasant to wipe out the hole that felt so unfamiliar each morning. His dream-self contemplated the difficulty of blowing his inverted nose and filled with dread at the thought of getting a runny nose. He involuntarily tossed his head forward, thinking about it.

The dream was disturbing enough that he consulted the only person he could count on to keep complete confidence. He summoned Harry Bennett to his office. Harry listened, chewing on an unlit panatela and pacing around the table in his office. "I think," said Harry, "that you're afraid of paying through the nose for something. I think you're worried about Edsel taking control of the company and you want to keep it for yourself."

Ford was not so old as to not see through Harry's damning of Edsel— Harry was already lobbying for the chairman's job when Henry retired. But that was something Ford understood, even admired—the guts to *stop at nothing to get what you want.* He wished a little of Harry had rubbed off on Edsel. Still, he gave Harry a cold stare. "You have any alternative interpretations?"

Harry saw that his gambit hadn't worked. He reverted to what he knew Ford liked about him, his bluntness and honesty. "Yeah. You're worried you're a Jew yourself. Somewhere back in the family line there's a Jew in the woodpile."

Ford's stare intensified, but Ford was looking through Harry, not at him, seeing in his mind the family tree, wondering who, if anyone, the Jew might be. Ford paced about, which was Bennett's habit, and Bennett joined in, relieved that Ford's glare was not intended for him. The two men were like gunslingers walking the requisite distance to turn and fire. But only one was packing a revolver. Only one was obsessed with Jews. Ford couldn't understand how Hank Greenberg could be so good, and he was relieved that Hank's bat had gone impotent during the Series. Hank was so upset at his performance that he punished himself, refusing food for twenty-four hours. Ford had a flash now, from the dream, of his nose being stove in with a baseball bat. If it wasn't Greenberg and the Jews, who could it be? He began casting for villains. Could it be, he wondered, the Negroes? Perhaps in the dream he was worried about Negroes polluting baseball, the way the Jews tried to pollute it with gambling in '19. No other candidates came to mind. Although Ford hired blacks, he was anxious at how their population had increased two thousand percent in seven years. Ford seldom seethed, but he could get a good simmer up, and now he was feeling a combination of righteousness and anger. He was also quick to make decisions when his feelings were clear. The Negroes had to be taught a lesson. He closed his fist and thrust his bony arm across his body. "I like Dean's idea—his All-Stars against Paige's. I want you to take care of it. Make it happen. Show those Negroes what a good white team can do."

Harry nodded.

"One more thing, Harry. That team cannot lose."

"Understood."

"I mean it, Harry. Do you know what it would mean for this country if word got out that the Negroes beat our best? It would be a national humiliation. You see how much depends on it." Harry understood from Ford's look that his job depended on it. He noted that Ford hadn't said they had to win, only that they could not lose. There was a difference.

"What's my budget?"

"No limit. Whatever it takes. Use the slush fund."

The fund was not unlimited, but enough. Not to buy the result, but to make it happen. Enough to make up the difference when Satchel's patron used his deep pockets to pack a revolver rather than the money for the black team. If Henry wanted to see a game, what did the fifteen-thousand-dollar team admission ticket mean? Harry wouldn't even tell Ford about the cash dispersal. The greater task, Harry would find, would be keeping Satch alive. No Satch, no match—he knew well. You made no excuses for failure with Henry Ford. The black team had a routine they called "shadow-ball," in which they played with an imaginary ball. Harry would shadow Satch, as well as Diz, right up until game day. Or night.

On Satch's advice, Harry would be in touch with the Kansas City Monarchs, to rent their portable lights. It took him a few more days to figure out the game's venue. Then it went off like, well, a light bulb in his head. If you wanted lights, you wanted GE. General Electric had a plant and a field for its team in West Lynn, Massachusetts, a Satchelesque stone's throw from Fenway Park. They also had the best lighting system in the country. It consisted of eight one-hundred-and-thirty-foot towers, each with a forty-four-inch-diameter bulb. Its Novalux projectors produced an astonishing 26,640,000 candlepower. The Monarchs' system consisted of six telescoping poles, each with six floodlights on the top and two on the bottom. Its one-hundred-kilowatt generator was powered by a two-hundred-and-fifty-horsepower motor, using fifteen gallons of gas per hour. Guy wires and stops held the light posts. The telescoping towers were raised by hydraulic derricks to a height of fifty feet. Each light was four feet across and used thousand-watt bulbs. Harry then learned that Herman Rosner in Brooklyn had a transformer that increased wattage by twenty-five percent. Harry had one brought to Fenway to be used with the Monarchs' system. Now they could use twenty-five-hundred-watt bulbs, or the Westinghouse CSA-24 bulbs, with twenty-four-hundred watts, that were originally designed to illuminate rail lines. Fenway would not have lights until 1947. It did have the Green Monster in left field, though it was not yet called that. It was covered with ads for Calvert whiskey, Lifebuoy soap, and Vimms vitamins. Until the beginning of the 1934 season, a ten-foot incline in front of the wall, known as Duffy's Cliff, warned outfielders of the imminence of the wall. When all the stars came out at night, on October 20, they'd light up Fenway, with a little help from the Monarchs and the General Electric Employees' Athletic Association.

Harry also set his sights on the portable lighting system used by the defunct Class B Northeastern League, which had operated all over New England, but his team of Ford engineers could not locate it. They then protested that the only thing they knew about lighting was headlights.

"You've got a couple of weeks to learn," said Harry. "I want every portable light in New England in Fenway Park. I want everyone in the dugout with a flashlight on. I want the fucking stars to shine on Boston, and if Henry's money can do it, dadgumit let there be light."

7

THE SEVENTH GAME

OCTOBER 9, 1934

"You should see Brother Diz pitch one of his good ones sometime. He can fling the ball so fast it seems to climb over itself in the rush. It takes sudden crazy shoots which are so sharp and wide that even customers can see the break, and it is plain that he gets a joyous emotional let-go when the ball obeys him well. He is easily nagged and seems to get quite cross when the hitters offer him impudence in the way of hits but unlike other temperamental masters of the business he does not let exasperation mar his work. Brother Dizzy sums up as quite a pitcher at this writing although another year or two may find him poor and forgotten with his arm squandered and long gone."

—Westbrook Pegler

It was a toe that eventually did in Brother Diz, but Pegler was on target with everything else. Like Damon Runyon, Pegler lobbied for racially integrated ball, but he disliked Jews as much as Ford did. He lit into Greenberg for skipping the game against the Yankees on Yom Kippur. In October Hank's mother reluctantly made the trip to Detroit.

She'd wanted to see the Giants in the Series, since she lived just a few blocks from the Polo Grounds. Schoolboy Rowe's father also made the trip, driving forty-six hours from El Dorado, Arkansas.

Westbrook Pegler was pulling for Diz and the Cards. Before the game, he and Damon Runyon brought Diz and Schoolboy together for an interview. Schoolboy posed for movie cameras, taking his windup. Then he kissed his dad on the lips and the old man spat out some tobacco. Pegler escorted Schoolboy over to where Diz was waiting, already in uniform, under which he wore a white sweatshirt with sleeves that came down to his knuckles, with long heavy socks with seven alternating stripes of red and white. His red-billed white cap was a half size too small, like Frisch's, while his glove was not much bigger than his hand.

Pegler put his hand on Diz's shoulder. "The Dean boys had quite a season. You were thirty and seven, and your brother won nineteen. Care to comment?"

"Well, I'll be doggoned. At times I just don't know how good me and Paul are. Imagine, back there in the spring when I said the Dean boys would win forty-five games, and none of your people would believe me. For pity's sake, I didn't even know myself then how good we were."

"You *are* good, but those Tigers have a powerful lineup. If you pitch today, how do you think you'll do?"

"Them Tigers are as tough to cut down as Houston honeysuckle. But what we wham down at them is liable to be tough to get ahold of. Paul's got a fastball that'd skin a rabbit from the kitchen to the barn, and mine ain't no freight train. Them Tigers'll be duck soup."

Runyon turned to Rowe. "How about you, Schoolboy? You've been described as 'high as the Alps and rugged as the Rockies.' If Auker gets into trouble, Cochrane's bound to bring you in. How do you think you'll fare against Dizzy Dean?"

Rowe pointed a finger at Diz. "I'll whip you sure."

Turning to Diz, Runyon instigated, "Sounds to me Schoolboy would like to turn this into a brawl."

Diz shrugged. "Schoolboy don't mean nothin'. He's just a cocklebur in a mule's tail. Pretty good pitcher, too. He ought to beat us every two or three years."

Schoolboy retorted, "Dizzy Dean can't hold my tobacco. He ain't got a pig's chance in winter of beating me."

"You sound a little peeved, Schoolboy," said Runyon. "Those Cards have been riding you pretty rough, especially Durocher. What do you think about him?"

"Durocher's got kind of a pungent personality, so he fits right in with the Cardinals. He's got more enemies than he has silk shirts. And when it comes to hitting, he might as well have a toothpick in his hands."

Runyon turned back to Diz. "Your turn, Diz. Frankie Frisch says Bill Hallahan is pitching the seventh game. How do you think he'll do?"

"Old Bill's got better curves than a farmer's daughter, and he's a little wild, so them Tigers had better duck when he fogs it through."

"And if you win today, what do you plan to do during the off-season?"

"Dogged if I know. Some duck hunting. Some barnstorming, I suppose."

"There was talk that you and Paul were hooking up with Barnum & Bailey."

Diz snarled. "Those carnival people wanted me to shoot Paul out of a cannon. I said, 'Shoot your own fanny out. Y'ain't shootin' my brother's.' "

Pegler turned away with the microphone and spoke to his radio audience. "All righty, folks. That's it, right from the horse's . . . mouth. Now let the game begin."

October 9, 1934, was a cold, blustery day, but sunny. The weather didn't matter for most of the 40,902 fans at Navin Field. To honor the home team, they rolled out a huge floral horseshoe on the infield. They didn't know that superstitious players thought flowers were bad luck. Schoolboy Rowe crossed his fingers and refused to come out. He was the most superstitious of the Tigers. Through most of the '34 season he kept a Canadian penny, a Dutch copper coin, and two Chinese trinkets in his pocket. In his shirt he kept four feathers from a three-legged rooster (note the correspondence to walks and strikeouts). In his glove he carried a jade elephant. In his hat he had the foot of a rabbit shot in a graveyard at midnight. When he went for his seventeenth victory in a row and lost, he chucked the lot of it, got a new rabbit's foot with stronger pedigree, a copper crucifix, and the carved ivory cross that Tommy Armour carried when he won the British Open. When the G-men also refused to come out for the presentation, the fans dragged their sorry horseshoe and sad asses away. It was an unintended preview.

At the edge of the Tiger dugout, Schoolboy Rowe let out a loud and uncharacteristic curse. "Fucking cocksucker, son of a bitch!"

Player-manager Mickey Cochrane looked concerned. "What's the matter?"

"Fucking bird just shat on me."

"Wash it off. It's not the end of the world."

"That was my right hand. My pitching hand."

"Then wipe it on Dean."

Schoolboy brightened up and walked to the Cardinals' dressing room. Paul Dean was putting on his glove when Schoolboy patted him on the back, wiping off the birdshit. Diz noticed. "What are you wiping on my brother's back? Looks like birdshit."

Schoolboy smiled mawkishly. "Yep."

Paul craned his neck to see his back but couldn't. Schoolboy didn't hang around for his reaction.

Diz smiled and called to Schoolboy, "You can wipe the shit off, but you can't wipe the mojo off. That bird shat on *you*."

Schoolboy's grin dropped right off.

At the other end of the dressing room Leo was pestering Frankie for the nth time about starting Diz. "I know you're leaning toward Bill, but Diz can do it. He's been our horse all year."

"I'm not leaning. I decided. Bill's starting."

"I talked to Diz. He's ready to go. He's not tired."

"He's had one day's rest. This would be his seventh start in nineteen days. Come on, Leo. It doesn't take a pencil-whiz to see he's overworked. Look at him. He's lost about twenty pounds. He's got a cold on top of it."

Leo frowned. "It's the seventh game, Frankie. This is it. No tomorrow. You've got to go with your ace. If they start knocking him around, take him out. But let's see if he's got it."

"I already told Bill he's starting. That's it. That's final."

Leo took a last shot at it with a big smile and a dose of psychology. He put a hand on Frankie's shoulder and spoke softly, "Frankie boy, this is your chance to be famous. Everyone thinks Hallahan's pitching, and at the last minute you outfox the Tigers and go with the guy they're all scared of."

"Hallahan's pitching!" Frankie shouted and walked away. Leo was six thousand in debt and needed the winner's bonus. He was convinced Diz was his meal ticket. He also had the lineup card in his pocket.

In his trademark black suit, diminutive, white-haired Commissioner Kenesaw Mountain Landis came into the Cardinals' dressing room looking for Diz. He saw himself as God's protector of baseball, and he was cut from the same stern Protestant cloth as Branch Rickey, all of which made him obsessed with gambling. He'd heard about the incident in St. Louis after game three, and he'd heard rumors of Diz hanging around with two suspicious characters. He turned his intent stare on the innocent Dean. "Son, I want to talk to you."

"Sure, Mr. Landis. What can I do for you?"

"I heard about that kidnapping attempt. I want you to be careful about the criminal element that is trying to invade baseball."

"Don't you worry, Mr. Landis. Everybody knows what you did to Joe Jackson. Hornsby don't even make his own bets anymore. He's got this guy in the clubhouse named Alabam . . ."

Landis cut him off. "Mr. Dean, this is not the time. You need to concentrate on the task at hand. Remember, if anyone offers you a thousand dollars for every game you lose, I want you to promise me that you'll kick him in the teeth."

"Yes, sir," said Diz, and Landis turned away. "But, if someone offers me three thousand, can I take it?"

"In that case I want you to take a Louisville Slugger and crack him on the head. Is that clear?"

Diz nodded. "And another thing," added Landis, "I just heard a rumor of some kind of postseason game between white players and Negroes. You know the rule about World Champions barnstorming—it's strictly forbidden. Now, I don't know if the Cardinals are going to win or lose this one, but regardless of the outcome, there's going to be no interracial play, so don't go getting any ideas."

Diz grinned. "You don't have to worry about that on my account."

Landis laughed at what he supposed was Dean's self-deprecating humor. "No, I don't suppose I do. I read the newspaper account of the hospital report after Rogell pegged one off your beezer. They said, 'X-rays of Dean's head reveal nothing.' "

"I saw a million stars when that ball hit me. Saw dogs, cats, but I didn't see no Tigers."

Landis registered the connection between "stars" and "no Tigers," but he had no idea whether the slight was intentional on Diz's part. Maybe Dizzy Dean was not the fool he had taken him for. Maybe he was as cagey as the depraved ex-lawyer he'd been seen associating with. Landis turned serious again, looked up into Diz's eyes and warned, "I also want you to steer clear of Clarence Darrow. I don't know what you're cooking up with him and I don't want to know. That man bribed a juror and he represents some of the nation's most reprehensible characters, and when the truth has them by the neck, he has them take the Fifth Amendment. You and Darrow and the Negroes—it doesn't add up to anything good." Landis shook his finger in Diz's face. "Remember what happened when Ruth defied me, and Rockefeller, too. He thought he could hide, but I hunted him down and subpoenaed him. Now, when this game is done, I want you to go back to Arkansas, hunt some ducks or whatever, and rest up for next year. Do you understand me?"

"Yup. The duck part, anyway. Can I be excused now? I got some business with the Tigers I've got to attend to."

"You're excused," said Landis, nodding.

Minutes later, Diz draped a tiger skin, complete with head, over his shoulder and ran past the Tigers' dugout, taunting them. Cochrane was going over the Tigers lineup with Gehringer.

"What the hell you going over the hitters for?" said Diz. "They ain't gonna get no runs off of me."

"Get out of here. Scat," said Cochrane.

Diz borrowed a tuba from a band member and played "Wagon

Wheels." The fans laughed. Then when Detroit was warming up, he stood behind Cochrane, watching Elden Auker warm up.

"Schoolboy's almost as fast as me, but Elden ain't as fast with the wind as I am against it."

"Hey, get the fuck out of here," said Cochrane.

Diz watched Auker throw a fastball on the inside corner. "That's the one to throw to Ducky, but Frankie's hands-be-dexterous. He'll murder that."

Cochrane squinted at the malapropism. Hank Greenberg turned and gave Diz a dirty look on his way to take a few hits. Diz grabbed a bat off the ground. He stepped in front of Greenberg. "Okay, Elden, now groove it in there." Diz looked at Schoolboy, staring at him malevolently from the dugout. "You know why they call him Schoolboy, don't ya? 'Cuz Diz and Paul took him to school."

Diz laughed, tapped the ground with his bat and said, "Let me show you how, Mo."

Like most players, Diz called Jewish players "Mo." He hit an Auker fastball off the wall. Then Greenberg stepped in and belted one over the fence.

Diz laughed. "That's hittin', Mo. My turn again."

He started toward the plate. Greenberg took a threatening step toward him and Diz looked at the other Tigers and tossed the bat. "You fellas don't know what this is for anyway."

Greenberg hit a soft fly to center. Diz pulled a cream puff from his shirt and tossed it at Hank. "Henry Ford gave me that, but I knowed who it rightly belonged to."

Greenberg tossed the cream puff in the air and hit it at Diz, who ran away laughing and ducking.

Durocher clapped his hands and whistled at the famed Tiger infield. "Where's that 'battalion of death' at?"

Frankie Frisch joined in, "They all died and went to hell, looked around, and nothing was different—still in Detroit."

Diz took a few steps closer to the battery of Auker and Cochrane. "Jeepers creepers, my slow stuff is faster than that."

"I already beat you guys once," said Auker. "I'm fixin' to do it again."

Diz clapped. "That's the spirit, Elden! You don't have to be an All-Star to pitch for the Detroit Tigers. It's too bad Hallahan ain't pitchin'. You mighta had a chance against him. But Ol' Diz is takin' over, so y'all might as well just go home and think about what to do with the loser's share. I hear it ain't that bad."

Cochrane and Auker stared for a moment at Diz. It was the first they had heard that he was pitching.

"Sorry to break it to you guys, but you'd have to find out sooner or later. Hey, Mo, what're you so white about? You boys are too tight. What you gotta do is unlax a little. Your troubles will be over in a couple of hours."

The surprised Tigers stared at Diz. Auker couldn't suppress a crestfallen look.

"Show me what you got, Elden."

Auker ignored him and threw his sidearm fastball.

"Hey, that ain't so bad. Just add water and you can float it in there."

In the bleachers, a woman named Antoinette was selling kisses.

"What the hell's that?" asked Leo.

"Kisses for a quarter," said Pepper.

"A quarter? What do you get for a dollar?"

"A disease, probably."

Leo laughed. "Probably where Babe got his bellyache."

Pepper looked toward the bleachers. "Looks like Damon Runyon lining up, and that kiss-ass Winchell."

In the dugout Frankie was pacing and scratching at the bald spot on the back of his head, trying to decide if he really should keep Wild Bill Hallahan in the lineup or go with Diz. He couldn't get past the fact that this would be Diz's seventh outing in nineteen days. Hallahan had started game two and battled Schoolboy Rowe for nine innings, before being lifted with the score 2–2. He had a reputation as a great World Series pitcher. He'd beaten the A's twice in the '31 Series. Suddenly, Pepper Martin ran by shouting, "Apples! That's it. I ate a flock of 'em before the '31 Series and felt like running around the moon."

He ran to Rickey's office and demanded apples, and Frankie followed him, bumping into Diz, who looked bedraggled, suffering from a cold. "If Shirley Temple comes down here to meet me, tell her I'll sing and dance with her, but I ain't shakin' hands. Not after what happened to Schoolboy."

Leo took advantage of Frankie's absence to hand the lineup card to Harry Geisel, the home-plate umpire. As he walked he scratched out "Hallahan" and wrote in "J. Dean." He was convinced that, in so doing, he was scratching out a six-thousand-dollar debt.

Henry Ford, with Edsel, Harry Bennett, Joe E. Brown, and Will Rogers, had a box next to Landis's. Ford was a rare fixture at Tigers games, convinced that baseball was primarily a Zionist conspiracy, but he still cheered for Greenberg. The Ford Motor Company had paid $100,000 for the rights to broadcast the '34 World Series.

A kid came by hawking programs for a quarter. "Program, sir?"

"No, thanks," said Ford. "I've still got mine from game two."

In a seat behind Ford was George Raft, an ardent Tigers fan, even though he was Durocher's buddy. He'd been out all night, at the club Balfour, drinking "Hanky Pankies"—a tribute to Hank Greenberg, with gin, vermouth, and orangeflower—and "Old Masters," a tribute to Mickey Cochrane, with Bacardi, grapefruit juice, and apricot brandy. George was normally shy, but by 3:00 a.m. he had the microphone and was singing, to the sound of "Making Whoopee,"

> And so it's fall, come on play ball,
> We'll beat those Deans,
> Dizzy and Paul,
> We'll hit their pitches,
> Those sons of bitches,
> They're only farm boys.

Then he led the chant: "Chew 'em, claw 'em, bite 'em, maul 'em, Daffy's dizzy, Dizzy's daffy, watch their hard balls turn to taffy."

The Musicians' Post of the American Legion, in tam-o'-shanters, red coats, and blue pants, played the National Anthem, which sounded like a cross between "Old Black Joe" and "Oh! My Pa-pa." Leo Durocher persisted in needling Schoolboy Rowe. "How 'm I doin', Edna?"

The crowd mixed boos and cheers as the Cardinals took the field in the bottom of the first. Diz led the charge, unnoticed by Frankie Frisch, who went to change into a dry jock. He'd wet his pants, as usual, just before taking the field. As Cochrane limped back to the dugout. Leo shouted, "How's our stricken leader?"

Now Frankie was back. He stopped short before reaching third base, noticing Diz on the mound. He turned and saw Bill Hallahan glued to the dugout bench. Frankie glared at Leo, who held the ball Rip Collins had just bounced to him. "For your own good," Leo said, then fired the ball back to Collins.

Immediately, the name "Judas" sprang to Frankie's mind, then the epithet "Jesus," an imperfect rhyme of betrayer and savior. Frankie wanted to spit it out at him—*Judas!* Inhaling to speak, his own breath hit his lungs like zero-degree air, stopping him. What good would it do now for Diz and the others to hear it? Better that they thought it was his decision.

The first two innings were uneventful. In the third Diz hit a Texas leaguer that Goosie came in slow after, not thinking that Diz would try for two. Buzzy Wares, the first-base coach, yelled, "Whoa! Whoa!" But Diz listened to nobody but Diz. Goose couldn't believe what he was seeing. He had a great arm, and Gehringer hadn't missed a tag in eleven years. Diz *slud*, and when the dust cleared, the umpire had his arms out wide. Goose threw down his glove in disgust, inspiring Damon Runyon, who wrote, "That Goslin is a tough bird, with a heart as big as his honker, the size of which got him the name 'Goose,' and with the smell of the chili and baked beans cooking around the ballpark, a big nose is no disadvantage."

Next up was Pepper Martin. He had no patience for walks and swung at pitches far outside the strike zone, but still managed to hit .289. He also led all third National League basemen in errors—nineteen. He knocked down ground balls with his muscular chest and threw erratically. Pepper ducked away from an inside pitch. The ball hit his bat and trickled toward first. Greenberg came in for it. Auker ran to cover, then decided he had a better chance at fielding the ball than Hank. In the end Hank got it, but the throw to Auker was late. Diz took third and needled Hank. "Hey, Mo. Come on in the clubhouse after the game and get your meal money. You're the best player we've got."

On the first pitch to Rothrock, Pepper stole second. Leo ran out of the dugout laughing and shouting to Pepper, "Initiative! Initiative!" He was making fun of Pepper, who copied Rickey's highfalutin vocabulary when Pegler asked him why he stole: "I got intuition and initiative."

With the count 2 and 0 to Rothrock, Cochrane decided to put him on and hope for a double play, which brought up the skipper. Frankie Frisch was thirty-six. He was a switch-hitting place-hitter who liked high balls when hitting righty, and low balls as a lefty. He used a small, light bat he could get around quickly, and choked up on the thin, bezeled handle. He contorted his body in his swing, lifted his right leg high, and stepped hard into the ball. He didn't hit like Ruth, or throw like Meusel, or run like Collins, or compete like Cobb, but nobody came closer to putting all those characteristics into one player than Frisch did. He couldn't get back on pop flies like he used to, but he was still the money player.

The Fordham Flash knew French wines and Italian composers as well as he knew baseball. But on the field, *Frisch* and *dirt* were synonymous. His cap was bent, creased, and soiled. Knees and thighs were a color entirely foreign to the uniform. He had a high nasal voice, perhaps in part because his nose took a bad hop to the right after a ground ball took a bad hop to the left and rerouted the nasal cartilage. Like Martin, he was a chest-fielder. He would have been a shortstop if his fingers hadn't been mangled from bad hops. Frisch was the right man for the crucial at-bat in the Series. Legs spread wide, he rubbed the toe of his left shoe on the back of his right sock, then did the same with the other foot. He choked up and wiggled the bat in a chopping motion toward Auker. After two called strikes Frankie knew he had to swing and pray. Geisel was giving Auker a broad strike zone. He fouled off four consecutive pitches. As Runyon wrote, Frankie was "swinging like a woman with four bales of laundry in her arms."

Gehringer shouted, "Uncle Charlie's got him,"—slang for an inability to hit the curve. Auker threw another sidearm curve and Frankie got a piece of it, slashing it over Greenberg's outstretched glove for a double.

Dean, Martin, and Rothrock scored, and Cochrane had seen enough of Auker. He called in Schoolboy Rowe to pitch to Ducky Medwick, a tough and not very bright Hunky who was even more disliked than Durocher. Batting cleanup, His Duckiness never saw a pitch he couldn't hit. He was a prickly guy who loved to fight, and when he did, he always got in the first punch. He went his own way, even on the base paths, and played left field according to his mood. He was a fast but dumb base runner who couldn't remember signals. Still, in 1934 there were only five or six better power-hitters in baseball. Rowe got Ducky to ground to Rogell at short, but the Cardinals rallied for seven runs, with Durocher collecting another hit.

In the fifth the Tigers still hadn't scored. Greenberg led off, and Diz had struck him out in the second. Common wisdom was that Hank killed high outside pitches but had trouble with high inside fastballs. Diz threw him two three-quarter sidearm fastballs that ran in on Hank for strikes. DeLancey called for the same pitch and Diz called him off. DeLancey called time and trotted out to the mound. Frankie came in from second.

"What's going on?" said DeLancey.

"I want to give him one high outside."

"That's his strength. Keep it inside," said Frankie.

"Frank, I don't see how a little old infielder like you could tell a great pitcher like me how to pitch to any hitter."

Frankie spit some Beechnut tobacco on his hand, scooped some dirt and worked it into the seam. Normally, that made the ball sail. "Throw that one inside, at his knees."

Geisel walked toward the mound and yelled at the trio to break it up.

"Here you go, Mo. High outside," said Diz.

Greenberg hit a screamer that almost took Diz's head off. Diz hung his head and glanced toward second. "You're right, Frankie."

Diz had the peculiar ability to go from outrageously truculent to aw-shucks penitent with no concern or remorse for the inconsistency, no feeling of lost face. Perfectly, utterly, childlike. A kind of bipolarity that had Branch Rickey plucking at his equally outrageous eyebrows, slamming his Bible shut, and hollering, "Judas Priest!"

Diz retired the side with no damage. In the sixth inning, with two out, Medwick tripled off the wall. He slid hard into third and spiked Marv Owen in the chest. Owen stepped on Medwick's leg, and when Ducky got up he took a swing at Owen. Both dugouts emptied. Harry Geisel and third-base umpire Bill Klem settled things down, but when Ducky ran out to left field in the seventh inning, he got pelted with anything fans could find—apple cores, bananas, hardboiled eggs. A kind of trash-fire-brigade line was set up, bringing food in over the left field wall and raining it down on Ducky, who trotted in to the refuge of the infield.

"They can't do that to you, Joey. Don't back off," said Leo.

"If you're so damned brave, you play left field and let me play shortstop."

"You're the hardest boiled egg in the Redbird nest. Go on back out there."

Ducky refused, and Landis summoned him, Owen, Cochrane, and Frisch to his box. Leo stood behind Frankie, close enough to hear what was going on.

"Mr. Medwick, did you throw a punch at Mr. Owen?"

"Yes, sir."

Landis turned to Owen. "And did you try to step on Joe Medwick?"

"No, sir."

Landis gave him the glacial stare. "I ask you again, did you try to step on Joe Medwick?"

"No, sir."

Owen didn't wilt. Landis looked avuncularly at Medwick. "For your own sake, son, I think I'll have to remove you from the game."

Frankie pounded his glove as he spoke, "I'm the manager of the St. Louis team. I say who plays and who doesn't."

"You may be the manager of St. Louis, but I am the commissioner of baseball, and you work for me. Now, I say take him out."

Frankie shook his head. "Klem can throw him out, but I'm not going to."

Landis was unruffled. "No. There is a safety issue here. You will take him out. You will do as I direct you, Mr. Frisch. You will take him out."

Durocher whispered to Frisch, "It'll cost Ducky two hundred if Catfish tosses him. You gotta do it."

Frankie bowed his head. "Okay, Joe, that's it."

"One more hit and I tie Pepper's record," Medwick pleaded, but he knew the case was lost.

Frankie put his arm around his shoulder. "Let's go."

Frisch replaced Medwick with Chick Fullis, who got Joey's twelfth hit, but it didn't matter. The Tigers would not score a run. Cardinals 11. Tigers 0.

"Well," said Henry Ford, "somebody had to lose." He turned to a glum Harry Bennett and looked at the bright side of things. "If Dean can do that to the Tigers on one day's rest, I'm not too concerned about the Negro team, are you?"

Indeed, Harry was. Reading the anxiety on Harry's face, Ford spun his old boater on his fist. "Darrow and I made a bet—loser eats his hat. I may be an old goat, but I am not partial to straw. If I have to eat even one bite of my hat, you will eat a Model A. I'll have it ground into powder, and I'll sprinkle a spoonful myself on your eggs for as long as you work at Ford. Understood?"

Harry grinned and snugged his own fedora on. "Not to worry." But Harry was worried. Elden Auker was not Satchel Paige. He could not bring down lightning. He did not, like Paige, live for baseball. Legend had it that, when spiked, blood would drip down Satchel's leg in little red stitch marks. Elden Auker was not, like Paige, in love with the pitch, with the very idea of "pitch," with its phases that might comprise a zodiac: rest, collect, cock, accelerate, fly, spin, concuss into silliness against a mitt. In love, too, with speed, deception, and submission—to a god who was perfection but permitted randomness, the certainty of lightning with the impossibility of predicting where it would strike, when an offering would be rejected outright, clouted to kingdom come.

There was no mythology about the Tiger pitchers, the way there was about Paige. No stories of balls leaving the pitcher's hand but never seen by the catcher, the batter, or the umpire. Hank Greenberg could hit a long ball, but there were no stories of one of his shots traveling out of Yankee Stadium. Greenberg was no Josh Gibson.

PART TWO
☆
CHOOSING SIDES

8

THE CRAWFORD GRILL

Satch's day began with the clear blue sky and ended in the smoke of the Crawford Grill, otherwise known as "Third Base," for many the last stop before home. Satch was cruising Wylie Avenue with Josh in his '32 Packard convertible that had once belonged to Bette Davis, wondering if the devil, noted for leading to temptations, had pulled on his foot, relaxing the pressure on the accelerator, down to the walking speed of a woman in red high heels with the air of a brassie who'd been around the block so often her arches were as calloused as her thighs.

"Hey, good-lookin'."

The woman smiled, glanced at him, but kept walking toward the Calvary Baptist Church. Satch cruised on to Harry's Crystal Bookshop, where Josh placed a dollar-bet on "805," the number that a few years earlier had ruined virtually all of Pittsburgh's numbers runners. Hundreds of people played the number corresponding to the month and the day—August fifth—and when 805 came up, only Gus Greenlee and Woogie Harris had enough cash to cover the hit. The others blew town, leaving Gus and Woogie the numbers bosses. Gus plowed his profits into his team, the Pittsburgh Crawfords, and into a new stadium, Greenlee Field.

Satch blew the horn and Josh got into the Packard. "Let's check out the Peacock room."

The Peacock room was upstairs at the Skyrocket Café, a hop house on the other side of the Hill, where the majority of Pittsburgh's blacks lived. The Skyrocket Café was the hangout for the rival Homestead Grays.

"You givin' up?" said Josh, referring to Satch's ostensible mission— asking Gus to bankroll his team.

Satch looked at his watch. "It's early. Better to let Gus get a few drinks in him."

"Let's see what's cookin' in East Liberty."

Satch drove through Brashton, Manchester, and East Liberty. They watched the jitterbugging on Shetland. Josh got a hankering for kielbasa and pierogies in the Polish district, but not Satch. All he ate was catfish, and this night he wasn't hungry at all. They ended up parking at the soup kitchen that Gus ran, across the street from the Crawford Grill. Josh was still hungry.

"You're not thinkin' what I think you're thinkin'," said Satch.

"Smells good. And you know that chicken fat's good for your arm. You said so yourself."

Satch shook his head. Josh had been inspired by the sounds of "Shortnin' Bread," wafting out when someone opened the door to the Grille. Satchel Paige wouldn't go near a soup kitchen, especially when it was Gus's soup kitchen and he had secretly jumped from the Crawfords to the Bismarck club.

"Sure you don't want to come in?"

"Ten bucks for a pint of whiskey? Too rich for my blood." Josh shook his head. "Besides, Gus is liable to bust a cap on your ass, and I don't want to get in the way."

"Cab Calloway and Lena Horne?"

"Twenty-dollar cover? I'll listen from the street. But she sure do have a sweet voice. Kind of bashful, too, what I hear."

Satch laughed. "Yeah, like a volcano's bashful."

"Let me borrow that shine. I want to read about the Series."

Satch handed Josh the rolled-up newspaper. Josh was rooting for the Tigers over the Cardinals. As a friend of Dizzy Dean's, Satch favored the Redbirds.

They could hear strains of "I've Got the World on a String." Satch got out and headed for the Crawford Grill, with October etiolating light shining on the huddled oak leaves, echoing the feeling Lena Horne had for her father, Teddy, who had invited her to Pittsburgh for a week and got her the gig with Cab.

On the second floor of the Crawford Grill three men counted, stacked, and re-bagged two roomfuls of pennies and nickels. The ground floor was packed to capacity with patrons dancing to Cab and Lena. The Cotton Club chorus girl was already starting to make a splash as a singer, but dancing at the Cotton Club was regular work, which was hard to come by, and with Hollywood already beckoning, Lena was not sure that singing was to be her true vocation. But with Cab and Lena, the Crawford Grill had never been so jammed. The top floor was set aside for dining, and Gus had just finished a whole plate of blue-point oysters. He got up to pee, and Jew McPherson noticed him limping slightly on the way back. Gus sat down to the main course of bear loin that chef Harry Winslow had prepared for him.

"What's wrong with your leg?" asked McPherson, who ate nothing, but shared Gus's bottle of Bordeaux. McPherson ran interference for state senator James Coyne, the kingpin of Allegheny County and Gus's longtime ally.

"Acts up once in a while. Took a load of shrapnel at Verdun. Still got about a pound of it," Gus exaggerated.

"Why didn't they take it out?"

"Woulda had me on the table for six months. Too much. They said it wouldn't kill me to leave it in and I believed 'em. Been right so far." Gus laughed.

The bear was cooked with morels and juniper berries in a brown sauce. Gus cut a piece, dabbed it in the sauce, and savored it.

"What kind of shrapnel is it?"

"I try not to walk by magnets."

"Iron." McPherson nodded and sipped his wine. "A lot better than lead. Lead will seep into your blood and poison you."

"Either way, he don't swim too good," said Woogie Harris, sitting down next to McPherson. Woogie was nearly as tall as Satch, with broad shoulders and a sunken chest, accentuating a belly that protruded far enough that you could place a shot glass on it with Woogie standing. He wore wide ties that tended to feature a sailboat motif, held to the curvature of his belly with an ostentatious diamond stickpin.

McPherson turned his glass by the stem and stared at it. "Elections are coming up soon. Coyne wants to know how big the third ward's going to be."

Gus was head of the third-ward voters league. His interest-free loans and his gifts of hundreds of turkeys at Christmas and Thanksgiving were motivated in part by sheer generosity. If a guy was really stuck, Gus would forgive the loan entirely, as long as the numbers dough was rolling in, which could amount to as much as $20,000 in a good week. But part of the generosity was to help garner the votes he traded to Senator Coyne and Alderman Harry Fitzgerald for protection, which was provided by the head of the Hill District's vice squad, Pappy Williams.

"He can count on eighty, maybe ninety percent."

McPherson smiled. "That's what I was hoping to hear."

Gus ran his fingers through his short, thinning, receding, reddish hair. "I was hoping Fitz would get Pappy Williams off my back. He busted us last week. Cab almost canceled on me."

McPherson took a slug of wine and sat back in his chair. "What can he do? There's a lot of pressure from all quarters on account of all those bodies they dug up at Greenlee Field."

Gus's reply was stifled by a mouthful of bear loin. He closed his fist around his fork and hammered it on the table, chewed for a few seconds, then swallowed. "That ain't my work. Ask Pappy. None of those guys were connected to me in any way. Fucking city hall ought to give me a medal for what I done, giving the Hill a real field. White folks don't do nothin' for the Negroes. PPA put a fence around an old dump and call it a ball field. A dump is a dump, no matter what you put around it."

"That's a pretty nice field now," said McPherson.

"It ain't nothin'. That's why I built Greenlee Field. Give niggers something to be proud of."

"Damn right," said Woogie.

"It's election time," said McPherson. "Coyne and Fitz have to please the white folks, too. Gotta look tough on crime. You wait a few months, it'll all blow over. Long as you pay the net you're okay."

Satchel Paige was dancing, and he was dancing with hot goods, dancing with Lena Horne. Though recently married, Satch had little use for fidelity. An affair was like a quick pitch or a spitter. If you could get away with it, there was no reason to abstain. Satch, of course, had the finest suit in the club. Off-pink, with a maroon shirt and a bright red tie. The man could dance, arms and legs moving and shaking in harmony. He drew a lot of eyes. Even with his legs bent considerably at the knees, he was taller than most of the men on the floor. He had learned a few jive moves from Bill Bojangles Robinson, who had been best man at his wedding. This night, Satch "might should" have been carrying a gun, as Bojangles always did, since Lena was off-limits on orders from her father, enforced locally by mobster Dutch Schultz. "Nobody hits on Lena, okay?"

Now, even in Pittsburgh no one was taking chances. No one, that is, but Satch. Disdainful of weapons, he had always relied on fast talking to get him out of a jam, and, if necessary, fast feet—something Bojangles never did, though he could. Negro League games often featured pregame sideshows, one of which was Bojangles running backward and beating guys running forward.

Lena Horne's father, Teddy, was a charmer, in his handmade shoes and collection of Sulka silk ties. Black parvenu. At home in black and white worlds. Born into upper black class. Light-skinned. Handsome. When it came to ladies, he was a human vortex. White showgirls. Black showgirls. Upper-class black girls. All of his siblings were college-educated professionals whom he disparaged as "briefcase niggers." Now his daughter was on the verge of stardom, in a forbidden world, one that he was right at home in, one he'd tried to keep her out of. Girls like Lena, he knew, were easy prey for the likes of himself. Lena had weaseled into the chorus line at the Cotton Club, where even light-skinned coloreds like Teddy usually couldn't get a seat. Her temperament was giving Teddy cause for worry.

Teddy also had a strange habit of speaking in proverbs and aphorisms. It made him mysterious and went over big with certain ladies. So when Satchel Paige was dancing with Lena and giving her his biggest, killer grin, Teddy elbowed Woogie Harris and said, "Trust no bush that quivers."

Woogie wrinkled his brow and turned to Teddy. "What are you talking about?"

"There's a nigger in the woodpile," he said, pointing to the shimmying dancer, whose identity he well knew. Teddy was intimately involved in baseball. He contracted players and led negotiations between various owners of the teams in the Negro leagues. He got his feet wet in baseball in 1919, when he was linked, along with Arnold Rothstein, to the fixing of the World Series.

Woogie took the hint. He nodded to his brother, Teeny, who approached Satch. "We got business," he whispered in Satch's ear.

"I ain't got no business with you. I got business with the lady."

"Anyone's got business with this lady's got business with the Dutchman. You catch my drift?"

Teeny was about 5'4". Satch stretched out to his 6'3" and lagniappe. "Why don't you drift on out of here, little man?"

Woogie approached Satch from the other side and whispered, "That's protected material."

"That so?"

"Dutchman's property. So, I got a new step for you, snake-hips—the Aleman scram."

Woogie lifted his jacket by the lapel to show the steel he carried. Lena sensed the tension, and she knew what it was about. The same scenario played out nightly at the Cotton Club, with a different cast of characters, enforcers readily identifiable as Schultz's henchmen. Lena excused herself. She approached the bandleader and nodded that she was ready to start. She took the microphone, wearing a white crepe dress and open-toed high-heel pumps. Her eyelashes were beaded with liquid soot for a Garbo effect. Chen-Yu lipstick provided the Joan Crawford effect, and an expensive Guerlain perfume showed the cognoscenti of scents that the girl had class. She looked at Cab and nodded that she was ready. Cab lifted the brim of the bizarre field-worker's hat with the Indian feather and looked at the band. "Are you all *reet?*"

A couple of voices said, "Yeah." Cab brushed something off the arm of his zoot suit and started a beat with his European black-and-white shoes, and Lena smoothed her way into "Night and Day," then an Ethel Waters–like "Stormy Weather." A sorrow spawned in the region of her heart from which dad was evicted. It resonated in her throat and came out as a tremolo, not a whole note—nothing could be whole—but a beautiful bluesy flat note nonetheless.

Teddy Horne ducked into a corner, which he did every time his daughter sang in his presence. It was peculiar. You could see it in his eyes, those moments when Lena was singing with that nonpareil clarinet voice. You wouldn't want to interrupt Teddy then. You'd be risking limbs if not life to interrupt his sky-long gaze when Lena hit a high blue note and held it, as if to torment him, to penetrate his thick skin and reach him when he might be a thousand miles away—the blue note of a fatherless daughter, and Teddy would be staring up at a cracked, cigarette smoke–patinated ceiling whose irregularities were pressed by a needy consciousness into service as stars, looking up at that filthy ceiling as if it were the Sistine Chapel. You could see then in Teddy's eyes that the water of life had dried up and he was asking himself the big question, "What went wrong?" over and over. Why had he virtually abandoned the daughter he loved, let her grow up without a father? The stylus was stuck in that groove, and even had it been nudged, no answer would have been forthcoming. There was just the overwhelming sadness of a life that had taken a wrong turn and kept going, and was now so far afield that there was no recourse but to keep going till he sailed over the world's edge. The words "I'm sorry" started up in a dry heave that would never come out. The narcissist kept drinking of himself and wouldn't dream of throwing it up. Notes were held only for seconds that seemed sempiternal. For Teddy, it was like lead poisoning, a chronic buildup, note by note. He felt as if the involuntary tightening of his muscles was squeezing the lead out of them, and he felt it dropping into his scrotum. What the blues would feel like—materialized. Blues balls. Then the song would carry Teddy back to the present, day and night, night and day, to the crooked reality of his life.

"Come up here, fool!"

Satch looked around, then pointed at himself. "Me?"

"Yeah, you." Gus made a wide sweep with his hand. "All these shakin' girls, and you go interferin' with Teddy Horne's daughter—you could be dead already, before I get my turn. Teddy's got a handshake with the Dutchman. The fact that you're living and breathing means one thing—you got the same rabbit's foot up your skinny ass as you got in that skinny right arm."

Gus had been looking for Satch himself. The word on the street was that Satch had already signed with a Bismarck, North Dakota team. Bismarck was an anomaly, an out of the way, semi-redneck town that lured black ballplayers with very good salaries. Players and management were no more faithful to their contracts than Satch was to his wife. Players simply followed the money. Owners who were complaining about one player jumping were simultaneously blandishing a player from another club to get him to jump.

Satch smiled and held out his hand. Gus reluctantly shook it. "I knew you was in a good mood. Cab Calloway at the Crawford Grill. You on the map now."

"I been on the map for quite some time. You just ain't been here to see it. You think you can jump the paper on Gus Greenlee, with impunity?"

"With impunity? Hell, no. I can jump all by myself . . ." Satch laughed. "Just kidding, Gussy. I know how you and Cum like those big words. But put yourself in my shoes. I got no pension. I got no retire-

ment. I got no Crawford Grill. No numbers. No booze trucks. I got a
wife. I got to look out for myself. This flipper could go dead tomorrow.
What do I got? I got nothin'. That's what I got. Man comes up to you
and offers to double your pay, what you gonna say to him?"

Gus leaned over the table. "I'd tell him Gus Greenlee's got a paper on
me. I got an obligation to the Pittsburgh Crawfords. I'm a team player,
and I'm not looking out just for me. Besides, if Gus catch up with me,
he gonna bust a cap on my ass but good."

"Gus, my druthers is playing for you. But you've got to pay a man
what he's worth. If you don't, the man is going to jump. That's just the
way it is. Business."

Gus gritted his teeth and shook his head. "You jumping the paper on
me *and* jumping on Lena Horne. That's two strikes. The third one you
take will be lead. You just lucky you ain't already floating in the Allegheny, chum."

Satch was seeing for the first time that other side of Gus Greenlee,
the side he'd heard about and been warned about but found hard to believe. "You ain't got to threaten me, Horse. I'm your man—Satchel
Paige." Satch gave him his biggest grin. "Just give me a little raise, and I
still be in Pittsburgh with the Crawfords."

Gus shook his head. "You ain't leaving town. You're staying right
here. Try and leave, and the next pitch you throw will be from six feet
under the mound at Greenlee Field. That was Willie Neal's resting
place, till he got relocated. I got that spot reserved for you." Gus
laughed hard and bit into his Dutch Masters. "Satchel, you just turned
white enough to play for McGraw. Did you think we didn't play rough
in Pittsburgh?"

Satch leaned back against the high booth's back and tried to com-
pose himself.

"Here, have some water." Gus poured him a glass of ice water.

Satch took a slug. "Look, Gus, I know you're a little ticked off, but
you're a businessman, right? Okay, you lost some money on me, but I'm
gonna let you get it back."

"Keep talking."

"We got a game. Black All-Stars against white All-Stars. Henry Ford is sponsoring the white boys. Now, I said to myself, who's the black Henry Ford? It's Gus Greenlee." Satch slapped him on the upper arm. "The patron saint of colored baseball—Gus Greenlee. He the man."

"Gus is gonna foot the bill," Gus deadpanned.

"Biggest-hearted guy in Pittsburgh."

"How much?"

"Five hundred for me. Three hundred for everyone else. Throw in travel money, run you about four thousand."

"What do I get out of it?"

"Exactly!" Satch smiled and eased forward to the edge of the bench. "You're a businessman. I wouldn't come to you unless I had a business angle."

"Cut the bullshit. What is it?"

"Wagers. Side bet with Henry Ford."

"Henry Ford don't gamble that kind of money."

"Okay. George Raft. He's connected to the white team. His asshole buddy Durocher's playing. He dropped twenty grand on the Tigers. He'll drop twenty more on this game."

"It's fixed?"

"Fixed? Hell, yeah. Ol' Satch is pitchin'."

"Against who?"

"Dizzy Dean. I beat him four to one with nothing like the team I got behind me."

"Who's Dean got behind him?"

"Bunch of Redbirds. Frisch, Martin, Medwick, Durocher. Few other guys."

"Like who?"

"Lombardi, Gehrig . . ."

"Gehrig? They got Ruth, too?"

"I think so. Except he claims he's retired."

"So, when you say, 'a few other guys,' they could come up with Foxx, Waner, and Greenberg, and you might not know about it."

Satch shook his head. "No way. Henry Ford hates Jews. Greenberg's out of it."

"But you're talking the best players in the world, and I should put up twenty G's against them. Are you out of your fucking mind? I ought to shoot you right now."

Satch leaned back, spreading his hands on the table. "Big Red . . ." Satch laughed. "Take it easy, man. I ain't askin' for twenty G's. I'm just sayin' you could make that. Four thousand is all it would take."

The stress aggravated the gout in Gus's big toe. He'd had to take his shoes off, but it seemed to keep getting worse, and it made him less patient with Satch. "Goddamn it! Wasn't a week ago you came to the Grille and jumped the broom with Janet. Next Saturday you be jumpin' the paper on me. You the jumpingest man alive. Where's your gratitude?"

Satch was getting irritated himself. "Where's my raise, Gus? I tried to negotiate with you, and you wouldn't give me nothin'. A married man's got obligations a lot more'n what he had before."

"If you go to Bismarck, you better pack your bags for good. Bring your long johns, 'cuz the wind is so strong out there it blows prairie-dog holes inside out. That's it for your options, unless you want to play donkey-ball for Ray Doan or play in drag for a bloomer girl team, like Hornsby did." Gus shook a stubby finger at Satch. "Mark my words. You'll never play in the Negro Leagues again. We got a organization, we got contracts, and we honor 'em."

The options were looking grim to Satch, and got grimmer when Woogie Harris bent and whispered in Gus's ear while staring at Satch. Gus's eyes dilated like a cartoon character's. He was versed in the languages of the eyes, including the dead ones. He was fluent in fear and conversant in intimidation. He shook his head slowly, with an affect of finality.

"You done it now."

"What?"

"That was Arthur Flegenheimer on the phone. Looks like all those alternatives you had are whittlin' down to one."

"What's that?" asked Satch, who knew that "Flegenheimer" was the name Dutch Schultz had jettisoned as unbecoming of a gangster.

"St. Peter's nine," said Gus, pointing heavenward.

Oh, Mamie Lena, where'd you get the ostrich-feather thing on your head that Raphael Leonidas Trujillo would die for, a whole aviary anchored to your temples. The feathers curl like the thick smoke of the Crawford Grill, like notes of soft, soaring jazz from the throat of the Cotton Club diva. And, mama, where'd you get that feather boa, the one I'd change places with in an instant, snaking down that caramel cleavage?

Lena saw Gus remove a long-barreled pistol from his waistband and lay it on his lap, clutching the handle. She sashayed to their table, mid-number, and forced herself between the table and Gus's belly and began singing "I've Got the World on a String," sitting on his lap, Gus's finger around the trigger.

There are ecstatic moments of music, like Marcel Dupré and Fats Waller at Notre Dame Cathedral in '32. Marcel took Fats up to the "God Box" and Fats sat down to play Bach's *Toccata and Fugue*. Nobody there to hear it but God. A communion. The "happy frog," behavin'. Two years later, Lena Horne was sitting on a lap on a pistol, not just singing her heart out but singing the mayhem out of the heart of a man known for misbehavin', searching for the notes that would rise and ring off the walls of the Crawford Cathedral and soothe one savage heart. Lena rolled her tush on Gus's lap, turned and looked into his eyes. Every phrase of her siren song was a road to take, a reverie, a plan, a thought; each change to a minor key unlocked a sadness to wallow in. Every line was a hand-me-down to the larynx from the place in her head where she heard the notes as through a keyhole, and imitated them, the notes then handed down to Gus, registered on the drums of his ears. Hand-me-down silk, mountains of it, ruffled with her vibrato.

The song ended on a low note ground into Gus's lap. Everyone but Gus, no one-handed Zen master, clapped, and the band toodled away on a new number. Couples took to the floor. Satch heard, as clearly as the hum of his be-ball, in the husky joy of Cab's hey-de-ho, intimations of the great game, and understood that the game too had its secret codes. Hey-de-ho! It made perfect sense. He wanted to shout it. He could not fathom why everyone was not wailing it. Hey-de-ho! It seemed the intersection of breath and life, revealing itself as sound.

"Gus, is that a pistol in your lap?" Lena said, smiling broadly and gyrating a two-seventy that brought a hint of a smile to Satch's face. Gus wiggled his hand free, taking care to remove his stubby forefinger, with its middle knuckle permanently swollen from a fight decades earlier, unsure whether an accidental discharge would penetrate his own thigh or Lena's backside.

Satch took advantage of the cover that Lena's dallying with Gus provided and mixed with the couples dancing. He wondered if he could steal out of the Crawford Grill the way Cool Papa Bell stole home. He watched Cab flailing his arms and stamping his foot, saw Gus brooding and plotting, saw Woogie with thunder inside his jacket, and Lena moving to the words of the song Cab's band was playing. He recalled Gus's prediction that he would be playing with St. Peter's nine, and he wondered what game it was that they were *all* playing, what God's game was, for surely the only divine plan for all of this was a fantastic game where no one knew the rules. How else could it all make sense? And when *the game* was over? Would Gus be joking with St. Pete about the universal numbers game that his earthly vocation was an ironic metaphor of, a game in which he'd hit, big time?

So many questions, so near the end. There ought, by Satch's lights, to be time for a man to figure it out. "Hey-de-ho!" shouted Cab. And the notes became urgent in that Gus didn't hear them. Wasn't listening. Satch could see the music pass right by Gus.

"This one is for all you Detroit Tigers fans. St. Louis Blues," said Cab, who took a moment to sip a "Diz Fizz"—a new drink created in honor of Dizzy Dean—two raw eggs in beer. Lena smiled, gripped the microphone, and began to sing.

Satch was momentarily buoyed by the feeling that he could get out of the Crawford Grill alive. But then what? Would he hear his name called? Would he even hear the shot if it entered his brain or his heart from the rear?

He savored the sounds of Calloway's band all the way across the room and out into the starry night, thinking of the warmth and the scent of Lena. He hadn't imagined the crash of the footsteps, that leather on cement could be so loud. He noticed the percussion his own shoes made on the gravel, followed by that of the executioner, the beat, he thought, of his own death. First, the footsteps. Then the beauty of a hammer's click. Which stopped him. He had to know. He turned and saw Woogie's arm rising, pistol at its extremity. He heard the beat of four doors slamming the way he imagined the four hooves of a galloping horse coming down, the solid thuds of a heavy, four-door Ford. He turned to his right and saw four unknown men with fedoras and black or purple trench coats on and nothing in their hands. Two of the men remained on the far side, behind the car's hood, and Satch could not see their hands. He couldn't recognize them. Woogie recognized the two in front as Eddie Fletcher and Sammy Cohen. They just clasped their hands in front of them as if that were message enough. Four to one. Woogie did not like the odds, or the chance that the two behind the hood held Tommy guns. Or the cool, professional menace, the presumption that gunless hands could force him to fold. It seemed the message was enough.

Woogie concluded that a dead Paige and two dead gangsters did not outweigh a dead Harris. He gave a cynical smile, holstered his pistol and turned, making a softer crunch in the gravel, *pianissimo*. Satchel watched the four men get into the black Ford after the briefest eye contact with him, and he watched the small rectangle of a Michigan license plate get smaller. Maybe there is, he thought, a guardian angel. At least for ballplayers. And the angel was from Michigan. Even God, he concluded, wanted this game to go on.

But Satch was wrong. It was Henry Ford who wanted the game to go on. And the guardian angel had a name. Harry Bennett. Harry had ears everywhere. Satch was alive and in the dark. He hadn't recognized Harry's emissaries—Eddie Fletcher and Sammy Cohen—one half of Detroit's Purple Gang.

By the next time he saw Harry, he had it figured out. Harry caught up with him as he let the screen door shut on Al's Barber Shop on Wylie.

"Satch!"

Satch recognized the voice. He shook Harry's hand. "That was the Purple Gang that saved me."

Harry smiled and nodded. Satch spat some tobacco. "Trouble is, I'm alive but the game ain't. Gus is out."

"I figured that." Harry started toward his Model A and motioned for Satch to follow him. He reached through the open window for a brief-case on the seat. He gripped a wad of fifties. "Keept this quiet. If Henry wants to see a game, he'll see a game, even if he has to pay for it. Slush fund. Nobody counts how much is in it, so nobody knows what goes out." Harry pulled back the lapel of Satch's sport jacket and stuffed the cash inside his pocket, then slapped him on the lapel. "Nobody knows how you came up with the dough. Catch?"

Satch smiled and put his arm around Harry's shoulders. "Let's get some lunch and I'll tell you about *el maestro*."

"Martin Dihigo."

"You've done your homework."

"More than you'll ever know."

9

THE BLUFF

"*Bokar Eight O'Clock*"—the label on the coffee had to be an anagram, thought Diz, but he could not figure out what for, at 10:30 a.m., the latest he'd sat down to breakfast in six months. Moe Berg had told him about anagrams. Had shown him a few. And Diz was hooked. He made a mental note to call Moe and ask him about Bokar Eight O'Clock.

He smelled the steam rising off the dark brew as he miscegenated it with Carnation Evaporated Milk, thinking, *what the hell was* evaporated *about it?* It was right there. Nothing was evaporated. It was canned milk. Why didn't they just call it that? Another conspiracy, it seemed, brewing right out of his Bokar Eight O'Clock, as if time stopped for coffee. As he reached for the warm toast, spread with margarine and grape jelly, the phone rang—another conspiracy, thought Diz as he picked the receiver from its cradle and heard the voice of baseball Commissioner Kenesaw Mountain Landis.

"Mr. Dean?"

"That's me."

"This is Commissioner Landis. First I want to congratulate you on your victory over the Tigers. You were as brilliant as indefatigable."

"As who?"

Landis paused, then proceeded to his second reason for calling. "I'm also concerned about your postseason activities."

"You want to go duck hunting with me and Paul?"

"No. What I want, and what the President wants, is to send a team of All-Stars to Japan."

"I'm sorry, Mr. Landis, but I'm booked up."

"I wasn't inviting you. It's your booking that concerns me, the possibility that you might be double-booking, for an illicit interracial game, the very players Uncle Sam intends to send to Japan. If rumors are pitches, Mr. Dean, I want you to tell me I just hit a foul ball."

"I'd say Uncle Charlie got you good. Uncle Sam's gonna do just fine."

"Then let me address any hypothetical interracial game. Such a game will not be sanctioned. Any player who takes part is writing his ticket out of baseball permanently. Do I make myself clear?"

"Sure, Mr. Landis. And don't worry about us booking Moe Berg. His horse collars wouldn't do us no good, and we'd never steal the only guy you've got who can speak Japanese."

Landis hung up. Horse collars—zeroes in the hit column—were what Diz had now for a game. He put down the phone and looked disconsolately at proto-gangsters John Henry Seadlund and James Atwood Gray, who'd spent the night on his living room floor.

"That was Landis. The game's off."

"Sorry to hear that," said James Atwood.

John Henry had other ideas. "Can I use your phone?"

Diz handed him the phone and took a bite of toast. John Henry dialed Chicago, where Darrow had driven after the Series.

"Hello."

"Darrow?"

"Speaking."

"Darrow, this is John Henry Seadlund. I just gave your secretary Landis's name 'cuz I thought you wouldn't talk to me again, seeing as I'm a criminal and all."

"I spend most of my time talking to criminals, especially at city hall. Make it snappy, John Henry. I've got work to do."

"Darrow, you gotta come to St. Louis. The commissioner found out about the game, and he says he won't sanction it, which means he won't let it happen. That concerns me and James Atwood 'cuz we're planning on holding Diz hostage till Henry Ford kicks in his ransom. And if there's no game, Ford won't need Diz, and we'll be out a lot of dough, on account of you, indirectly."

"I've got nothing to do with this. Landis made the decision. I told you he was a prick."

"Still, you're the only one smart enough to talk him out of it. So you've got to come out here."

"I'd be aiding and abetting a felony."

"You'd be aiding one if you don't. I've got half a mind to plug Elmer just to show you we mean business."

"John Henry, listen. Number one—I don't believe you'd do that. And two—I'm going to call the St. Louis police as soon as I hang up this phone."

"Wait a minute." John Henry held his hand out to James Atwood and said, "Give me the gun." James Atwood handed it to him butt-end first. John Henry cocked the hammer. "Darrow, are you still there?"

"I'm . . ." Three shots gave Darrow a start. He jerked the receiver away from his ear, then placed it back at a cockeyed angle.

Diz put his hand though the obliterated lower-left-hand quadrant of the window screen. "Hell, now flies are gonna get in."

John Henry raised his voice. "If you're not on the first plane out here, I'm gonna put the next three in Elmer. He doesn't really matter, except maybe to you."

"Yeah," said Elmer Dean excitedly and loud enough for Darrow to hear, "shoot me!"

"All right. Don't shoot the kid. I'm coming. But I'm not promising any results. Landis won't care who you threaten to shoot."

"You'll think of something. You're the famous Clarence Darrow. The monkey guy and all that. You're the most famous lawyer there is."

"I'm retired from law. And you couldn't find a worse advocate to plead to Kenesaw Mountain Landis. We don't exactly get along, professionally or privately. I want your word you'll let Elmer be if I don't convince that white-haired dwarf to let the game go on."

"You can count on us. You ought to know that by now. But just remember—we're psychopaths. Can't be hanged for anything."

In Detroit enough cars had come off the assembly line at the Ford plant to keep Henry in croissants for the rest of his life, but Henry ate simply. Toast and butter. He enjoyed eyeing the crystal crock and resisting its superfluous jam. He indulged in frugality, but the toast had to be hot enough to hold the butter in various pools on the toasted surface, uncongealed.

He had a vision of an engine block with a piston that would thrust the toast out of the heating element when it was done. Eight pieces of toast popping in synchrony as the crankshaft pushed each piston in its turn. Henry ruminated on the pieces of eight that would flow from his invention as he watched his chef click his pocket-watch, then pull back the silver doors with H and F elaborately engraved on either side of the cantilevered device with ebony handles that ingeniously carried the bread slice that had to be turned over and returned to the central heating element for thirty more seconds.

Henry alternated bites of toast with sips of tea from a cup he found too ornate, with a handle he found too dainty and ineffective, but china didn't afford many choices, and it was his wife's domain, so he didn't complain. As soon as Harry Bennett arrived, Wagner rolled in a serving table with duck pâté, assorted hors d'oeuvres, and melon, which Ford sometimes indulged in after toast. A servant in black tie rushed in. "Urgent call, Mr. Ford. You said if anybody called about Dizzy Dean . . ."

Ford ignored him and addressed Wagner. "Didn't I tell you I wanted the melon in balls? Not squares. Not rectangles. Not some shape that God Himself never imagined. Balls. Do you understand?"

Wagner nodded and picked up the serving spoon Henry had thrown on the table.

"Now, give me the phone." Another servant brought the phone.

"Ford, here. Who's this?"

"Never you mind who's this. We've got Dizzy Dean, and if you want to see him alive, you'll follow the instructions I'm gonna give you."

"I don't give a fig about Dizzy Dean. And I don't give a shit about you. About the only person I can think of who might is J. Edgar Hoover, and I'm going to give him a call."

John Henry Seadlund laughed. "Sure. You don't care about Dizzy Dean. So who's gonna pitch that game you got coming up with the niggers?"

"Just how in blazes . . ."

John Henry interrupted, "We got Dizzy Dean, you rich prick. That's how we know. And we want twenty thousand dollars for him."

"What makes you think I'm going to pay that?"

"Ain't no game without Diz. We heard all about how much you want to beat the niggers and how you're paying for the whole white team to be there."

"Listen, you imp. As far as I'm concerned, baseball is a Zionist conspiracy. Before this month, I hadn't seen a game since 1919, and I shouldn't have bothered to see this Series. Dizzy Dean beat our Tigers, and if you want to kill him, that's fine by me. And as for the game you're talking about, the reason I'm funding it is the Negroes are teaming up with the Zionists and I want to shut their mouths for good. And I can do that just as easily with Schoolboy Rowe or Carl Hubbell. So you can put your little gun between Dizzy Dean's eyes and blow what little gray matter he has out the back of his head. I don't give a damn."

Ford slammed down the phone and inspected the balled melon Wagner had just brought. He picked one up and pitched a strike against a windowpane. "Goddamn it! These are perfect and I've lost my appetite. Get my dog. I'm going for a walk."

Harry Bennett wiped his fingers on a linen napkin. He grabbed a couple of melon balls and was pushing his chair back when Ford motioned to him to sit back down. He pushed his bowl in front of Harry, took a handful of cereal, squeezed it into a powder. "Remember what I said." Ford pointed at the powder. "That could be your Model A breakfast." Ford picked up a silver pitcher. "Milk?"

Harry shook his head.

"Now, I want you to go to St. Louis and see if what those hooligans said is true. Find out who they are, and take care of them. I want Dean to pitch that game and nobody else."

Harry replied as he always did, "Yes, sir."

On the other end, John Henry was dumbfounded. He held the receiver between his ear and the carriage whose shape resembled some of the discarded melon pieces in Henry Ford's trash can.

"What did he say?"

"He told us to stick it."

"He don't care what happens to Dizzy Dean?"

"Sonofabitch doesn't even like baseball," said John Henry.

"That sonofabitch. I'm like to blow up one of his plants," added James Atwood.

"They already tried that. He's got spies all over. And Harry Bennett."

James Atwood nodded pensively. His lips constricted as if he was going to spit. "When you're that rich, you can thumb your nose at death."

"And buy Carl Hubbell."

As soon as Ford got back to the house he asked for the telephone and called St. Louis.

"Is this Paul Dean?"

"Reckon so."

"Paul, this is Henry Ford. I didn't call to wish you congratulations, though you deserve it. You played a fine series."

"We beat a fine team in those Tigers. They're the second best in the world."

"Paul, I called to talk to you on another matter. I can't reach your brother, and I just got a telegram from a couple of knuckleheads who say they've kidnapped him. Have you by chance seen him recently?"

"No, sir. But I don't think he was kidnapped. If anyone was kidnapped, it'd be our other brother, Elmer. He was gone for four years. Cotton-picker picked him up in a Chevy coupe. He was just going to get some lunch. Jay and I lit out after him, but the buzzard ran a red light and that's the last we saw of Elmer for four years . . ."

"Paul, have you seen your brother?" Ford repeated, petulantly.

"After the game yesterday. He looked to be in a big hurry. Said he was looking for Elmer. So don't you fret, Mr. Ford. Elmer always shows up sooner or later."

"Well, you'd better start looking for him, and Jerome, too. If you want to call in Hoover, just let me know. I'll contact him personally."

"You don't have to bother Mr. Hoover. I ain't worried none. Diz can take care of himself. He's a big fellah."

"All right, Paul. You have a good off-season."

"Mr. Ford?"

"Yes."

"I'm gonna shoot me some ducks this afternoon. You want any? I could send 'em up your way."

"Thanks, Paul. We've got our own ducks."

Harry Bennett was 5'6", with reddish, slicked-down hair. He had the look of a white man with a conk. The Ford Company psychologist who examined Harry as a condition of being hired described his worldview as, "Don't shit on me, and I won't shit on you." Harry argued for, "Don't shit on me, and I won't punch you on the beezer." They agreed that Harry was not the kind of guy who pleaded, "*Please* don't shit on me." He acknowledged that sometimes he raged with shit, like the time he found his stolen motorcycle locked in a Navy parking lot and went back to the barracks and got an awl and a wire-cutter to wreak a shit-load of revenge. The psychological report acknowledged Harry's ingenuous apology for the oblique embrace of life that his philosophy entailed. "I do feel diminished," he said. He promised the psychologist to be more proactive. "I'll slip out of my hammock and even take off the shit-protector, sit on the plank and give you three tosses for a dollar."

"Hire him," said Ford. "He's just what we need."

Occasion thrives bandit-like on the dicey border of cause and happenstance. Thus for Harry Bennett occasion was all one needed. The occasion, betimes, of sin—the turf that Harry made slippery with more greenbacks than most Wall Streeters or gangsters had ever seen. If a little could go a long way in 1934, then Harry's slush account was the unmoved mover that could move a jury to acquittal. It was the kind of thing Darrow saw time after time in Chicago, the thing that moved him to bribe his own juror, but with the clumsiness of an anarchist manqué. Darrow lacked the cunning sleight of hand that Bennett had. He also lacked the backup Harry always had, the heaviness of hand that could break jaws. If Harry couldn't beat you with his hands, he always had a revolver tucked in his waistband. A target sat on a filing cabinet in his office, and a bell would go off when the bull's-eye was struck with an air-pistol pellet. He once shot the high-hat off the head of Prince Louis Ferdinand Hohenzollern, the kaiser's grandson, who dared to break Ford's rule about hats in the inner sanctum. And he shot the cigar out of the mouth of another visitor who smoked where Ford banned smoking.

The one subject Harry Bennett never flunked in school was history. Only fools, thought Harry, thought history dead. Seeing men challenge Ford and lose their jobs, one after another, only a damned fool would not learn from that. The smart guys, the guys who thought they knew a lot, were all gone because they weren't savvy enough to see that if you argued with Ford you were history, that if you wanted to cross the old man you did it in a way that could not be traced back to you.

Because he kept his mouth shut and said yes and got any job done, he had Ford's confidence to a greater degree than did Ford's sons, or even his wife. He knew more about Ford's private thought than anyone. He knew that knowledge was power. He was the J. Edgar Hoover of the Ford Motor Company, and as such he could never be let go, in Henry Ford's lifetime. He knew too much. The union men who'd been roughed up. The ones who died of happenstance. The juries bought off.

Harry would borrow books from the Ford home. History books. He was enthralled by the fall of civilizations—the Incas, the Mayans, the Romans, the Greeks. He remembered reading about the Mayan ball games, how the captain of the winning team was beheaded. The Mayan empire was not the Ford Motor Company. If there was one thing America had learned from history, thought Bennett, it was that the losers lost their heads, not the winners. The Mayan game was one Harry could play. He'd be the lowest-scoring player in the game's history.

He was, in Ford's mind, a perfect destruction machine. But then, so was a reaper, a tiller, a harrow—those machines Ford had been in puppy-love with. They cut and broke and killed, but with a higher purpose, like religion, and perfect machines were his religion. Part of Henry Ford worshipped Harry Bennett. A machine, after all, did things non-Bunyonesque men could not do.

To inspire himself, to revel in the *migliores artistes*, the giants on whose shoulders he stood with steel-tipped shoes for breaking shins, and to intimidate those permitted into his inner sanctum, Harry Bennett had a room, opened by a switch beneath his desk, full of functional weapons, an armory of sorts, with a fantastic collection of derringers, pistols, rifles, garrotes, Aztec obsidian axes, scimitars, even a guillotine and a functional electric chair where he would sit for high tea, hatching his plots or chatting with a visitor who needed convincing about something. Harry would entreat the guest to take just enough juice to make his hair stand on end—"a thrill"—Harry offered, ingenuously. No one ever accepted. But most recusants actually believed that Harry had experimented to find the correct hair-raising voltage, as if the machine were a kind of carburetor mixing the oxygen, lean or fat, for a kind of idle they could barely imagine.

Over high tea in an electric chair, he had to fight the impulse to do a mental accounting of all those he had maimed, killed, and injured, the way that other men counted all the women they'd had sex with over a lifetime. That other kind of reminiscing, in Harry's view, was for retirement. In mayhem one needed to be proactive.

Harry rose from the electric chair with no particular inspiration on how to locate the hooligans who might be holding Dizzy Dean. He would first have to verify the alleged kidnapping. He rose with an ironic but irrelevant thought that he articulated to himself, "They use twenty-four hundred volts to electrocute a man. Only takes four thousand to move a trolley. Go figure."

Ten hours later Harry Bennett called to inform Ford that he'd arrived in St. Louis and would get on the case first thing in the morning. He updated him on the plan to play the game at Fenway Park at night. The Detroit night was chilly. Ford closed a window, feeling the burden of having Dizzy Dean's fate in his hands, wondering if his bluff had been the right move. He was wishing he were Harry Bennett—ruthless, entirely his own man. He crossed the hall to the antechamber and put on his pajamas and red silk bathrobe. Sliding his feet into slippers, he had a vision of Durocher's shoes, black and pointy. He envied him, this late, out cutting a rug in those high-waisted pants with that energy, abandon, lust, disdain, sliding the way they say one did on Polly Adler's satin sheets. He sighed, ruing that there was no one to complain to about being Henry Ford. He turned on the Victrola. Put on Caruso. Imagined himself Rudolfo, jewing the Jew-landlord out of the rent. Dying for love, without an automobile in sight. Arias instead of Klaxons. He sat in his black leather armchair wanting to give to the poor, the lame, the unwashed, the shoeless, the shiftless—something unimaginable, the way he gave them the five-dollar-an-hour wage, he wanted to give them his life.

And to the hooligans allegedly holding Dizzy Dean he would give a dose of Harry.

As if all roads have led to St. Louis. While Harry Bennett took a cab to Dizzy Dean's hotel, just blocks away Clarence Darrow said hello to his old nemesis, baseball Commissioner Kenesaw Mountain Landis.

"You know why I'm here, Squire, don't you?"

"Squire" was Landis's nickname, but almost no one called him that to his face.

"I think I do. The cat is out of the bag, counselor. And the jig is up, so to speak." Landis retreated to the oak desk that appeared immense with the diminutive man behind it. He looked Darrow in the eye. "No interracial play, and that's final."

"That was the verdict, but it is now under appeal."

"Let's be square, Darrow. There's no love lost between us. It wasn't a sin of omission that I didn't attest to your character when you were tried for jury tampering."

Darrow hung his coat on the elk horns that served as a rack and began to speak without looking at his adversary. "The trouble with you,

Judge, is that you never get off of that high, righteous horse of yours. You fell in love with your own image, and you made the mistake of believing that your image was a little closer to God's than is the case for the rest of us. Now you're the biggest cheese of all—Commissioner of Major League Baseball. The problem is there's a lot of little mice who aren't white and who are going to take a bite out of you. You fancy yourself a trust-buster because you went after Rockefeller, but you're the head of the biggest trust this country has ever known—baseball. And when I finish my work with the NRA, the last legal thing I do will be to come after you. I'll go to the Supreme Court if I have to, but I'm going to see Negroes playing in your league before I die."

Darrow's threat had more to do with personal animosity than commitment to black baseball. Landis swiveled in the high-backed chair that made him look even slighter than he was. "You and your gambler friends can forget about Negroes playing in the Big Leagues, and I'm going to tell you why. I tell you this *in camera*, expecting your complete confidentiality"—Landis swiveled again, and then added parenthetically—"though I have no right to expect that of a man who remains unacquitted of bribery and a man who has his clients take the Fifth."

Darrow pivoted on his right heel and had a momentary image of Teddy Roosevelt, which he took as a good sign. He lit a cigar and let himself sink into the Roosevelt persona. He looked Landis in the eye and nodded agreement to the request for confidentiality. Landis eyed Darrow even more coldly. "It's this," the commissioner said with his right hand raised and his thumb rubbing against his fingertips. "As you might have expected. No grand conspiracy, no smoke-filled rooms, none of that Chicago City Hall business you engaged in. It's all very simple. I know you blame me, as do a lot of other socialists, libertarians, and anarchists, along with the muckraking press, but I'm no more racially prejudiced than you are. My chauffeur is a Negro, and I've seen to it that he and his family will be taken care of for life. I watch the Negroes play every chance I get. It's a different game. It's elemental. And fast. Full of chicanery, but that's to be expected. I enjoy watching Bojangles racing against a horse, the shadow-ball, the clean comedy of the agile coon."

Darrow slumped in his chair, the way he had a habit of doing during a long prosecution closing argument.

"I'll get to the point," said the commissioner. "History may not be kind to Landis. When integration happens, and it is bound to, people will look back at Landis and ask why he didn't make it happen sooner. But my hands are tied. My tenure as baseball commissioner is in the hands of the owners. I can stare down Ruth and Hornsby, because it's good for the game, which means that in the long run it fills the pockets of the owners. But if I cross them on the Negro issue, they'll lose their shirts, and I'll be out of a job. I'm not against Negroes playing in the Major Leagues, and never have been. Find one public statement to that effect."

"You outlawed interracial barnstorming, for one."

"That was for the good of the game. Satchel Paige was embarrassing our teams. Babe Ruth was the best thing that ever happened to baseball. What good would it do to millions of white kids, who grow up idolizing the Babe, if they find out the Negroes have one guy who can strike out Ruth almost at will, and another guy who can out-slug their idol?"

"It would do a lot of good for a million Negro kids. They need the role model more than the white kids. Think of what Jack Johnson meant to them."

"Jack Johnson set off race riots."

"And white rioters precipitated the Ossian Sweet fiasco. When I saw what your institutional justice was doing to that man, I became an advocate of Negro causes."

Landis laughed. "The cause that motivates you is not Booker T. Washington; it's George Washington—on a dollar bill. You wouldn't have defended Sweet if the NAACP hadn't come up with the cash."

"I'm not denying that I was fairly compensated. But I would have taken that case for the money Detroit's black ballplayers ponied up, passing a hat." Darrow shook his finger at Landis. "And now I'd like to pay them back, not with money, but with something it can't buy—the integration of Major League Baseball."

Landis leaned forward, putting both fists on the desk. "Integration will come, but at its own speed. Have you ever asked yourself how it got that way in the first place? How it got segregated?" Landis rubbed his thumb and forefinger again. "It wasn't just Cap and the good old boys who put the kibosh on integrated play. It was money. Those white boys on the fringe knew that the colored boys would get their jobs, if they let them. And the middling boys would look better if the coloreds were excluded. It was an insurance policy for everyone. So they bought into Cap's philosophy, his bigotry, which admittedly wasn't a big step for a lot of them. Everybody had something to gain. Even the Negroes. Satchel Paige makes more in his league, pitching three times a week, than he would in the Majors.

"Now that's the history of it. As for now, for why Negroes won't be in the Major Leagues this year or next, there's two answers." Landis spread his hands as if his desk were a keyboard and he were trying to play the lowest and highest notes at the same time. "The first is . . . *money*. The owners of those parks are making a fortune renting their stadiums to the Negro teams when they're away. The Senators made a hundred thousand last year. And the second reason is . . . *money*. If the Negroes come in, there will be a bidding war, first for the Negroes, then for the whites, who'll insist on making more than the Negroes. Look at Paige. The only player who ever made more was Ruth. So how are you going to get Paige to play in the Major Leagues? You've got to pay him what he's worth. And he's worth as much as Dean. Maybe more. What do you think is stopping Branch Rickey from signing Negro players today? . . . Sam Breadon. He won't even pay Dizzy what he's worth, let alone Daffy and Ducky. Is there a conspiracy? Collusion? Not overtly. But de facto, yes. Are you following me, Darrow?"

Darrow nodded.

"So when you come spewing righteousness and threatening upheaval in our national pastime, I won't have it." Landis assumed the lecturing posture that Darrow hated in the preachers of Kinsman, Ohio, where he'd grown up. But it struck Darrow as funny to be lectured to by a white-haired dwarf, after dealing with the likes of William Jennings Bryan.

Landis continued, "You defend the men that try to bring this country down. And you don't do it just for the money. You've got some kind of Antichrist bone in your head."

Darrow swiveled and laughed. "So that's it. I thought it was callus mastoiditis that had me down after the Haywood trial, but in fact it was an Antichrist bone in my head. I'll tell my doctor when I get back to Chicago. Right now, I'm going to do something I've wanted to do for thirty years. That's telling you to mind your own goddamn business. These fellows are going to play a game. It happens to be a game that I love. It's going to be the game of the century, and you won't even be there." Darrow smiled at the thought of Landis being left out.

Landis seethed. He looked at Darrow with his best Andrew Jackson imitation and prepared to give him hell. None of the affect got through Darrow's thick skin. He'd seen too many judges puff themselves up, too many prosecutors try to intimidate him, and the commisioner had the look of an escapee from a Goya painting.

"Let me make myself clear, in case you don't understand plain English. There'll be no interracial play. The boys know it. They'll respect it, or there'll be consequences. I've made that clear."

"You don't mind if I sit over there, do you, Judge? You've got all the chairs here below the pedestal of your desk, and I'll be carrying on my foolish dialogue from on low." Darrow sat in the leather chair next to Landis's desk. "Consequences, yes. But I don't believe you have any idea of the magnitude thereof, and I don't think you'll want to risk them." Darrow stretched his legs and crossed them. "I'll come right to the point. The fellows on both sides feel pretty strongly about this game. On one side we have Henry Ford and Harry Bennett. And on the other . . ." Darrow looked away and smirked, irritating the bejesus out of Landis. "Is there such a thing as a lame duck commissioner?"

Landis's brow wrinkled. Darrow continued, "If I don't have your word tonight that the game is on, negotiations for the real Major League of baseball, an integrated league, will begin at once."

Landis kicked himself, shuffling his feet under his desk. He grimaced and was angry at himself for visibly grimacing at Darrow's words.

"Every player on Dean's team will resign from your league and they'll form the nucleus of the new league. They'll draw every player who has ever felt cheated by the unfair labor practices of what has hitherto been called Major League Baseball. Players will be paid fairly for their labor. They will not be blackballed if they don't like the contract offered them by the team they have been playing for. Their services will be fairly compensated. The new prospective owners are more than satisfied with the prospective earnings. They do not feel the need to gouge and exploit. They are glad to be part of the integration of baseball and they are more than content with the larger audience they will now reach. This league will put your league out of business in less than three years. No one but the racists will want to play for you. Exploitation has never been a strong incentive."

Landis laughed, showing the tips of his lower teeth. "Do you really expect me to believe a cockamamy story like that? What new owners? And those players are all under contract. They'll be sued and they won't make a dime."

"And we'll countersue. All the way to the Supreme Court."

Landis laughed. "You were never worth a damn as an attorney in any court that didn't have a jury."

"Well, I am officially retired. So I'll be getting some help. But you've made baseball into a monopoly. With the public behind us, and that means every Negro in this country, we'll win an antitrust case. Your labor practices are direct descendants of slavery, so you can see how that will play out in the court of public opinion. As for the new owners . . . this is confidential, mind you, but so far we've got Adrian Anson, Howard Hughes, Jack Warner, Benjamin Siegel . . ."

Landis leaned his one-hundred-and-thirty-pound frame against his desk. "You don't mean Bugsy?"

"Benjamin Siegel of Beverly Hills."

"That's Bugsy Siegel, dadblast it!" Landis slammed his fist on his desk. "He's a criminal. A gangster. That's the element I was hired to get rid of. His type will kill baseball. And Jack Warner! I don't know what's worse, turning baseball into a den of iniquity or a spectacle for entertainment. This is our national pastime you're messing with!"

Darrow gloated and did nothing to hide it. He'd made up his phony list of owners to provoke just this reaction in Landis. He had the son-ofabitch. He leaned forward and erased the gloat. "Now, realistically, here's what's going to happen. These things always enter a bargaining phase. The present owners will make the necessary concessions to stay in business, and they'll be furious at you for getting the whole thing started by stopping this game. You'll be canned."

"You're bluffing. You're making the whole thing up."

"We've also got a consortium of Negro owners who'll put together two more teams. Gus Greenlee and Rufus Jackson of the Grays, Tom Wilson in Baltimore, Alex Pompez of the New York Cubans, Robert Cole of the American Giants . . ."

"That's a consortium of gangsters."

"Do you think they'll steal more from the players than the present owners, one of whom has expressed quiet interest in buying into the new league."

Landis scoffed. "You expect me to believe that?"

"Why don't you call Adrian Anson and confirm it? We go way back. We were members of Mayor Gunne's 'kitchen cabinet.' Adrian's a highly principled man who wanted to build a utopian Chicago. Translate that into baseball and what do you get?"

"I still think you're bluffing."

"Do you think I'd drive all the way to St. Louis just to waste my time trying to con an old fogey like you?"

Landis thought on it. That did seem preposterous. But it seemed unlikely that negotiations for a new league could be happening without his getting wind of it. He shook his head. "I'm calling your bluff."

Darrow stood up slowly. He had arthritis in his hips and shoulders. He spoke without looking at the judge. He had bluffed juries where men's lives were at stake. "You've got till when I reach that door to convince yourself of that." He turned and looked at the commissioner, but said nothing.

Landis shook his head. "I put my trust in Providence, and I'd trust the weather before I'd trust you."

"I can understand that. They're two sides of the same coin. Just as fickle."

Landis fixed Darrow with a stern gaze. "You're an Antichrist, Darrow."

"I'm an honest broker, Commissioner." Darrow theatrically cocked his head and squinted at the squire. "Now that I'm retired, I kind of wish you'd go back to being a judge and leave baseball alone. Baseball doesn't need to be tainted with divine retribution, which is what you represent. You've got the hair and pallor of a man who's died and come back"—Darrow turned stagily and stared Landis in the eye—"with a message. And it *ain't* a happy one. It's 'Guess what, boys! It's not just coal in your stocking on the other side. No, sir. You'd better watch out, all you niggers and miscegenists, too. God is right out of the Old Testament, and He's swinging a stocking full of shit. And He swings it like the other big Jew, Greenberg, swings a bat.' And whether you or I get to heaven or hell, I don't care. As far as I can see, in any case there's just one way out—the door."

He turned again and had his hand on the doorknob when Landis squeaked out a tepid "Okay . . . but there are conditions. I'm not a bigot, Darrow. I canceled interracial play because I didn't want those colored boys embarrassing us."

Darrow withheld the sigh of relief, even with his back to Landis, for fear that his body language might give something away, but inside he gloated. Landis landed on his feet and walked around his desk, ostensibly reading the marble tiles beneath his feet.

"Here's the deal. The white team will be comprised of no more than seven Major Leaguers, and no more than five from any one team. That way, if we lose, we can say they didn't beat a real Major League All-Star team, and they won't be able to say they beat the World Champions. Is that clear?"

"I'll have to ask the players."

"Take it or leave it. There'll be no more negotiations."

Darrow knew his answer, but wanted Landis to squirm. He opened the door, took a step out, turned, and said, "I'll take it." He held out his hand. Landis hesitated, but only for a split second, for effect, then shook his hand firmly. Frankly, he was dying to see the game himself, and Darrow's gloating notwithstanding, he knew that through Harry Bennett, via Henry Ford, he'd be informed of the game's venue.

10

THE PLAYERS

The young man at the far end of the room had a pistol in his hand, so Harry Bennett reached for his own, but loosened his grip when a stream of water emerged from the pistol's nose and Elmer shot at a bee that had accessed the room through the hole John Henry had blasted in the screen. The bee settled on the jam-spotted handle of the revolver on the table that neither of the erstwhile kidnappers made a move for.

Clowns, thought Harry. *Worse than amateurs.* James Atwood didn't bother to get off the couch to shake the hand that Harry extended. And when Pat Dean appeared and offered him some jamoke, Harry realized that the whole thing was a farce.

"I'm Harry Bennett and I'm here on behalf of Henry Ford. I thought I was going to free Dizzy Dean."

Diz laughed. "Hell, Pat ain't no ball and chain. We ain't been married that long. You come back in a couple of years." Pat frowned and slapped Diz on the arm. Harry stared at Pat's white apron as she ran her fingers along the frills. He loosened his signature bow tie, which he wore instead of a standard tie because he'd almost been garroted once with his own cravat.

James Atwood lay motionless on the couch where his 5'7" frame fit perfectly. The throw pillow forced the tuft of blond hair up only a few degrees more than when he was standing. He put his hands behind his head, watching Elmer and the bee, thinking of the rabbit he'd shot and posthumously named Jack, about the uselessness of his death and the bee's. How little it takes to reform, he thought. How instantly it happens. How much lighter one feels, as if the couch's pillows were clouds. Which made him think in contrast of a jail cot. He savored his comfort, every moment counting. Besides, the October air blowing through the window couldn't possibly be sweeter anywhere other than where he lay. And as if Newton's second law of motion had an equivalent in Plato's realm of ideas, as James Atwood basked in thoughts of reformation, Harry Bennett was cooking him up a different fate. Relaxed in the moment, James Atwood noticed John Henry in counterpoint, muscles taut, sitting upright in his chair, as if preparing to flee, which reminded him again of his rabbit—being stalked.

Harry tried to hide a snicker, moving his finger through the air from John Henry to James Atwood. John Henry's expression mixed scowl and smile. "We never intended to kidnap Diz."

"That would have been ungrateful," added James Atwood through clenched teeth that added a vibrato to his speech. "And we're grateful to Diz for including us in his parade."

"We were going to share the money with Diz. Them Cardinals don't pay him half what he's worth," John Henry asserted.

"In other words, you're shaking down Mr. Ford because he's got deep pockets."

"We're not shaking him down. The tight sonofabitch refused to pay up."

The logic, Harry realized, was too convoluted to straighten out. He wouldn't even try. He accepted Pat's offer of coffee and watched Elmer drown the bee while a rectangular box of sunlight framed it like a coffin. Turning in the hooligans would only bring unwanted publicity. He had plans for them, now that they were in his debt. He saw, especially in the eyes of James Atwood, the anxiety that a jail term could provoke. Harry smiled. He himself was relieved. Coming as executioner, leaving as savior, with two recruits—saviors-in-waiting, saviors of a different kind, while Elmer tossed the bee carcass through the hole in the window.

It started, for Harry Bennett, as a rumble—what he went into, in his head, when he was all ears and Henry had thrown open the gates to any means, any degree of violence, to get a job done. He heard it, and went into it, and became something feral. The intelligence of the senses poured into him. He plotted, planned, intrigued, and he got what he was after.

What he was after now was the team that would beat the Negroes. He was after any knowledge money could buy. Something told him that the meeting with the team's core had to be in the team's clubhouse, in Sportsman's Park, and he arranged it under Branch Rickey's nose. Diz was there, and Leo, Frankie, Pepper, and Ducky. Harry was content to sit back and let the players pick their own team, but there was one player he would insist on, if push came to shove—Gehrig. That left two non–Major League spots, plus a tenth man in case someone got injured. And Harry had his insurance player, in case the Negroes got cute.

Harry turned his chair backward and sat down. "So, boys, what'cha got?"

Diz lifted his loose cap with its bent brim with white lines of salt from his sweat that looked like a time-lapse photo of the foam-edge of waves that came in, a little farther each time, with an advancing tide. "There's us five, from the Gashouse Gang, and we only get two more Major Leaguers. One of them's got to be Gehrig, in my opinion. I don't know about you guys," Diz said.

Harry held back a smile. The four other players looked at each other and nodded. "He won the Triple Crown," said Pepper. "Hard to argue with that."

"I got another no-brainer," said Frankie. "For one of the non–Major League slots, we get Ruth. The Yankees released him. He says he's retiring. I know he can't hit like he used to, but he still hit .288. And there's one thing, doggone it, that the man *can* do—he can beat you. When the chips are down, I don't know about you, but I want the greatest hitter the game has ever known to have the stick in his hands. He's gonna get three cuts. And he's convinced every cut is gonna put the ball in the upper deck. And one more thing—suppose Diz takes a liner off the arm. Who's gonna pitch? Leo? Pepper?"

"I pitched in Texas," Pepper protested.

Frankie looked at him and affirmed what he had thought—Pepper was not serious in his protest. He just wanted recognition that he could pitch. Harry looked around and noted the consensus, and wrote "Babe Ruth" on his list. "Speaking of pitching insurance," said Diz, "I had a harebrained idea. I mean, I'm the pitcher on this team and all, but either for backup or maybe we use this as a chip with Landis and parlay it into another Major Leaguer—what I'm thinking of is this—we get that girl that struck out Leo and Ruth and Gehrig, let her pitch one inning. And then if we lose . . ."

"You can't lose," said Harry threateningly. "You're not allowed to lose."

"I was just saying that if we did we could say the Negroes beat a girl pitcher."

Leo wrinkled his mouth into something between a smile and a grimace. "She struck me out last year fair and square, but I don't know about Ruth. Might have been a stunt."

Frankie shook his head. "Those Negroes can hit. She might get them out. Anyone can get lucky. On the other hand, they might wallop her from here to Tuesday. We might get in a hole and never get out. That guy Paige can throw."

"So it's nix on Jackie Mitchell?"

Pepper nodded, not looking at Diz. Leo nodded and walked to the table and took a Rheingold from the bag.

"What about the other Babe—Bloomer Babe. Didrikson? I seen her throw a ball from the center-field wall to second base on the fly," said Pepper.

"Center field where? The sandlot on 14th Street?" Harry laughed.

"No, seriously. She won the Olympics baseball toss. Threw it three hundred feet."

"There's no baseball toss in the Olympics," said Leo scornfully.

"Well, then it was somewhere else, but she won it. And I've seen her throw. She mows 'em down. Pitches for the House of David. Those guys are good. She started an exhibition against the Yankees. Bucky Harris says she can handle the apple with some of the boys."

"Wouldn't that beat all, if we had her start against the Negroes, pitch one inning then Old Diz comes in?"

"Don't think she throws hard enough," said Leo.

"I don't know if speed's the question. I mean, throwing a ball three hundred feet, you gotta have speed."

"That's an outfield throw."

"It's physics, Leo," said Frankie. "The distance you throw depends on the initial velocity. The faster it goes, the farther. And vice versa. The girl can throw it fast, all right, but does she have stuff?"

"What I heard from the Yanks is she's got a dandy curveball," said Pepper.

Harry laughed. "I tell you, though, Hitler'd love it. An Aryan woman beating Negro men."

"Don't tell Hitler," said Diz. "He's a big-mouth. The press would get wind of it and we'd be in horsefeathers."

Pepper looked around. "No reason not to give her a tryout, right?"

Nobody said no. "I'll get her out here tomorrow," said Harry. "And I'll have Gehrig on a plane tonight."

"I don't know about this idea—broads pitching," said Leo, wiping his mouth.

"Bet she can beat that little pop-gun arm of yours," said Pepper, smiling.

"Yeah? How much?"

"Twenty bucks. From center field."

"I don't care where the fuck it's from." Leo lit up a cigar.

Harry removed the Havana from his mouth. "You still don't have a catcher."

"We've got one Major Leaguer left. I say we get Cochrane," offered Leo. "He's the best."

"Didn't we put him in the hospital?" said Pepper, laughing at how Ernie Orsatti had knocked the Tiger catcher almost unconscious in game six of the Series.

"That Ernie Lombardi's got my number," said Diz. "I'd like to see him paste a few of Paige's."

"He's as good a hitter," said Ducky. "But Cochrane's a lot better defensively, and those niggers bunt."

"Y'all can forget about Cochrane. I ain't playin' with no Tigers," said Diz with an air of finality. Nobody challenged him on it.

"So, it looks like Lombardi," said Harry. "Any objections?"

Ducky and Leo looked hard at Harry but didn't say anything. "Okay, Lombardi's catching," said Harry. "Now we need a centerfielder and a sub, in case someone gets hurt. Neither one's a Major Leaguer. What's that leave us?"

"Hottest prospect I know is a kid named DiMaggio, in the Pacific Coast League," said Leo.

"That's a pretty good league, what I hear. Wouldn't make any sense for baseball to stop at St. Louis," said Diz.

"They got some players out there. Augie Galan came from out there. Frank Crosetti. Lombardi, too."

"So, what about DiMaggio?"

"I heard the Yanks were gonna bring him up next year, but he blew out his knee."

"So he can't play?"

"I don't know. I think he's playing. The Yanks just don't want to take a chance."

"What's he play? We need an outfielder."

"A little outfield," said Leo. "Mainly he plays shortstop. But he bobbles too many balls to play infield for the Yanks. He'll play outfield. Don't take my word for any of this—I'm just telling you what Cy Slapnicka told me."

"Okay. Just tell us what he told you."

"Cy says he's still getting used to center-field, but he's got the speed to make up for his mistakes."

"What about hitting?"

"Boy, can he hit. Big kid. 6'1", 185. Had a streak of forty-seven, forty-eight games. Broke the league record. Hit one off Bobo Newsome.

Cy says he's got the best swing since Paul Waner. Could be the best natural player since Joe Jackson."

Pepper's eyes lit up. He rose an inch off his haunches and snapped his fingers. "Joe Jackson!" Pepper looked around at the heads that were letting the thought register. "Why not?"

"Joe's been out of baseball for, what, fifteen years?"

"The Majors, yeah. He's playing semipro in Greenville. I just heard some good old boys talking about one he hit last year down in Georgia. Five hundred feet, they said."

They all wanted it to be true. The legend they'd grown up with who could still play. The greatest natural hitter in baseball hitting against Satchel Paige in the greatest game ever played. Joe Jackson redeeming himself. Landis tearing out all of his white hair. But no one quite believed it, not even Pepper.

"Anyone got any better ideas?" said Diz. Frankie and Leo shook their heads.

"Okay, that's it."

"No, there's one more thing," said Harry. "Landis wants the midget."

"Nittols?"

Harry nodded.

"Landis never said anything to me about it," said Diz.

"Me neither," said Frankie, who suspected, correctly, that it wasn't Landis's idea but Harry's, and Harry didn't want to own up to subterfuge, which was the name of his game, and everybody knew it. But how do you say no to the money-man?

"We got nothing to lose, right?" said Harry. "We don't have to put him in, right? But if we get two on, it'll put a scare in 'em. Paige will have to put the ball over, 'cuz if he walks a man, he knows what's coming. Besides, I don't trust those Negroes. They might bring Bebop."

"Is that the midget who plays for the Clowns?"

Harry nodded.

"Not a bad idea," said Leo.

"Okay," said Frankie. "I'll get Nittols. Leo, you take care of DiMaggio and Ruth. Harry's got Gehrig and the other Babe. And Diz, you're a good old Southern boy. You take care of Jackson."

"Don't know if he's gonna believe me when I call him."

"They got phones in Greenville?"

"Hell, they got phones everywhere now, Leo."

"Then they've got a telegraph," said Frankie. "Harry, you wire him five hundred dollars. That'll make a believer out of a guy who's probably getting ten bucks a game."

Harry stopped at the door and nodded. "See you guys in a day or so with the lowdown on Paige's team. Anything else?"

"Yeah," said Ducky, looking at Leo. "How about a scouting report on that kid—what's his name—before we sign him up?"

"DiMaggio. No problem. I've got a friend out there who played minor-league ball with me in Springfield. I'll have him check him out."

Diz unstraddled the bench and led the players out. Harry called out, "Leo, better act fast on Ruth. He's headed to Japan with Moe Berg and a bunch of All-Stars."

Leo laughed. "Japan? What the hell do they hit with, chopsticks?"

Two days later Babe Didrikson Zaharias stepped out of the cab outside Sportsman's Park with a small duffel bag. She slung it over her shoulder, eschewed the driver's offer to help carry it, and gave him a twenty-five-cent tip. She walked up to Frankie and Leo and extended her hand.

"You know who I am. Which one of you is Harry?"

"Neither. I'm Frankie Frisch." Frankie shook her hand and was impressed with her grip. "This is my right-hand man, Leo Durocher. Harry's on his way from Pittsburgh. Got some business there."

Leo shook her hand. "Pleased to meet you. I thought you might be taller."

"I thought you'd be, too."

"Touché," said Frankie, laughing, trying to deflect any sensitivity Leo might have about his height. But Leo just laughed. He could read the good humor in Babe's voice and face. He'd thought she might be an Amazon, but all of Babe's accomplishments came from a 5'5", 140-pound frame.

"Say, how far can you really throw a ball?"

"I thought you guys were looking for a pitcher."

"We are. Some guys are making a side bet."

"Well, at the AAUs I threw two-hundred and ninety-six, but I can beat that."

A security cop opened the door to Sportsman's Park.

"You want to change up?" asked Frankie.

"You don't think I play in this fluff, do you?"

Frankie smiled. "You can use the visitor's locker."

Babe could see some players in uniform on the field. "Say, who are those fellas? They look pretty good."

"Some of the Gashouse Gang—Pepper Martin, Dizzy Dean on the mound. Medwick, Ruth, Gehrig . . ."

"Holy shit! I mean, golly! Is that who I'm pitching against?"

"Suppose I said you'd be pitching to a bunch of guys called Diablo, Maestro, Mule, and Turkey. Would you know what I'm talking about?"

"Sounds like barnstormers. Cubans, maybe."

"I'll warm you up, then let you pitch to a couple of All-Stars."

Alone in the visitor's clubhouse, Babe changed into a male uniform. It fit well enough, but she couldn't get used to it, didn't feel comfortable in the itchy woolen uniform that offered no resistance to her hands as she wound up, not brushing against bloomers. She rotated both arms five times, then she did a one-arm push-up. She'd heard that Pepper Martin could do ten.

Butterflies, she reflected, was not an accurate metaphor for the feeling in her stomach. It was more like a balloon held underwater and rising, then getting somehow sucked down again, agitated on the washboard of her stomach, and recirculated. She knew she could make the throw from left field to the infield. She'd done it before, but never with this kind of pressure—an All-Star team watching, most of them probably wanting her to fail.

Walking onto the field she saw a full, pale moon already rising in the sky over left field. She imagined its transit, much the same as that of the ball she would toss, just slower, steadier, certain. She'd heard a prediction that some days before Kingdom Come the moon would be sucked in by earth's gravity and would crash—somewhere near the pitcher's mound in Sportsman's Park, she imagined. She looked at the moon again and inhaled deeply, saying to herself, *If you can do it, old man, so can I.*

She trotted toward the left-field wall, and Diz wound up histrionically, leading her with a long, high toss that she shagged, putting it in a high gear that left the other Babe shaking his head in disbelief. "That bitch can run."

"Beat your fat ass any day," said Leo.

"Anything over the infield dirt, I win," said Pepper.

"You're on," said Leo, signaling Babe to throw.

Babe took a step and a hop and let it go. The ball had a perfect arc for distance. Not a line-drive throw like the other Babe's. It landed on the grass, two feet past the infield dirt, and bounced to the backstop. If Leo hadn't moved, it would have hit him. Pepper smiled. "Twenty bucks, Lippy."

On the mound, Babe let the sounds engulf her. She concentrated on the fragments of speech—that was what settled her, gave her confidence to face the men. They all spoke English, their mother tongue, so that made them all the same. They became genderless vocalizers of words in patterns she viscerally understood. What she loved hearing was the *"Shit!"* following a swing and a miss. The *shit* of a foul ball, a pop-up, an agonizingly slow roller that spoke for itself, saying, "Stupid! Stupid!"

The ballpark, for Babe, was like church. It could be filled to standing room only, or she could be the lone worshipper. And if God had to choose a house, wouldn't it be one without a roof? One that let the stars in? One with the color of grass? With a diamond at least approaching the size of a ring for His finger?

And if she prayed hard enough, if she prayed as hard as sometimes she raged, would God in return whisper to the breeze in His house, which she venerated, an answer to her prayer—*What do I throw to the Iron Horse?*

Frankie put on catcher's gear, and the other players took ten whacks apiece. Leo didn't do much, as was expected. Pepper hit one off the wall and another over it, then Babe started pitching the corners more, and Pepper didn't do much, but Frankie started worrying about Babe's control.

"Get 'em over, Babe."

Babe nodded, and the Iron Horse stepped up. Babe threw him a fastball and he hit it over the fence. She threw him a curve and he hit one down the first-base line and off the fence on one bounce. She threw another curve way outside, hoping to catch the corner. Gehrig stepped into it and hit it over the left-field fence. The next pitch was a fastball that came back at her just as fast. She ducked and the line drive rolled to the center-field wall.

Frankie lifted his mask and trotted out to the mound.

"You know, Miller Huggins once said to me, 'there's a lot of guys with a strong back and a weak mind. You've got a strong mind and a weak back, but you'll be there when those guys are long gone.' I'm gonna tell you the same thing. Use your head. You're not gonna throw too many by Lou Gehrig. Change him up. Throw two changes in a row. Catch?"

"Yeah, I guess I'm not Carl Hubbell," said Babe, kicking dirt.

The changeups netted two ground balls, but Gehrig went seven for ten. Ruth and Medwick also hit some long balls, and Babe looked discouraged as she walked to the water bucket and the players huddled by home plate.

"So, what do you think?" said Diz.

"I think she's got good speed, good placement, decent stuff. I think she'd win a lot of games in the Pacific Coast League," Frankie offered.

"Not a Major Leaguer?"

Frankie raised his eyebrows and looked around, focusing finally on Ruth, the elder statesman of the group.

"If you're asking me, she's not ready for that lineup. Gibson, Charleston, Stearnes, Wells . . ." Babe shook his head. "Too much depth in that lineup. There's no Leo Durochers in there. They could get on a roll, then we've got to play catch-up with Paige. I'd rather go with a minor-leaguer."

"Leo?"

Leo nodded confirmation of what Babe said. "Those guys are used to hitting that kind of meat. They'll whack her around like nothing."

"Ducky? If you were a gambling man . . ."

"If I were a gambling man I wouldn't be playing for Branch Rickey, with Landis looking over my shoulder. Are you insinuating something?"

Frankie shook his head, thinking he shouldn't have said anything that could get Medwick's defenses up. "I'm not insinuating anything. I'm just what-iffing."

"Well, I say get the dago. Just make sure he can bunt, 'cuz he won't even get the bat off his shoulder against Paige."

Frankie gave Babe Didrikson Zaharias fifty dollars of Harry Bennett's money for trying out. She took being cut better than Frankie imagined she would.

"This is a hell of a team you've got. If the other guys are this good, I'm not sure I'd want to go up against them. Who are they, anyway? I didn't recognize any of those nicknames."

"I'm not allowed to say. Kind of like the Lone Ranger."

"Masked men?"

"Yeah. Kind of."

Frankie was one of those guys who showered right away. He didn't care to hang around the clubhouse drinking, playing cards, or listening to Pepper Martin's "Mudcats" jam. He went straight to the showers. He was a little paranoid, a little neurotic, and a little touchy at times. He couldn't stand the inane whistling he heard in virtually every locker room he'd ever been in. Now Ducky was whistling, some half-assed measure of quasi-random notes. Sometimes Frankie would hear a whistled tune, then some half-assed chirping would kick in, as if the whistling asshole realized he'd started whistling a stupid tune and disguised it with an atonal series of notes. Later, Pepper was whistling "Birmingham Jail." At least it was a recognizable tune. But all the others—were they covering up their locker-room nakedness with notes? Covering up their self-consciousness at being naked with a group of men? But the last thing that Frankie would do would be to make public his private annoyance at whistling. Then they'd whistle him to death. Instead, he counted the tiles between the wall and his left foot.

Harry Bennett knocked on the clubhouse door. Pepper put down his guitar and let him in. Harry habitually walked with his hands closed into fists. It gave pause to everyone he encountered and led some to wonder what the devil was wrong with Harry. Harry didn't know. Whenever he tried to figure it out, he ended up liking himself less, so he stopped trying. Harry would be the first to admit that he was a hard man. Hard enough that he himself regretted the extent of it. The only virtue in it for Harry was that it was better than being soft. Of this he was fairly convinced, but he never followed through to any conclusion his examination of the virtue, or lack of virtue, of being a soft man. He was satisfied with the face validity of the superiority of the hard man. Zarathustra over Gandhi, in less than ten rounds.

The reason that he walked about with his fists clenched was probably that he saw every man he encountered as a potential opponent, weeding out those over fifty or under fifteen. He scanned the Gashouse Gang, sizing them up. Leo was smaller than he was. Pepper and Frankie were scrappers, but not much else. Diz was not known for winning too many fights. Pepper took him out of his pugilistic reverie before he got to the new gang members, Ruth and Gehrig.

"You don't play nothin', do you?"

"Afraid not," said Harry. "You guys been going over the lineup?"

"The ones we know. Played against some of them before. Broke even, I'd guess."

Bennett laughed. "You'd be wrong."

"Boys, I've got some notes for you. This is just for starters. I've got a real know-it-all coming later. Now pay attention, 'cuz these notes cost me a few C's. Paid the best colored pitchers I could find to get their book on these guys."

Pepper was excited. "What'cha got?"

Harry pulled an old crate over to the bench where the team sat. "Start at first base. Buck Leonard. Kind of young. Just coming into his own. They say he's gonna be the black Gehrig. Plays deep at first, so you can bunt up the line. If he's got a weakness in the field, it's throwing to the pitcher covering."

Harry glanced again at his list. "Second base is Dihigo. Martin Dihigo."

Pepper swiveled his head. "Di-he-go? I don't know. Did he?"

Babe laughed hardest at the pun.

"He's the ringer. From Cuba. About 6'1", 190. Don't know who to compare him to. Nobody like him in the Majors. He could be the best they've got. They say he's the real thing. A young Joe Jackson. Power. Average. And he plays every position but catcher."

"What the hellfire's so hot about playing every position? He can't play but one at a time," said Diz.

"Yeah," said Pepper, impressed with Diz's logic.

"And as far as I know, he only gets three strikes, like the rest of 'em, right?"

"Yeah," said Pepper, as if to urge on the preacher at a revivalist meeting.

"I don't want to take the wind out of your sails," said Harry, "but he not only plays every position, he plays each of them better than anyone else. Maybe even as pitcher. He had an 0.89 ERA one year, in Cuba. Satch once said Dihigo was better than he was."

"All Satch does is throw fastballs," said Ducky.

"Yeah, and all Caruso does is sing," said Babe.

"Seriously. It's fastball, fastball, fastball."

"That's the way it was with Johnson. Nine pitches and the inning is over."

"He'll sneak in a curveball, too," said Harry. "But Babe's right about the fastball. Especially under bad lights. He struck out a guy in Kansas City, under the Monarchs' lights, on a pickoff."

Diz wrinkled his brow and gave Harry an incredulous look.

Harry laughed. "Honest to God. He threw to first. The guy swung. The ump called 'strike three.' Said, 'If you're stupid enough to swing at a pickoff throw, you deserve to strike out.' "

"You believe that stuff?"

"It happened. I can tell you the day, the time, and how many Paige struck out."

"How's that?"

Bennett pulled out a checkbook and slapped his hand with it. "The fatter the checkbook, the more you know. He's a lot like Diz. Same height, a little skinnier, almost as nutty. A real showman, but he backs it up. Throws the same speed as Diz, mid-nineties or better. Then there's the hesitation pitch. It's a real corker. Plants his foot and you expect the arm to come around all in one motion, but it doesn't. There's a kink, a half-second delay, and it wreaks havoc with your timing. Hitters get distracted by that foot up in the air. Says he picked that up throwing rocks at white kids in Mobile. The other kids would think it was safe, then bingo. Babe, you wanna tell 'em about the game he pitched against you in '29?"

"Don't remember."

"You don't remember he struck out twenty-two?"

"That's 'cuz four of them were him," said Leo, laughing. Babe slapped him with his cap.

"He had 184 strikeouts in 196 innings that year. This year he was 13–3 with a 1.90 total run average. That's not just earned runs, but total runs. Think about it. And like Diz, he had one game with seventeen strikeouts."

Diz nodded. "That Paige is the best pitcher I ever seen, and I been looking in the mirror for a long time."

"He's a magician," said Harry. "Winds up with a baseball and throws a pea." He looked at his notes again. "Okay. Shortstop—Willie Wells. Doesn't have the best arm in the world, but he's accurate and covers a lot of ground. You'd have to take Willie over Leo 'cuz Willie can hit. Good power for a shortstop."

"I remember him," said Babe. "Stole home in back-to-back barnstorming games against us in '27."

"Who's on third?" asked Pepper, eager to know who he was matched up against.

"Squatty, Hooks, Dandy, Danny, Talua, Mamerto, Ray. Two-thirds of an unbeatable All-Star team, all the same player, Ray Dandridge. He fields like Leo, only better, always gets the runner by one step. Kind of teases them by giving them a chance. But they're always out. He's a killer on bunts. Takes the ball in his bare hand and fires it sidearm without looking."

Diz nodded. "Yup. I played against him once. He was on bunts like a chicken on a June bug."

"Had four errors last year—the whole year, not just a season."

Ducky laughed. "Pepper's got that many in one game."

Harry continued, "Now, outfield, that's really something. Left field, Oscar Charleston. Some say he's the best ever. Hard to tell. He's a little past his prime, but he's still fast. In the army, they clocked him at twenty-three seconds for the two-twenty. Wasn't anybody faster, in the whole U.S. Army."

Ducky raised his hand. "Was that with the spear or without it?"

When the laughter subsided, Diz offered, "It's just one-twenty round the bases. Two-twenty ain't gonna do him any good."

"Just don't let him on base, Diz."

"Don't you worry, Mr. Bennett. The onliest running that boy's gonna do is from the dugout to the plate and back, and that goes double for that Cool guy."

"Cool Papa Bell," Harry informed Diz. "You've got to keep that scat bastard off the bases. He stole a hundred and seventy-five bases in '33. He stole second, third, and home, consecutively, against a Major-Leaguer. And he stole home twice in the same game, against another Major-Leaguer. He's a switch-hitter, but he gets a better jump batting lefty. Not a great hitter, but he *is* a great bunter. He'll run right into the ball, drag bunt it and get a step ahead. If he's fast to first, he's even faster to second and around the horn. Does the circuit in about 12.3. Beats out infield hits. You've got to get rid of the ball the moment you field it. Okay? And when he gets on, if he takes a big lead, he's probably not going. When he plays it closer to the bag, that's when you've got to call a pitchout. Okay?" Harry looked at Frankie, who called most of the plays for the Gashouse Gang, even pitchouts. He'd signal to DeLancey, who would signal the pitcher.

"They say lightning ain't as fast as Bell. Scores from first on a single."

"They only got one ump in that league. They can cut across second," said Pepper. "And the way they bunt ain't even legal, practically. Take a swing then loose the grip and pop a bunt."

"Yeah, he's another rabbit," said Babe. "He was playing against Gehringer and the Waners. Bill Walker was pitching. Bell was on third. He took a big lead and taunted Bill, 'I'm gonna steal it.' And on the third pitch he did. Charlie said, 'I seen Cobb a lot. But I never seen anything like Bell that night.' Before the game in '27, he came up to me with a big smile and told me he'd won the home-run crown."

"What?'

Babe laughed. "The guy won the home-run crown on inside-the-park jobs. He claims he hit twelve out and eight inside the park, but I never saw him hit a long ball. He's not that strong, but he's got a grip like Oscar Charleston. Never had my hand squeezed by a little guy like that." Babe laughed again. "The funny thing is they got the speedy guy, and he won the home-run crown, and they got the slugger, Gibson, and he led the league in base-stealing one year."

"Funny? Or tragic?" said Harry, looking up and down the bench. "Bell is even faster than Oscar used to be. The whole infield's got to be in on the grass. And he still beats out bunts. And if he gets on, he'll steal you blind. Steals second on routine pickoffs—takes off as soon as the pitcher starts to toss it to first. In center field, he covers more ground than a circus tent. Catches flies like a frog. Plays way up. Dares you to hit one over his head. Texas leaguers don't exist when Bell is playing. Sets up a hundred feet in back of second, dares you to hit one he can't catch up to. Except for Gibson, of course. When Gibson is up, he's back against the wall like everybody else.

"Gibson's got an easy, fluid swing. Waits on the ball. Got the best wrists in the game. Then puts that weight into it and it's gone. And that's with the Negro ball. A Wilson. Cheaper. Not wound as tight. Doesn't travel as far. If he gets ahold of a Major League ball, you won't find it, except in the next county. Now, the good news is he's not the catcher Lombardi is, or Cochrane or Hartnett. Got a good enough arm, but he misjudges pop-ups sometimes. As a catcher in the Majors, he'd be ordinary. As a hitter, he'd give the Babe a run for it. They call him the black Babe Ruth, but he doesn't lift it like Babe."

"Doesn't turn into a pretzel when he misses," joked Diz.

"He just socks it out there thirty feet off the ground on a line. You know how far the fence is in center in Comiskey?"

"About 435," said Gehrig.

"He hit one over the wall into a loudspeaker there. They had to pry it out. And he hit one out of Forbes. First man to do that." Harry looked at Babe. "Know who the second was?"

Babe shook his head.

"Oscar Charleston. And there isn't a third."

"What about the right fielder?" said Ducky.

"I don't know who they'll start—Turkey Stearnes or Mule Suttles. Both tremendous hitters. Hit the long ball. Stearnes is faster, though. I'd give him the edge because of his speed. That's what you've got to watch out for. Mule goes 6'4", 240. Hits the ball as far as Josh. Hit three homers in one inning once. Not the fastest guy out there, or the slickest fielder. Jake Stephens hit one that was going out. Mule jumped up to catch it and got hung up on a spike in the fence. They had to cut him down."

Harry got off the crate and paced back and forth, collecting his thoughts and relighting his cigar. "Now, I don't know how to break it to you, so I'll just lay my cards on the table. I talked to Damon Runyon, and asked him where to get a hypothetical handicap on the game. You guys understand 'hypothetical,' don't you?"

Harry looked at Diz, the lowest common articulation denominator, and Diz showed no sign of incomprehension, so Harry continued, "He put me in touch with a couple of guys, and they've all got the Negroes as the chalk horse." Harry paused and looked at each of the players with steely eyes. "Man for man, these guys are a lot faster than you are. Position by position, the guys in the know give them the edge. You take first with Gehrig and left field with the year Ducky's having. Pepper and Frankie are even up, and the pitching is a standoff. The rest go to the Negroes. The Judge is hurting you with the seven Major Leaguers rule. Jackson is way over the hill, and the kid, DiMaggio, is too green. Replace them with Simmons and either Waner or Foxx, and you take back the edge, theoretically. Believe me, if Branch Rickey had a bucketful of whitewash, none of those guys would be playing in the Negro Leagues."

Diz was oddly silent. Ruth was hunkered down with a bottle of beer. "I still think we'll kick their ass," said Frankie, "but if we don't, it's 'cuz we're handicapped."

Harry stared at Frankie almost contemptuously. "There's handicaps all over the place. You know who the coloreds have the toughest time with? . . . Charley Gehringer. He plays like them, only better. Those bookies say this team would be stronger with Gehringer on second."

Diz defended his teammate. "Frankie's an All-Star. Besides, these guys are used to playing with each other. That's an advantage. Especially on the double-play ball. Anyway, Frankie is just as good, in my book. And I ain't playin' with no Tigers. You can forget about Gehringer and Cochrane."

Harry nodded and walked to the door. "Suit yourselves. I'm just giving you the lowdown. Hope those tips help. They cost me. And, anyway, I've got a surprise for the niggers." Bennett exited, then reached back inside with a large revolver in his hand. "Those coloreds play like rabbits." Harry spun the cylinder. "Minus one." He closed the door behind him.

"What's he mean? He gonna shoot somebody?"

"Looked like a magnum, or a .45."

"I hate that," said Frankie. "Guys with power who like to be cryptic."

"What's cryptic?"

"Cagey. Leave you guessing. Makes them feel more powerful."

"Maybe you better look out, Frankie," said Babe wryly while relighting a cigar.

"What do you mean?"

"Maybe he's gonna shoot you. Maybe you're the 'minus one.' The man wants Gehringer on second. You're in the way." Babe pointed his finger with his fist closed, like a pistol, and made a "kapow" sound with a puff of smoke out one side of his mouth. The smoke thing got Diz and Pepper laughing. Frankie didn't find it funny.

"That's it. I quit. Get Gehringer," said Frankie, getting up.

Babe chuckled and slugged his beer, watching Diz get up to block Frankie's path.

"You can't quit. You're the heart of this team. The skipper."

"Do you have any idea how dangerous Harry Bennett is? He's got unlimited money to go with unlimited balls and a boundless bad temper. The guy can do anything he wants and get away with it. He's Henry Ford's right-hand man. Face it, anyone with a million-dollar slush fund is above the law."

"So what?"

"So, what's five hundred dollars? I want to live."

Diz scratched his head. "Frankie, you're not talkin' sense."

"Minus one? With a gun in his hand? You don't think that's a threat? Babe did."

"Aw, I was just getting your goat. Don't take it to heart," said Babe, relighting his Havana. "You're what they call 'paranoid.' Rickey said that about you. I heard him."

"Maybe you all ought to be a little more paranoid. Look at you, Diz. Those guys from New York were going to kidnap you. You just got lucky."

"That's different."

"Right. There's no ransom here. And I end up dead."

"Oh, hell . . ." said Ruth.

Frankie sat on the end of the bench and stared at the wall. Paranoia— Frankie would give it up if he could be guaranteed that whatever replaced it would feel as comfortable. Not that he was dumb enough to walk around all day deliberately with a stone in his shoe. It was the comfort of mild discomfort that you were used to that was hard to give up. It was like pissing in your pants and no one knows it but you, and it's warm, if only for some moments.

"No one's out to get you, Frankie," said Babe. "Not even Harry Bennett."

"Yeah? Then what's it mean? It's got to mean something."

Frankie packed up his stuff. Diz was tying his shoe and suddenly stopped. "Remember the All-Star game? You kept sayin' they'd stab you in the back. Runyon and those guys."

"Keener did. He flipped on me."

"Who started at second?"

Frankie looked away. "Who'd he talk to—Knowledge something or other?"

"Knowledge Clapp."

"What the fuck kind of name is that?" said Pepper.

"He's a whiz kid. Knows everything. Puts odds on anything," said Diz.

"I'm gonna give him a call."

Frankie started for the door.

"Hey, Frankie, ask him something for me, huh?" said Leo. Frankie turned. "If the guy knows everything, ask him how come some guys wipe their ass and it sounds like they're shining their shoes?"

"Ask Ducky," said Babe. "He knows shit from shinola."

Everyone laughed but Frankie, who was thinking, *It must be me. I must wipe my ass like an asshole.* And he thought, *If I was Ducky, I'd say, "I'll wipe my ass with you, motherfucker."* It was the only time Frankie ever wished he was Medwick. The first time any Cardinal, besides Medwick, wished he was Medwick.

"I'm serious," said Leo. "Sounds like they're sawing wood. All that friction on your asshole—that's gotta hurt."

"I'm getting sick, Lippy," complained Diz.

"It's like they all went to the Shinola School of Ass-Wiping." Leo just would not let go. Diz grabbed a role of toilet paper and fired it at him.

"Stick it in his ear!" hollered Babe, laughing.

Leo ducked, and the roll careened off the top of his head. Babe put Leo in a headlock, leading him to the sink. "Someone ought to wash your mouth out," he said, jocularly.

Leo squirmed out. "Wash your drawers out, you big ape."

Babe had gotten a lot of shit from Tris Speaker and some other Red Sox for taking a shower then putting back on the same underwear he wore during the game. His response was to stop wearing underwear altogether.

"Give me my watch back, you little shit." Babe opened his locker and grabbed a bar of soap.

"I never stole your watch."

"And Lou wants his ring back."

Gehrig looked at Babe, embarrassed that he had implicated Leo in the theft of his ring without any real proof. He took his wallet from his locker, hoping that Leo wouldn't say anything and that Babe would let it drop. Leo put on his three-hundred-dollar suit, with the pockets sewed so as not to ruin the line of the pants.

"And tell Boney Pradella if I see him I'm gonna kill him," said Babe, heading for the shower with a towel that was stiffly challenged to engird him. Boney was Leo's alleged accomplice in the thefts that occurred before the Yankees sent Leo to the Cards via the Reds.

"What the hell's this?" Babe picked up Leo's glove with the stuffing torn out the way Rabbit Maranville did. "Looks like a gutted possum."

"Looks to me like Babe just got hungry," said Diz, laughing. Leo snatched his glove from Babe's hand and threw it into his bag.

"Didn't Lippy lead the league in errors?" asked Babe.

"That's 'cuz he gets to balls no one else does," said Pepper, who was normally not a Durocher supporter, but who felt some Gashouse Gang solidarity. And because he thought it was true. Leo was, as Babe called him, "the All-American out" at the plate, but he was a spectacular fielder.

Babe flipped up Leo's collar. "Look at this. Three-hundred-dollar suit, and a shirt made by a shoemaker!" Babe knew his collars. At Saint Mary's in Baltimore, he had been a joiner—putting the collars on thousands of shirts. "No wonder you get nothing but horse collars."

"Knowledge Clapp?"

"Yeah."

"This is Frankie Frisch. Listen, I've got a question for you. It's got to do with . . ."

"Frankie Frisch?"

"Yeah."

"What did you hit in '33?"

".303."

"In '30?"

".346. Why?"

"Just wanted to make sure you were Frankie Frisch. Frankie Frisch never called me before."

"I just want to ask you, as a favor—in that game Harry Bennett ran by you, the hypothetical one, who's on second?"

"For the white guys?"

"Yeah."

"Frankie Frisch."

"You sure."

"I'm sure."

"Just one more thing. It's a numbers question."

"Right up my alley. Shoot."

"Does 'minus one' mean anything? Does it have some special significance?"

"Not to this Knowledge. You might try some other guys in your area. Sleepout Louie, Cigar Charley, or the Dancer. What's the context?"

"There's a guy . . . Okay, it's Harry Bennett. He's got his hand inside the door and he's holding a gun . . ."

"Sounds like Harry."

"And he says, 'Minus one.' "

"That's it?"

"He closes the door and leaves."

"You're not helping me much with the context."

"The larger context . . . baseball."

"Now you're talking. What kind of gun?"

"I don't know. Big one. Someone said . . . I don't know, magnum, I think."

".357?"

"I don't know."

"Gehringer."

"Gehringer?"

".357 minus one. Gehringer's batting average—.356. "

Frankie's end of the line went silent.

"Now you owe me one."

"What do you want?"

"Where's the game?

"Like I said, it's hypothetical."

"Okay. So, if the hypothetical game were to be played, where, hypothetically, would it be?"

"Honestly, I don't know."

"Gotta be somewhere with lights."

"Why?"

"They're trying to keep it a secret. So it's got to be a night game."

"Hmm."

"So, I want a ball, with all the hypothetical players' autographs. And, Frankie, even Gus knows about the game, so let's not be cute. If you tell me where it is, I'll tell him someplace where it's not—catch? Then Satchel won't get killed."

Frankie gave an ironic, paranoid laugh. "That would even things up."

"What do you mean?"

"Minus one for both sides. I'll call you if I find anything out."

Frankie hung up. Knowledge was still holding the phone, his mind ticking, when he said to no one, "Unless it's Foxx . . . Hit .356 the year before last."

11

HOLLYWOOD

It was about the flint of ambivalence and the steel of charisma. It was about the fire in the seat of Darrow's pants when Leo could not get ahold of the charismatic George Raft, his Springfield, Massachusetts minor-league teammate. "I've called him about twenty-five times. He's not answering the phone."

"Did you read what Louella Parsons said about him?" said John Henry. "If I had his sex life, I wouldn't answer the phone, either."

Darrow folded the newspaper, threw it on the table and addressed John Henry and James Atwood. "All right, you bums, pack your bags. We can make Hollywood in thirty-six hours, nonstop."

It was about *trompe l'oeil*—fooling the eye. And the ear. But not the way the French masters did it. Darrow fooled the eye and ear the way corn silk got substituted for tobacco by generations of adolescents. What you saw was no longer what you got. It was as if the old man had been husked of his indolence. He saw himself again as a man with a mission. The way he saved Ossian Sweet and overturned popular thinking about evolution via the Scopes trial, he now had invigorated himself as the savior of black baseball. With one difference. There was no money in it. For the first time that he could remember, he was fighting for a cause with no material motive. Landis had been right about that, and Darrow had a legacy to think of. If Landis saw the financial motive going all the way back to Sweet, historians would see it, too. It was, in fact, why poet Edgar Lee Masters left Darrow's law firm in a huff. Masters was for a while Darrow's alter ego. Darrow always wanted to write, but the only thing he did well was declaim. Maybe now he could re-write history.

He could not keep still. He fumbled for his keys, searched for his glasses, refilled his cup with coffee, as if constant motion would keep him alive, as if his mission were all that urgent, as if he'd been listening to Satchel Paige's oft-repeated "Don't look back; something may be gaining on you." Entering what would be the last year of his life, Darrow knew exactly what *something* was. He had not only not to look back, but also to keep moving forward. There were things on his mind. Suitcases, spark plugs, spanners, brake rods. Things in his mind's eye, things that didn't fool it, but occupied it, or took it off things to *come*, things like *kingdom*.

"Darrow, you got ants in your pants?" John Henry asked.

"Does anyone have a better idea?" Darrow asked with a tone of arrogance, as if to remind the crew that to refute the man in whose esprit the red ants of rationality swarmed was a waste of time. "You need a scouting report on DiMaggio, firsthand. You trust Raft because he was a minor-leaguer, and as a friend of Leo's you trust him not to spill the beans to Winchell or Parsons and the rest of the Los Angeles gossip mongers. You have no viable alternatives, and time is at a premium. James Atwood, you've been on that couch like a fly on a cow pie. Pack your other shirt and let's go. I'll need both of you to spell me driving." Darrow shook a finger at Diz. "I know you're sitting on Harry Bennett's bankroll, and these hooligans need a job. Fifty bucks apiece ought to keep them happy."

"We gotta pay you, too?" Diz asked, scratching his head.

Darrow smiled. "Roosevelt is paying me. He just doesn't know what for."

John Henry put his cup in a sink crowded with things that needed to be cleaned. He washed his hands and lingered, staring at the pots and pans and thinking "panhandle," that section of Oklahoma that reaches across the top of Texas, wondering if they would drive through it, perhaps at night when its geography would mirror the stars above it—the Big Dipper, the Drinking Gourd that slaves followed to freedom. He thought of the other constellations he would see in the western sky. Cancer. Gemini. Taurus. He associated people with their most likely horoscopic star cluster. Gemini would be James Atwood and himself. Taurus—that would be Harry Bennett, kicking to stardust any constellation he would see in the western sky. Cancer—he refused to think about it. John Henry mentally took the Fifth. He already had five silver dollars in his pocket. Harry had that dramatic flair. A clinking down payment on a job John Henry would do at the greatest game ever played. He didn't know that Harry had also hired James Atwood, giving him his five dollars in the form of a bill. Secrecy was the way Harry operated. One hand of Gemini did not know what the other was doing.

Wrinkles were part of the fabric of John Henry's and James Atwood's clothes, so it didn't matter that they stuffed their worldly belongings into a Cardinals duffel bag that Diz gave them. PROPERTY OF THE ST. LOUIS CARDINALS now included a revolver. Stuffing was something that Elmer enjoyed, so he added his assortment of socks and shirts and announced that he too was going. James Atwood tousled Elmer's hair. "They say it's good luck to rub his head—a kid like that."

Pat Dean was relieved to hear that Elmer was leaving. "Don't forget your glove. You might catch one that DiMaggio hits."

"If he does, it won't prove nothing," said Diz. "Scouts sit up close, in foul territory."

Darrow was the first out the door. The sense of adventure that had kept him in St. Louis had been undermined by John Henry's fondness for a sofa and James Atwood's ability to entertain himself for hours on end with nothing but a jackknife. Pat smiled while bidding a silent good riddance to the two slugs who had taken up residence in her living room.

James Atwood insisted on driving first. Darrow put on his hat and got into the rear of his Rolls. James Atwood looked over his shoulder. "I thought you was fed up with us *cyclo*paths."

Darrow spoke through a half-sheepish smile as James Atwood accelerated in first gear. "I get up every morning. I read the obits and I feel good—not that my name isn't there—but that so many sons of bitches are." James Atwood accelerated toward a crow standing on a carcass. "You know why people die? Why men are mortal? Because they deserve it. Man is not a dunghill covered with snow. He is a dunghill, period. And you know who the biggest dung beetle of all is? Me. Landis was right. The crooks of Chicago all say, 'There but for God and Darrow go I.' You may be a couple of psychopaths, but we're in the same ark."

"Yeah. A Rolls-Royce."

They drove Route 66. Missed the panhandle by miles, with four pieces of silver jingling in John Henry's pocket. The fifth he had lost to James Atwood on a bet that the Rolls could not do one hundred miles per hour. James Atwood spent his waking, non-driving hours flipping the silver dollar the way Raft did in *Scarface*.

Whenever the hum of the wheels on the road produced a tone signaling about sixty miles per hour, Elmer would begin to sing. He had a surprisingly good voice, but after the tenth repetition of "Home on the Range," James Atwood was ready to strangle him. "Don't you know nothing else?"

He did. He had a surprising repertoire of lullabies, impressed on him by Pa and Ma Dean, trying to sing him to sleep after he tried and failed to cut off two fingers to emulate Mordecai "Three Finger" Brown. The driver, trying to stay awake, didn't appreciate the lullabies on the thirty-six-hour jaunt, but the others did. At night, Elmer had his glove on his left hand, part way out the window, poised to catch the baseball-shaped moon, so that when they arrived in Los Angeles the glove's webbing had nearly as many insect carcasses as the radiator of the Rolls.

Darrow was sore and cranky when they arrived, cruising a steamy Hollywood Boulevard. In the drizzle he walked slowly enough to give John Henry the impression that he was on the way out. Even on the level sidewalk he looked like he was going downhill. Darrow felt John Henry's eyes on him, but he couldn't explain the collusion of age and arthritis and disease in a body set in motion out of desire for a cookie or a bathroom, how what precipitates out of the collusion is pain. On the scale of desire, John Henry had nothing on the man. Desire. It was no less strong in old men than it was in young. It just bifurcated—the bathroom and kitchen to one side, the bedroom to the other.

James Atwood parked the car and they got out, looking for a luncheonette. An attractive redhead dashed out of an insurance building in front of the four men. "I'm drenched," said the Ginger Rogers lookalike, full-busted, lipsticked, rouged, in high-heel pumps and a flimsy hat hung with a spider-web veil, held on by a hat pin hard-pressed to hold the hat to the bun of her hair in the strong wind. She spoke to no one in particular, just a friendly proclamation to the world at large, a world populated in part by the coterie of Darrow, John Henry Seadlund, James Atwood Gray, and Elmer Dean. On top of that world strutted John Henry Seadlund, his mouth preempted by Darrow yanking on his arm.

"What? I was just gonna offer to share my umbrella."

"Mr. Seadlund, you don't have an umbrella. And no offense, but you need your head examined."

John Henry smiled and slapped him hard enough on the back to knock the wind from him and make him wince. "You know something, Darrow? You're right."

The redhead shuffled quickly toward a group of people waiting for a bus. John Henry had no umbrella. He had a fedora for the rain and a pistol for anything else that annoyed or threatened him. The pistol was no equalizer, but it jacked him up mentally, to where he felt he could look anyone in the eye—especially women, to whom he'd looked up from the moment he flicked on the light switch in his room on a hot August night in Fenco twenty years earlier. At eye level on his bed his mother had collapsed. His room had the best breeze in the house, and the eye-levelest thing about his mother was the patch of darkness left by the receding light where the skirt was drawn up to her waist.

Instinctively John Henry flicked off the light and called to his mother as if the light event had never occurred. On her feet, she smoothed down the hair on his head and asked, "Did you see something you were not supposed to?"

Reflecting on the event twenty years later, John Henry would say, "Yes, through no fault of my own." But at the moment it happened, John Henry preferred to pretend that it had not, and puzzled over what he knew was an unfair question, and he felt to this day the prick of his own original sin.

At that moment John Henry stopped and jerked up so abruptly he had to take a step backward to keep from losing his balance. His whole field of vision suddenly turned into a broad band of fiery orange. It was like opening the door to a blast furnace, but the flame-like color did not have the form of fire. It was the bright, flat, univocal orange of a Wisconsin August sunset, intensified by several orders of magnitude. John Henry shook his head, and the vision disappeared as instantly as it had arrived. But it scared him, the way it could take over his conscious perception. Armageddon redux. It scared him that some part of his mind might be watching this second feature while the other part watched *Daylight on Hollywood Boulevard.*

"Where do we go from here?" asked James Atwood.

"We find a telephone directory, and we find Raft."

"George Raft won't be in no telephone directory."

"Oh? Why not?"

"He's a Hollywood guy. Those guys are different."

"They use carrier pigeons?"

"They're famous."

"I'm famous. I'm in the directory."

"But you're not George Raft."

The argument was getting circular, which was the way people walked, they said, in the desert, without knowing it. Darrow spied a phone booth and made for it. The way he saw it, you could have a pocket full of dimes and dime-sized holes in your shoes, or you could have empty pockets and an address, something temporal, something that reminded him of his own condition. El Royale. Just the thought of it. The hint of exotic. El Royale. What goings-on might go on at El Royale on Rossmore?

"The Hollywood Reporter"

by Louella Parsons

Should I be surprised by George Raft's outlandish generosity, an instance of which I shared with you in my last column? A working girl of my acquaintance, who happens to be intimate with many of Hollywood's leading men, and ladies—did I say that?—and a source of things that I cannot reveal in this column . . . she is, well, one of those thousands of starlets who never quite make it off the casting couch but find that there are ways to supplement a starlet's meager income that leave her days free for casting calls, bows, stoops, bends backward and forward . . . Well, having established this lady's credentials, I'll get to the meat—she carries an address book that happened to be left on our lunch table at the Beverly Wiltshire when she went to the loo, and so I had a peek. I will not at present reveal all of the astonishing notes therein, at least for now, but if you were *in-like-one-of-her-clients*, you'd be a swash-buckling and no doubt satisfied man. But next to his name was *$10*, and the same figure was affixed to the names of a whole col-umn of stars, except for Raft's, next to which was *$20!* These, dear reader, were notes of what to expect from the John, or George. It seems that our coin-flipping gangster by himself is keeping a large part of Hollywood's doormen, coat-check girls, and waiters in the black. Such generosity does not go unnoticed or unrewarded. If you gentlemen readers aspire to Raft-like exploits in bed, you'll need to rival not only his generosity but his prowess. To wit, a chorus girl acquaintance of mine revealed to me that George did a line . . . a chorus line . . . among whom she numbered, by himself in one night. This chorus numbered seven, and when the girls were

in their cups and out of their knickers, they had their way with
their screen idol, one at a time, in hourly shifts, for seven hours.
Not a full working day, but who is complaining?

Right after he moved into El Royale, Leo Durocher's old minor-
league buddy George Raft disconnected the bell, since it rang at all
hours of the day and night. He also unplugged the telephone for days
on end. Every hooker in Hollywood had his address, and George was
known to send them away with ten bucks just to be polite. He let them
knock. If they were persistent enough, he'd open the door. Leo Costello
was a persistent knocker, though not a hooker. When his knuckles got
sore, he used the butt of his pistol.

"Remember me?"

George stared at him, finally matching him to a little guy he worked
with at the El Fay Club in Manhattan.

"Yeah, I remember. 'Hoochie,' right? You're a long way from New
York. You catch the wrong train?"

George never liked Hoochie. He liked him less now. Everybody had
their hand out, and judging by his clothes, Hoochie had both hands out.

"Doin' pretty good, huh? *Scarface*—I saw that one." Hoochie wagged
his finger. "That coin thing. You took that from Feets Edson."

"So, what can I do for you?"

"Guy like me, I'm kind of an embarrassment, wearing these brogans
while you prance around in those pointy, fifty-dollar jobs you can see
your face in. Even when you were driving for Owney you had that black
shirt and a white tie, velvet collar on that camel wraparound. Remember that? I showed you how to drive on two wheels under the Third
Avenue El, and how to avoid the torn-up pavement and stay on the
trolley tracks from 59th to 110th? Remember?"

George reached into his pocket and peeled two twenties off a roll.
"Here's for the driving lesson."

Leo lifted his hands in the air. "It ain't the lesson. It's what I know
that the public don't. How we picked up Owney's stuff at the brewery
on 26th Street and delivered it to Dutch's guys at 110th. Then we'd pick
up the receipts for *Diamond Lil* and hand 'em over to Owney person-

ally. Not something a Hollywood big shot would want anyone to know. Am I right?" Leo smiled, showing bad teeth. "Hey, you know me, Georgie. I know how to keep my mouth shut. But I owe these guys five bills. Know what I mean?"

"So you want five Cs to keep your mouth shut."

"That ought to do it."

Leo smiled. George stuffed the two twenties he had in his hand into Leo's vest pocket, then grabbed him by the lapels. "Listen, you small-time chiseler, there's forty bucks for telling Louella Parsons and Walter Winchell and anybody else about my driving for Owney. It'll help my image."

George shoved him backward and threw him down the stairs. "You show up here again and I'll have the cops on you. They don't like New York hoods showing up in Hollywood. Just ask Dutch."

Darrow and company walked up the stairs that Leo "Hoochie" Costello had been thrown down a half hour earlier. John Henry rapped persistently on the door. Raft opened it and started to shut it, but John Henry wedged his foot in the door. "Hey, wait. Leo sent us."

George realized the futility. He opened the door and stepped forward. "So, you're the muscle." He looked derisively at John Henry and James Atwood, puzzled by the incongruity of Darrow and the half-wit. "Go ahead. Take your best shot."

"Nah, we ain't here to hit you. Just looking for some help." John Henry held out his hand. "I'm Jay Hanna and this is Paul." Raft reluctantly shook their hands and smirked. He knew baseball well enough to recognize the names.

"Okay, Diz. Daffy. And who's that, Dummy?"

"Yeah. But my real name's Elmer."

Elmer extended his hand and George shook it. "Okay. Three fucking clowns and the circus manager. Does this look like the Big fucking Top?"

"Hey, don't talk to me like that. What the hell are you, some kind of fag in them high pants and pointy shoes?"

Darrow elbowed John Henry out of the way. "Excuse my friend, Mr.

Raft. We're actually here seeking your assistance in a baseball matter. Leo Durocher . . ."

George smiled and held his palm vertically in front of his face, then theatrically slashed at his misconception. "*That* Leo! I thought you were the goombahs of a schnorrer I just threw out." He studied the situation for a moment, then said, "Come on in."

The contingent entered Raft's palatial quarters. George led them to a huge yellow sofa.

"I'm Darrow. And, no, I am not the *pater familias* of the Dean family. I have no connection with them besides friendship, or something along those lines. I used to be a lawyer, and I've been engaged by some baseball people, including the Deans and your friend Leo Durocher, to check out a prospect in the Pacific Coast League. Kid by the name of DiMaggio. Supposed to be tearing up the league, and Leo says you know baseball pretty well—you could tell them if the kid was the real deal or not."

George lowered his gaze, grimaced, and turned his head to the side. He took his right hand from his pocket and gestured with it. "I'm making a movie now, with Carole Lombard. We're on the set every day. I start at five."

"That gives you most of the afternoon free," said John Henry.

"Five a.m.? I've got time for lunch, and that's about it."

John Henry and James Atwood sat on the yellow couch. James Atwood bounced once and struck the cushion with his open hand. "Pretty fancy couch."

"That's a gift from Jack Warner. It's the original casting couch from Warner Brothers. Had it refurbished. Lot of history on that couch." George smirked. James Atwood didn't know what to make of it. The only casting James Atwood knew of had to do with fish, but he suspected this was something else, so he just nodded. When John Henry sat down, his jacket opened and Raft could see the pistol at his waist.

"Hey, I thought you guys were legit," Raft said to Darrow.

Darrow put a hand on his brow and sought the nearest chair. "Let me try to explain this. I don't know if I *can* explain it. Do you have any water?"

The old man, at least, was legit, thought Raft. He looked like he was going to pass out. "Sure," said George. He went to the bar and poured a glass of water from a pitcher. He put four ice cubes in it. "You boys want anything?"

"That looks like top-shelf whiskey."

"V.S.O.P. Gift of Owney Madden. You guys know Owney?" Raft hoped to throw a scare into the two hoods in case they had anything nefarious in mind.

"I heard of Owney, but I never been to New York," said James Atwood.

George handed Darrow the glass of water.

"Mr. Raft, I've been completely on the level with you. I'm in the midst of a very complicated situation, the essence of which is we are on a quest for the best minor-league player in the country. You can call Leo right now and verify it. I can't tell you exactly why, and I have no explanation whatsoever for my colleague's carrying a gun. All I can say is that this has become a very, very strange universe. And without your help, we will have come all the way from St. Louis for nothing."

"I can't call Leo. The phone's been busted for days."

"That's why he ain't been able to reach you," said James Atwood.

"Come on, Darrow," said John Henry. "Level with him—about the game."

Darrow gave John Henry a cold look. "You know what will happen if word gets out."

George hoisted his pants at the knees and sat down. "Well, let me make it simple, fellows. I'll help you out on one condition—you tell me what this is all about."

John Henry crunched an ice cube from his whiskey glass. "Okay, I'm telling. I ain't coming all the way out here for nothing. There's going to be an All-Star game between whites and Negroes. Only the commissioner won't allow more than seven Major Leaguers on the team, so we've got to find two more guys. Leo's hot on this guy DiMaggio. So, are you in or out?"

Raft swiveled on his chair and opened the newspaper. "Who's DiMaggio play for?"

"San Francisco Seals."

Raft pored over the sports section. "You're in luck. Seals play tomorrow afternoon. I'll get away even if they fire me. Hell, these prima donnas don't show when they've got a hangnail. I've got a ballgame to scout. But right now, if you'll excuse me, I've got to get to the set."

"What's the movie?"

"Doesn't have a definite title yet."

"Who's in it?"

"Me."

"Who else?"

"Carole Lombard." George looked up at the ceiling, shook his head wistfully, and let the name drip silently off his tongue again: "Carole Lombard."

That evening George was in his own three-hundred-dollar suit, as usual. The studio had nothing as good. What he wore was what he was filmed in. No one would mess with his style or his taste. He wore the highest pants in town, and any kid in Hollywood who even pretended to be a dancer imitated his wardrobe, not Astaire's. Fred once asked him, "How do you get your hands in your pockets without breaking an arm?"

His jacket too was tight across the shoulders and tapered sharply to the waist. On his chair was a fedora and a brown coat with large, darker brown checks. His shoes were pointed, Cuban-heeled, black and impeccably polished, for which he paid generously every day.

Carole was wearing the kind of gown for Carole-kind-of-women, the kind of garment you don't want to see Little Orphan Annie in. In gowns, as in baseball, you've got to know how to play to your strengths. You wouldn't put a plugged nickel on the tensile strength of Lombard's gown straps. That gown had "London Bridge" written all over the label. You could fold it up and wear it for a hanky in your lapel. And if gowns were boxers, this one would be disqualified for not throwing nothin'.

The Travis Banton creation, a diaphanous *terciopelo* afterthought cut very low about the neck, tumbled back to reveal what was already more than hinted at, breasts that had an almost noble arc and attitude, that seemed the Platonic archetype on which all other breasts were imperfectly modeled. There was nothing to do but stare. But at what? How to choose? Did the breasts outdo the thighs, the legs, the arching back that angled into the full, saucy rump that was partly visible through the backless gown that mysteriously stayed on?

The music started. George twirled her. She spun and draped back on his arm, nearly weightless. Her arms windmilled back and one leg raised slightly off the ground. George was astonished by the lightness of her body, what a gossamer she had become, in movement. He thought of how her circle—the Countess di Frasso, Darryl Zanuck, Gable, Harlow, Cooper, Louie B. Mayer—would dine at the Trocadero and discuss Einstein, the mad scientist who theorized that speed approaching its limit made mass negligible. Something like that had happened to Lombard's unearthly body. When it came to rest, necessarily, before being impelled like a hardball off the bat of his arm, it was the essence of sleek. That moment froze in everyone's eyes. Had they been given the opportunity to choose the visage they would die with, it would be Lombard's near-naked body hung in promise over Raft's arm, her neck as vulnerable as beautiful, with her head hung back, her eyes closed, her blond hair flowing. If the gods wanted a sacrifice, would this not sate them for millennia? And if Einstein was right, her body possessed some unfathomable speed. On some metaphysical plane on the dance floor of the studio, Lombard's body intersected with a Dizzy Dean fastball, and *there* was all that was good in the human.

"I need a drink," said Carole when the song ended.

"I don't drink," said George.

"On the set?"

"No. I don't drink, period."

"Not even water?"

"Water's good."

"I've got three kinds of water, including tap, in my dressing room."

"Tap's fine."

Carole made herself a whiskey and soda and gave George a tall glass of tap water that was filled with ice.

"I hope you like it cold. I do."

"Cold's fine."

Carole's shoulders shuddered and the dress fell to the floor. As George had suspected, she had nothing on underneath. She stepped out of it, kicked it to the side, and went about her business, mixing peroxide and water and carefully touching up her pubic hair.

"Maybe I should go."

"Sorry. This won't take long. It's so boring." She looked up. "You didn't think I was a natural, did you?"

George pushed up his lip and shook his head, then realized that was not what he meant to say, with his expression. "I mean, I wouldn't have known. Wouldn't have guessed."

"I don't know why, but it's always such a shock when you've got blond up here and black down there. I don't want to shock anybody, so I touch it up. Kind of like Gable in *It Happened One Night*, you know, when he takes off his shirt and he's not wearing an undershirt? The whole country was shocked."

Carole shook her blond head and went back to work. "Not that I'd want to be responsible for a million dames painting their pussies." She laughed. "Ta-da. All done. Want to grab a bite at the Brown Derby?"

"Sure."

"But I'm picking up the tab, after what I've put you through."

She put on golden cotton panties, which shocked George. He couldn't imagine her in anything but silk. But in fact, she seldom wore undergarments of any kind. She forwent a brassiere and threw on a dress. He was amazed that a person could dress that fast, and he said so.

"That was fast."

"I'm hungry," she said, finishing her whiskey and soda. "You can't tell anybody, though. Promise?"

"That you're hungry?"

George had that deadpan delivery that made occasional sarcasm and wit indistinguishable from sheer ignorance. It was part of his charm.

"No, silly, the paint job."

"My lips are sealed."

"You never even touched your water."

George extended his arm. She took it.

"Mind if I drop off this coat?"

"No."

They took the elevator to George's dressing room. The elevator man stared at George's clothes and hardly noticed Lombard. "That is some suit, Mr. Raft. And that coat." He shook his head side to side with a wide, closed-mouth smile. "That coat speaks to you."

With hardly a moment's thought, George handed the man the coat. "Stop in for the suit later."

It was typical Raft generosity. But when they got out of the studio Carole began to laugh.

"What's wrong?"

"Nothing. That was so generous. The reason I'm laughing is . . . last month that man said the same thing to Gable."

"That con!" For a moment George was mad, but his anger quickly turned to laughter. "I was had . . . by an elevator man." George shook his head. "Hell, I'm going to give him the suit anyway."

Carole stopped. "Clark didn't give him anything." She thought she saw something in the normally far-off gaze of George Raft.

At the Brown Derby, Carole ordered a tuna sandwich on rye, took the top slice of rye off, ate the tuna with a fork, then put the top slice back on the empty sandwich. George had a Reuben and asked for an extra pickle. He had a Coke with just a little ice. All of this was noted in precise detail from a corner booth by Louella Parsons, who would have given as much as any American male would have to have been in Lombard's dressing room when she dressed up "down there" with peroxide and water.

"THE HOLLYWOOD REPORTER"

by Louella Parsons

. . . The tab couldn't have been more than ten dollars. But the tip was—get this—fifty simoleons!—I can't spell that, but I saw it with my own eyes. I didn't need to count it because it was a fifty-dollar bill, and I know Ben Franklin when I see him. I don't know if gentlemen do prefer blondes, but apparently big tippers do. And with a figure like Carole Lombard's, a girl could be bald on top. Anyway, there is only one way to know if a lady is really blond, and if a lady is really a lady we'll never really know, will we? And a lady wouldn't ask a lady to hold her breath, but I would advise her to read the next installment. This lady digs, and is not afraid to get dirt, or peroxide, on her hands. I'm taking a tip from George, and who knows what Ben Franklin may turn up!

"Say, there's a ball game tomorrow I'd like to take you to," said George. "You interested?"

"I love baseball."

"Swell. I've got to scout a kid named DiMaggio. Supposed to be a world-beater. A few acquaintances of mine are coming, too, if you don't mind."

"All right. If you promise to buy me a hot dog and a beer."

"Peanuts, too."

"You're a regular old shoe, George." Carole slapped him on the shoulder. "But there's one condition. I'm having a party the day after tomorrow, and you have to come."

"Sure."

She couldn't wait to see a ball game. Get out of Hollywood. See some Seals. And of course, *DiMaggio*—it sounded like a rich sauce, an Alfredo, the way it dripped off the tongue. *DiMaggio.* You almost had to slurp it, long strands of spaghetti hanging from your mouth. *DiMaggio.* It sounded like it would stick around for a while.

12

THE CLIPPER

The quest began in a '32 Packard. George drove. He parked ten blocks from Oaks Ball Park, which was filling up with the fans who knew that DiMaggio would be in New York in a year. The pilgrims stopped at a light. Across the intersection on San Pablo Avenue, a cute college girl jogged up to her companions, ponytail flapping. John Henry stared across the street as if this were the OK Corral and the girls were the Younger sisters. He elbowed Darrow, standing next to him. "Look at those tits. You think they need an education? They could teach you a thing or two." John Henry pointed at the model manqué, who giggled, saying something inaudible to the other girls while focusing her eyes on John Henry, a proto-James Dean, mobster manqué.

John Henry continued, "You think Moe Berg is smart 'cuz he speaks ten languages? Those tits are speaking languages Moe's never heard of. They're speaking dead languages. They're saying 'Rub me up' in Eskimo. The Eskimos have twenty-six words for 'snow.' I bet Moe doesn't know how many they have for 'tits.' Jesus, if I was a broad, I'd be getting my oil changed twice a day." John Henry slapped Darrow on the shoulder. "So, whadaya think of them apples?"

"Impeccable."

"Peckin' ain't what I had in mind."

A middle-aged redhead with piercing blue eyes hollered at John Henry from a shack where she mongered newspapers, Kewpie dolls, and souvenirs. "Take your hands out of yer pants, Buster—I'll sell you a donut for a penny."

Chastened, John Henry pulled his hand from his pocket and looked at James Atwood, who was hanging onto John Henry's shoulders to keep from falling down laughing. "You hear what that carrot-top said to me?"

James Atwood snorted a laugh that turned into a razzing sputter. John Henry turned to the lady. "You can keep yer fuckin' donut."

The redhead put her hands on her hips and grinned more widely at the unintended irony in the deflated riposte, which chagrined John Henry even more. "And you can put it where the sun don't shine."

The woman raised a chocolate donut and grinned even more widely at John Henry, who turned away feeling as if he had run a red light and every car in sight was honking at him. The light changed. John Henry, seeing the whites of their eyes and the swells of their bosoms, was the first man off the curb into the wild, urban, zebra crossing of Hollywood.

Carole maternally took Elmer by the arm and crossed with him. James Atwood couldn't keep his eyes off her. He found himself thinking again of high school geometry class, how antithetical Carole's body was to Mrs. Pearly's, as if Carole, autodidactic geometrician, had redefined with her hips "the acute angle." Nor could Darrow keep his eyes off her, though he knew he was invisible. Old age was humbling. Was obscene. But in other ways it was not as the young saw it. Old age—he reflected— was not the one-way ticket to infinity, from birth to death and beyond, in that straight-line vector. No. Old age was shrinking. From both ends to the middle. Old age was a redefined vanishing point. Invisible. Bubble man. Propelling his shrinkage across the intersection as the light turned from stop to caution then to go.

At the next light George bummed a match from the man next to him. More than just ritual, it had the cowl of religiosity, the insinuation of sex, even homoeroticism, the way George and legions of men in the thirties would cup their hands around the stamen of cigarette, and bend their heads to the explosion of light offered by a perfect stranger, the puff, the glow, the withdrawal, the ecstasy of exhale. The recipient of the flame would nod first, then the donor, shaking out his light, the signal for the distaff eyes to contact. Then they'd part, till they could do it again, two strangers, gad to the incantation, "Hey, buddy, got a match?"

George exhaled, then thoughtlessly hawked a loogie onto the face of John Henry's shadow. John Henry bristled. "You just spit on my face!"

"That's your face? Looks like a shadow to me."

"All the same. You coulda spit somewhere else."

"No offense, bub."

John Henry looked at his violated shadow again. He still didn't like it. He slid his hand slowly inside his jacket to reassure himself that the pistol was there if he needed it. The pistol, he thought, was his own guardian angel. One he could squeeze.

Darrow noticed John Henry's hand-check and he knew that John Henry had a pistol. He also worried that John Henry might shoot a man over misplaced spit.

"John Henry, why don't you just move a foot this way, and the spit won't be on you anymore," said Darrow.

"He's got to apologize first."

Raft had been pushed around and baited by head cases his entire childhood in Hell's Kitchen. His reaction was instinctive: Never show a bully weakness. He just stood there staring down John Henry, the way he did in the movies. Darrow didn't know much about George's childhood. He didn't read the Hollywood press. He didn't understand why George would put his life in danger over spit.

"George, this man is a borderline psychopath." As he said it, Darrow realized there might be an element of psychopathy in Raft as well. Raft wasn't sure what a psychopath was. So it was timely that James Atwood spoke. "That means they won't hang him, no matter what he does."

James Atwood smiled with the expectation of carnage. Darrow's instinctive move was to turn the sidewalk into a courtroom, where he made a living of manipulating opinion. He instinctively pled to Raft, who had his eyes fixed on John Henry. "George, you wouldn't spit on the American flag, would you?"

"Course not."

"Can you tell me what the flag is made of?" Darrow cross-examined.

"Who cares?"

"Precisely. It doesn't matter that the flag is made of cotton. Or linen. Or silk. Or whatever material Betsy Ross happened to have at her disposal. I don't care what it is made of. The object itself is meaningless. What matters is that it's a symbol—of your country. And for John Henry, it's the same thing—his shadow is a symbol of his being, his selfhood, his manhood, if you will, and when someone spits on his shadow's face, it's an insult, the same way it would be if you spat on the American flag. Catch?"

Darrow could see both John Henry and George relaxing after his declamation. The magic was still there. His invocation of the flag was serendipitous. He didn't know that George had two brothers killed in the war and that he felt guilty about not going himself. But two in a family was Uncle Sam's limit. For the flag, George would stand down.

"All right. I'll apologize for his face. Still think it'd be a good idea to move, though."

John Henry was relieved that George hadn't called his bluff. James Atwood was at first ambivalent, but then felt good about it. "Glad John Henry didn't have to kill you. Wouldn't be no more George Raft movies. I want to see you get Cagney next time. He sure dies good. And that dancing with Carole. I could be your stuntman for that."

How fragile, thought Darrow, life was; how reckless these young men were with something so precious, evanescent. But he knew he could never make them see that. It was something a man had to see for himself. He couldn't honestly remember how he felt when he was their age. Now when Darrow looked at the sidewalk terrain that John Henry's shadow had vacated all he saw was the depth of the fissures. A man could get lost in them.

George held out his hand to John Henry, who stepped forward to shake it.

"Hey, look," said James Atwood, pointing at the displaced shadow of his companion. "John Henry's got a hole in his head."

The humor was lost on Darrow, who was completely elsewhere. He was thinking of his only son, an atavistic burgher who had abjured law, how his progeny was evidence of regression to the human mean, one notch closer to the likes of John Henry Seadlund and James Atwood Gray. How these men would live on while he perished, and how they would populate the world in his absence, and how it didn't matter.

Carole and Elmer waited in front of a luncheonette for the foursome. George looked at the clock mounted in a Coke sign above the luncheonette. They had a half hour to kill. He held the door and the gang entered. The counter-girl was a sultry Rita Hayworth look-alike, with heavy eyelids that refused to widen as she stared into the handsome faces of George and John Henry, spilling words that for John Henry were like honey. "What would you like?" The intonation cascaded downward from word to word, to the final, sultry, almost inaudible, breathless, *"like."*

"10W40 for me."

"What's that?"

"Coffee," said John Henry, with a proud smile that marked him as a bumpkin. Cute, but a bumpkin.

"And you?"

Darrow looked at John Henry, then back at the waitress, in some strange thrall to his youthful companion. His mind was turning faster than the dynamo of a Tin Lizzie. Would he respond as Darrow or as John Henry's protégé in a brave new world?

"10W30."

"Let me guess . . . tea."

Darrow nodded and smiled into his jowls. A thin, sophisticated smile. The waitress took Carole's order for a Coke, while John Henry was irritated at the cookie jar that was blocking his view of the Rita Hayworth bust, his eyes forced to feast on biscotti and sugar snaps. Visions of sugar snaps crumbling in his fist filled his head, squeezed the way Oscar Charleston reputedly could make the seams of a cheap Negro Leagues ball pop.

John Henry whispered to Darrow, "Get a load of those."

Darrow shook his head and frowned. He looked at John Henry. "Some men have a mind like a steel trap," he said, thinking of how the

New York Times had described him. "You, John Henry, have a mind like a grease trap at the world's sump outlet."

John Henry laughed, which disconcerted Darrow all the more. He pressed on, "No, let me revise that—you have a mind like a Geiger counter, which, when you come down to it, is a pretty stupid instrument—it's got a one-track mind, so to speak. A constant buzz about one thing—radiation. The one and only thing it perceives. And for you, all breasts are uranium."

"You got something better to think about?" John Henry countered. Darrow puzzled over the simple query, and he had no simple answer.

Something about the way the sandy hair mopped atop John Henry's head reminded Carole of her cat. It was short of laughable, but John Henry was playing brinksmanship with the subdued wildness that was short above the ear and on the back of the head, but was unleashed as it moved to the summit. It had a windblown look even in a luncheonette. The hair did not brush straight back. It seemed to be moved against its will, bent back at a rounded ninety-degree angle. It spoke wildness, rebellion. It spoke volumes to Carole, who walked over and sat next to John Henry and spoke, "Your hair is absolutely wild."

"Thanks. I like yours, too."

James Atwood took out a small jackknife whose blade he had honed to razor sharpness and began to pare his nails. Carole was both enthralled and repulsed. The miniature sliver-moons of James Atwood's nails were being pushed into a huddle that James Atwood knew was utterly worthless. A little token of himself. His smithereens.

Carole took the swiveling stool next to James Atwood. "I thought we might get acquainted."

James Atwood couldn't even look at her. He blushed, staring at the knife in his hands.

"What are you thinking?"

James Atwood looked up at Carole and smiled. "You know what you are? You're one of a kind. Like a flower we got in Kansas. It's called Slipper of Venus. That's the Greek god of love. It grows in the swamps with the sphagnum moss. And not many knows where to find it. But I do."

"That's sweet, James Atwood."

As James Atwood watched Carole sip her Coke, the words of "The Prettiest Girl I Ever Saw" ran through his mind.

"Know what I am?"

"A kidnapper and a gangster," said Carole with a smile.

"Before that."

"A cute farm boy?"

"A megalomaniac. That's one word."

Carole smiled. "You'd fit right in in Hollywood."

"You mean they had their heads examined, too?"

"Can't say that they did, but they ought to."

"So you know what 'megalomaniac' means? Most folks don't know and I have to tell 'em."

"I have a good idea."

"Well, it means I'm hellfire for power and too big for my britches. They put it all in one word."

Carole nodded.

"Did you ever have your head examined?" James Atwood asked.

"Yup. For lice."

James Atwood laughed. "I mean for what's inside of it." He laughed again. "Heck, you know what I mean. You're just joshin' me."

"You're right, James Atwood. I hope you don't mind."

"Oh, heck, no. You're a movie star. I'm privileged just to talk to you."

"When you get to know me, you'll know I'm just plain folks like you. When you're on the big screen, you seem bigger than life. Your head gets swelled and you walk around like it's just as big as it is in the movie theater. It's a trick sometimes to shrink it down to where it's reality-sized."

James Atwood couldn't help smiling broadly. "You and me got something in common." He spoke in a slow monotone that was almost hypnotizing. It sounded almost theatrical, affected, but was in fact natural. The manner of his speech captured Carole's attention much more than the substance. It was like a kid's windup toy that was about to stop at the next phoneme. It was as if each syllable struggled up and over the

cog in a sprocket and you were never sure there was enough energy behind it to topple it over the tongue. Altogether it was a slow mixture of
Sydney Greenstreet and Jimmy Stewart, and Carole toyed with the idea
of suggesting that he have a screen test, but James Atwood lacked the
charisma of his buddy, his partner in crime. There was in fact something disturbingly vacant in the eyes of James Atwood, but that too on
the screen could translate into menace. Carole prudently waited on the
suggestion.

"You'll never guess who I grew up with."

"Tell me."

"Johnny Appleseed."

Carole gave him a disbelieving look. James Atwood waved, as if to
erase the literalness of the tale. "That's just a manner of speaking. My
grandfather grew up in an orchard that Johnny Appleseed planted, and
he knew him. My whole family revered Johnny Appleseed. They gave
me the same initials—J.A. But I wasn't no Johnny Appleseed, so they
hated me. Johnny Appleseed was some kind of saint, like St. Francis.
He could walk barefoot in the snow with no shoes on and not freeze his
toes. And he could stick pins in his flesh and not feel pain. I think he
stuck pins in his toes when they was frostbitten—that's why he didn't
feel nothin'. Then he went nuts—wearing just a coffee sack with arm
holes cut out and walking around with a stew kettle on his head. But
you couldn't say nothin' agin Johnny Appleseed in my house or you'd
get it with a belt. And I got it with a belt anyway 'cuz I was nothin' like
Johnny Appleseed. And frankly speaking, I think the Bible is a lot of
horse manure. Johnny Appleseed would run around with his Bible,
shouting, 'News fresh from heaven!' Then you know how he died?
Caught a chill. After all that. How do you figure?"

"You're such a chatterbox, James Atwood. You know that? I'm glad I
got the chance to talk to you. I had you pegged as a quiet, morose type.
You're kind of like Sydney Greenstreet. There's a guy you'd figure was
quiet as a mouse in real life, but Sydney will talk your ear off if you give
him a chance."

"Let's have another Coke."

"Sure."

James Atwood waved his hand to catch the soda girl's attention, then pointed to the two empty Coke glasses. The girl nodded and smiled in understanding.

"I almost died once, from a chill. Me and John Henry. And you know what I thought about?"

"What?"

James Atwood nodded as if in agreement with the words he'd uttered in his head prior to speaking them out loud. "Johnny Appleseed. It was John Henry that saved me. He's the real Johnny Appleseed. Kind of a hero. At least, to me."

Carole turned to look at James Atwood's silent, brooding friend, feeling more intrigued. Next to him, Darrow opened his book, then looked up at Carole Lombard in a golden dress. How much art could a man take in one day? On the page the preacher, Elmer Gantry, spoke of resurrection, while the living Lombard walked with them, abreast of them, in front of them—while the living Lombard had a Coke with them at an ordinary soda fountain, soda drawn by an ordinary soda jerk with a white apron. While Elmer Gantry silently ranted and the women spoke in tongues and their tongues rolled on Gantry's in the mosquito-colored hay, among the stooks, in gullies, in furrows, in hysterical need of what could not be spoken in ordinary language. Not even by Darrow. Not when they were on a quest. When the grail was a young ballplayer named Joe DiMaggio.

For a moment nobody had anything to say to anyone. Five men and a beautiful woman. A moment of pure perception, a magical Buddhist moment of clocks, Coke machines, levers, buttons, counters with their small, inevitable spills. Then John Henry looked scornfully at Darrow's plate, shook his head, and said, "An open-faced sandwich is like old people making love." Pure perception dissipated. The bubble was popped. The background reemerged—a forest in which young Joe DiMaggio was lost. And had to be found. "Barney Google with the Goo-Goo-Googly Eyes" was on the box, and the soda jerk turned it up. He liked the jaunty rhythm and humor and the sound of the words.

George said, "That's my friend's song. Billy Rosenberg. Changed it to Billy Rose. We grew up together in Hell's Kitchen. He hustled me and Leo Durocher at pool, and we were hustlers ourselves."

Carole was taken by his ingenuousness—the megastar moved by his friend's song on a jukebox. She smiled at him, fixed him with her eyes for longer than casual allowed, and he fell for her like a ton of bricks.

"You know "You Gotta See Mama Every Night"? He wrote that, too."

Suddenly it seemed Hell's Kitchen was the place to grow up. Raft, Rose, and of course Owney Madden and Feets Edson. Carole smiled again at George's boyish, authentic enthusiasm. She felt like a kid again herself. Off to see the Wizard. Of swat.

It had been raining intermittently since they got to California. It followed them for the duration of the eight-hour jaunt from Los Angeles to Oakland. But as game time approached, the clouds uncoupled and fled. The last of them, in the shape of an overstuffed catcher's mitt, drifted over the left-field wall. By the time the organ began playing "Take Me Out to the Ball Game," the newly painted, dark-green Oaks Ball Park had become a fishbowl covered with bright blue.

They paid seventy-five cents for seats in the small section that had protection from the sun, an arched canopy behind home plate. With a ticket they each also got a ham sandwich. Carole gave hers to John Henry, who was miffed because, even though they had gotten to the park early, progress to their seats was slowed by a barely ambulant lady loaded down with hot dogs and beer and Cracker Jacks and a lot of lard in the can. John Henry followed Carole to their seats and watched her lower her buttocks onto the seat. He turned to Darrow, who followed him, and shaped Carole's ineffable butt in the air with his hands. "What I like about movie stars is the way they make something out of nothing. I mean, the way the hearth of the ass sweeps out of the tiny flue of the waist. Something out of nothing, you know? The way God did it."

The busy hands of God, thought Darrow. It sounded convincing.

*   *   *

DiMaggio recognized Raft immediately but couldn't fathom the reason for his appearance, so his facial expression was still the affect-less pucker of a flounder out of water when Raft extended his hand and explained the parameters of the game the rookie was invited to, the game that also had chosen him. All Joe had to do, explained Raft, was hit a few balls pitched by Leon Day after the game. An audition of sorts. It seemed wrong to Joe, a crosscurrent to the game that had swept him up. Gable didn't audition. Chaplin didn't. Why DiMaggio, born to play ball the way the naked cherub in the stone fountain George had bought his mother was created to piss?

"Who's Leon Day?"

George laughed and moved to his right so that the sun would not be directly in his eyes. "I'd never heard of him, either. The guy who is funding the game, guy by the name of Harry Bennett, he works for Henry Ford, he insisted that you try to hit Day. He says Day is the third-best Negro pitcher, after Paige and Slim Jones. Says Day could be number one in the starting rotation of half the Major League clubs, if they allowed Negroes to play."

DiMaggio rolled the bat on his shoulder, then stretched his thick fingers and regripped the handle as if playing an arpeggio on a flute. "Ed Walsh is pitching for the Oaks. He pitched for the White Sox and he stopped my hitting streak at sixty-one games. That ought to be good enough."

Raft put his hand on Joe's arm like a manager trying to calm his starter down. "I understand. I don't like auditioning either, but I already paid Day, and Harry calls the shots. So, are you in or out?"

Joe stepped back and took a swing, his way of thinking. Raft was thrilled just watching the swing close up, the imaginary ball leaving the bat with the same arc as the stream from his mother's cherub's stone phallus. In other words, the stroke spoke for itself. In the language of swat, DiMaggio had said yes.

Carole, Darrow, James Atwood, Elmer, and John Henry took their seats under the canopy. Ten minutes later they were joined by George, who bought peanuts for everyone from a vendor in a natty blue uniform with white piping. The eleven-thousand-seat stadium was packed. It took John Henry little time to realize that he was sitting next to a braless woman. He looked around him, reflecting on how much was superfluous. The post that almost occluded their view. The dangling gold crucifix that minimally impaired John Henry's.

DiMaggio had had a big year with the San Francisco Seals, and the Seals had a sometimes ugly rivalry with the Oakland Oaks. They played a lot of doubleheaders. The morning game at Seals stadium and the afternoon game in Emeryville at the Oaks' home park both drew around ten thousand fans.

At the start of the third inning Seals manager James Caveny sidled up to DiMaggio, who was pulling his bat from the rack. "See that blonde there?" He pointed. "Behind first base."

DiMaggio scanned the seats. She was hard to miss.

"Know who that is? Carole Lombard. And the guy sitting next to her—George Raft."

"I know," said Joe.

Caveny slapped him on the back. "Hollywood's here. To see the great DiMag. And the four guys on the other side of Lombard—don't know who the heavies are, but the old guy must be a scout. He came down asking about you."

"Scout? I'm going to the Yankees."

"Maybe he's a Yankee scout. Wouldn't say what he was. But I told him you're the real thing."

Joe lifted the bat to his shoulder and watched Ed Walsh Jr. warm up. James Caveny looked alternately at the infielders taking their practice throws and at Lombard. "It's all yours, Joe. Twenty years from now you're gonna have a broad like that on your arm, waltzing into Cooperstown. And I'm gonna be in Laguna Beach, listening to the game on the box. But I'm gonna have something you don't have. When a guy puts down a squeeze with the bases loaded I'm gonna get a tingle. Always have. Because I love the game. And you don't. You play because you're good at it. It's your meal ticket. You and Cobb. He didn't love the game either. Played the way he did because of his old man. I think he killed himself. Now that's something, huh? The two greatest talents in the game, save Babe Ruth, and neither one of them really gave a shit about the game. They just had the talent. Not God-given, just talent."

"What do you mean 'not God-given'?"

"I mean there is no God. If there was, why would he waste all that talent on a guy who doesn't love the game? Aw, fuck it. Why am I wasting my breath? Just get up there. Earn all that macaroni you're making. Buy your old man a new boat."

"I already did."

"Hit one out, Joe," Caveny said, walking to his place on the bench.

"I already did."

"I know. I still feel the tingle."

George Raft's imagination was in overdrive, with the otherworldly Lombard by his side: *What could be better than to go to a ball game with you, have a hot dog with you, one long squiggly line of mustard down its length, but spare me the tumbling dice of relish, that emasculated form of a pickle. I love to watch you getting your lips around a hot dog and looking at me with those eyes and getting the mustard on your fingers. And now it's my turn to bite that dog in your fist, then wash it down with thin beer that doesn't matter because we are at one with the conspiracy of enjoying thin beer and watching it go down each other's gullets with the funny motion the throat makes, so funny it could be sex itself, feeling almost drunk on the thin beer or on you getting drunk on me.*

James Atwood opened his pack of Zeenuts, tossed the contents into his mouth and looked at the card, hoping it would be DiMaggio, who batted cleanup. It was. James Atwood felt like he'd just hit a number. "Look, it's him! Christ, he looks like a squirrel. What a greaser. Those teeth."

"Teeth can be fixed," said Carole. "Look at Gable. Besides, what do you care what he looks like. He had a sixty-one-game hitting streak last year. That's a record. And I think he's kind of cute."

Chastised, James Atwood opened a small bag of peanuts, feeling squirrel-like himself, shelling then popping a nut into his mouth. John Henry looked at James Atwood with lowered forehead and raised eyes

and laughed. "You're a real crackerjack," he said, sotto voce. James Atwood punched him on the arm, without looking.

If a body could be all sinew it would be DiMaggio's body. Tall, thin,
with some filling out to do. He strode quickly to the plate, dug in, and
straightened up, twirling the bat once and staring at the left-field wall,
then taking two quick warm-up swings and crouching for the pitch. Of
the long-ball hitters in the Major Leagues, Satch later rated Ted Williams and Joe DiMaggio as tops. With Williams Satch felt there was no
way to be confident of getting the man out or neutralizing his power.
He just threw it up there and hoped for the best. Satch always felt that
he could get away with pitching Joe outside, that Joe couldn't pull his
fastball on the outside corner, which didn't mean that Joe couldn't hit it
for an extra base, but he wasn't going to put it out of the stadium. Not
so with Ted. He could pull anything.

Joe took the first pitch from Oaks' star Ed Walsh for a ball. Oaks an-
nouncer "Mush the Ragman" reproved the call on the radio. Joe had
forgotten about the Hollywood fan club behind first base. But now he
heard a woman shouting encouragement from that direction and he
looked over there. He couldn't be sure it was her, but he wanted to believe it. He dug in, took a practice swing, and waited for the next pitch.
He ducked and stepped back. A wasted pitch. 2 and 0 now. Even in the
Pacific Coast League pitchers took offense to a hitter digging in. Dizzy
Dean was a fanatic about it. He once hit seven batters in a row, on purpose. If you dug in against Diz, you could be guaranteed that the next
pitch was coming at you. You only hoped it was not coming at your
head. Joe liked to dig in. He wouldn't let any pitcher intimidate him.
Two years later he hated the satin sheets at Polly Adler's, the famous
New York brothel. He'd slide right off, trying to dig his toes a hold. He
politely requested cotton sheets, which came to be known as "DiMaggios."

Meat and potatoes. Pasta with calamari. The fastball he expected was
coming right over the heart of the plate. The decision was instant. The
sinew flexed and uncoiled. The sound and feel of the ball off the bat
told Joe before he could see the arc of it that it was going out. Two at-
bats, two home runs. He would end up three for four. A single struck so
hard that it went through the first baseman's legs before he could lower

his glove to field it, and a line-drive out to third. Less than spectacular work at short and in center field, but he got the job done in the 8–3 victory. Joe trotted in to the visiting team dugout after the last out, ostensibly to shake hands with some of his goombahs but actually to get a better look at the dame who was watching him all the way.

The crowd was filing out. Darrow stood up and looked at George, who motioned with his hand that Darrow should sit down. "Hang on. When everyone's gone, we're gonna see what he can really do. I've got Leon Day coming. He's gonna throw some balls to Joe. If he can hit Day, he can hit Paige."

A half hour later the stands were deserted and the players had left, too. All but Joe, who emerged from the dugout like a groundhog after hibernation. Then Leon Day appeared on the mound with a big bucket of balls. Twenty pitches later, the rookie had managed two foul balls and one liner over second. Leon walked over to Raft, who looked away and frowned. George couldn't bring himself to ask Leon directly what he thought. He just raised his eyebrows as a signal for Leon to begin.

Leon laughed. "Well, he can't hit a fastball, he don't raise no Sam with a curveball, and if you throw him a changeup he's liable to break a leg."

DiMaggio was shagging the missed balls directly behind home. He had ten in the bucket, and when Leon started up the ramp to the exit, Joe hollered, "You won that round, Leon."

Leon looked at him and Joe held the bucket up. "Round two."

Leon looked at Joe, then at Raft. "Twenty balls, twenty dollars. That was our deal. I pitch for money, not fun."

George looked around at the balls scattered on the field. "How many you got, Joe?"

Joe looked in the bucket. "About ten."

George handed Leon a ten-dollar bill. "Dollar a ball. They've got to be all strikes."

Leon shook his head at Raft's folly, smiled, and gladly accepted the ten-spot. "You're wasting your money."

"Nothing I can do about it now." George smiled, then looked at Joe and nodded, acknowledging that the deal was on. Joe handed Leon the bucket, then stood in the batter's box, kicked at the dirt, and dug in just where he wanted to be. Leon fired a perfunctory fastball down the pipe and Joe hit it sharply on the ground, just to the left of second, a hit against all but the best shortstops playing him not to pull. Leon didn't take any care to disguise his gripping the ball for a curve, and Joe waited on it, hitting a line drive to center. Leon turned to see how well the ball was hit. Then he set himself for the next pitch. Joe had seen enough of Leon to know that he'd be saying to himself, "The kid got lucky on that one. This one will be a real breaking ball."

It was, and Joe put it in the right-center-field bleachers. Carole was jumping and clapping. It was odd how the tide could shift so completely from the pitcher to the hitter, or vice versa. Joe knew that Leon would now be saying to himself, 'Okay, you hit my curve. Now try my fastball." If Leon had taken the time to think on it, he would have realized that Joe would be guessing fastball. But it wouldn't have mattered. Leon had to test his fastball on the kid. It was a matter of pride. Power versus power. The fastball came in on the inside corner and went out just as fast, into the left-field seats.

Now Joe guessed that Leon would not give him a pitch in the zone where he could apply any power to it. *Curve, low outside,* Joe said to himself. And again he was right. He hit a sinking liner down the first-base line that rolled to the wall.

At this point Leon realized that the kid had his number and he would have to mix it up, outfox the kid, to get back the upper hand. Joe fouled off a fastball down and in, then swung and missed a changeup. He hit the next fastball right at Leon, who caught it and returned a slider that Joe dribbled to short.

One more ball. Leon held it up to signal that it was the last. Joe guessed that Leon would not take the chance of giving him anything he could hit out. And the last pitch would not be off-speed. Curve or slider, then. Leon had an excellent curve. A money pitch. It would be a curve . . .

Joe swung late on the slider, hitting another slow roller to short. Joe slammed his bat on the plate. Leon walked in and shook his hand. They didn't exchange words. Joe had hit two homers off Leon Day and was disgusted at himself. That alone was a good sign.

Leon approached Raft. "Okay, he's a hitter. Guess-hitter. Maybe he got lucky, guessing them pitches. But a guess-hitter's gonna guess right some of the time, against anybody. With Satchel, all he's got to do is guess the location. 'Cuz it's gonna be a fastball, eight out of ten."

Leon turned and looked at DiMaggio leaning on his bat with one hand, waiting on the verdict. Leon looked back at Raft and nodded with an incipient smile. "The kid could be something." Then he turned and walked out the exit.

After the hitting exhibition Raft treated the gang to the price of admission to *Scarface*, which was playing in Oakland, then refused to see it with them. Carole pleaded, but it did no good. George never saw himself on screen. He was too self-conscious and self-critical, so he and Carole took in a show at the last vaudeville house in town while Darrow and the others watched the movie.

John Henry and James Atwood were partly to regret seeing the film, because Elmer emerged with a new trick, flipping a coin the way Raft did throughout the movie, the way James Atwood had done in the Rolls-Royce on the way to Los Angeles. Elmer was proud of being able to duplicate Raft's mannerism, and did it incessantly, despite credible threats from John Henry and James Atwood. After the show, George stopped at the telegraph office and sent the following message to Leo:

Scouting Report: Joe DiMaggio

Tall, thin. 6'2", maybe 185. Shortstop. Some center field. Not real comfortable out there. Unsure where to play. Good eye for the ball, chases everything down before it drops. At the plate he takes a big cut and hits it long. Can he hit a Major League curveball? Probably better than you do already, but that's not saying much. Can he play for your team? Yeah. My instinctive reaction? This kid is going to be one hell of a ballplayer. Get Rickey to make a deal with the Yanks now. Give them anything. Give them you! The Yanks are looking for him to fill Ruth's shoes. It would have been interesting to see the two of them together. Would the Babe have taken him under his wing? Or pissed on him? I won't miss this game for all the tea in China. The Negroes will think they're looking at a minor-leaguer. This is no rookie. This is Joe Jackson twenty-five years ago. Just a little wet behind the ears.

"THE HOLLYWOOD REPORTER"

by Louella Parsons

All right. The dope is this. No one, not even my sources in the FBI, knows who the three thugs are who are keeping company with Clarence Darrow, Carole Lombard, and George Raft. But they've registered at several motels as the Dean brothers: Dizzy, Daffy, and Dummy. And get this—there *is* a third Dean brother— a retarded kid named Elmer, and one of that trio looks amazingly like the two Dean brothers, who favor each other both in looks and pitching skills. But that duo are in St. Louis, so, so much for that angle. The trio clearly have something to hide and certainly are sinister in appearance. Young Joe DiMaggio, meanwhile, has no comment, which leaves Louella all the more suspicious. Something is afoot in our national pastime, and it has a base-filching, Gashouse Gang aura to it. Why is it that Clarence Darrow's phone bills include long-distance conversations to ex-client Ossian Sweet, a successful Negro physician? Why does Darrow himself have a Negro physician? Is there anything to the rumor of another monkey-gland operation? Do these Negro doctors have some access to monkey glands that our own white doctors do not? Questions, questions, questions! Louella has been waiting for a tip that clears this all up. But so far, nothing. Something big is going on underground. And if it takes a sighted mole to sniff it out, Louella is your animal.

13

SOIREE

Carole and her roommate Fieldsie spent the whole day working on the party. Fieldsie was thin once, not quite a year earlier. But thin in the way that wide-bodied people are, so that they look fat even while thin. So why bother. Forty pounds lighter, she auditioned for Ernst Lubitsch, who called her *toro*. She never got comfortable without the ballast. Four months and forty pounds later, she was her old self, following her shrink's orders to try to love her body, skipping a naked fandango at Carole's soirees.

Like most of Carole's parties, this one was a theme affair. The living room was transformed into a hospital ward, filled with trappings rented from surgical supply houses. A dozen white iron beds were scattered about the place, with a star's name on a hospital chart attached to each bed. On some stars' charts a plummeting graph was drawn, and the doctor's signature line read: "Louella Parsons" or "Walter Winchell," Hollywood's rival gossipmongers. A buffet dinner was rolled in on an operating table. Anyone who was anyone arrived in an ambulance.

John Henry and James Atwood had been put to work on party preparations, John Henry outside and James Atwood inside. "Let's take a break," said Carole. She got them both Cokes, some pound cake for James Atwood, and picked up the newspaper.

Carole continued to read as James Atwood spoke. "I like the funny pages. But I don't understand the front page. Don't read that. Lot of things I don't understand, like how come a radio works. That beats all. I heard about the secret of the Incas, and I'd like to know what it was, but I'd put that second to radio. The Incas' secret didn't help them none, 'cuz where are they now? You don't hear about the New York Incas or the St. Louis Incas. I guess they're all gone. And if they was still around, I'd bet they'd like to understand the radio, too. I took one apart once and didn't find nothin' special in it. So it's a mystery how it just plucks somebody's voice out of the air that's a hundred miles away, maybe more." James Atwood smirked. "You know, when I was a kid, and the first telephone came to town, there were folks who thought the telephone wires were hollow. That was the only way voices could travel through 'em."

Carole smiled. "That's funny. My grandfather laid the first international cable. He would have gotten a big chuckle out of that."

"You mean across the ocean?"

Carole sipped on her straw. "Hm-hm."

"I don't usually tell folks about not understanding the radio. I'm afraid they'd laugh at me like we laughed at those guys who thought the telephone lines were hollow."

"Well, I'm honored. But to tell the truth, I don't understand radios any more than you do."

James Atwood breathed a great sigh of relief, as if the burden of thousands of voices had been lifted from his shoulders, his head. "Say, you know what I always wanted to know?" he said excitedly.

"What?"

"In the movies, when it's snowing, you can tell it's not real snow, but what is it, if it's not really snow?"

"Well, that's a big secret, James Atwood. I think Hollywood learned it from the Incas."

James Atwood smiled. "You're joshin' me."

"Yes, I am. But it is a secret. Promise not to tell?"

"Promise." James Atwood raised his hand in a Boy Scout salute.

Carole whispered. "It's corn flakes."

"Corn flakes?"

"Ssh! Not so loud. Bleached corn flakes.'

"I'll be damned. Corn flakes."

A fly crawled on the counter between James Atwood's Coke and Carole's Coke. James Atwood shot out a fist and grabbed it, then threw it to the floor.

"You've got fast hands."

"Wanna know how we used to catch flies back in Ossage?" James Atwood did not wait for a response. "I'd pour a line of molasses across a table, then sit there. The flies would light on it. Then I'd grab up the bunch of them. Folks make a custom of catching flies like that, where I'm from. There's all kinds of flies, you know. Horseflies. Deerflies. Greenheads. Blue flies. All kinds. None of 'em any good. And blackflies is the worst. You want some of my pound cake?"

"No, thanks."

"I hate to eat solitary."

Around 8:00 P.M., Gable picked Carole up. They went for dinner, then a drive. The party started at nine, but she didn't want to be there till ten. Fieldsie could handle the early arrivals, usually the starlets and hangers-on who were looking for free booze.

"So, who's coming to this party of yours?" Gable asked.

"My friends, George, the usual crowd. Sidney, Cesar, Basil and Ouida."

"Why did you invite *them?*"

"Basil and Ouida?"

"The biggest stuffed shirt and stuffed bra in Hollywood. They're so full of themselves, and so boring, and unrepentant about it. They throw a party and expect everyone to wear a monkey suit."

"That's the point. To show them what a fun party is like, Clarkie."

She smiled at him. Carole was the only person who could get away with calling Clark "Clarkie." It just wouldn't work with anyone else. He disliked the name, but he liked her for it. It was . . . he didn't know exactly how to put it, but it was something like balls. Whatever women had that could be like balls, that's what made Carole special, to him. Great tits and ass were ubiquitous. Carole had what he thought of as character. The scar on her face, for example. The marred, imperfect beauty that didn't prevent her from carrying herself as a beautiful woman. He admired that. He didn't entirely understand it, which was in large part why he admired it. She was different. He liked different.

The Cadillac convertible sped along Mulholland Drive. The speed and the Cadillac made the stars more accessible, somehow. He looked up at them, admired them. He felt like a million bucks, with Carole in his Caddy, the stars and the moon somehow his present to her, which made him remember the other present he had for her.

"I almost forgot," he said, reaching into the backseat for the small, wrapped box. He had trouble reaching it, and veered toward the ravine.

"Clarkie, be careful."

"It's all right. I've got it."

He handed her the box and turned to see her expression. She undid the bow and tore off the paper. She shook it to see if she could divine its contents. Paperweight was the only thing that came to her mind. The size of the thing had her baffled. And Clark wouldn't give her a paperweight. She pushed back the tissue and removed from the box a shrunken head.

"Like it?'

"It's a skull."

"From Brazil. Amazing, isn't it? Nobody knows how they do it."

"But Clark, it's a human head. What did they do, did they . . . I mean, are they cannibals or something?"

"How would I know?" Clark had hardly finished his sentence when he saw her arm jerk up and the head fly into the ravine.

"What are you doing?"

"I don't need another skull. This one's good enough. Why did you think I would want a skull?" she said testily.

"It's shrunken. It's unique."

"Oh, Christ, Clark, stop! Stop!"

She put her hand on his arm. He put on the brakes. "What's wrong?"

"Turn around."

"What?"

"Turn around." Carole pulled the wheel to her, and Gable came to a quick stop. "We've got to go back. That's a human skull and it's got my fingerprints on it. If the cops find it they'll think I murdered a baby."

"No one's going to find that. It's in the ravine. Nothing in there but jackrabbits."

"Clarkie, we're going back."

"How are we going to find it?"

"I threw it by a road sign."

"But it's night."

"We'll find it. Just go back."

Gable turned around and parked opposite the road sign indicating a sharp curve. Clark and Carole kicked through the underbrush for ten minutes.

"The only way we'll find it is to step on it," he groused.

"Here it is!" Carole saw the skull on the rocks and pebbles, just below a pipe that carried runoff from the high side of the road down into the ravine. She handed it to him. It clearly gave her the willies just to touch it.

"Put it back in the box."

"Don't you want to wipe your fingerprints off first?"

Carole liked his childlike demeanor. When he laughed or smiled, it was hard to stay angry at him. "Who would give a lady a shrunken head?"

"Me, obviously. Come on. I'll make it up to you."

"You're so cheap. That's the problem. You'd never think of diamonds."

They walked back to the car. Gable offered her his hand up the steep incline. She managed by herself. He slipped as they approached the road.

"You're such a lunk."

"Is that why you like me?" He thought of saying "love," but nixed the idea.

It was past ten when they pulled into the spot where their ambulance was waiting, equipped with a driver, a block from the house. Gable looked at Carole's well-lit front lawn. "What's that man doing?" he asked with a deliberate irascibility.

"Watering the grass."

"Why?" Gable said incredulously.

"To make it happy and healthy."

"Grass isn't happy. It's not human. It can't talk."

"No, but it's pretty good at listening." Carole gave him a look that meant he was to see the point of the implied comparison. Gable shook his head. It seemed he always had these kinds of conversations with Carole.

"You drive me crazy, Carole. But that's what I like about you. You're so natural. No bullshit, like all these other dames all over Hollywood."

"Clark, what's natural for an actor?" He bit on his mustache, thinking of an answer. Nothing came to him.

"Acting," she answered for him. "I'm acting all the time, pretending to be natural. It's a lot of crap, actually."

Clark was on the one hand completely confused. But on the other he understood perfectly. *What a dame,* he said to himself. He liked a dame who was quick, a dame who could put him in his place. They changed into their party attire and got into the ambulance, which arrived with sirens blaring. Carole was carried in on a stretcher by her "bodyguards," John Henry Seadlund and James Atwood Gray.

Guests who were not already in doctors', nurses', or orderlies' uniforms were given hospital gowns, open down the back and tied top and bottom with strings. The house itself was designed by Billy Haines with parties in mind. It had a good-sized swimming pool. The drawing room was hung in velvet, six shades of blue. The furniture was Empire period. She had an oversized plum satin bed with threefold mirror screens on either side. And she had the loan of unemployed, neophyte gangsters John Henry Seadlund and James Atwood Gray to help put the party together.

The phone was ringing as she rose from the stretcher. Fieldsie answered it and handed it to Carole. She hung up and frowned. It was Louella Parsons, calling to warn that W. C. Fields was coming with a diarrheic pig on a bicycle. It was part of an old vaudeville act he once did. Fields was obviously plowed, already.

"What's wrong?" asked John Henry.

"W. C. Fields. Nasty old man is coming to the party with a diarrheic pig, on a bicycle."

"The pig is on the bicycle, or he is?"

Carole swatted a throw pillow with Chinese characters onto the floor and pouted, legs tucked under her, on the couch. "What does it matter?"

John Henry consoled her, "Don't you worry, Miss Lombard. I'll take care of Mr. Fields."

"You will?" Her legs swiveled to the floor. She pushed herself up off the couch and gave him a hug that was every bit as melodramatic as the line that followed, "Oh, Johnny. That's swell."

Acting had become a part of her quotidian repertoire. The star born as Jane Peters was playing Carole Lombard twenty-four hours a day. But she was genuinely happy to have two bodyguards out waiting for Fields when the party was under way. She also knew that there was a good chance Fields would be in such a stupor that he might completely forget where he was going. Odds were even that if he started out for her house he might end up in Baja.

George Raft was at Carole's pool table, taking everyone's money at 8-ball. It figured, they all thought, for a gangster—probably spent most of his formative years in a pool hall, if he hadn't been born in one. George put down the cue. There was no one left to be had. He walked to the swimming pool. A dragonfly crashed the meretricious blue surface of the bottom-lighted pool. Did it take this as a misplaced sky? On the other side of the pool, Carole tested the water with her foot, sending a wave across as Gable slithered up. As they talked George felt jealousy welling up. He still wasn't comfortable starting a conversation with a beautiful, classy dame. Gable had nothing to say, but he had the nerve to say it anyway. The waves kissed off the long sidewall of the pool, de-livering the dragonfly to the sucking side-pocket and a faster oblivion.

I got George's attention and extended my hand. "I'm Walter Win-chell. We've never met, formally."

George shook my hand and smiled. "Yeah, I remember you. We were in Dave's Blue Room that night and some guy comes in and says he's going to kill you. You're lucky he chickened out."

I smiled. "I still don't know if it was Owney Madden or Dutch Schultz that put the hit on me."

"I'll bet it was Dutch. He was pissed about your column about Mad Dog Coll. I wouldn't have been in your shoes for all the tea in China."

Louella saw that I had George's ear and trundled over. "George, you made it. And Walter—this *is* a surprise."

"Lollipops, you look divine."

Louella smiled and turned to George. "I just loved you and Carole on the set of *Bolero*. The dancing was exquisite. You must read my review."

"I never read reviews." George lied.

"I did," I said. "When they catch Dillinger, the judge is going to sentence him to read it twice."

George started to laugh, then thought better of it and turned it into a cough. Louella put her hand on George's shoulder, her mouth near his ear, and spoke in a sotto voce loud enough for me to hear. "Watch out. If Walter pats you on the back, it's to find the best place to put the knife."

At that moment, about midnight, three shots rang out. The band stopped playing and the place went silent.

"It's either Fields or the pig," said Carole.

"Triage!" shouted Errol Flynn, glass raised high. And those who were able to get on their feet raced out the door behind Flynn.

"Wait! You forgot your rapier, or your épée, pee-pee, whatever," said Louella's husband Docky Martin.

"Did you shoot him?" Carole asked John Henry Seadlund.

"Nah. Just scared the shit out of him and the pig. Don't think he'll be back."

"Three cheers for . . . what's his name?" Flynn asked.

"Johnny. He's my bodyguard," said Carole, putting her arm around him.

After the cheers and forced imbibing of half a bottle of champagne,

Johnny the bodyguard was offered enough jobs to set himself up permanently in Hollywood, if he could get kidnapping off his mind.

"Carole! Carole!" Ernst Lubitsch was melodramatically peeling through the crowd with his perpetual urgency.

"Lubsey."

Lubitsch put his arm around her and escorted her to a private corner. "Carole, you can't run off to San Francisco with that gangster, that lothario. Think of your reputation."

"Fuck off, Lubsey. I'll go where I want and with whom I want. Who do you think you are, my chaperone?"

"I'm just looking out for your career. You can't be seen with a two-legged clotheshorse with a patent-leather smile," he said, referring to George Raft. "And we need to make some Lombard pictures."

Carole waved at the smoke from Lubitsch's sempiternal cigar. "I've made Lombard pictures. About forty of them."

Lubitsch waved his arms. "No, no. Those are just pictures with Lombard in them. I want to make 'Lombard' pictures." He conducted her name with the cigar as baton.

"Our timing's just been off. We'll get together one of these days."

Fieldsie rolled by, naked, on roller skates, her hair in a mikado-tuck, with a tray of canapés held head high. Lubitsch did a double take. "Isn't that your housemate?"

"Triage!" shouted George Burns, echoing Flynn. "Someone get a sheet, quick. No, make that two."

A tall woman put her arm around Carole. "You are the most voluptuous creature. I just love those tits." It was Billy Haines in drag. "And who is this divine man. No, wait. Don't tell me. It's Ernst Lubitsch, the great director." Lubitsch was smitten.

Louella's husband Docky stumbled up and put his arm around Raft, more than half in the bag. "You're going to see DiMaggio again tomorrow." He noticed the surprise in George's and Carole's faces. "Oh, come on. This is Hollywood. Nothing is a secret. Listen, I can spare you the trip. That spaghetti could hit a slow-pitched ravioli out of the park."

Docky staggered off, fading fast. Billy Haines pulled Carole away. "There is something you've got to see."

Errol Flynn practicing mouth-to-mouth resuscitation on two women. The gag was being used all over the house, but no more expertly than by the pool, where half of the swimmers were naked.

"Who is that?" asked Billy, stepping over a passed-out naked body to get to Flynn.

"Docky Martin."

"I suppose *that* is Louella's *column*," Billy said drolly, pointing at his groin.

Carole laughed. "That's clearly what she writes about."

"Corinthian?" said Billy, tongue in cheek.

"Definitely not Jewish," said Travis Banton, who designed gowns for Carole and sets for deMille. He put an arm around Carole's shoulders. "Speaking of columns, my dear, you should have known Phidias." He sighed wistfully, slapping his forehead. "I should have known all the Greeks."

Fieldsie skated up to them and stared at Flynn, working hard at re-suscitation. "Get me in line! Who *is* that?"

"Nobody, right now. But he's going to be Errol Flynn," said Billy, loud enough for Flynn to hear. "And he's going to be on the marquee, on top of Carole Lombard, if she can get him off of me."

Carole sat on a deck chair, crossed her legs, and dangled her shoe.

"Nice party," said Flynn. "Drink?" He held up a bottle of champagne.

"Would you drink it from my shoe?"

Flynn threw off the shoe with abandon, high and end over end, but with the touch of a pickpocket. He grouted out her toes with his tongue.

"Oh, my. I think my cork just popped." Carole held out her glass. "Fill me up, please."

Flynn emptied the bottle into the glasses of Billy, Fieldsie, and Carole, then put it down. Carole picked it up, put it on its side and spun it. It pointed to Fieldsie, who puckered up for Flynn, who obliged, while Carole stole away to the closet by the pool. She took out a stack of pillowcases and carried them on her arm, throwing them to guests to store their clothes in while they swam.

"Pool time," she called. The call was answered. Soon there were thirty naked people in the pool.

Cecil deMille, who was clothed, squatted by the edge of the pool. "Who are those gangsters of yours?" He addressed Carole. "They're so authentic. I think we could use them."

"George dug them up somewhere."

"I might have known."

Carole noticed Max Sennett and Eddie Cline rolling in a stretcher filled with custard pies. She laughed. This was not planned. She hoisted herself out of the pool, leaving an admiring circle of dicks dangling in the water. Billy Haines caught her eye, as did Fieldsie. They all made for the pies. Carole couldn't find Lubitsch. The next pie-target on her mental list was Basil Rathbone, who had the nerve to come to her hospital party in a tux. Billy hit Basil's formally dressed wife Ouida in the kisser. Soon pies were flying everywhere. Carole stuffed one in Fred MacMurray's saxophone, while Billy got him in the face. Samuel Goldwyn got more than his share. Gable looked Carole in the eye, custard dripping off his mustache, and hit her in the crotch with a pie. She gasped, then laughed. "Custard, anyone?"

Clark didn't miss a beat. Carole histrionically leaned against a marble column entwined with marble fig leaves and wrapped herself in her arms, imagining Flynn tonguing custard from between her toes, which involuntarily curled up as Gable stooped to get his fill of custard. Sidney Greenstreet squared off in a duel with the steely-eyed Raft. They swaggered around and drew simultaneously, hitting each other in the face.

I was scribbling this all down, and of course so was Louella, though it was all too hot for "The Hollywood Reporter." A bird circled above us on the patio.

"Dollar to a wooden donut that bird shits on somebody," said Billy.

"I hope it hits Louella's bald spot."

Louella budged in front of Billy. "Who *are* you?" Billy said indignantly.

"She's the famous gossip columnist," said Travis Banton.

Billy snapped his fingers and gaped. "You're Walter Winchell."

Carole and everyone else laughed.

"Louella Parsons," said the somewhat plump but not unattractive columnist with clear skin, brown eyes, and teeth that had undergone Hollywood-style work. "Who are *you?*"

"I'm Babe Ruth. And I've got a stomachache. Wanna have a go?" said Billy with fey intonation and looking down his extended wrist. Everyone knew that Ruth's famous stomachaches itched somewhere below the belly, and those itches were her husband Docky's specialty.

"You're an actor?"

"Sometimes. Mostly now I do decorating. Interiors."

"Your name?" Louella pulled from her pocket a small book and a pen that were always with her.

"Billy Haines. With an 'i.' "

"You ever heard of the Depression, Billy?"

"Why, of course. Hasn't everybody?"

"You know what it is?"

"Oh, dear, what could it be?"

"It's your career."

"Bitch!" said Billy, walking away. Louella would not be outdone in the nasty/snide department. Fieldsie laughed, with her back to Billy, not wanting him to hear.

Gable withdrew from his custard cleanup operation and picked up a bottle of champagne. "Do you do nails, too?" Carole asked, extending her hand.

The crowd moved to the dance floor, where Fred MacMurray played a cleaned-up sax with his ex-group, the California Collegians, as Joan Crawford threw on a nurse's uniform and pulled Ray Milland onto the floor. Joan was Carole's only competition in the Charleston. The two of them competed at the same dance halls and were always finalists, Joan coming away with the majority of the trophies. Joan was disappointed that she could not locate George. Ray could cut a rug, but he couldn't compete with George. No one but Astaire could.

It took some time, but finally MacMurray and his band were cooking. You knew it because the guys were smiling and nodding at each other, pumping each other up for solos. And it all got louder, beckoning people to dance. The rhythm was flowing through the room and out onto the patio, where Carole looked up at the stars and felt sad that, while their light made it down to Hollywood, MacMurray's band's beautiful reciprocating sound would peter out before it got five hundred yards back up toward the stars.

Everyone was being drawn to the ballroom, and nearly everyone who could stand was dancing. Someone saw George by the pool table and said, "Hey, George, dance for us!" But George sipped his beer from a bottle and shook his head. He couldn't dance without his signature pants. His pants were as important as his shoes, and the latter he'd worn deliberately for dancing. But he had on intern's pants, with a drawstring tied into a bow, and he wouldn't be caught dancing in them.

The requests kept coming. Finally, he acceded and entered the coat room, changed into his custom-made, high-waisted pants, from Charvet et Fils, 18 E. 53rd Street, and listened involuntarily to the grunts of Gable and an unidentifiable woman against the far wall of the deep coat room. When George reappeared, it was almost scripted that Carole was at the fringe of the dancers, alone, in her Travis Banton gown. George grabbed her by the waist and spun her onto the floor where a circle opened the way a dog in a hay field would turn round three times and flatten himself a space. They dived into a Charleston. George began with controlled but sharp arm movements, while his feet moved at three-quarter speed, faster than anyone on the floor, but paced so that he could hit it when the song moved him to.

The high-waisted pants seemed to lengthen his legs, made him sort of a glorious freak. The suspenders over the naked chest accentuated the continuum of vertical movement, so that George had the aspect of a carefully constructed Claudesque composition in motion. And the motion counterpointed the composition, dominated it, but the tension accentuated the motion. And now the feet were at full tilt, sliding, popping, slamming the floor, but laying off smartly when he moved Carole through spins and turns where all eyes would be diverted to those curves, those buttocks, the beautifully sculpted, athletic legs.

The dance floor gradually unmobbed, dancers drawn away like iron filings by the magnet of perception itself. The desire to watch something extraordinary overwhelmed the individual and collective desires to express the self to music. Now, there was only Hollywood's number-one dance couple, George and Carole. Even their names fit as symmetrically as their bodies—six letters, each with a silent "e," and when the Charleston was over, MacMurray let silence hold sway only for a few moments before signaling the band to begin a tango. It was to be one of the best performances of their careers. Hot and sultry? Think hotter and sultrier. George circled Carole like a matador, making it clear that the purpose of the high-waisted pants was to scabbard the ersatz sword. And the female impersonating the bull was a dazzling mix of reluctance and compliance, with the right touch of woundedness and pounce. The sweat dripping through the mascara spoke both *massacre* and *be massacred*.

Who was I dancing with, thought George. And, *who was I dancing with,* thought Carol. The unforgiving, frightening answer that came to each was that it was so good, so perfect, *I could have been dancing with myself.* That's when each one knew s/he had to make love to the self s/he was dancing with. Neither one too bashful to tell the other, with eyes. Stepped on—not bitten by—the love bug. So daintily that its heel could have been lips, its instep the arch of their tango'd backs, the ball of its foot, well, the ball would be nothing other than one of the two jingling, high-rolling dice in the high-waisted pants of the dancer whose number came up again and again in his mind as he rolled her over and over until both of them were crapped out. That's when he noticed that his hand in hers was sweaty, and her back against his other hand was sweaty. Then the steely-eyed Raft looked into the lambent eyes of Lombard and they both turned into adolescents, with the crowd imagining the only proper climax to the performance.

When the dance was over and the spectators let out their breath, Carole was still draped almost horizontally over George's arm, staring into his eyes, and the couple, as if in a more ancient mythology, had turned virtually to stone. As she spun back to vertical, Carole could not differentiate need from desire, and knew only that the mix of the two emotions composed ninety-nine percent of her mind at the moment.

The remaining one percent was ratiocination, operating as chattel to the majority, realizing that the reason Clark was not in the circle was probably that he was fucking a starlet in the cloakroom. Clark had a thing for cloakrooms. They simulated an audience. So her own bedroom would be a safe bet for the fast fuck for which the public foreplay was finished. MacMurray was into his next tune, and the dance floor refilled. The room buzzed again with voices. The silent "e" partners dashed up the stairs to interlock consonants, blur vowels, and practice the protophonics of grunt and moan.

"Hard and fast," she said.

George didn't say anything, though his trademark was slow and steady. Table manners, his mother taught him. Bed manners, he was an autodidact. He had, he knew, the kind of manners that only came from professionalism. George was a gigolo and loved being a gigolo almost as much as he loved being a dancer. And the one followed from the other. What he didn't understand was that bed manners were largely an extension of table manners. When George spread Carole's legs and knelt on the floor to worship and feast on her beauty, he kept his elbows on the sheets. And when she protested, "No, hard and fast," he relinquished. It was a role he could play, too. So he rolled her. Harded and fasted her.

Downstairs, Fieldsie threw off the nurse's garb and skated into the kitchen where James Atwood was sitting on a crate with a bottle of hooch. She cleared off a space on the marble counter and lay on it, sighing. "This is the coolest place in the house."

Lubitsch came in, looking for a bottle opener, blowing clouds of cigar smoke.

"Who's that?" said James Atwood, waving away the smoke.

"Lubitsch."

"Lou who?" said James Atwood, with wonderment at the mix of matter-of-fact tone and profanity.

"Lubsey. The director." Fieldsie put quotation marks in the air around the last word.

"Never heard of him."

"You've heard of the Depression?" Fieldsie echoed Louella in a loud enough voice for Lubitsch to hear. "That's Lubsey's career." Coked out and feeling good about her witticism, she smiled at James Atwood, who was staring at the triangular hedgerow between her legs.

"Like pussy?"

"Uh-huh."

"Are you really a gangster?"

"Yep."

"Wanna fuck me?"

"Sure."

"THE HOLLYWOOD REPORTER"

by Louella Parsons

As you might have expected, I have investigated this Raft/baseball connection to death. And so far the score is: Forces of Conceal-ment 1, Louella 0. I have just plain struck out. The principals in-volved claim to have principles that forbid revealing anything juicy to the likes of Louella Parsons. They are just a hard nut to crack. But the game is still afoot. It ain't over till Mr. Arbuckle sings the national anthem in Sportsman's Park. And he's still got his chops in a donut. Which brings us back to Mr. Raft, who often has his chops in the same donut that got our dear Fatty into so much hot water. I'd like to rinse their mouths out with sodium pentothal. You, John Q and Jane (Peters) Public, deserve it. What I have been able to ascertain is that Branch Rickey and George Raft share one, and probably only one, characteristic—they're both early risers. When George is on a set, he's up at five a.m. And when Mr. Rickey wakes up it is always five a.m. Which might lead you to wonder if Mr. Raft is always an early riser . . . Take it from my Hollywood girlfriends—off the set the astonishing Mr. Raft is up, and at it, at five. And sometimes at six and seven. How could a girl take it? I'd be at sevens and nines. A little interval training for Mr. Raft, please. A proper girl does not need a marathon man. These habits, I'm told by Mr. Freud and his ilk, are traceable to potty training, and I will check in with Mrs. Raft—not his estranged wife Graycee, but Eva Ranft, his mother, on that subject. Did you know that every time she sees *Scarface*, and that's about once a week, whenever George's character is in trouble, she stands up in the theater and shouts, "Run, Georgie, run!"

14

HUMPTY DUMPTY

Storm clouds played catch-as-catch-can as Satch and Josh docked the boat in Ciudad Trujillo, formerly known as Santo Domingo, at around five p.m. on October 15, five days before the game. The breeze behind the hulking clouds ruffled the waters and seemed to unsettle the comically uniformed official. The jumpy-eyed man jabbered at Satch and Josh, telling them they had to cough up some cash, and fast, if they wanted to forgo the diplomatic niceties of having passports stamped. Satch pacified the man. Then he and Josh took a taxi to the Grand Hotel Dominicana, with orders from Harry Bennett to get Martin Dihigo out of the country within twenty-four hours. Harry was ambivalent about their success. He didn't want to appear to be subverting the blacks' efforts to field the strongest team possible. He also had a hard time believing that one Cuban could spell the difference between victory and defeat. Plus, the whole adventure got the ex-Navy man back on the water, which he loved, while appealing to the pirate in him. Still, twenty-four hours was all Satch and Josh would have to pull off the extradition with his help. Beyond that, they were on their own.

"*El inmortál*" or "*el maestro*," as he was variously called, Dihigo *was* Cuban baseball. 6'3", 190 pounds, graceful, powerful, broad shoulders tapering out of a thin waist. Dihigo's versatility was even more valuable on a team that had only ten players, especially if the pitcher got injured. Only Josh and Cool were ahead of the Cuban slugger on Satch's "must-get" list. Satch also knew that getting him out of the Dominican Republic was a risky proposition. Dihigo himself might need some persuading, and Satch was always the master of that. Even if Dihigo was willing, Satch knew that Trujillo disapproved of players jumping teams as much as Gus Greenlee did. Even the appearance of jumping to the States would sit badly with the Dominican dictator, who had more resources than Gus did to prevent it. He had an army.

Much of Ciudad Trujillo was tacky. Even the clouds over the city could be tacky. English has no verb to express cloud behavior, the way French has *moutoner*, but if necessity is the mother of invention, the sky would give birth to a homonymic variation of the verb: *to tack*. The shame of it was that Ciudad Trujillo needed only a nudge to be phenomenal. "It would be great, if . . . ," but *dios* left the city bereft of a subordinate clause. Tacky. Unto the nocturnal birds and insects that sounded like scratchy wiper blades. A plague of cicadas greeted them. Immodest *bestias*, they flew into the faces of Satch and Josh, alighted on their arms as soon as they exited the taxi at the Grand Hotel Dominicana, one or more of them crushed with every step. The women all wore ground-dragging skirts, and now it was evident why—the panic of a bunch of *bestias* suddenly taking off and flying straight up.

A boy from the Grand Hotel Dominicana grabbed Josh's and Satch's suitcases as soon as the taxi man removed them from the trunk. The three of them watched a younger boy drop both of his eggs on the Ciudad Trujillo sidewalk, look up and around with muted concern, then toddle back into the Mi Pan bakery and mumble in the frontierless interior language of three-year-olds. The baker indicated, with fingertips that collapsed like a trap door, that the rains might come at any time, in buckets, "the tears of the gods," he said. He took from the boy a tattered, perforated bill of a denomination too small to purchase anything. He rolled the bill into a cigar shape, handed it back to the boy with a gum drop and sent him away with a pat, shoes slapping the sidewalk like raindrops.

Across the street from the Grand Hotel, a robotic acolyte pulling on a bell-rope, a bald-headed prelate shilling, wrought iron, ribbons and the rubbish of the previous night's parade in honor of the big game between Ciudad Trujillo's *Escogido* team and San Pedro Macoris's *Estrellas Orientales*. Satch and Josh entered the hotel lobby and headed for the rickety elevator. The operator's broken sandal strap slapped the floor like the tail of an animal on its nethers. It was the day of the big game, the operator informed Josh and Satch on the elevator that only worked when operated by Manuel, who clutched the slide with one hand and with the other clasped the overhead track at its limit, closing the circuit, electricity surging harmlessly through him, ungrounded. He looked, from the dark of the elevator's recess like one of those perfectly outlined silhouettes in a gray wall through which a cartoon character had crashed, leaving a perfect, sharp, carved image.

As they passed each floor's translucent rectangle of coop-wired glass, Manuel momentarily came back, somebody's celluloid. Satch wondered if the explanation of closing the circuit was fanciful or just plain bullshit. Or maybe his Spanish, like Josh's, needed subtitles. Manuel also told them that he had been a pitcher with *Escogido* until he broke his fingers in the elevator.

A quirk of architecture in the Grand Hotel Dominicana forced Satch, Josh, and the boy carrying their bags to exit the elevator and ascend a half-flight of stairs above the top floor, into the domain of sheets drying in the skylight, before descending another half flight to their room. The descent was signaled by an old, cheaply framed movie poster of Greta Garbo, held with blistered, discolored Scotch tape to the slanted stucco over the stairwell. In this small Dominican heaven Garbo lived— bleached out, stained, her once-warm, white neck looking like the underarm of a much perspired-in blouse. The boy leading Satch and Josh to their *cuarto* looked up at the *gringa* goddess and tripped, busting his *huevos* on the stairs. In this occult corner of the Grand Hotel, a few kilometers from the Tropic of Cancer, another prostrate young man perplexed in short pants and bowed to a white pietà. Satch looked at him and smiled, head turning from side to side, knowingly. If he spoke better Spanish, he'd tell the kid about the hook slide and the Polly Adler sheets that two years hence would come to be called "DiMaggios," emblems of Joe's whole repertoire of dealing with women.

Josh and Satch unknowingly carried half a dozen cicadas on their backs. The *bestias* alighted in the ballplayers' room and crowed from corners to the night's sybaritic feats elsewhere. Josh and Satch would sleep without sheets in the air that besogged the concrete. In this air came other *bestias* that bit, hummed softly, played with one's blood the craps of dengue, malaria.

A finger in the hole where the bathroom doorknob once was made an impression on an unsuspecting roach. Satch was astounded by the catholicity of puddles he surveyed through the window. In the background a ten-year-old Dominican Louis Armstrong held a high note while outside in one of the puddles something moved—two antennae surveyed the air then disappeared. The good ship *cicada* was lost as the young Armstrong's breath gave out.

Satch and Josh were hot and worn-out by the trip. So when Satch, who never did anything on time, suggested putting off the search for Dihigo till after a plunge in the ocean, Josh readily agreed. There was a beach just a block from the hotel. They changed into swimming trunks, and Satch asked at the desk for a tube.

A stream flowed into the bay at the far side of the beach. The good and vulcanized ship Satch shoved off, ass dragging over rocks and detritus. On his left, jutting out of the jetty, was a stone tablet as flat as the one God gave to Moses. It would serve, he thought, as a reasonable tombstone. But now it was the shitter of seagulls, who inscribed it in earthly white cipher.

The sun would not long remain up over the water, and the gibbous moon was gaining over the hotel. Satch saw some kids throwing stones, pitchers in the making, and he recalled his own stone-throwing education, learning to hesitate in his delivery so that white kids would duck, then straighten up, then get hit, get to be part of the larger collage of the artist performing his way out of Mobile.

Between the grunt and snore parameters of this long day, Satch watched the wealthy, white and high-*yaller* adolescent girls strut in pairs and decided that the collective word for them should be an *orgullo*, a pride. Between the perfection of sunrise and the blood-orange setting, he decided that the collective word for clouds should be a "chaos," and soon he would watch a chaos of clouds fret over the boundaries of self and not-self and swab inconstantly over a sky going blue to black, with a moon going imperceptibly to half and perceptibly to bright white, then under.

At dusk a dark hubcap slipped past Satch and Josh in thigh-deep water. The stingray was followed five minutes later by an eighteen-inch shark, a baby driven by plans it was too young to execute, making a dry run, shark acting-out. The ventral-finned pickle flirted with Josh's shins, trying out different angles of attack, as if posing—slash, backslash—modeling, those keyboard characters substituted for cuss. Moments later, safe on a sandbar, Satch and Josh watched a veritable mushroom cloud approach, gobbling the lighter gray scudders, a strange, sudden collusion of clouds all becoming one. It seemed a premonition. Josh liked that feeling of just-before-storm more than the storm itself—kid-on-deck anticipation, where all things were possible before the reality of facing some proto-ace with intentions of mowing him down.

Then the mosquitoes came, saturating the air, their constant high whine eerily mimicking President Trujillo's high falsetto when he was emotional, when someone was going to feel his wrath, the brush of the *cantaclar* (the iron whip he was so fond of) on his back, the theme song of the Republic of Malaria.

Back at the hotel, Josh, who was afraid of lightning, showered first and rushed down to the bar for a beer. Satch, as usual, dallied. The only Spanish he knew was picked up from the other Cuban slugger, Cristóbal Torriente, in a *latino* bar in New York: *Dos cervezas.* Torriente had said it every time they were empty, and Josh got to know it, to like it. *Dos cervezas.* The pronunciation was not elegant, but the ambient helped to disambiguate. In a bar, anything that sounded like "two beers" should bring two beers, no? So in every *latino* bar in the U.S. or south of the border, Josh ordered two beers, which worked out if he had company, and just as fine if it was only himself. Except for strikes, two of anything sounded better than one.

The problem in the Dominican Republic was pronunciation. The natives were not used to the Gibson drawl. In the bar at the Grand Ho-tel Dominicana, Josh ordered his *dos cervezas*, and the waiter kept re-peating it with a questioning intonation and no movement toward the bar. Josh started to get irritated, and barked *"dos cervezas"* like an um-pire calling "ball four," and pointing to the bar like an umpire pointing to first base. If the man understood baseball, he'd understand that call. The waiter nodded petulantly and came back with twelve opened beer bottles.

"Doce cervezas," he said, putting them on the table before Josh. It was a hot night, thought the Crawfords' slugger, so what the hell. The first four went down in one relatively continuous swallow. Time to burp and contemplate the fate of the remaining eight. Satch would be down soon, he thought, and he'd be spending a lot of time at the bar *pissoir*, to which he momentarily repaired.

The *pissoir* was not a room per se, any more than the bar was just a bar. It was a cathouse, as most bars were. The way you'd find vending machines in U.S. bars you'd find *putas* in Dominican Republic bars. Still, Josh did a double take at the *pissoir*. It consisted of a five-foot-high wall coming perpendicularly out of the back wall of the bar. One eight-inch step up to the wall itself, which had a thin, rusted pipe running its length, parallel to the floor, with holes in it to let water drip down the wall onto which one pissed. Piss *al fresco*, with the *señoritas* walking by the other side of the wall, looking at you with your dick in your hand, and smiling. Josh couldn't help smiling back. Dominican ambient at its best.

A short, busty *señorita* was giving him the eye. She walked to the wall and stuck a cigar in his mouth, then took a matchbook from her largely exposed cleavage and lit it. Josh didn't know quite what to make of it. There was some connection between the cigar in his mouth and the dick in his hand and the *señorita* who was smiling at him, and it all made him smile. The girl had panache. She also had the clap, but that would not be a problem for the slugger. Satch would tear him away to watch Dihigo, who had the clout.

He went back to his *doce cervezas* minus *quatro*, thinking that the name of the bar—La Cigarra—meant "cigar," when in fact it meant "cicada." Still—what a magical language—you ask for two and get twelve! The possibilities went to his head. Would it work with money? With women?

The waiter walked by, giving him a strange smile and waving in a way that seemed to Josh almost a salute. Josh smiled back and saluted. An hour later Satch slapped him on the back. "What'chu doin? We gotta get Dihigo."

"It wasn't me, horse. Honest. All I did was order two beers and the guy brought twelve."

"Man, you pitiful. How we gonna get Dihigo tonight?"

"We ain't. He can wait. We gonna have steak tonight."

"Yeah? How come?"

"Bullfight yesterday."

"What about Dihigo?"

"We don't even know where he lives. We'll get him at the park, tomorrow."

The next morning, not early, Josh was awakened when a cheap warped print of Van Gogh's bizarre stars fell off the wall, reminding him of the blackboard that fell in the one-room schoolhouse he attended in Buena Vista, Georgia. The blackboard had taken too many Klan potshots and too many screeches from white chalk, and so the vault one day cracked and dropped at Miss Jeffcoat's feet, leaving grammar rules in shards, imitating Humpty Dumpty, whose rhyme Josh had been reciting. "Humpty Dumpty"—that sobriquet given to piss-poor ballplayers.

"Hey, Satch, wake up."

"Why?"

"It's nine o'clock."

"I wouldn't get up at nine o'clock to see Lincoln free the slaves. Besides, this is the Dominican Republic. No one is up at nine."

Someone swept, someone hammered, someone looked to see if it was discreet to pee, someone walked the streets hawking newspapers. The sweeper was skinnier than Satch, nearly as slender as her broom handle. She spoke to a hammock vendor about the big game, and hammock-man's eyes came alive. He guffawed at San Pedro's chances, while the radio urged them to do the Hokey Pokey and the young sweeping-girl held her broom by the far handle end and swung it like a baseball bat, removing the night's accumulation of dust from a spanking pink toilet bowl in a loose crate with easy, compromising slats. She turned and noticed Satch watching her, unequivocally beautiful and smiling whitely.

On the second floor across the street a small boy in pajamas, who looked to be sleepwalking, proceeded to the edge of the patio and let fly a stream of urine over the wall into the dark street with a seven-year-old's nonchalant satisfaction at the graceful arc, high as his head.

Satch had convinced Josh that they'd be wasting their time hunting Dihigo in the morning. He had to play in the final game with San Pedro in the late afternoon. They'd just get there early and clue him in. Manuel told them that the best beach was a fifteen-minute bus ride from the city. It was where they'd find the high-class *señoritas*. At the bus stop a man ran across the street and into an alley with no one chasing him, looking deranged, and shouting, "They already killed my brother and all my family. Tell them I am not Ellobin Cruz but Anibal Vallejo."

No one said anything. The man who was not Ellobin Cruz vanished, leaving Satch and Josh spooked, a reminder of what went on behind the scenes of a dictatorship. Josh and Satch watched a smallish man, wiry as a chicken, pull a cart down an unpaved side street, in *caballo* traces. Half-man, half-horse. He was stuck. But it hardly registered on his face. He tugged. Rested. Tugged again, until Josh couldn't stand it any longer. He eased the man from the harness and stepped into it. He heaved, and the cart laden with wood launched out of the mud at the bottom of a small incline. Josh pulled it to the top, halfway down the block, while kids cheered, uttered encouragement he did not understand, and flexed their bony biceps, which he did understand.

The man muttered, *"Gracias."*

"De nada," Josh replied. He, too, learning.

It was 1934. In the U.S., baseball was still the national pastime, though football and basketball had already made inroads. In the Dominican Republic, there was only baseball, as there was only one God, which was more than a trinity. It was father, son, holy ghost, and *beisbol*.

Out of the alley where Josh had helped the cart-man, there emerged a man in a baseball uniform, in his early forties and not a god or even a demiurge, though not from lack of trying. He was 5'10" and lanky, muscular in that sinewy way, ironwood arms and legs, and looked bigger than he was. The energy was still there in the body. He was an athlete. You could sense the quickness with which he would still move to a ball and the rifling speed of his release. Kids looked at him and tried to touch him, as if touching his fantastic muscles would heal them of their own reflex slowness, the unsnap of their skinny arms. But his face was telling another story. The story of a fall from the grace that was *Las Estrellas* or *Escogido*. It was etched in the split seam of his lips. *Has been. Almost was.* He had a name, but few knew it. Call him *beisbolista*.

After a breakfast of scrambled eggs that came mixed with minced *habaneros*, they headed for the bus. Satch stopped at the first corner to get his shoes shined.

"That's the fourth time since you got here."

"The kids need the money."

"Just give it to them. We gotta get to the beach, then get Dihigo."

"Can't just give it to 'em. It's not American."

"We ain't in America."

"It's like Moe Berg says, horse. Baseball is culture. We gotta teach 'em the American way."

"They teachin' you, Satch—Dominican sense of time."

On the bus. A four-year-old started wailing.

"I like kids crying, sometimes," Josh said, looking out the window at a restaurant that no one had eaten in, a hotel where no one stayed.

"You smoking reefer again?"

Josh shook his head. "When they crying, they need you. That feels good."

Satch did a double take. "That's fucked up, man."

Satch's words rang hollow to himself as he said it, and he didn't have the words for the nuance he felt.

Josh did. "It's like when you burn one in and it hurts, but it's good. It's like the hand needs the ball."

Satch's mind wandered to the variety of offerings that came from his outsized hand, all meant to deceive. Why he was a pitcher *and* a philanderer. "Remember the guy we saw, the ballplayer? The man's a hero."

Part of that made sense to Josh. Part was not enough. "Okay, man, give it to me. Why's he a hero?"

"Why he's a hero? 'Cuz he didn't make it." Satch looked Josh in the eye. "He's still trying."

"What else is he gonna do?"

Satch looked around at the men pulling wagons, sweeping sidewalks, begging. He nodded in their direction. "You think some of them wasn't ballplayers?"

Josh smiled. "Guess that makes you a hero, too. Makes both of us heroes."

Satch gave a halfhearted chuckle, his head bobbing in inchoate agreement. Josh sat back and raked his upper lip with his lower teeth. "Don't know how much longer I can."

Can what? Satch wanted to ask, but didn't. He figured Josh meant he didn't know how much longer he could go on, but he didn't want to make him say it. He didn't want to hear it. "If you made it to the Bigs, you'd gain something, but you'd be losing something, too."

Josh held his breath momentarily to avoid breathing the noxious emissions of the bus they were passing, then snarled. He wouldn't dignify Satch's assertion with a comment or a question, and he knew Satch well enough, knew that he'd expand on it on his own.

"What you'd be losing is the anger that makes you so good, what makes you hit the ball so hard, like you're punishing it 'cuz it's white."

Josh punched the aluminum back of the seat in front of him so hard Satch thought he'd dent it. "I'd hit it just as hard."

Satch smiled at the corner of his mouth, turning his head sideways. "Wouldn't be the same. You'd be losing what your life is all about."

"What my life is about? You can have what my life is all about. Hell, you already got it. You can keep it."

Satch's attention was diverted to a woman with a tin container of bananas on her head. Josh could see Satch's mouth turned down in a frown. "You been listening to Willie and that DuBois stuff."

"I listen to everybody," said Josh, "but I make up my own mind."

* * *

At every bus stop they were mobbed by *tigritos* selling *chicles* and sucking on sugarcane. Naked kids with distended bellies were everywhere, untended. Older kids played catch with papayas or lemons or something like a stuffed sock, with milk cartons fashioned into gloves. The kids who lived near the truck depot sometimes had gloves made from the tarps that covered the trucks, pieces of which were cut and stolen at the risk of their lives.

The bus driver looked at Satch in the rectangular mirror that had a purpose on an American schoolbus but served none here. He readjusted the position of the machete on the dashboard in front of the steering wheel. Satch recoiled, and the driver laughed. He spoke so slowly Satch could understand him.

"Is okay, *gringo,* is okay. Is not for you. Is for the ones who have something and call us 'barefoot.' The truth makes us fight. Maybe that's why we fight all the time. Here is the beach. You get off here. Hey, maybe I see you at the baseball game, no?" With his gold chains and gold watch and tailored clothes and big smile and good *gringo* looks, Satch saw *señoritas* smiling everywhere. Starry nights were on his mind, where all knowledge was private, all desires pocket-sized.

Josh pointed at an elderly obese woman sunning herself on the beach. Her skin resembled the yolk of a Chinese thousand-year-old egg. She overwhelmed a beach chair like an immense yellow yolk over a depression-sized serving of hash, everyone dreading the consequences, should she break—envelopment by runny flesh. Then she rose, bent over to grasp a bag, exposing a chiaroscuro of crooks, crannies, spandrels undreamt in the architecture of flesh.

Decay had hit a growth spurt in the cove. A fraction of hammock hung from a palm tree, thin ropes bleached to bones of an exotic skeleton—Venetian-blinds manqués. They spread their towels on the beach. A noisy PT boat passed, driven by a man in full military uniform. With him in the boat was a girl Satch took for one of Trujillo's minions. The boat pulled a water skier across the bay, throwing up a plume of polluted water like a rummaged peacock tail or a cherub pissing off the boat's stern, while the boat missed the head of a fallen water-skier by the width of a losing lottery ticket stub.

The PT boat slowed down and approached the shore. Through the knee-high surf came gamboling a tall girl with a floppy hat and a buxom girl with one thinner, polio-stricken leg, both of them beautiful. They spread a *petate* and blankets commensurate with their economic and political status in the city. The shorter girl's breasts in Satch's eyes more than compensated for her leg, and she listened to the tall girl with the floppy hat talk about her waterskiing with the arrogance of a Shibe Park luxury box and the composure of a chain-link fence.

Satch was juggling two oranges. "Think I can make an orange curve, horse?"

"I'm not catchin' an eighty-mile-an-hour breaking orange without a glove." Josh picked up a length of sugarcane and took a batting stance. "Try to get that one by me."

Half of the orange disintegrated on impact and the other half flew all the way to the ocean. Everyone watching was stunned. Satch lowered his voice. "Throw me some flies, that way."

Satch made a couple of impressive diving catches, each one closer to the two Dominican beauties. The next catch put him practically on their *petate*.

"Ay, coño," said the short buxom girl with the thin leg.

"Como se llama, mama?" Satch asked the taller girl, the one who had been waterskiing. She watched the gold chain sway on his neck, then rolled her eyes with a look that retained a note of flirtation, and turned her attention back to a not-too-outdated Hollywood tabloid, in English, with a number of slang expressions underlined in pencil.

Satch read the embroidered red letters of the white towel spread over the cane-sliver *petate*. "La Reina de Beisbol Escogido, 1930," which he could understand—"Queen of Baseball Escogido, 1930." Red was the color of Trujillo's team. *Escogido*—The Chosen.

"Te gusta el beisbol? Yo soy pitcher."

"Enséñame un hombre Dominicano que no es pitcher."

"What's she sayin'?" asked Josh.

"Something about a man who's not a pitcher." Satch lifted himself to a sitting position. *"Tu—la reina?"* he said, pointing at her.

"Ex-reina."

"Uva pasada," said her glum but just as comely companion, with a dose of friendly sarcasm. Satch understood *uva pasada*—raisin, but not the complexity of the comparison.

The *reina* slapped her companion. *"Callate, negra,"* she said with the mock anger of an intimate friend. She noticed the complete puzzlement on Satch's face. "She means I'm resting on my laurels," she said in English and with, thought Satch, a slight wiggle of the well-made laurels.

"You speak English," said Satch with a tone that started in the interrogative and ended in the declarative.

"I had an Irish nanny."

"Es muy negro," said the companion with a scornful look.

Satch smiled. "I'm a nigger? You bet'cha. You got a little brown sugar in those *nalgas* yourself."

"Qué dice?" said the companion, who understood as much English as Satch did Spanish. The *reina* smiled and declined to translate. She addressed Satch, "She really didn't mean that. She's just jealous."

The companion did not contest it. Satch changed the subject. "What's a *reina de beisbol?*"

The queen laughed. "We take baseball very seriously here. It's another religion, actually. It's like voodoo to our neighbors, the Haitians. When we play the series with San Pedro de Macoris, there is a *fiesta*, and a parade, and when there is a parade there is a queen. Four years ago, I was elected."

"Escogido," said Satch, proud of his Spanish pun.

"Escogida," she corrected his gender error.

"Por que hablas con los negros norteamericanos?" said the companion.

"We ain't any Negroes, we're *beisbolistas*," said Satch.

"That's right. We *beisbolistas*," said Josh, squatting.

"Vayanse correr las bases, pues," said the companion. "Like she said, all men *beisbolistas* in *La Republica Dominicana.*"

Satch put on a serious look. "We ain't sugar-ballers. We're professionals."

"Como se dice 'arena'?" the companion asked the queen.

"Sand."

"You put the sand on me, my face."

"Sorry, Miss, we was just playin'," said Josh.

"Showing off," said the queen.

"I want water to wash my face."

"I'll get you some," said Josh, standing up.

"No! No, you. *El flacito.* He did it," she said peevishly.

"No problem." Satch got up. "You want something? Beer? Coke?" he asked the queen, who shook her head.

"No the restaurant," said the companion. "I no want water of the restaurant. I want *coco*-water." She pointed up at the coconuts hanging from the top of the palm tree that shaded their blankets. *"Agua coco."*

You needed a death wish to get to the *cocos*. You needed to be a fourth-story man, straight up, to get them. You needed to have either a death wish or a stupid-bone in your head to sit under a coconut tree. When a *coco* hit your head it was traveling at the speed of Satch's change-up, and your head would be no match for a *coco*.

Skimpy, scraggly, these palms. If there was a verb form of *hilarious*, palm trees would utter it through the split, many-times forked tongues of green at the top of the sixty-foot trunks. Josh shook his head. "Don't do it, Satch. You'll fall down and break your ass. We got the game, remember?"

"Don't seem to be much to it. One foot after the other. All those other guys do it."

"You'll break yer ass, man. Humpty-nigger-Dumpty. I ain't lettin' you do it."

But Satch was already three steps up and moving like a native. "Nothin' to it, man."

Halfway up he stopped, looked down, and was having second thoughts.

"Go, monkey," said the companion, smiling for the first time.

"Come on down or I'll put those *cocos* up your skinny ass!" said Josh.

Satch looked up and down, then up again. He got a second climbing wind and proceeded slowly up the tree. The locals stopped whatever they were doing and watched, laughing and shouting things in Spanish that Satch couldn't understand. They had never seen a *gringo* climb a palm tree, but it made sense that the first one would be black. Satch reached a group of coconuts and dropped three. He didn't want to have to repeat the climb in case the girl wanted another. The *cocos* thudded in the sand, not entirely accidentally, next to the companion.

"*Coño de mono!* Yump! I geeve you a beeg kees." She was, in spite of herself, impressed at Satch's athleticism. Satch had his limits, even for a kiss. He climbed down and hopped in the sand, grimacing. "That hurts my feet." He picked up a *coco* and waved to one of the guys with machetes. "*Jefe!*"

The man efficiently sliced open the *coco* for the companion, who drank some of the liquid and washed her face with the rest.

"Some of the *campesinos* think that the coco water is, how do you say, *aphrodisiaco*?"

"Never heard of that one."

"*Qué lastima, flacito. Grandote tambien,*" said the companion through a laugh, then added, "*Corta-cañas del Norte.*"

"What's she complaining about now?"

The *reina* smiled and shook her head. "She just wants someone to take her to the game. And if you climb trees like a Dominican, she thinks you're not really baseball players. You're cane-cutters."

"My friend thinks that because you are so black you're really not professional baseball players."

"We got our own league," said Josh.

The queen looked at Satch. "If you're really a pitcher, you will throw that *coco* into the ocean."

Josh shook his head. "Here we go again."

Satch hefted the *coco*. "Don' try it, Satch. You'll hurt your arm."

Satch nodded. "Ain't worth it."

Josh felt relieved. Satch held out the *coco*. "You got to bail me out, horse."

Josh turned away. "Me? No way. I'm not throwin' my arm out for a couple of broads."

The queen turned over onto her stomach. "Then you and your supposed pitcher friend will have to go back to your little towels and play in the sand."

"Give it a toss, horse. You can shot-put it that far." Satch felt him wavering. "Come on, man. I see the Fordham Flash stealin' on you."

Josh gave a scornful smile, then gripped the *coco*, wound up, hopped a couple of steps and let fly. It landed in the sand ten yards short of the surf.

"Man, that was pitiful."

"Too bad," said the queen, taking a bottle of toe-polish from her straw bag and opening the top. Satch had already taken off after the *coco*.

"Forget it, Satch. You're not throwin' your arm out for some pussy."

"Am I a cat?" said the ex-queen of the game, making claws with her fingers and the one painted toenail, smiling, not understanding the slang. Satch started back, tossing the *coco* up and down in his right hand. He stopped fifty feet from his battery mate, wound up and threw, saying, "Catch this, horse."

He threw a strike that Josh caught like an egg, to cushion the impact. "Gimme another."

"Get me a glove, then I'll give you another." Josh pulled a sliver from his left palm. Satch picked the *coco* from where Josh had dropped it.

"Let me," said the companion, in an unexpected gesture of sympathy. Josh let her apply her sharp nails to the sliver while Satch wound up. The *coco* flew high and the timing was serendipitous. A wave came in, bringing the tide mark a meter or two farther in, with enough water that a splash went up as the *coco* splatted into the wet sand. The *coco*-tree climbers and beach-detritus cleaners jabbered to each other. It was a truly stupendous throw, after which Satch grabbed his shoulder and Josh shook his head fearfully.

"Ay! Mi amor!" said the queen.

"Increible," said the companion.

"What's that mean?" asked Josh.

"It means we're in like Flynn. They've never seen anything like it."

"Neither have I. How's the shoulder?"

The girls were now squeezing Satch's arm. Satch smiled and said, "That ain't nothin'. Feel the big boy's."

The ex-queen's companion felt Josh's biceps. *"Grandote."*

"You will play for *Escogido*, today, no?"

"Baby, Ol' Satch'll do anything that pleases you." Satch grabbed his arm histrionically and grimaced. "Thing is, I can't pitch worth a damn without some lovin.' "

"Yeah. Me, too."

"You no pitcher," said the companion.

"I'm the only one who can catch that smoke he throws."

Satch looked at the companion. "Honey, you know who Babe Ruth is?"

"Coño. Sí. I know who is Babe Ruth."

"Well, when you're looking at Babe Ruth, you're looking at the white Josh Gibson."

"Yosh Geebson. *Honron,* yes?" The companion smiled, squeezing his arm. Josh looked at her quizzically, not understanding *"honron."*

"Home run. Yes, indeed," said Satch, clearing it up for Josh. "Y'all get your things and come with us. We got some game preparation to do. I see a no-hitter comin.' I'm feelin' the inspiration pumpin' through me right now."

"What about Dihigo?" said Josh.

"Ay! You know *el maestro?"*

"El rentado," said the companion, with her typical saturninity. Both San Pedro de Macoris and *Escogido* had paid large sums to bring in ringers, said to be "rented" for the occasion.

"All the time, baby. *El maestro* and us go way back."

Josh's question went unanswered. Somehow, he didn't feel like asking it again. The girl was squeezing his biceps and smiling, mumbling, *"Honron."*

"Amigo," said Josh, smiling and touching her with his forefinger just above the breast.

"Amiga," she corrected him, touching herself squarely on the breast. *"Amigo,"* she said, touching his.

"Buenos amigos," you and me, baby.

He was learning. *Dos muchachas* would be the next phrase he memorized. He was right about the lingo, he thought, with some satisfaction. *Dos* was everything. *Dos* was the magic. And *doce* was not far behind. *Dose* of everything but the clap, please God.

They walked on the sand's unique, random, pink speckling—like jimmies, that made it look almost edible. Satch's eyes were drawn to the single strap on the tall girl's unique bathing suit, a fashion misstatement that struggled to support a compensating generosity that incited a few *"mamacita"*'s from the beach's aristocratic, *macho flaneurs,* ultimate arbiters of beach taste, of that which hung in the balance.

"You girls got names?"

"Inmaculata Altagracia Troncoso de la Paz."

"Flerida Inocencia Arismendi Molina."

"You ain't got names. You got a whole team."

15

GET DIHIGO

The exhaust from the diesel trucks outside the stadium was so thick that Satch and his party put handkerchiefs to their mouths and closed their eyes as long as they could, getting through it. Satch brushed small black particles of soot off his white linen suit and Panama hat. A large circle formed just outside the main gate, around a cockfight where a lot of money exchanged hands. The fights were fast, and it seemed to Satch that the white cocks always won. His shoes already having been shined five times, he bought a packet of *mani* (roasted peanuts) from a different *tigrito* every hundred feet, letting the kids keep the change. By the time they got to the gate, they had a small army of *tigritos* chasing after them.

Satch looked at the larger-than-life-size painting of Trujillo and his wife, which graced the entry to the stadium. The dictator was 5'7" and 130 pounds, about the size of Kommissar Landis. The artist had blown him up to about six feet, whitened his skin and straightened his hair significantly. Satch almost expected the portrait to exude the smell of the president's perfume, the application of which was the only thing liberal about the man. He was in full military regalia—epaulets, red jacket, and a bicorne hat with long ostrich feathers. *If I looked like a mad scientist's attempt to cross a pullet and a human,* thought Satch, *I wouldn't hang my portrait in a baseball stadium.*

Inmaculata Altagracia Troncoso de la Paz kissed him on the cheek and went to pose for a photo in the gallery of ex-queens and finalists for this year's honor, from which Trujillo would take his pick of partners for the coming week. Flerida and Josh waited as Satch stopped at the men's room, where he read the *graffito* on the wall in front of him: *EnEste Letrino Trujillo Es El Jefe*—"in this latrine Trujillo is the boss." He figured that the "r" was missing from "Erneste," and that the dictator's full name was Erneste Letrino Trujillo. It was a mistake he might have paid dearly for.

The afternoon sun made playing right field, or right center, one of the toughest jobs in Ciudad Trujillo. Whereas most Dominican teams had few or no left-handers, *Escogido* was stacked with them, and some of them would go to the plate with a fungo bat and try to sky balls to right field. You didn't wait to tag up on a fly to right, you just took off, with a high probability that it would drop. The *Escogido* right fielder was so often a goat that his position was called *cabrero*.

Flerida, Inmaculata, Satch, and Josh took their seats. Satch had bought scalped seats on the third-base side, as close as he could get to the home-team dugout, where he could razz or encourage Dihigo. They were also in eye- and earshot of the presidential gallery, where Trujillo sat with the new queen, his wife, Deputy Aybar, lackeys, soldiers, sycophants, and assorted hangers-on. A well-placed bomb would have wiped out the whole Trujillo family—his brother Hector, known as *el Negro*, with whom the president didn't like to be seen in public because of how dark he was; his brother Pipi, who ran the fruit monopoly; his sister, Japonesa, who ran the lottery; and his son Ramfis, who was made a colonel at age three. Like Trujillo, Secretary of Foreign Affairs Arturo Lograno was making his annual trip to the ballpark. Not that he was uninterested, but getting his three hundred and fifty pounds up stairs and into ordinary seats was a problem. Lograno refused to ride in cars, citing a preference for old ways, but the truth was he couldn't fit. An open carriage, an entire seat of which he filled, was the only way he could get around. He was further renowned for his custom-made chamber pot, made from a converted *olla*, a kind of crock used to ship olives from Spain. It was five feet by two feet, not much smaller than the secretary himself, a man full of a whole lot of shit.

Trujillo's cultural informant at these games was Dr. Jose Enrique Aybar, Deputy of the National Congress and an avid baseball fan. Aybar was a soap-box jockey, a cynic, and a dentist, whose one requirement for an office was that it be on *Tiradentes* (tooth-puller) Avenue.

Trujillo himself was in a foul mood, recovering from an operation for urethritis, for which Dr. Marion had inserted surgical tubes in a delicate area. He had trouble standing, then when standing he had trouble sitting. In short, transitions were problematic for the dictator. He sat now with a glass of sour milk and a plate of tortoise eggs, the former because he liked it and the latter for virility. Arturo Lograno did not want to be among the presidential party. He knew that the combination of pissing pain and losing the San Pedro game spelled trouble all around. The president had already threatened to surgically remove fifty pounds of flab from his belly, and he had broken one of Trujillo's favorite seventeenth-century Spanish chairs just by sitting on it.

"Hey, *bombilla*," said the president. "I have an idea. If we get three men on and need a run, I'm going to put you in to pinch-hit. Your belly will completely cover the strike zone." Trujillo laughed, which signaled those around him to laugh, until he winced with pain in the groin. *"Ay, coño!"*

He watched the transvestites doing *merengue* on the dugout, with a mixture of entertainment and repulsion, the latter not strong enough for him to put a stop to it. It was a tradition he could live with, and he was smart enough not to take from the masses a pleasure that didn't cost him anything.

Soldiers surrounded the stadium on the outside and the field on the inside. Controlled democracy, both on the field, where the rules were the same for everyone, and in the stands, where the spectator could root for either team and not be shot. For two hours, democracy was allowed to rule in the game of the people, the game that had replaced bullfighting, the pastime of the *conquistadores*, whose descendents tried to ban the game, fearing the literal use of bats and balls as instruments of rebellion.

On the field, *brujos* representing Ciudad Trujillo and San Pedro went through a ritual duel, each putting the evil eye on the opponents. A fair amount of money was spent on charms and spells for the big game, as well as divining the winner, but much more was spent on rum. Among a crowd of ten thousand, one thousand or more bottles would be sold, which pleased the president, who personally controlled the rum industry.

Trujillo himself was not a big drinker. Before the game, while most of the men around him had shots of rum, he had his glass of horsetail tea or sour milk, then lit a votive candle to the Virgin of Altagracia, the patron saint of the Dominican Republic, put a *caprelata* (voodoo charm) around his neck, and opened the immense closet that contained the latest installments of his wardrobe of ten thousand ties, two thousand suits, and five hundred pairs of shoes. All of this with mincing steps because of the tubes that he volubly cursed, and every time he had to piss he threatened to have Dr. Marion executed. Lastly, he put on the watch that was a present of Eleanor Roosevelt, who had visited the Dominican Republic the previous March.

The first inning was an *escon*—derived from the English "skunk"—a scoreless inning. With *Escogido* behind 1–0 in the third, Dihigo came up for the second time, having walked in the first. Originally from Cuba, Dihigo wore number "8" on the back of his uniform, which signified "death" in Cuban kabala. He thought it would intimidate pitchers. *El inmortál* also found walks an indignity. With a 3-0 count, he would swing at anything. The San Pedro pitcher, Luis Tiant, knew it, but this time at 3-0, Dihigo made it a matter of *machismo*. He defied Tiant to burn one anywhere in the strike zone. *"Manigüero!"* he taunted the pitcher.

"What did he say?" asked Josh.

"He called him a busher."

The fan behind Josh was allergic either to baseball or to the tamales he was eating, for he sneezed as often as Tiant threw strikes, and with each sneeze Josh felt particles of wet tamale embedding in the back of his neck.

Dihigo framed a strike zone with his hands and made an obscene gesture, telling Tiant that he couldn't get it in. Tiant, a skinny left-handed finesse pitcher with a good curve and a better screwball, could be hit when behind in the count. He threw his fastball and Dihigo hammered it to right center. It was over the center fielder's head and off the wall, but he lost it in the sun and had no idea where the carom would go. He chased after the ball and threw to third, but Dihigo easily slid in for a triple. Time out was called so that he could pick up the gold coins being thrown at him. He ignored the ribbons also thrown by the *señoritas*. He put about ten coins in his pockets.

"Martin, they be calling you 'Pirate.' Loading your pockets with pieces of eight," shouted Josh.

Flerida laughed and pointed at Dihigo. *"Pi-ra-te!"*

Satch yelled, *"Manigüero,* that stuff will slow you down."

Dihigo recognized the voice. *"No, señor.* I will run faster because they will be chasing me for the gold, not the out." He didn't need to run. Tiant struck out the side and Dihigo took the mound to face Cristóbal Torriente, leading off for the *Estrellas.*

Soldiers were stationed all over the stadium. The one by the left-field foul pole was not much taller than his rifle and might have weighed a tad less than the combined weight of his carbine and bandoliers. He stood, as ordered, at attention, a Buckingham Palace guard without the big funny hat. In the Dominican sun, "attention" took on a definite Dominican tilt. Still, it would not have been a wise idea to muff it entirely. As part of the presidential guard, his posture and attention made a statement, especially when eyes might be on him, like when a fly ball headed to left field. A fly ball then could be a pivotal moment in a man's career, in his life, as it was when Torriente connected with a fastball and sent it toward the area the soldier was guarding. It didn't take long for him to realize the ball was heading right for his *cabeza.*

Memento mori and Eureka moment, rolled into one. *"Jijole, caramba, y ching!"* he said to himself. He had orders not to move, but not against shooting. In the Trujillo era the ethos was *when in doubt, shoot.* In a flash the guy had the carbine on his shoulder, and *blam, blam, blam.* Strike three. The ball passed just over his head and into the bleachers.

"Shoot that *coño*," said Trujillo. "He can't shoot."

Deputy Aybar had a way of humoring the president and toning things down. "*Presidente,* you know how bad the sun is out there. Besides, they're all cheering him. Maybe we should just let him catch Dihigo's pitches with his bare hands."

Trujillo laughed. "*Muy astuto.* Let the punishment fit the crime. *Muy astuto!*"

Aybar discreetly told a lieutenant to remove the soldier from his post and send him back to the barracks. Satch watched with amusement and some degree of jealousy. On a skeet ramble, he could hit ninety-seven out of a hundred clay pigeons. He wished it had been him. He knew he could have hit the ball. The thrill of it—ten thousand people watching you blast a baseball from the sky. Satch shook his head and smiled. Soon enough, he'd have his chance.

"I just saw a guy fall off the roof!" Satch said with his voice nearly cracking. He found it strange that play wasn't stopped and that nobody seemed to care.

"It's on account of the flags," said Inmaculata. Satch looked at the Ciudad Trujillo and San Pedro flags planted on the stadium roof, with cliques of fans guarding them. "It is *macho* to pull down the flag of your opponent, but of course there are consequences." Inmaculata nodded in the direction of the guy who fell.

Satch looked at the prostrate man, then back at Inmaculata. "You act like it's nothing. That guy is probably dead."

"The way they think in the *barrio* is that at least he died for something. The others just starve to death."

Satch was getting rattled. He looked at the eucalyptus trees towering over the stadium, with men who couldn't afford a ticket in the highest branches.

By the bottom of the seventh inning, when Dihigo came to bat again, *Escogido* was behind 3–2, thanks to Torriente's home run. *El Tiante* burned one in. "That sounded low," shouted Satch. The umpire called a strike.

"Tiant is good, man," Satch said to Josh. "Nips the frosting off the cake."

Josh nodded. "Don't too many get on."

Because of his *macho* disdain for walks, Dihigo became a good bad-ball hitter, but he sometimes bit at pitches that were way off. When he swung and missed for strike two, Satch let him have it. *"Coño!* Don't swing at that shit, Martin!"

No one called the great Dihigo *"coño"* without attracting attention. He attracted Trujillo's. "Who is that *gringo* who keeps shouting at Dihigo, the one in the Panama hat, with all the jewelry around his neck?"

Deputy Aybar stared at the tall black man and his jaw dropped. He picked up a pair of binoculars to be sure he wasn't fantasizing. *"Dios mío,* that is Satchel Paige, the Quixote *del Norte."*

Satch was alone with Flerida. Josh had left to pee, having drunk *dos cervezas.* The floor of the capacious and busy men's room was covered with more than an inch of water and urine. It really didn't matter where he peed, but he made his way to the wall, walking gingerly. If he was careful, the liquid he tramped through would not spill over the sides of his white shoes. He rolled his pant legs up anyway, as a precaution, while Porfirio Garcia swung and missed for strike three to end the inning.

The situation began to look dire for Trujillo's team. The president was no fan of baseball. He preferred horses, and went to the San Pedro series for political reasons, not for sport. His idea of sport was more along the lines of the Roman Colosseum. Still, any literate and sentient Dominican would have heard of the great *Norteamericano.* Major League and Negro League players both played winter ball in the Dominican Republic. And of course, when it came to *rentados*, the names of many of the greats came up. Trujillo put down his sour milk and demanded the binoculars of one of his lieutenants. He focused on the *gringo*, then smiled. "Enrique, take a squadron and bring *Señor* Paige to the *Escogido* dugout. Make him a reasonable offer, then put a uniform on him. Take one off one of those *pendejo*s on the bench if necessary. Then put him on the mound, and shoot Dihigo."

"Sí, comandante," said Dr. Jose Enrique Aybar.

Trujillo laughed. "I'm joking. Don't shoot Dihigo. Feed the right fielder to the crocodiles. He struck out twice and missed an easy fly ball. *Coño.* Then put Dihigo in right field."

Deputy Aybar had no intention of shooting anyone, though Trujillo would have no compunctions about shooting Cristóbal Torriente and Luis Tiant himself if the game results displeased him. "But, *Señor Presidente*, we cannot stop the game. He'll have to go in next inning."

Trujillo stood up and fired six shots into the air and spoke over the loudspeaker. "Time out! Seventh-inning stretch! Have a beer, some *chicharones*. Support your Dominican economy!" He laughed and holstered his pistol. "And do not forget that all cows are to be milked to music, to increase productivity. *Viva la República Dominicana!*"

The crowd roared its drunken approval. Merengue broke out again, on the roofs of both dugouts. "Speaking of stretch, Enrique. If we lose this game, put the whole team on the rack. Then Tiant. I can't stand to see that ridiculous motion striking out our *Escogidos*. He looks into center field, then into the heavens and doesn't even look at the batter when he throws the ball. Straighten him out."

"*Sí, comandante.*"

Satch noticed two soldiers not much taller than their guns standing at one end of his row and another two at the other end. The ones to his right were saying something that he could not pick out through the din of the fans and the foghorn. But the soldiers were persistent.

"Inmaculata, tell those guys there ain't no room in here."

"A *reina* does not talk to soldiers. You tell them."

"Ain't no room in here," said Satch. "Scoot, scat."

One of the soldiers aimed his rifle at Satch while another, with a gold epaulet hanging by threads, motioned for him to come.

"I think they want you," said Inmaculata. "You'd better go."

"Okay," said Satch, squeezing down the row. "What did I do?" He addressed the officer with the pendant epaulet. "Another parking ticket? I don't even drive down here."

A soldier jabbed Satch in the back with his rifle. "Is it the visa thing? Columbus didn't have no visa."

"*Vámonos,*" said the officer.

Satch flicked the epaulet with a finger. "Gotta get that thing fixed. Kind of limp, know what I'm saying? Looks like a toilet brush. The gold ain't foolin' nobody."

Satch was pushed, this time with a hand. He looked back at Inmaculata. "Tell Josh I be back soon as I take care of the visa thing."

"Farewell," said Inmaculata, forlornly. The word choice worried Satch. This should be a technicality that a few dollars could take care of handily.

Inmaculata Inocencia Altagracia de la Paz never quite recovered from seeing Trujillo personally execute six men here in the stadium. Now she saw the *desparecidos* whose last breaths filled the visitors' dugout. They all became very real, displacing the *Estrellas* of San Pedro de Macoris. She saw the tall *gringo* in the Panama hat take his seat unnoticed at the end of the bench and look directly at her, from beyond. She swooned and was caught by Josh, back from the loo.

"You okay? Where's Satch?"

Inmaculata pointed at the visitors' dugout. "I think he's thirsty. They all are," she said.

Puzzled, but thinking that Satch had gone to get something to drink, Josh looked at Flerida. "Visa," she said, rubbing her fingers together in that universal sign for money. Josh took his seat, uneasy. He waved to the *cerveza* man and bought two for himself. Inmaculata watched Trujillo's gaily costumed *brujo* cautiously approach Satch, who looked out at the field with the disinterest common to both the damned and the eternally saved.

Between innings and during timeouts like this, an old man planted grass in right field, by the stadium wall, with a machete. Squatting more than kneeling, with a barrow full of divots, each the size of a small birthday cake with green, cotton-candy frosting. These he broke into handfuls and planted in the rocky soil-simulacrum, at intervals, so that the field was a mosaic of rocks and divots that looked like haystacks cropped into a clown's bald head. They did not take. The field looked stitched together, the imported patches poorly sewn together, as if to deny any consanguinity of green. Secretary of Foreign Affairs Lograno looked at the man and shook his head, thinking that the whole theory, strategic hamlets of grass, was supremely improbable.

And Trujillo was wondering if he should switch his title from *generalissimo* to "Kaiser," which he'd just read came from "Caesar," but *generalissimo* had a grander sound, more syllables, and a magisterial suffix with an explosive rise in pitch. Maybe he was just window-shopping, on the *Avenida de los Dictatores*, for a new dog tag. Just trying it on. Maybe *Mahatma*, as Branch Rickey was called, would be a more resplendent fit.

The dugout Satch had been escorted to was cracked, pitted, eroded, crumbling, and decaying all at once, and it was less than ten years old. The stucco, once white, was now of random coloration, with mosses and fungi and other growth vying for dominance, while dirt and mildew built up on the sun- and humidity-eroded walls. Some of the holes were spaced so as to be unmistakably bullet-born. Others were the result of angry batsmen. Iron bars were affixed to the outside walls on both sides of the dugout, on mysterious rusted tracks that at least hinted at secondary usage of the dugout and of the stadium. Satch had a vision of the prisoners sitting here, waiting to take their turn to come up out of the ground. And they would have a name, this team—*The Croaking Lazaruses,* each one coming up with his life on the line. Satch saw them, these Latin Caseys, dissidents, looking at each other from the home and the visitors' dugouts, wondering who would be the next, blindfolded in the *on-deck* circle—an accidental irony, or the stroke of some cynical *generalissimo?* The metaphors were relentless on this field of nightmares. The present beckoned Satch, the timbre of the pop of the bat sounded like Torriente. It sounded long and deep.

Aybar found Satchel taking his time buttoning his uniform. "*Señor* Paige, it is an honor to meet you. I am Deputy Enrique Jose Aybar." Satch shook his hand.

"It is lamentable that the honor must be accompanied by a message from the president. Alas, I must tell you that the president says that every hit San Pedro gets is a tickle for you from his *cantaclar.*"

"What the fuck is that?" drawled Satch.

"I'm afraid it is an iron whip, and the tickle is to your testicles. I am also to tell you that any *señorita* of your choosing will be waiting at your hotel, if you win. Stick and carrot."

"We call it carrot and stick."

"The president has his own ways of doing things."

Satch laughed. "Yeah, he milks cows to music, divides the country among his family, and kills Haitians, mainly because they're black like me."

"You have your dynasties, just as we have ours. First, Teddy. Now Franklin. And what the president does to Haitians is the same thing your country does all over the region. Your government sends the marines to kill anyone who might interfere with your sugar companies that pay Dominicans a peso a day and treat them the way the Spaniards treated their slaves. Do you see any difference, *Señor* Paige?"

"I'm a ballplayer, not a politician."

"You know, the Dominican Republic has only one foreign policy— don't piss off Uncle Sam. Do you know what your Secretary of State Hull said about Trujillo? 'He's an SOB, but he's our SOB.' *Comprendes?* How things work? And what do you think of the way you have been treated in the Dominican Republic, as opposed to your country? Have you been called a nigger here? Been told you can't sleep in a hotel or eat at a restaurant?"

"Been kidnapped to play a baseball game," Satch said, trying on several *Escogido* hats, each one several times.

"So when you call it 'carrot and stick,' you think you are the more advanced nation, ethically? A peso a day is a fine carrot, and it keeps the peasants so weak and malnourished you don't need a stick. That is a fine carrot, is it not, *Señor* Paige?"

"Like I said, I ain't no politician. I just don't like bayonets sticking in my ribs."

"The fact is, your government doesn't give a shit about Dominicans, or Cubans, or Haitians. It doesn't give a shit about its own people— except the wealthy ones, and the ones who aspire to wealth and play by the rules. Your government is nothing more than a corporate plutocracy."

Satch put on his own voodoo charms. "Better than a pimpocracy. And as for me, I'm just a guy getting by. I ain't the government, so don't go complaining to me." Satch slammed his locker and noticed that there wasn't a lock. He looked a foot down, into Aybar's eyes. "I'm like all those kids out there in the *barrio*, just lookin' for a way out, and baseball's my ticket."

Aybar put his arm against the locker, blocking Satch's path. "But you can't get all the way out. The way is blocked by a fundamentally unjust system. You can't play in the Major Leagues of baseball, and you never will. You deserve to be in the Hall of Fame, but you never will. Your government has offered you a carrot, and you've taken it. You get by, *Señor* Paige, but that's all you get."

"Speakin' of carrots, what am I gettin' paid for this gig?"

Aybar laughed, then shrugged and lit a "Pride of Havana" cigar. "If you win, *el presidente* just may give you his yacht. Fans will stuff your shirt with more money than you've ever made in one baseball game. But if you lose, well, I don't advise you to lose. Did you know that *el presidente* is also a *curandero* (healer)?"

"No."

"*Pues, sí.* He invented *la aspirina Haitiana.*"

"Which is?"

"*El presidente* was interrogating a Haitian who complained about a headache from soldiers beating him, so *el presidente* put a bullet in his head. And you know what? No more headaches!" Aybar laughed. "I say that only because you will face the Cuban ace, Cristóbal Torriente, this inning. I advise you to give him a Haitian aspirin. They say that when you throw hard, the ball looks like an aspirin. *Precisamente.*" Aybar slapped Satch on the shoulder. "You and *el presidente* have much in common. He hates to lose."

Satch looked in the direction of Trujillo and Lograno. He shook his head. "Look at those fat cats."

Aybar looked at Lograno, draining a bottle of beer. "Secretary Lograno is a disgusting fat man, but he was my catcher in 1915. I was a pitcher, like you. Many *poncheos.*" Aybar threw an uppercut with his right hand. "Strikeouts. You know why he was a catcher? Because he was so fat, even then. We were poor. Most of us didn't have gloves, so the catcher had to let balls bounce off his stomach."

Satch laughed, thinking Aybar was pulling his leg.

"You laugh, but it is true."

Satch glanced at the visitor's dugout. "How did San Pedro get Torriente and Tiant?"

"They're *rentados*. Like Dihigo, and you. Both sides bring in ringers for the series. It's a tradition. It is also bankrupting us, but it is a tradition that we win. Do you understand, *Señor* Paige?"

"I'd feel better if you cut all that *Señor* Paige shit. Call me Satch."

"Esatch." Aybar slapped him on the back as they started to walk out. Satch stopped suddenly when an eerie-looking guy with long, curled hair jumped in front of him. He stared at the two *caprelatas* on strings around Satch's neck. He grabbed one and tore it off. The string burned into Satch's neck.

"Ow! Sonofabitch! Give me that."

Aybar stepped between the two men, with a hand on Satch's shoulder. *"No es caprelata, es wango."*

"What's he sayin'?"

"That's not a good-luck charm. Somebody fooled you. That's a *wango*—it's for bad luck."

"Who's this guy?"

"That's the president's *brujo*. They call him *el diablo*. Trujillo believes it is enough for his *brujo* to put his hand on a man's heart to divine from the rhythm of a single beat his deepest character, his fate."

The *brujo* put his hand on Satch's heart and leapt back. *"Caramba! No le toces el corazón de ése!"*

Satch laughed, picked up a glove and trundled to the mound. Aybar called to him, "Esatch, can I get your address, please?"

"What for?"

"If the sharks get you, the president will want to send his condolences and a basket of fine Dominican fruit. It is his custom."

Satch gave him a big-time frown and ambled to the mound at his normal, glacial, pace. The uniform was too short for him, and he looked ridiculous in it. The fans—the ones who did not know Satch—laughed. The San Pedro dugout was not laughing. It was buzzing with apprehension.

Dihigo, who had pitched a very good game, was startled to see Satch walking toward him. "Martin, baby." Satch shook his old friend's hand.

"Qué pasa, man? *Rentado?"*

Satch nodded. "Long story. The short version is I'm pitching and you're in right field. We meant to see you last night, but a couple of things got in the way."

Martin laughed. "You couldn't have seen me if you tried. I was in jail all night. The whole team was in jail."

Satch looked at him quizzically.

"Trujillo didn't want us carousing before the big game. And he doesn't trust the San Pedro people. He's afraid their minds work like his. You know—a couple guys go missing."

Satch shook his head in disbelief. "When this game's over, horse, we got to get out of here. And you're coming with us."

Dihigo grinned. "That's what you're doing here. You want me to jump. You see the way Trujillo is? You don't jump his team the way you do up north."

"After this game, he won't need you. This is your World Series, right?"

"This is the San Pedro series. But the stakes are higher. I mean, if you don't win, they might shoot you."

Satch laughed. "You're kidding, right?"

Dihigo shrugged. "With Trujillo, you never know. I'm just glad you relieved me. The last thing you want to be is the losing pitcher when *Escogido* plays San Pedro. The last guy . . ." Dihigo shook his head.

Satch felt his entrails sinking but sucked it up with a false bravado. "Don't worry. They ain't gonna get a loud fart off of me. This is the ninth inning. Three up, three down. Then you, me, and Josh will get on the boat and head for the big game."

"What game's that?"

"The biggest game ever played. Black All-Stars against the White All-Stars. Two hundred bucks and all expenses."

Dihigo shook his head. "It's not worth the risk."

"Two hundred dollars, man. That's a lot of *aguacates*. You can live for a year down here on a hundred dollars."

"Just strike these guys out," said Dihigo, turning toward the field.

Satch grabbed him by the sleeve. "Okay. Three hundred. You've gotta play, horse. I'm counting on you."

"Three hundred dollars for one game?"

"One game, *maestro*."

Dihigo smiled. "There's just one thing."

"What's that?"

"After you strike these guys out, we need two runs."

Satch wiped the sweat that was already pouring down his forehead. "The boat's in the harbor. The *Coco Loco*. Meet you there an hour after the game."

Dihigo walked to right field, and Satch took his warm-ups. When Josh noticed, he sprayed beer from his mouth. "What the hell is going on?"

Inmaculata had had her head down and her hands over her eyes, in some kind of private mourning Josh didn't understand. When she saw Satch on the mound, she brightened up. She hugged Josh and ran toward the *glorieta*.

"What the hell is going on?" Josh repeated.

Inmaculata was in a panic, fearing the worst if the home team lost. She tried to break through the cordon of the presidential suite.

"*El gordo, señor presidente, el gordo! Es* Yosh Geebson!"

Trujillo was perturbed. "Who is that *coño*? And who is Yosh Geebson?"

The ex-*reina* waved her laurel crown. "*Soy yo.* Inmaculata Altagracia Troncoso de la Paz, *reina de* 1930." Inmaculata broke through the guards who noticed that she had the president's attention. She ran mincingly in high heels and curtsied. "Excuse me, *señor presidente,* but you must get the chubby one. Is the black Babe Ruth."

Deputy Aybar already had the binoculars to his eyes, scanning the seats where Paige had been sitting.

"What's she talking about?" Trujillo asked Aybar.

"*Bateó la mitad de una naranja desde las cabañas hasta el mar!*" (He hit half an orange from the cabanas to the sea.)

"Half? Where did the other half go?" Trujillo laughed, and his circle laughed with him.

"*Á demonios, senor presidente.*"

"The *cabañas* to the ocean. That's quite a shot."

Deputy Aybar made the sign of the cross on his chest. "It is the Colossus himself, Josh Gibson."

Trujillo grabbed the binocular from him. "Let me see." He saw Josh with his arm around a girl. "*Coño.* The Negro is with Flerida Molina, my niece."

"Yes, Flerida is with Geebson."

"It looks like Sancho Panza to me. But if you say Yosh Geebson, it must be. Take him. Give him a bat. He'd better know what to do with it."

At this point Josh was looking at the presidential box. He noticed all eyes on him and a goon squad heading down the stairs. He wasn't sure what to make of it, but the worst-case scenario projected through his head. He ran.

"Wait!" yelled Inmaculata. "They just want you to play."

The fans, packed ten deep, impeded his progress. He threw locals left and right but he couldn't break free. Three bayonets convinced him to follow the squad to the dugout.

The first batter up was Tarzán Marsans, the leadoff man. A slash-hitter, he led the *Estrellas* in hitting. Satch mowed down the first two batters on six pitches. They were as close to aspirins as Josh had ever seen him throw. The catcher's hand stung, but it never felt so good. Satch had told the catcher, Oms, to forget the signs. He was just throwing his signature fastball wherever Oms put the target, and he was never off by more than a centimeter.

The next batter was Agapito Cienfuegos who, like Frankie Frisch, prided himself on virtually never striking out. Shouts of *"Pito!"* and *"el Pitón"* mixed with foot-stomping and the beating of sugarcane sticks on anything that would make noise. The sticks were alternatively sucked on and banged. If you were deaf you could gauge the decibel level of the foot-stomping by the degree of *cucaracha* panic, especially under the grandstand. Three men in acid-eaten shirts and pants had a foghorn hooked up to a car battery. They cranked it up when the *Estrellas* scored, homered, doubled, or stole a base. By the seventh inning, when the operators were completely soused, it could be set off for anything. Now it was blaring for Cristóbal Torriente. 5'10", 190 pounds, with bulging muscles. One of the greatest hitters of the era, in '34 he was near the end of his career. He would die in 1938 in New York of acute alcoholism. His penchant for drink was what kept Satch from re-cruiting him for his team. Now he was a little slower in the field, but his hand speed was still there. San Pedro had hired him to put the ball in the seats, and despite the humid air that kept almost everything in the park, his first time up he put a Dihigo fastball over the fence.

Because pitchers were not used to facing lefties, Torriente had an ad-vantage against them. But not against Paige. Satchel had faced Torriente in a previous stint south of the border. He knew his strengths and weaknesses. Torriente was a power hitter who took a big cut. Satch was one of the few pitchers of his era who never threw deliberately at hitters. He was always afraid of killing someone. Oms called time and urged Satch to waste one, a Haitian aspirin, putting the slugger on first to face the lighter-hitting Gomez. But Satch had once walked two men delib-erately to get to Josh and then struck him out. He relished the con-frontation with Torriente. It was what he lived for.

Satch looked up at the presidential gallery and smiled. "This one is for *el jefe*—Erneste Letrino Trujillo," he shouted.

Trujillo had been distracted by his wife and only half heard what Satch said. When the stadium erupted in laughter, he said to Aybar, "What are they laughing at?"

"The *gringo*'s bad Spanish, *comandante*."

"What's going on?" Josh asked Santos Avila, the manager.

"Your teammate just called the president a shit-house." Josh felt his shoulder blades involuntarily hunch together.

"Don't worry," said Avila. "If the president had heard him, he'd be dead by now."

Satch set Torriente up by backing him off the plate, throwing a rare slider. It started out at Torriente's head. He backed away as the ball dived and almost hit his elbow. The next pitch was a fastball on the out-side corner. Torriente was taking all the way, but it wouldn't have mat-tered. He wiped some dust from his left eye and blinked, realizing that if he blinked at the next pitch it would be past him before his eye re-opened. The 1-1 pitch nicked the outside corner. It jumped about six inches, like the previous fastball. Virtually unhittable. When Satch had it going like that, the batter was best off following Cool Papa Bell's lead, taking a half swing just to make contact. The home-run hitters could only pray that they'd get the bat around fast enough to catch one. Prayers made for poor batting averages. The last pitch was identical. Torriente never got the bat off his shoulder. He just shook his head. Each of the fastballs had come from a different angle—overhand, three-quarters, and sidearm.

Escogido was still one run down, with Dihigo leading off the inning. Josh couldn't find a uniform that fit him. Avila, a *gordo* himself, took matters into his own hands, stripping off his own uniform.

"You're up after Vallejo," said Avila. "Pinch-hitting for Hernandez."

"I ain't warmed up."

Satch heard the commotion and came over. "You warmed up with a *naranja*, horse. Get up there and hit one." Josh heard a pistol shot and figured that Trujillo had called time again.

Deputy Aybar appeared with another three-man goon squad. "Gibson?" He extended his hand and Josh shook it. "I'm Deputy Aybar. I have a message from the president. He says you will hit the ball into the ocean or you will be deposited there, with the *tiburones*."

Dihigo singled and stole second when Casamayor struck out after fouling off four pitches at three and two. Vallejo, batting sixth, came up, and took two wicked breaking balls for strikes. Dihigo shouted, *"Coño! Es una bola de ensalivada!"* (spitter) to the umpire, who ignored him. Vallejo managed to foul off another big breaking ball, and the umpire walked to the mound, followed by the catcher.

"He's right. That's a spitter you're throwing."

"Okay, it's a spitter, but Dihigo keeps stealing my signals," said the catcher.

The umpire nodded. It was a fair trade-off. Vallejo struck out swinging at the next pitch. Dihigo was beside himself at second. A group of six soldiers walked past the San Pedro dugout and stood against the stadium wall. The umpire walked to the mound again and warned Tiant, "I think you'd better stop throwing the spitter." Tiant looked at the soldiers and nodded.

The coach called back the batter in the on-deck circle, which was more of an ellipse, and Josh walked slowly to the plate carrying a forty-six-ounce bat. He dug in and stared at the sidewheeler. After what Aybar said, the one thing clear in his head was that he was not going to walk. But Tiant didn't want to give him anything to hit. The first two pitches were curves way outside. Josh figured that Tiant would come inside with a fast one. He did. Josh rocked it deep into left-field foul territory. The crowd roared. Tiant took off his cap and wiped the sweat off his brow. The big guy could get around on his fastball, even with the tree trunk that posed as a bat. The catcher, Nemesio Mendez, called time and jogged out to talk to Tiant. Josh knew he wasn't going to get a strike now, but he didn't know if he could trust the umpire. He felt like Frisch in the crucial at-bat in game six in Detroit. He looked at Satch, who gave him the take sign. Then Josh realized that no ump was going to cross Trujillo's team on a close call. What he didn't realize was that Tiant and Mendez had seen enough of Gibson and decided to either put a scare into him and back him off the plate or put him out of the game. Tiant threw a curve behind Josh's head. He ducked but got plunked on the top of the head. It was not so much stars as a thousand lightning bugs that Josh saw the instant the ball struck. If hills could feel, Josh's head felt like a strip-mined West Virginia coal-field hill. He heard Mendez saying, "You no hit *dat* one." Josh made no sign of recognition. Mendez bent and cupped his hand between his mouth and Josh's ear. "You no hit *dat* one." When his vision started to clear up, what he imagined looking at was a contour map of Africa. The sand his face lay on was the sea abutting the black-rimmed ivory continent of home plate. At the moment when reality kicked in with a new, throbbing pain on his skull, he thought of Mrs. Jeffcoat's classroom in Georgia again, the blackboard in ruin on the floor, Humpty Gibson Dumpty now rising to his feet and surveilling the landscape like Stanley and staring at the base path upriver to the first sack.

Trujillo was furious. He had counted on Gibson's bat. He whispered to Aybar, who then ran out to the field to deliver the president's message to the umpire, Napoleon Mosquito Canónico, who removed his mask and turned to the Deputy. "Listen," said Aybar, "the president wants Gibson to hit, one way or another. That pitch must be called a strike."

"It hit him," said Canónico incredulously.

"Rule 2.00—A legal pitch that touches the batter in the strike zone is still a strike. The runner is not awarded first base. That was strike two. The count is two and two."

Mosquito Canónico and Deputy Aybar stared at each other for a few seconds, while Josh got to his feet, dusted himself off, and started toward first base.

"*Estrei!*" hollered Canónico, loud enough to be heard in the *glorieta*.

Josh stopped and turned in disbelief. Aybar was holding his bat by the fat end and smiling. "You hit *dis* one."

Now Tiant was in a jam. He knew who Aybar was and he quickly figured out what had transpired. He couldn't walk Gibson. He had to pitch him something he would bite at but wouldn't wallop. He threw a screwball at the knees that he thought was strike three.

"*La tercera bola!*" hollered Canónico.

Tiant checked Dihigo, who read the pitcher's mind and said, "Don't even think of wetting this one."

The catcher gave a curveball signal, and Dihigo shouted in English, "Curveball!" Tiant did not know that Josh made his living on curveballs and bad pitches and had once reached for an outside pitch with one hand on the bat and deposited the ball in the right-field seats. The pay-off pitch was a sweet curve that broke from your house to mine. Josh waited till the last possible moment and practically took the ball out of the catcher's mitt with his powerful wrists.

The ball had nipped the outside corner. And got no farther. No farther north. It traveled a good deal farther south. Out of the stadium, but short of the ocean. Mendez couldn't believe he had hit it. Trotting the bases, Josh kept thinking "ticket." That ball was his ticket home. Trujillo stood up and clapped. The ex-queen, Inmaculata Altagracia Troncoso de la Paz jumped and shouted, "G-e-e-bson!"

Rum-inspired fights broke out all over the stadium, which was not unusual. Soldiers rushed onto the field, while San Pedro fans hurled rum bottles at them, then broke chairs and threw the pieces at the soldiers who dropped their rifles, picked up the wood and threw it back at the fans. Meanwhile, winning gamblers were yelling for Gibson and

Paige, stuffing their pockets with gold and silver coins, and Dihigo made his way to the *glorieta*.

Trujillo shook his hand and embraced the winning captain. "*Señor Presidente,* I need to ask a favor. My grandmother died, in Miami, and I have to go back for the funeral."

Trujillo was nearly illiterate, but he had a phenomenal memory. "*Coño,* that's what you said in '28, when you went back to Havana."

Dihigo was at a loss for words, and Trujillo's mental machinery was clicking. "That's why the *gringos* are here. They want to take you *al norte* to play for them. *Coños!* Deputy Aybar, arrest the *gringos*. And you," he said to Dihigo, "be glad you won the game, and get the fuck out of my sight."

Dihigo nodded. "*Sí, señor presidente.*"

He started to walk away. Trujillo called to him. "One more thing— if you try to leave we'll find out if you really are *inmortal.*"

Dihigo had no confidence in the mercurial dictator. He felt he'd be safer in the U.S. He headed for the harbor, hoping Paige and Gibson would get out of the stadium before they were arrested. They didn't. They were put in straitjackets and tossed into an old hearse that served as a paddy wagon.

"We're in some shit now, horse," said Satch.

"I've been in it before. These guys got nothin' on the sheriffs in Georgia."

"They got us in straitjackets, horse. And that Trujillo don't fool around. We're shark bait."

"You think we should run for it?"

"I would, 'cept I'm kind of tied up, if you know what I mean."

"I been in one of these before. Was kind of drunk, you know? They had to immobilize me. But not for long."

Satch squirmed uncomfortably. "What I want to know is what they expect you to do if you gotta piss? Bet they never thought about that?" Satch stopped squirming and looked at Josh. "What did you mean— 'not for long'?"

"I busted out."

Satch laughed and repeated, "Busted out . . . That's a straitjacket, man. You ain't Houdini."

"I ain't lyin'. I busted out. I was pretty drunk. Tore a wheel off the car and hit a cop with it. The other boy took off." Josh shook his head. "I was out of control, man. Still don't know how that wheel came off."

"Well, you'd best get out of control again. I don't want to be wearing cement shoes."

Josh got to his knees, inhaled, then flexed every muscle in his arms and torso. His face screwed up demonically and his torso turned slowly back and forth. Several seconds went by and Satch was holding his own breath. Then he heard some seams pop. Josh breathed out and inhaled again, flexed, and the ripping sound was louder, longer. Josh had the straitjacket in his teeth and was pulling up while working his arms free. Satchel bit onto the torn seam and pulled, ripping it another few inches. Josh's head was nearly invisible, inside the restraint, and moments later he had it off. He helped Satch out of his, and peered out the back porthole window of the paddy wagon. There were two soldiers on guard, expecting nothing. Josh kicked the door open and leaped at a diminutive soldier, knocking him down and trampling him, one foot on his chest, which produced a gasp, and the other foot on his face.

Satch jumped out and hit the other guard in the face with his right hand, and regretted it. Pain shot up from his knuckles as the soldier staggered back into some corn stalks. Satch grabbed the rifle from his hand and took off after Josh. They didn't stop till they reached the boat, where Dihigo was waiting.

"Man, it's a good thing you didn't have spikes on. You did a Bojangles on that guy's face."

The *Coco Loco* had what looked like a half-mile lead on the Dominican PT boat, World War I vintage, speeding toward them.

"Whose idea was it to get a slow boat, yours or Bennett's?" Josh asked.

"Mine. I wanted to enjoy the trip."

"You chose a slow boat? *Coño!* They're gonna start shooting any second," said Dihigo.

Satch had the boat at full throttle. They were losing ground, rapidly. "Relax, horse. We'll be in international waters before they get us."

"You think they give a shit about international water? You're gonna have international water coming out the holes in your chest."

"We can always run up a white flag. Surrender."

"I don't think they play that way here," said Josh. "That's fucking Captain Hook in that PT boat. I don't think he knows what a white flag is."

Josh's and Dihigo's fears came true. Within a minute they could hear bullets, and the PT boat had closed the distance between them by half. They were not going to make it to international water. And now a bullet tore a hole in the hull. Then another. The three players ducked out of sight, and in a few moments the boat took a few hits on the stern and started sputtering. Then there was a loud noise and the *Coco Loco* was up on its starboard end, almost to vertical. The ballplayers rolled to the low side. When the boat righted itself they saw another PT boat headed for the Dominican one at an alarming speed. They had been hit and almost upended by its wash. Now the fast boat's fore-mounted machine gun was clacking, and the Dominican boat made a sudden turn and headed back to the harbor. The new PT boat turned and pulled up alongside the disabled *Coco Loco*. A lone American threw them a line. It was Harry Bennett.

"Get in, maties." He extended each of them a hand. "You must be Dihigo. Welcome aboard."

Satch smiled. "Fucking Harry, the lone ranger! Now I *know* God's a white man."

"I thought you might run into a little trouble. We always do. It's cash in advance with these characters."

"Let's advance the hell out of here."

Bennett smiled and bit on the Havana Perfecto between his teeth. The ex-Navy man was loving this. "Used to have a Johnson." Bennett laughed and threw open the engine doors. "I replaced it. This baby's got twelve cylinders. One of Henry's prototypes. Was just sitting in a back room at the Rouge, so I thought I'd try her out. When this was on a car, it was so powerful Barney Oldfield refused to drive it. Too unstable—

what he said. Does a nice job with a PT boat though. Those suckers might as well be sailing the *Maine*, trying to catch us. Did an ender in Miami, testing her out. An ender is a wheelie in a boat, case you didn't know."

Bennett bit on his cigar. Josh looked toward the harbor, then back at Bennett. "They may be slow, but there's three of them now, and they're headed this way."

"Ee-ha!" shouted Bennett. "Satchel, you're the shooter. Jesus, what Meyer Lansky wouldn't do for a boat like this."

Bennett gunned the new PT boat, borrowed from the Navy. Then he turned and headed for the three Dominican boats.

"What'chu doin'?" stammered Dihigo, frightened into a falsetto.

"I want to see what Satch can do with that cannon. Fires about ten thousand rounds a minute, maybe a second. Best money can buy. I take that back. Money can't buy that gun. It's a prototype. Newest machine gun in the U.S. Navy arsenal. Henry had to pull strings with the Secretary of the Navy for that baby."

The Dominicans were already firing at them. "Pull that trigger, Satch."

Satch fired as Bennett headed straight at the middle boat of the Dominican three. Its gun apparently jammed and Satch was filling it with holes. It veered to its left and nearly collided with the PT on its port side. Bennett laughed. Satch fired at the third PT, which was clearly outgunned. It too turned away. Bennett made a hundred-and-eighty-degree turn and nearly endered again. "Yahoo!"

Havana was just hours away.

16

KNOWLEDGE

The Miles Standish. The Kenmore. The Ritz. The Parker House. Whores—all of them. Babylon's legacy to Boston, to any metropolis. How else to explain the players' love of a room not one's own? A different man, or woman—it didn't matter—every night. Insatiable. They loved it. Whites only? Some loved it even more—the Cobbs, the Ansons, the Hornsbys. Barnstorming the South was the worst. Having a car as big as Satch's had its advantages. A front seat almost long enough for a lanky player in full stretch, for the pitch of himself into slumber, cutting the perfect hesitation pitch with z's.

It was October 19, the night before the game. Satch again was lucky. Gus Greenlee came looking for him at the Parker House two hours before he arrived, then checked himself into the Ritz-Carlton, had champagne and a Victrola brought to his suite.

The clouds onto which a month earlier Gus had projected the ghosts of Willy, Rabbit, and the others he had killed were a manifestation of the black cloud that followed him like the dialogue box of a cartoon. In it were written no words, just slash marks and symbols representing curse, representing much of Gus's reflective life. They spelled out all that was taken from him, down to Pappy Williams raiding him almost weekly now and Satchel Paige jumping his contract. It all had to stop somewhere. If Paige was not going to pitch for the Crawfords, he might as well be dead. That was the unwritten stop-loss in Paige's contract.

Gus looked at himself in the full-length mirror. Sized himself up the way Harry Bennett might. More than a bit of corpulence. Broad shoulders and chest. A more than expansive belly, in spite of his diet. He longed for the holidays, when he could let himself go. He hadn't killed in nearly a year. Oh, to just let it go. "Satchel Paige dies." What a story it would be. Everyone telling it—Runyon, Winchell, Parsons. Round and round it would go. Like the angel of death, twirling her partner. Round and round. All fall down.

Gus listened to a plaintive Lena Horne and thought about the mutt that stopped belonging to Willie N. one night in 1929 when Willie passed away and Woogie carried him in a gunny sack to keep the blood from staining his shoulder and to keep body parts from being lost in transit to Willy's final resting place in Greenlee Field. The mutt followed his master decorously and watched Willie's left leg hook over the lip of the shallow hole while his pant leg receded and the whiteness of his ankle shone in the moonlight. Watching the mutt approach, Gus wondered, cynically, if it would tear a morsel from the "roadkill." He wondered too why Woogie, being Woogie, didn't bash it with the shovel but stood instead looking almost penitently over his shoulder as the mutt licked the exposed ankle, and Gus wondered if the dumb dog's licking was a vain attempt to resuscitate his master, or a final kiss, or just a serendipitous salt lick.

Gus listened as hard as he could to Lena but did not hear the answer to the three-part multiple-choice question that had grown out of all rational proportion. Three doors with a tiger behind none of them. Just a dead dog. Now Gus's platter was stuck in the groove, and Gus did what Gus always did. Pulled the platter off and snapped it over his knee, as he had done five years earlier with Willie's spine, which gave him a case of the *willies* in a way that no one could understand when any old mutt sniffed at his ankles. He fluffed the pillow with the pistol under it, with the bullets meant for Satch, and lay down with the light on.

* * *

While Gus snoozed, Babe Ruth got out of the taxi at the Miles Standish Hotel, a dame on his arm. He wore a camel-hair cap and coat and smoked a cigar. Babe and the brassie walked slowly up the red-carpeted sidewalk to the lobby. An attendant approached, and Ruth stopped. That was his mistake. A water-balloon hit him on the shoulder. He cursed, looked up, and saw movement but no faces. He ran into the lobby and accosted Diz. "Where's Martin?"

Diz saw the water mark on Ruth's expensive coat and smiled. "He got you, too?"

"You think it's funny?"

Ruth poked Diz on the chest with a single finger and Diz had all he could do not to step backward from the impact. He was stunned by how strong the man was. The single finger in the white glove reminded him of the white end of the scallions Babe relied on the way Popeye relied on spinach. In Cuba, power hitters Dihigo and Torriente were both called "spinach." Diz reflected later that maybe Foxx and Gibson could drive a man backward with a finger, and maybe Ted Lyons, too. Lyons once picked up the bambino and deposited him in the upper berth of a Pullman because he was blocking his path to a craps game in Lazzeri's cabin. Babe got a kick out of it. "Hey, he's picking up the baby," he said. He always called himself "the baby."

James Atwood took a linen napkin from a table and sidled up to Babe unnoticed. *I could be an assassin,* he thought. How easy. Even the Pope's scarlet robes could not have been more resplendent, thought James Atwood, than Babe's camel-hair coat. Only when he was close did he notice Babe's diamond-studded tie clasp and pearl cuff links. Pepper's antics had been funny, but they were not right. This earthly god, ostensibly pissed on by the lumpen man in the moon.

"I can dry that off for you."

Babe took James Atwood for a coconspirator who was mocking him. He raised his arm, threatening a swat. "Get out of here, you little shit, or I'll croak you."

Bitterly disappointed, James Atwood considered stabbing Babe with a cheese knife within easy reach on the small antique table that also held a dripping ice sculpture of a baseball player who had as strong a resemblance to the Babe as the chef could manage. Deciding first that the cheese knife would be ineffectual and second that the rest of the team would be miffed, James Atwood swallowed the indignity and scowled. "Ah, you stink worse than that cheese anyway."

James Atwood had unconsciously rolled the linen napkin into a rattail. He flicked it unthinkingly at a fly on the cheese and was pretty sure he had gotten it. Responding to the blonde's tug on his arm and her plaintive look, Ruth repented his boorishness. He reached over and rubbed James Atwood's head with a white-gloved hand.

"Not bad, kid."

Seeing the Babe smile, James Atwood's spirits soared. He felt like the folks Billy Sunday put his hands on. He felt like reeling. His allegiance to the white team was sealed. Now it wasn't just that he was on Harry's payroll—Harry had flown him and John Henry to Boston. It went deeper. He'd been touched.

Ducky Medwick walked up innocently, followed by Leo, hands in pockets and whistling. Babe looked menacingly at them, and Ducky's eyes widened, but he was not looking at Babe. Babe turned and saw Frankie with a suitcase in his hand.

"You're back!" said Ducky, slapping him on the shoulder.

"Hey, you quit," said Babe. "We already got Gehringer. Ducky stuffed him in a locker in Fenway Park."

"What changed your mind?" Ducky asked.

Frankie put down his suitcase. "I figured I'd left about ten pounds of skin on National League diamonds, and I figured there wouldn't be any room in the Gashouse for a guy who was afraid to lose a few on an American League diamond."

Babe patted him on the back. "You were just paranoid anyway. Harry wasn't going to hurt you."

Frankie looked at his watch. "He's got about twenty-four hours to try."

Leo shook Frankie's hand. "Glad you're back, Frankie, but I can't call you skipper anymore. We thought you were gone, so the players elected me captain."

Frankie smiled. "The truth is I don't want the job. You're the skipper now, Leo."

Babe's lady friend cleared her throat impatiently. Babe excused himself and had already forgotten about Pepper, who waited for Babe to
get to the elevator before signaling to Frankie at the reception desk.
"Psst!"

Pepper poked his head out from behind an ionic column in the
lobby and waved to Frankie to come over. Then Babe got on the elevator and Pepper rushed over and shook Frankie's hand. "Hey, I got some
venison in the trunk."

Pepper had driven his new pickup from St. Louis to Georgia, then to
Boston.

"What did you do, run it over?" said Frankie.

"I ain't no scavenger. I shot the bastard."

"Where?"

"On the Wilbur Cross Parkway, outside of New Haven."

"You shot a deer on the Parkway?"

"A deer's a deer. Don't matter where you bag him."

"I guess it figures. It's probably deer season and the smart ones get
out of the woods and head for Yale."

"Yeah, the ones that couldn't get into Fordham."

The water-balloon gag stopped with Babe. Pepper was itchy. Normally,
he'd work off the excess energy with his Musical Mudcats, playing guitar
or harmonica, with Diz on certain vocals. Now he turned it into mischief.

"Hey, remember that thing we did at the Bellevue-Stratton in
Philly?"

Diz smiled. "You're not thinking what I'm thinking?"

Pepper and the Gashouse Gang had wreaked havoc on a Rotary lun-
cheon in Philadelphia. Now the American Psychological Association
was having its convention in Boston, and there was a plenary session in
the main meeting hall of the Miles Standish. Pepper's plan to break it
up, putting on overalls that painters had left in an alcove of the lobby,
was interrupted by a man in a bow tie and suit stepping into their path.
He was carrying a gun, albeit concealed. Harry Bennett held out his
hand like a stop sign. James Atwood tried to control the momentum of

a full, open can of paint, but some spilled out, threatening to add yellow to Harry's two-toned, black-and-white cap-toed shoes.

Harry jumped back. "Whoa! Guys! Slow down, hey! . . . Boys, put down those paint cans. We've got to talk. There's someone you need to meet. You've all heard about him. Boys, this is Knowledge Clapp. Just flew in from Pittsburgh. He's going to give you the lowdown on pitching to Paige's team, personally. I want you to get the rest of the team together and meet me in my suite in ten minutes. Okay?"

"I think Babe is occupied," said Diz.

"If he wants to play, roust him. If he'd rather get laid, we can replace him."

"I'd rather get laid," said Pepper.

Harry smiled. "You don't have any choice."

Ducky laughed and slapped Pepper on the back, while Knowledge Clapp opened a closet door and peered inside. Harry had made Clapp's trip well-worthwhile, but he was coke-paranoiac and understandably petrified of Gus Greenlee, who was in Boston looking for Satch. Knowledge continued opening doors, looking behind him, and throwing long glances down halls not taken.

What were the odds that the red-haired man that Knowledge kept seeing was a phantom? If it could be at the end of one hall, then at the end of the next, parallel hall, the odds would have to be pretty high. Pittsburgh's high priest of odds should have taken comfort in that, but in fact he felt aggravated and frightened. He took a deep breath and changed mental tack. He decided that if the phantom kept slipping through walls it must be afraid to confront him directly. Knowledge squeezed his fists and inhaled deeply through his nose, as if the minor vortex he created could swirl up the phantom and jar him the way his nose candy did. He saw a long raccoon coat on a hanger and assured himself there was not a red-haired man in it. He took stock of his situation and convinced himself he was safe. He took a pill from his pants pocket and swallowed it, and the known world came sharply into focus.

Harry had the penthouse suite. The main room was big enough to hold the whole Cardinals team. The liquor was hidden away. In its place were coffee and tea. The team was surprised by how young Knowledge Clapp was. He was wearing a cheap blue suit, white shirt, and a red bow tie that Frankie suspected Harry had given him. He had finished one semester at college, majoring in probability and statistics, then found that he had a talent for handicapping horses and a hankering for white powder. He quit college and went to work for Gus, handicapping and memorizing names that corresponded to about five hundred numbers. Soon Gus couldn't do without the kid, and the kid couldn't do without the powder.

"Frankie Frisch, right?" said Clapp, extending his hand first to Frankie, then the rest of the team.

"Glad you got that right," said Leo, "or they'd have to take back your nickname."

Diz said, "If you know as much as they say you do, then you know what an anagram is, right?"

Frankie Frisch's head swiveled ninety degrees. He couldn't believe that Diz knew the word. Knowledge nodded.

"Well, I've got one for you—Bokar Eight O'Clock. That's got to be an anagram some smart-ass made up to make folks think they need coffee when they see it."

Knowledge went as still as any piece of furniture in the room. He looked like he'd been sprayed with liquid nitrogen and if he fell over he'd shatter. His eyes seemed to withdraw. No one said anything, transfixed by Knowledge thinking. In his head sixteen wheels, each with sixteen letters on a face making the wheel not exactly circular, spun, creating combinations that perplexed him. He felt his head spinning. He looked plaintively at Diz. "Too many letters."

He still hadn't moved any part of his body but his mouth. Now he turned his head and looked at the door. "Excuse me. I'll be right back." He stepped out, took a large pinch of coke and rubbed it into his gums. Then he took a second pinch and walked back in feeling a lot better.

Diz felt guilty about messing with Clapp's head. Diz waved at him. "Don't feel bad, Knowledge. I asked Moe Berg, and he didn't even try, and Moe's the smartest guy I know."

Knowledge smiled and made eye contact with all the players. "The first thing I've got to say is this meeting is confidential. It never happened, okay? Or I could be in trouble with some people."

"I'm sure Harry made it worth your while," said Ducky.

Clapp looked at Ducky. "Confidential. And everybody's got to agree to it." He looked at each of the players, who nodded their consent, including Ducky.

"Okay. Harry asked me to find out everything I could on how to pitch Paige's team. The Grays and the Crawfords I know pretty well. For the other guys, I got some help from the pitchers I respect. So, let me start. I want you guys to take notes."

Harry passed out paper and pencils.

"You can skip Ducky," said Pepper. "He can't write."

Ducky was three players away from Pepper, or Pepper wouldn't have dared to say anything.

"I'll take notes for him," said James Atwood, trying to be helpful.

"I can write, dummy," said Ducky.

"Let's start with Ray Dandridge—he's a spray hitter. A lot like Arky Vaughan. Never under .300." Clapp stared at Diz to make sure he was taking notes. "He's a first-ball hitter, and he loves curves."

"How about Gibson," said Frankie. "He's the one I'm worried about."

"He's the one everyone's worried about. Nobody knows how to pitch the guy. If you walk him intentionally, put the ball way out. He's been known to reach out and hammer one over the fence. When he crouches, he golfs low balls. When he stands up, he hits anything above the waist. So pitch him the opposite. Some say Uncle Charlie's got him, but Satch says he murders curves, especially outside. And if you pitch him inside, he'll kill the third baseman. So fastballs high and outside look like the way to go. He may hit them, but they'll probably stay in the park."

"No off-speed, either," said Babe.

Diz looked at him. "How do you know? You ain't pitched in years."

"Matty said . . ."

"Matty?"

"Yeah, Matty. Christy Mathewson."

"Ain't he dead?" said Pepper.

"No. He ain't dead."

"Yeah, he is," said Diz. "Been dead for ten years. I read it."

"So who gives a fuck if he's dead? I want to make a point, all right? He was twice the pitcher you are. He wrote a fucking book about it."

"About what?" asked Leo.

"Pitching. What the fuck did you think? Custer's last stand? The point he made is that you can't get a late swinger out on a change of pace. He'll pull it into the seats. That's Gibson. He's a wrist hitter. Waits till the ball's practically in the catcher's mitt before he swings."

"Babe ought to know. Jackie Mitchell struck him out with a change of pace," Leo cracked.

"Struck out, my ass," said the Babe, petulantly. "That was publicity. That was no strikeout."

"You struck out. So did I," said Gehrig with little emotion.

"Hey, that broad can't fan me. You struck out. I took a dive. What do you think she is, Hubbell? She's a broad."

"If it was publicity, why didn't they come to Meusel and me?" said Gehrig.

" 'Cuz you still ain't the drawing card. Even with your Triple Crown. Hell, I hit .298 and they still come to see me."

"Yeah, strike out."

"Yeah. They're paying to see me strike out. They ain't paying to see you do nothing."

Gehrig sneered. "And tomorrow night, they're coming to collect."

After a few moments silence Clapp continued, "I think Babe's right. Satch just fires Josh fastballs, up and down. Keeps him guessing where the be-ball is going to be. Bill Foster says his only blind spot is a six-inch band at the belt buckle. And I'll tell you how the Grays play Gibson: put the right fielder toward center, and the left fielder toward center, then put the center fielder as far back as he can go. Put his back right on the wall. Same thing with the infield. Pinch 'em all toward the middle, then throw the ball down the middle. What they did in Cuba— they cut down the left-field fence and put a man out where the bleachers used to be. So that's what you should do. Give that man a big glove and a telephone, 'cause he's gonna be too far to see the ball when it's hit."

"Okay, we have an idea how to pitch him—which is, basically, don't pitch to him—walk him. But you really don't think we should put the center fielder against the wall, do you?" said Frankie.

"You guys all played in Griffith Stadium. Four-hundred and five down the line, then there's a twenty-five-foot fence and twenty-five rows of bleachers, then a hot dog sign? Josh hits that sign all the time. Center field—how many guys hit 'em over that fence? Four-hundred and eighty-four feet. They got a forty-five-foot fence and trees in the back. He puts it in the trees. He's hit the ball out of every park but Yellowstone. So if I were you, I'd have all three outfielders up against the wall."

Clapp glanced at a pocket-sized, well-worn, black leather notebook, then looked up. "In a different way, Cool Papa Bell is just as tough as Gibson. Gibson will wreck you with his bat; Bell will wreck you with his feet." Clapp stared at Diz. "You've got to bear down on him, blow fastballs by him. Don't get too picky. Right down the pipe. If he can hit it, hat's off to him. He'll bunt a lot. Frankie and Lou will have to be in on the grass. I mean, way in. If he gets on, he totally disrupts the game. He was unofficially clocked in twelve seconds—first to home. I think the Major League record is 13.3. He'll steal every base, make you alter your delivery, and the infield has to adjust to the stealing threat, so that leaves bigger holes to slap a ball through. The infield's got to come up on him. The saying is that if the ball bounces twice, just put it in your pocket, 'cuz you're not gonna throw him out. When he steals, he's got a hook slide that he calls a swan slide, just a little kink in it that makes it different. And one more thing, when he's going, he hitches his pants up. If he takes a big lead, he seldom goes. He steals out of a normal lead."

Clapp looked at his notes again. "Buck Leonard. Doesn't bunt much. Stands way off the plate and likes to pull, so the only way to pitch him is outside. He's a power hitter, but he's raw. Throw him high curves and junk. He feasts on fastballs. Hard to get one by him."

"Next, we've got Turkey Stearnes. You guys ever play against him?"

The players looked at each other and shook their heads. Leo said, "I think maybe I did, once, maybe. I don't know. They all look the same to me."

Everyone but Frankie laughed. Harry continued, "Stearnes is an in-credible long-ball hitter for a guy who's not that big. Paige pitches him outside low. Other pitchers say you can get him out with changeups and high fastballs. Anything over the plate is gone."

"What if he can't see it?" said Diz, who did not expect Clapp's answer.

"General rule in the Negro Leagues seems to be if you can't see it, bunt it. They'll bunt you to death. But Stearnes strikes out a lot, going after those bad balls. And when he misses, there is a Pentecostal wind."

"Pentecostal wind—I like that," said Leo. "I feel it just sitting next to Babe."

Clapp laughed, then slapped his hand with the little leather note-book. "Charleston—you've got to brush him back and try to let his temper get to him. Willie Wells. Word is, he's gun-shy. Throw one at his head, and he'll back off the plate. Then fire everything over the outside corner. Okay? Mule Suttles is another one you've got to go after, Diz. Uses a thirty-seven-inch, fifty-six-ounce bat. You should be able to get the fastball by him. But what smart guys do is throw at his feet. He's got bad feet. And he's scared of taking a ball off the foot. So make him dance a little. He'll back off, too. Now, if I had to sum it all up, I'd say victory depends on two things—keep Bell off and put Gibson on."

"What about Dihigo?" asked Diz.

"Don't know much about him. Plays down in Cuba. Knowledge has its limits."

Maybe it did, or maybe Knowledge was playing some of his cards close to his vest. Harry shook Clapp's hand and let him out. Five min-utes later he burst through the door and looked at Diz. "*Black crook.* If you leave out the 'eight' and the 'o', it's 'black crook.'" His mouth showed something like a smile as he left. He associated the anagram with "Gus Greenlee," but Diz looked at his teammates and said, "The base filcher, Cool Papa Bell."

Harry Bennett put Satch's team up in the Parker House, which was a sight better than the chinch parlors the Homestead Grays were used to on the road, places like the Woodside Hotel in New York, which had a club downstairs that kept them awake half the night, and where the bugs were so bad the players had to sleep in chairs with the lights on.

In his room, hat down over his face to shut out the light, Oscar Charleston could have been anybody—anybody in pinstripes. Baggy woolen pinstripes, short-sleeved to the elbow, and plus fours over the knees into long black socks. The uniform signified what you were, as long as you wore it. This man would not much longer be a Homestead Gray, not much longer a full-time player. Maybe that was why he slept in his uniform. Maybe he felt it all slipping away. Maybe he was the tails side of the Babe Ruth coin. It certainly wasn't for comfort. The wool was itchy. But then there were those who thought that Oscar slept in an itchy uniform just so that he'd wake up meaner than he went to bed.

Play with fire? How about eating Oscar's chicken. A mess of fried chicken, half gnawed on, half rolled up in a brown paper bag on his bed. Itch notwithstanding, Oscar was a sound sleeper. You could sit on his bed and eat his chicken and he wouldn't wake up—if you had a pain wish. Oscar was known for squeezing a baseball so hard some seams would pop. Granted, that was the Negro League ball, a Wilson, not as well made as the Major League Spalding, but in a fight Oscar's favorite hold was a grip of an opponent's testicles. Or you might chow down on Oscar's chicken if you had a death wish, or maybe . . . maybe if you were a gambler with a strong sense of intuition, like Satch . . .

"Don't do it, Satch," Cool warned him. "I'm tellin' you. I played with Charlie in the Dominican Republic. This skinny shortstop didn't like the way Charlie'd slud into him, so he pushed him. Charlie laid him out with one punch. That brought the second baseman into it. He wasn't much bigger, and Charlie laid him out cold. Then a bunch of soldiers ran onto the field and pretty soon the whole platoon was flattened. No lie. That's the way it happened. He was one-man mayhem. Even Mule backed down from Charlie. Smokey Joe, too, and you know how big he is. One time, three Klan guys came up to us, in Georgia. We'd just whipped the local boys. Everyone jumped on the bus but Charlie. He jumped off. Walked up to the three guys and stared at them. He's got those lion eyes. Like a gunfighter. He tore the hood off one of 'em and the other two turned tail and beat it."

"Cool's right," said Josh. "You know how Lefty Gomez hates Negroes? He's a tough character. Dusted Ruth off all the time. Well, he dusted Charlie in Bloomsburg, and when Charlie charged the mound, he turned tail and ran. He asked Jimmie Foxx to help him out, but Jimmie respects Negroes." Josh laughed. "I got a kick out of that. Got a kick out of beating Gomez, too."

"That's one side of Charlie," said Satch, "but there's the other side, too. One time in Pittsburgh we was tryin' to get some food, and the waitress said, 'We don't serve niggers here.' When Charlie gave her that look, we all got scared what he might do, but he just said, 'That's okay. I didn't order one.'"

Josh laughed, and Satch noticed the loaded pistol that Oscar kept under his pillow, a gift from a grateful Cuban politician. It was a very calculated risk Satchel took to bring Oscar into the fold, to make him feel, for once, part of a team, not the outsider with a grudge against everybody. Satch got the whole team around Oscar's bed. He took a bite of the chicken and passed it around. Buck bit into it like it was the Last Supper. When the chicken was eaten, Satch put around Oscar's neck a necklace made of the chicken's bones. Then he bounced a ball off Oscar's forehead. Oscar opened his eyes.

"Charlie, you awake?"

"How could I be fucking your wife if I wasn't?"

"My wife liked it so much she gave you a necklace, man."

The superstitious Charleston saw the necklace and freaked. Tore it off and noticed the empty bag his chicken had been in. He inspected it and tossed it aside, then reached under his pillow for his gun.

"You ate my fucking chicken?"

"Go ahead, shoot me, nigger!" Satch said, with *sangfroid*, and the team laughed. Oscar backed down. He lowered the gun, but Satch lunged for it, pulled it toward him and the gun went off. That is, the hammer hit the chamber, with nothing in it. Satch had emptied the pistol. He laughed, and the team broke up. Oscar sat up, half enraged and half something else. Satch's gesture was asking Oscar who he was, and it gave him no time to let thinking obfuscate the response from the heart. Oscar looked at the gaggle of teammates. He saw them as a choir. He saw himself on his deathbed and asked himself, *How do you want to go? How will they remember me?*

"You motherfuckers!" Then Oscar laughed, with the motherfuckers, and he felt self-conscious about the grin widening into gulleys, furrows, craters. But he couldn't stop grinning.

Dandy guffawed, then laughed that snort laugh. "You . . . you know what you look like? . . . The man in the moon."

The team laughed louder. Willie slapped his thigh and nearly fell down. "The man in the moon!"

The team slapped Oscar's head, shoulders, and legs, and said their goodnights. Oscar called them back. "Wait a minute. We've gotta talk about Dean's team. This is as good a time as any."

Oscar sat up on the edge of his bed, and nine players sat around him on chairs or on the floor.

Josh smiled. "Shit, it wasn't two years ago we beat Stengel's All-Stars five out of seven. You remember that? They had Hack Wilson . . . who else they had?"

"Manush, I think," said Mule.

"Heinie Manush, Heinie Meine, Heinie Schuble. They had Heinies coming out the hiney, and we kicked their hineys."

"Mm-hm. You not lyin'."

"Ever since we beat Ruth's All-Stars six out of seven and Willie Foster threw that perfect game against 'em, Judge Landis been runnin' with his tail between his legs," said Josh. "Our guys hit the same or better against white pitchin' as they do against our own. Knowledge Clapp said so, so you know it's true."

"I think it was on account of the Hillsdales beating the A's three games to none, and the last one eighteen to three, that's why Landis won't allow no more interracial play," said Turkey Stearnes.

Oscar looked around with a frown. "If you're all through patting yourselves on the back, we can get down to discussing these guys in particular. They happen to be the cream of the crop. Ruth, Gehrig—the two best of all time. Not much to be said about them."

"Durocher and Martin may not be the best ballplayers in the world, but they turn the double play and they come to kill you," Satch offered. "It's the attitude. That's what makes 'em winners. That's why they won the Series and the Tigers are crying in their beer. Don't underestimate Durocher and Martin."

"Martin was an All-Star, and Durocher wasn't far behind," added Cool.

"I've played against Martin," said Oscar. "Got an inside-out swing. Slices balls to right field. Doesn't run through first base—slams on the brakes and skids to a halt, which would kill an ordinary man's knees. He's one strong sonofabitch."

"Associated Press Athlete of the Year in '31," Mule added.

Satch nodded. "You guys know anything about Frisch?"

"Yeah. He's bald in back, like Charlie."

"He's a complete player," said Willie. "He don't hit for average like Gehringer, but he's got more power, and he's better defensively. The guy always makes contact. Once had only ten strikeouts in 617 at-bats."

"How do you know that?" Josh asked.

" 'Cuz Willie had ten against me in one doubleheader," said Satch. Willie snarled. *El Diablo* didn't like being ragged on.

"He's fast, too," added Cool. "Stole forty-nine bases one year. Set the National League record."

"When was that?" Satch asked.

"Don't remember."

"I think he's lost a step. The only threat they have on the bases is Martin. And maybe the kid, DiMaggio. Everyone else is slow as shit."

"Like Lombardi," said Josh, laughing. "Hits singles off the walls. That's how slow he is. But he's a hell of a hitter. If he could run, I'd take him over Cochrane or anyone."

Satch tried to be objective and see himself as the right man for the greatest game ever played. Slim Jones would get a fair share of dissenting votes. Satch never had a season like Jones's—22-3—beating Satch head to head, twice. Jones threw just as hard, but like Bullet Rogan, he'd wear down a bit by the ninth. Rogan, only 5'6", had to put everything into every pitch. Satch didn't. He'd save his fastest stuff for when he really needed it, saved his arm wear and tear by alternating overhand, sidearm, and underhand, using different muscles. Then he had those tricky deliveries—sidearm, looking at third base till the ball was out of his hand. And the hesitation pitch that had guys swinging before the ball was even released. That not only got him free strikes, it made the batter feel stupid, which gave Satch an edge.

Like Wells and Durocher, Satch and Diz were two sides of the same coin. Both a little on the nutty side, Dean more than Paige. Both the biggest drawing cards in their respective leagues, and savvy enough to get paid for it. Dean versus Paige was a sellout. They each got a percentage of the barnstorming gate, and on a per-game basis they made ten times what they earned in league play.

Physically, they were similar. Paige was an inch or so taller, and skinnier. Both were primarily fastballers, but Dean had a better curve. Satch had more variety in his deliveries, but the many names he had for his pitches were mainly variations on a fastball. A slightly different motion, slightly different grip, but the ball still roared in at ninety-five plus, rising or sinking. Both had fabulous control. Satch would put a postage stamp on home plate and hit the corners. Dean had a tremendous strike-out/walk ratio. Some guys didn't want to walk, fearing that the next time up the wrathful, nutty pitcher might put one in their ear. If Diz wanted to hit you, he hit you. Ducking didn't do much good. If he really wanted to bean a guy he'd throw behind his head. Instinctively ducking back would literally put the ball in his ear.

Josh watched Cool massage his calf muscles. His legs took a beating both from sliding and from shortstops coming down on him with their sharpened spikes when he stole second or tried to break up a double play.

"Cool, why don't Jesse Owens race against you?" Josh asked.

"He'd rather race those horses that Gus gets for him, gun-shy ones that rear up when they hear a starting gun," Cool answered.

"You can beat Jesse Owens no sweat, but Bojangles can beat you running backward, with a twenty-five-yard spot," said Satch.

Cool stood up and shifted his weight from left to right, several times, testing the feel of the shoes. "Just bring your money, man."

"I'll bring it, too," said Josh. "Bojangles beat the guy who beat Jesse in the hundred, with that twenty-five-yard spot. You better watch out, Cool. Bojangles comin' to take your job when he's done dancing." Josh let out a big laugh, and Cool laughed, too. Neither Josh nor Satch was going to bet against Cool. They just liked teasing him. Then again, nobody ever made money betting against Bojangles. It would have been a good race.

"Anything else you guys want to add?" said Oscar.

Some shook their heads. Nobody offered anything.

"Okay, then. See y'all tomorrow."

The players again said goodnight to Oscar.

"Goodnight, old man," said Satch, the last man out.

Oscar called him back. "Leroy, come here. I got something to tell you."

Satch closed the door and walked to the bed.

"They say Oscar Charleston's a mean man. And I ain't denying I got a mean streak. But it ain't me."

Satch's brow furrowed. He reassured Oscar. "Sure. It ain't you . . . Who is it?"

Oscar pulled at his uniform shirt where it was joined with buttons, as if to bare his heart. "It ain't me. It's Oscar. Sometimes I be in here looking out and I say, 'Oscar, why'd you do that?' Or, 'Oscar, why'd you say that?' It got really bad about five years ago. My wife was gonna leave less'n I saw a doctor. So I made an appointment with this head doctor, and I learned something."

Oscar leaned forward and his voice broke into a loud gasp. "It ain't even me! *Oscar* is a condition . . . And God wouldn't have nothin' to do with it, so the devil picked it up and breathed life into it. And it had to have a name, so devil called it Oscar Charleston. Actually, it's two conditions, but I roll 'em into one 'cuz they's both Oscar. One's what they call paranoia. That means you see enemies everywhere you turn. The other is depression. That's like the blues, only it's what they call 'chronic'—you got it all the time. Then the devil felt sorry for this miserable thing he made, so he said 'I'm gonna make it up to you, Oscar. I'm gonna make you the best black ballplayer ever lived.' And I don't know if he was telling the truth, but if he was off, it wasn't by much.

"Now, we got a game tomorrow, and you got ten players, and I know you're frettin' about who's going to start and who's going to sit. So let me make it easy on you. Oscar sits. Those guys, Mule and Turkey, they're young. They can run. I ain't as fast as I used to be, and to tell the truth I don't even like playin' all that much anymore. The only thing I love is the big moment. When the chips are down. Other guys are getting tight and Oscar's getting goose bumps, dying to get his at-bat 'cuz he know that he'll come through in the clutch. So pinch-hit me when the chips are down, okay?"

Satch nodded. "Just one thing. We got eleven players. I signed Bebop."

Oscar turned up his lip. "What the hell did you do that for?"

"Heard Dean's got Nittols. They play their midget, we play ours. Just an insurance policy."

"Like, bases loaded?"

"Only if they do it first."

"If Dean's on his game, bases may never get loaded."

Satch nodded and walked to the door. Halfway out, he looked back. "*Condition,* tell Oscar that was some mighty fine fried chicken."

Satch laughed. Oscar picked up a shoe and threw it at the door that closed behind the skipper. A few minutes later, Cool knocked on Satch's door and asked for some gin. Satch gave him a pint. The joke was that you could flip the switch and Cool would be in bed before the light was out. The truth was anything but. After a game, Cool's arthritis would kick in. He was in pain most every night. Cool peeled a lemon, mashed it, and poured the juice into the gin bottle with two teaspoonfuls of sugar. He shook it up and took five slugs, as he did every night, for his arthritis. In the morning, when he got up, he took five more slugs, before a hot bath. Then he cut sponges and taped them around the wounds on his legs.

Cool Papa Bell was not alone in the ailment department. The doubleheaders with a six-hour bus ride in between, and the all-night bus trips right after the second game of a doubleheader, with only baloney sandwiches and a six-pack for dinner on the bus, all got to any player. Mule Suttles didn't fit on a bus seat. His knees were as sore as his back.

Before he played he stretched out an inch at a time. Just off the bus he could barely touch his knees, and any sudden motion would throw his back out completely. Eventually his long arms reached his shins, and five minutes later his toes. Oscar Charleston had a permanent neck burner from his head hanging and bobbing as he tried to sleep on the bus. In the on-deck circle he'd twist his neck—kind of like a turkey— three times in each direction. Then he'd lurch his head to each side, feeling minor pain but loosening his neck enough that when he clouted a ball, finishing with a short twist of the neck, he wouldn't be paralyzed for three to four seconds, waiting for the intense burn to subside enough for him to run the bases.

Satch went back to his room. He had his own rattlesnake oil, and he rubbed it into the right shoulder he had injured on the boat and by throwing the *coco* into the sea, and he rubbed it into the sore right hand he had thrown at the guard's chin. He had trouble raising his arm to comb his hair. He fell asleep thinking on how this night was different from any other, thinking *Take me out to the ballgame. Take me back to the womb. Don't let me out till they integrate. But whatever you do, don't do it till tomorrow night. Till the wee hours, when I'm skunked past soreness, when we've won.*

That's when Satch realized that for the first time in many years he had been talking to God, and snored himself to sleep, thinking about the big game and about making it to the Major Leagues, thinking . . . *wouldn't it be funny if guys like Branch Rickey and Kenesaw Mountain Landis came up to the pearly gates with their season-tickets presumptively in hand, and Peter said, "You guys got it all wrong. You should have taken inscrutability more seriously, for self-righteousness is the big one. And you could never imagine what a kick I get out of pulling this golden lever to the trapdoor you jokers are standing on."*

17

CAROLELOMBARDCAROLELOMBARD

G ame day, October 20, began with unusual warmth and a light breeze bringing the scents of rotting green apples and burning leaves through the window that John Henry had opened to spit out orange seeds. The smells were opiates. John Henry was lost in meditation, connecting the dots of the leaves on the porch and glimpsing the eternal as they blew away. One of those days. He raked his bushy hair with both hands, feeling bifurcated. One side of his head was feeling housebroken and it was not a bad feeling. Nostalgia seemed right for such an October morning, a chapter of his life culminating in the game. On the other side there was a job to do. Easy money—what John Henry had always been drawn to.

He rolled a cigarette and smoked it, contemplating the heads and tails he had made of his life, considering pissing around the sofa and the Victrola, marking his territory like a tomcat, then lying in the sun coming in at an angle that was neither hot nor cold, watching the peculiar staccato dashes of squirrels up and down the trunk of the huge oak in the yard. He stabbed the waxed cardboard seal of the milk bottle with a chef's knife and levered it off. He drank the cream off the top, then poured some in his coffee.

The house that Carole was renting in Weston, Massachusetts for a week was both cozy and witchy, a tawny brick affair, the bottom half of which was largely blocked from sight by yews, hemlocks, and assorted esoteric shrubbery. The top half, below the slate roof that tapered to a squared-off point, was mostly covered with ivy. With an immense chimney, the house had the air of a place you'd warn kids named Hansel and Gretel not to wander to. The spooky shrubbery obfuscating so much of the house gave it a nestled, squat appearance, like a Lewis Carroll cat with its outsized tail wrapped around it.

Carole had flown in with John Henry and James Atwood and invited them to stay in the ten-room house. Being alone was not something she was used to, and everybody could use bodyguards. Carole rented the house because for a week it was no more expensive than the Ritz, but what really mattered was that it had a tennis court and the Ritz didn't, and Longwood tennis finalist Sarah Palfrey was in Boston. In California, Carole played with rising star Alice Marble, who had been the mascot and ball girl for the San Francisco Seals.

John Henry watched a big cumulous comforter, thinking of how cozy it would be to pull all that fluff over himself and Carole. Then sail over the edge of the world to the strange sound of Vivaldi's *Four Seasons* tripping down the stairs, notes falling over each other in a rush. It sounded ominous, a whole gunnysack full of cats dropped off a bridge and smelling water. The music seemed somehow to imperil his cloud, which refused to move any faster despite the urgency, and John Henry felt like a conductor with a baton in his hand when he needed a paddle. He felt impotent. Then hungry. He picked an orange from the fruit bowl in front of him and cut through the skin with the chef's knife, then peeled it. That's when Carole first glimpsed him that morning, the music coming from her open bedroom door, John Henry grasping the knife overhand, cigarette dangling from his lips, coffee steaming before him. He seemed to her a live piece of folk art, or an artist mocking himself, with the grotesquely unnecessary twelve-inch blade gutting the orange. She had to stifle a laugh, but at the same time there was an aura of engaging warmth about him, and a wild sense of life. She stared at him staring at a cup of jo, smoldering—which was what John Henry seemed to spend a lot of time doing. Smoldering, so that the oval kitchen table could have been an ashtray, the long mop of John Henry's hair the intact ash of a cigarette lit and left on a semicylindrical holder. There was a Rodin-ish intensity to the handsome, brooding young man in trousers with suspenders over a T-shirt, a pack of Chesterfields perched in the short, rolled-up sleeve.

After salutations, Carole took an orange and began to peel it. John Henry's unsophisticated exuberance over a bowl full of oranges made her smile. He watched the juice accumulate at the base of the convoluted crystal dome the oranges were squeezed on. He watched the pure juice come through the strainer, leaving the seeds and pulp behind.

Carole filled two short glasses. They drank synchronously, looking at each other. She found herself drawn to John Henry the way that all the glitterati were drawn to criminal elements, the way that Hollywood had its tongue out for George Raft, for the real thing. She was at the same time afraid of him, while that fear drew her to him. This was *realer*. When she thought on it, she told herself it was the professional actress in her that wanted to understand the character, to be able to use it. In many respects, John Henry seemed like a puppy. So Carole's query, "You're really a kidnapper?" was imbued with incipient flirtation.

"Yes, ma'am. But other than that, I'm a regular guy."

"How many folks have you kidnapped?"

"Just one."

"Who was it?"

"Some guy. He deserved it though. Like he had a tag on him that said, 'Do something to me.' Like the Lord put the tag on him."

" 'Do something' doesn't necessarily mean kidnapping."

"I never meant him any harm. Even if he hadn't paid up, I'd have let him go."

"So you're a big bluffer."

John Henry cogitated, then owned up to it with a closed-mouth smile. "You won't tell anybody?"

Carole returned the smile with about thirty perfect teeth and tussled his curly hair. "What kind of work do you do when you're a regular guy?"

"Anything. Everything. Been a whistlepunk, shovel stiff, river hag, automobile mechanic, you name it. When things got really rough, I'd steal dog biscuits from the city pound."

John Henry took a match from the box and placed the head in the long ash that had just dropped from his cigarette just to see if it would ignite.

"You like playing with fire?"

John Henry pushed his lips together and gave the slightest nod, thinking it was funny that he hadn't been fully conscious of what he had been doing or that Carole might be noticing. "I set a field on fire once. Just to see what it would be like. There was a hornet's nest in the tall grass and I wanted to see what they would do, too. My father came running over with a big canvas tarp, trying to smother it. He got burned pretty bad in the process, mainly on his thigh. I could see his pants on fire, and it scared me bad, but I kind of felt like laughing, too, seeing a man with his pants on fire.

"He'd always been healthy as a horse, till then. He went into a decline. Everything went wrong. He got emphysema, and his leg hurt, and he got a hernia. But they say every cloud has a silver lining, and this one wasn't no different. It was really my emancipation. My father didn't have the energy to beat me no more. Before that, every day of his life, my father beat me. He used to get a stick and a belt and make me choose. If I didn't, he'd use both, one after the other. After he went into his decline he looked at me like I was going to beat him, get my revenge. But I didn't. I loved my father. Don't know why. Just did."

John Henry drained his coffee, put his cup down and poured some orange juice from the pitcher into the cup. Carole chuckled. "I can get you a glass."

John Henry smiled. "I like it this way. You get the taste of the orange juice and the smell of the coffee at the same time. It's like something for nothing. Like getting something you're not supposed to get."

"You like feeling guilty?"

The question made no sense to John Henry. He looked at her, and when she didn't avert her eyes he stared at the ashtray, twirling a matchstick with the thumb and forefinger of his left hand. He gave a combination of laugh and sigh. "Maybe I played with fire 'cuz I had nothing else to play with."

Carole's head buzzed. John Henry seemed to turn everything upside down.

"You ever play with fire?" John Henry's tenseless question left Carole uneasy. She'd been burned a few times. She stared at the box of matches John Henry had just flipped with his thumb. He took a Chesterfield from the pack in his sleeve and rolled it on the table under his fingers, unnecessarily and out of habit, as if the barely audible crush of tobacco leaves meant something. Now he was lighting it. The blue tip of the wooden match exploded into a teardrop-shaped flame. She felt the same push and pull, to and from her gangster, that left her gaping and staring, a smile slashed across her face with a pallet-knife. She didn't know if she wanted to get close to the *reformed* gangster or titillate herself with a quick slap and tickle with a *real* one.

John Henry hawkered out the kitchen window he'd opened to spit out orange seeds.

"Good aim."

"I can hit a spittoon from ten feet."

"I'll bet Dizzy Dean can't do that."

"No, but I bet Pepper Martin could."

"James Atwood says you met the whole Cardinals team, at Henry Ford's."

"Yup. Met Ford, too. Didn't care for him much. Don't care for any of those high-hats. All high and mighty with finger bowls and all. I told Ford to put his finger bowls up his ass so's he wouldn't have to use no Montgomery Wards like the rest of us."

"You didn't actually say that."

"No. But I wish I did."

John Henry experienced a blinding flash, as though someone had flicked on the light for a fraction of a second in a dark room. He'd had it before, several times, since the kidnapping. What he saw repetitively in his mind in the blinded aftermath of the flash, like a shade snapping up and being pulled back down, was Carole's satin robe falling off her shoulders, leaving the top half of her body jaybird-naked save the gold chain around her neck. Satin that should fall on itself and then on the floor with a susurrus fell with a sound that was magnified by the intensity of the effect on his eyes. John Henry projected for the thousandth time on the screen of his mind the naked imagining of her flesh. His face had a tempered glow to it. He looked to Carole like the incarnation of sundown at a Minnesota iron mine. Then the face turned somber.

"Sometimes I think I done wrong. Everything I done is wrong. I done a lot of people wrong, including a girl near as pretty as you. I might have froze her to death. Sometimes I feel like I'm lookin' into the gates of hell, and the angel of the Lord is standing by like an escort."

John Henry was wondering if Carole ever wondered what it would be like to take inside her the angel of the Lord. If swords went to ploughshares, why shouldn't ploughshares evolve into steely shafts fit for any girl-next-door? And if God was always a man, *why not, why not, why not?*

Carole held out her hand. "Come on upstairs and talk to me while I get ready."

"For what?"

"Tennis."

John Henry followed her into a spacious room, one whole wall of which was glass, facing east. She carried the black teapot with gold Chinese characters on it, and two porcelain cups.

"Hey," he said, getting his first good look at the left side of Carole's face in good light, "you got a scar."

"You should see the windshield on Heinie Cooper's Bugatti."

"You smash it?"

"Disintegrated it."

"I never noticed, in the movies, even when your face is so big."

"Johnny, there's a lot of things you don't know about a girl till you get up close." Motionless for a moment, Carole looked him in the eye. Nobody called him Johnny back in Ironton or Fenco, but he liked "Johnny" when Carole said it. He decided he'd let her do it, exclusively.

"Like what?" he said.

"Like whether she bothers with undergarments."

John Henry half-snorted a laugh. "Yeah, I noticed that about you. I mean, that you never wear a bra. But I can't tell nothing about the under-rompers. Ain't seen nothing up that way."

"That's because a gentleman isn't supposed to, Johnny." Carole looked at her watch. "It's ten o'clock. Where the hell is Sarah?"

Carole pulled back the curtain to look out another bedroom window. Sarah Palfrey and Alice Marble were the only women she knew who could beat her at tennis. Ginger Rogers and Kate Hepburn could put up a decent battle, but always in a losing cause. Carole was arguably the best woman athlete in Hollywood. She'd learned archery from Jessica Barthelmes, polo from Spencer Tracy, and as a kid in Fort Wayne she even got boxing lessons from lightweight champ Benny Leonard.

Carole sipped her tea. John Henry watched her dip the tea bag again in it, loop the string around the bag and spoon, then squeeze, depositing the spoon on the saucer, a little wet Ahab lashed to his silver whale. Tea bags had always turned him off. In his own personal Rorschach, John Henry saw a tea bag and thought "maiden aunts with doilies." But his whole worldview was altered when he saw Carole sipping tea. China appeared on his map. Ceylon became a mysterious rendezvous. Tea was for two. Carole and John Henry.

"Sarah has stood me up. Can you play tennis?"

"Sure. I played hockey, semiprofessional."

"Johnny, you know the difference between hockey and tennis, don't you? Hockey has a puck and it's played on ice. Tennis has a ball and it's played on a court."

"Sure. I knew that. You're supposed to wear shorts, too, but I don't have none."

Carole didn't miss a beat. She dropped her shorts, stepped out with her right foot and then the left, with all the nonchalance of practicing a new dance step. She handed them to John Henry. "See if these fit."

John Henry was so flabbergasted he almost did not notice the blond patch. He did notice the mole on her behind as she turned and walked to her closet. She stopped halfway there and turned her head back. "Now you know everything there is to know about me."

For a millisecond the entire field of John Henry's vision was the same curtain of orange flame he'd seen in the snow of southern Minnesota. The sky cracked open with black lightning. Then it was gone, as instantly as it appeared. John Henry was for the second time in minutes visually stunned. His head snapped back. Carole didn't notice. She kept her backside to him. She felt his eyes on her and enjoyed the feeling.

"I seen Armageddon twice now."

It seemed to Carole that John Henry's voice rose like a preacher's. "Did you like it?"

"No, ma'am."

"I don't believe in Armageddon."

"What do you believe in, then?" he asked.

"I believe the world is what you make it."

"You don't believe anyone's judging you?"

"Sure. Hedda, Louella, and Walter. I read the papers every day to see what they think of me."

"I think you're swell."

"That's 'cuz you're looking at my ass."

"No. I really think you're something."

Carole pulled on another pair of shorts and gave him a big smile and a peck on the cheek. John Henry could see very clearly the scar on her cheek. It reminded him of the shape of the sky cracking open. He put the thought out of his mind and inhaled her scent. He expected perfume, but she was fresh air. John Henry laughed.

"You know what you smell like?"

"What?"

"Fresh air."

Carole smiled and tweaked his cheek. "You're the sweetest kidnapper I know. Get those shorts on and let's play."

John Henry had no ass at all. So though the shorts were extremely tight, they fit, with the side-zipper halfway closed. He was, however, hung. Carole took a long look and brushed past him. John Henry could not believe he was playing tennis with Carole Lombard, and after a minute it was clear that John Henry did not play what the rest of the world knew as tennis, but he did go after balls like a man possessed. The game turned into serving practice, with John Henry chasing down balls with the same sense of urgency and obedience as a Labrador retriever. He carried her racket and balls back upstairs. She entered her bedroom and left the door open. John Henry peeked in to say he would wait downstairs.

"John Henry," she said flatly, "I want my shorts back."

She already had the cotton blouse up over her breasts, and it reminded John Henry of something being born. He couldn't tell what part he liked best—seeing her midriff contracted with the flesh exposing itself so fast, or the tease, the time to savor every centimeter, as the blouse slowed, tight over her breasts—so nonchalant, an identical mix of melon and pear, then over the regal neck. John Henry Tantalus, forcing his eyes to move as slowly as dripping honey, dripping unnaturally, uphill, from the exaggerated arch of her foot up past the knee, with the anticipation of Burton nearing the source of the Nile. That river, back upstream, he'd read, does amazing things. And why shouldn't it—with that jungle? Delta at the source—unnatural again. But John Henry was getting used to that. He had to say that he liked it. He looked at her with a benign, almost saintly glaze to his eyes, near-blinded by the conflation of her naked body with Armageddon, reeling in a vision while by rote disrobing himself.

"Is this enough?"

Out of the blue. John Henry almost panicked. *Enough what?* The sight of her almost undid him, never mind the question. Some kind of Madonna, some shining, full-length halo, some radiance about her. And John Henry's mind asking—*Is what enough? What? Your body? Do you mean—did you take enough off? It's all off. Is that what you meant? Facetiously? Do you mean—is it enough just to look at your body? To worship it? Yes. Yes. No. Yes.* This was not the time for ambiguity. Not when he had not yet peeled off his boxers. Not when she had been reading his mind, his insecurity, and had beaten him to the verbal punch with regard perhaps to the size of his genitals.

John Henry chortled, "What? What?"

Carole strode toward him and pulled down his shorts. She looked at him. Divine yet pixieish. Or devilish and smiling, finger on the lower lip of her open mouth, signing a question.

She was touched by the answer. Then by the sight of his lips silently mouthing, *Carole Lombard Carole Lombard!* Trochaic tetrameter. The meter, he found shortly, matched his own rhythm, and hers. A fast rhythm. But, what the hell. What was a man to do with *Carole Lombard Carole Lombard?*

What sadness does is drip. Sadness and joy could share the same foxhole, though. Maybe they have to. Maybe they're assigned that way. Joy, I suppose, rises. Can't say that I really know. But sadness does drip.

Sadness—it's in the eyes. Some will see it in the shoulders. The droop. Then they stop looking. As if sadness were a shelf contained by the bookends of eyes and shoulders. All the major works on it. *Job* is there, central vowel elongated as if put on the rack, even without his silent *e* that had gallivanted off with Carol*e*.

In the coupled silence John Henry experienced the familiar, comic flop, tiny shock of falling out, then the familiar hanging. The self being reintroduced to self. With so much to talk about.

"You're a hero, John Henry."

He tittered. "Oh, heck, it was nothing."

"No." Carole laughed. "I mean at my party, with the pig."

John Henry breathed deeply and audibly and found himself, on exhalation, a different if not a new man.

John Henry tried the broad elbow-joint of a low limb of the massive oak, then a pile of leaves and branches, and finally the ladder-like end of the long woodpile. No matter where he sat or lay he could not find a spot that was unequivocally uncomfortable, so heady and distracting was the afterglow of his tryst with Carole. He chain-smoked a pack of Chesterfields, craving emotional normalcy, fighting the indulgence of basking in the sweetness of the experience.

James Atwood both sensed and understood John Henry's feeling.

"I've got a stone you could put in your shoe, if you want to."

"What are you talking about?"

James Atwood unfolded the blade of his jackknife and threw it end over end into a log. He changed the subject to something he had words for. "I saw you carrying on with Carole. Did you think I wouldn't?"

"I couldn't give a shit one way or another, James Atwood."

"You ain't good enough for her, John Henry. She goes for guys like Clark Gable and George Raft."

John Henry laughed. "You're jealous."

"I ain't jealous. I'm not looking to plank Carole. I respect her too much. She's one of a kind. Like a flower we got in Kansas, called Slipper of Venus. That's the Greek god of love. I know you better than anybody, John Henry. You're nothing but a cyclopath, and I don't want you doing Carole like you did that girl you stole the car from."

"She was a whore."

"Could be you treat all women like that. Carole's a lot more than a pair of tits."

"I seen you looking at her tits, and I hear you jacking off at night. You're just a loser, and now you're a sore loser."

"If I'm a loser, you're a loser, too. I heard Carole on the phone to Gable. You're out of the picture. That was a one-time thing. Carole's not wasting her time on a loser like you."

"We'll see about that."

"You're lucky I owed you one, for my toes," James Atwood said with a hard toss of the knife into the same log. "We're even up now. I'm warning you to stay away from Carole. You cross me and you'll be sorry you did."

The sky grew more ominous as James Atwood vaulted the fence and headed down the road. John Henry did not take the threat seriously. He lit up another cigarette, content to ignore the corpse of a squirrel rather than load it onto the blade of a shovel and catapult it over the fence and onto the road James Atwood had taken. The low-pressure air could not have been sweeter. Chesterfields never tasted better. The robins chattered to each other about his exploits. The living squirrels, holding acorns and spilling shards, were giving him two thumbs-up, while upstairs in the witchy house Carole had prepared her own bathtub brew of emollients and bubble-bath, including one-half of a lime and a teaspoon of rue that a Cuban fortune-teller insisted was *her* herb, along with a few accidental drops of gin and tonic. Glenn Miller's orchestra came through the radio, and out of the bubble-brew came a perfect tanned leg, draping over the tub's edge as if for a breather. Her back slid down and her rump fitted the contours of the tub in a series of three short motions, high to low, matching the intonation drop of the three-syllabled name uttered in her cranium—*John-Hen-ry.* How it seemed to glide. A three-bagger. *John-Hen-ry.* She contemplated calling his name out the window, getting out of the tub wearing nothing but bubbles and wrapping him around her like a towel.

Suddenly, the squirrels were razzing John Henry, loudly, their teeth chomping through acorn shells and making that husky squeak from their throats. *Maybe,* thought John Henry, *I should go up for more.* For a moment he thought he heard his name being called. He stood up, listened intently, and heard nothing human. He grabbed a thin bat-like log from the woodpile and took a few practice cuts. He picked up a fat green apple, tossed it up and disintegrated it, then dropped the log and took the first step toward the doormat gleaming like home plate.

"THE HOLLYWOOD REPORTER"

by Louella Parsons

If anybody doubts this lady's ability to dig with Sam Spade, then read no further. But, oo-wee, if I don't have some blisters on my fingers and if my arms aren't tired from flying to St. Louis to Chicago to Washington, D.C. to check on my sources, and have I got some lowdown for my fellow Hollywood gardeners! If you've kept up, you know which leading man who cuts a rug with the likes of Astaire and who makes even Louella's old heart skip a beat is seeing which leading lady whose skin is so perfect the Gods (female) are making excursions to earth to check out the anomaly and whose figure almost makes one forget the fleet-footed man with the marcelled hair who does such a mean Charleston that he used to bind his feet with chicken wire to cushion the impact of hitting the floodlights with what our Germanic brethren might call uber-exuberance, so I don't even have to remind you that George Raft and Carole Lombard are unofficially an item, which must have Mr. Gable in a fine stew. But even this female version of a private dick does not know for sure why Raft and Lombard have been spotted with distinguished attorney Clarence Darrow, who should be in Washington heading the NRA, but instead is cohorting with the couple as well as with three thugs who must be part of Raft's circle when he was growing up in Hell's Kitchen with the likes of Owney Madden and Feets Edson. Why did this sextet purchase tickets to a Pacific Coast League game? Surely, Raft's pal Leo Durocher has something to do with it. And what of the rumor that Darrow is going to be commissioner of a rival league to Major League baseball, one that allows Negroes to play? Could the sextet be checking out young Joe DiMaggio and other stars of that league-to-be? One has to wonder, given Raft's past, if Arnold Rothstein is at it again, for rumors are that Shoeless Joe Jackson has disappeared from his hometown and has been sighted in St. Louis and Boston. Commissioner Kenesaw Mountain Landis would not comment on any of this, and if his reticence is any indication, something is brewing between Tinseltown and Beantown, and it's not beer. If this is the kind of heady stuff that tickles your throat, keep your eyes peeled and your glass at the ready. This tale's yet to be told, and if you think sand crabs dig fast, you've got to see Louella's pencil. Oh, Mr. Raft, for just one Tango! And Miss Lombard, I've discovered who your hairdresser is . . .

18

FLY ON THE WALL

Errands. Errands. Errands. Satch hated them. Most of all, bringing presents to his sister-in-law in Duxbury. Clara Howard was a showgirl, working in Boston's West End. Scollay Square, mostly. Joints that were a rumor conduit through which word of Satchel's philandering passed. Clara was content to chew him out, without passing the news on to his wife, Janet.

The game was at 8:00 p.m., and Satch thought he had plenty of time. He brought Josh with him, thinking that Clara's bite would be less tenacious, her brimstone less cataclysmic, with Josh in tow. Satch handed Clara the teddy bear. She thanked him. He turned down the offer of tea. He had a game to play. Clara gave him that cynical, disbelieving smile that said *you're full of crap and we both know it, but I'm not going to make a pillar of fuss about it.*

Satch read her expression. "No, it's true. Ask Josh."

Josh nodded. "All-Star game."

Janet cast her eyes up at the darkening sky and sighed. She didn't bother to point out that no park in Boston had lights.

"They're bringing in lights," said Satch, reading her mind.

"Well, I'm sure we'll read about it in the morning paper."

"I don't think so, Clara. It's kind of a secret. It's hard to explain."

"I'm sure it is," Clara said with the same patronizing smile. Satch was now at the edge of the porch, and Clara was holding the screen door. She did a kind of double-take lunge toward Satch, unsure whether to hug a chronic, pathological prevaricator, but one of the family nonetheless. Of what use would mercy and forgiveness be without the likes of Satch to bestow them on? Clara hugged him and whispered, "I'm not sure God loves you, Leroy, but He probably likes you."

Satch looked up into the drizzly, secular sky where the first stars were itching to come out, to wink. "Yeah, He probably do."

When the rain clouds began to dissipate and the first stars did come out, Satch wished on one. He thought of saying a prayer, unable to shake off Clara's fear of the Lord the way he'd shake off Josh's signal for a curve. Star photons were coming at him at the speed of light. Fear came even faster. Especially when the Lord was on the mound. But the urge to pray was checked. At that moment, Satch figured, there was more to fear from Dizzy Dean. And from Oscar Charleston, if he was late to the game.

Something about an October flower, some version of black-eyed Susan, invited picking. Josh began pulling off the petals, trusting his luck and wanting to send Satch a message. "She loves me, she loves me not . . ." His cheeks were pulled back in a broad smile, and Satch was not sure if the ersatz black-eyed Susan represented Janet, or his mother-in-law, or all of the women he consorted with, but he was sure that Josh was teasing, if not taunting. Still, when Satch slapped the flower from Josh's hand it was not the allusion to his failed intimacies that Satch objected to. It was something more primitive, a worldview that saw things as evenly distributed—petals, balls, strikes. A pitcher needed an edge, a ball/strike ratio of around 70–30. He needed three-leafed clovers depetaled with *he-strikes-out, he-strikes-out-not, he-strikes-out*. Pulling petals, Josh was messing with mojo, and Satch felt already tainted. He'd have to drive even faster than usual to outrun it, to contravene it. Speed cured all.

Josh eased down in the shotgun seat of the Packard convertible as Satch left a strip of rubber in front of Clara's house. "Why you always in such a hurry, Satch? If you want to go long and far, you got to go slow."

"Yeah, well, we got as far as Fenway to go, and it ain't far."

Satch was doing about fifty in a thirty-mile-per-hour zone. The siren sounded so far away he paid no attention to it. He didn't check the rearview mirror, believing, as he often said, "Don't look back; something may be gaining on you." It was. It pulled abreast of him. The driver was a cop. He was waving his hand for Satch to pull over. Satch stopped. The cop got out of his car and walked up to the Packard. "In some kind of hurry?"

"Got to get to Fenway Park. I'm pitchin', and I'm late."

The cop smiled. "If the game goes to extra innings, you might get in. Speed you're doing, you're gonna be cooling it."

"Officer, this here's an important game. I gots to be there."

The cop pulled out a ticket book and began writing. "It's October, buddy. All the important games are over. And I don't like niggers pulling my leg."

Josh put a restraining hand on Satch's shoulder. Satch nodded to indicate that he was under control.

"You realize this is a one-way street?"

"I was only going one way."

"You a wise guy?"

"Nope. Just in a hurry. You wanna write me that ticket?"

"I'm going to have to take you to see the justice of the peace."

"Justice of the peace? You at war or something? Declared war on colored folks?"

"Mind your tongue, Leroy. You and your buddy follow me."

"Wait a minute." Satch took a ten from his wallet and held it out the window. "Can we make this go away?"

"You got four more of those?"

"Where is your integrity at, man?"

"You keep that tongue wagging and I'm gonna break it."

Satch looked at Josh and whispered, "*Break* a tongue?"

Josh scowled. "Just do what the man say."

The cop stopped at a barber shop, got out, and walked to the Packard.

"We don't have time for no haircut."

"The barber's the justice of the peace."

"I'm thinkin' the barber is a barber, 'cept he's your brother."

Josh gave Satch a good clout. "Let's pay the fine and get out of here."

The cop held the door open. The barber shop was small and poorly lit. There were two old, throne-like, enamel-based swivel chairs, with fifty pounds of overly elaborate but functional wrought iron, and reddish seats patched in many places with tape. Long black leather straps hung from the arm rests for stropping a razor.

"You sure this ain't your brother?"

The cop gave Satch a push, then looked at Josh and decided not to push him.

"Looks like a clip joint to me," Satch said.

"You want to play baseball tonight?"

This time Josh pushed Satch inside. The barber was short and bald. He was evening off the sideburns of a thin-haired man. Kind of a good-looking fellow, if you ask me. He had a pair of glasses in his hands, resting on his lap, over the long, blue, pin-striped apron. Tissue was wrapped around his neck under the apron to keep the hair from going down his neck. A steely-eyed guy. Close-lipped. Never opened his mouth, even to breathe, the whole time Satch and Josh were there. Never turned, either. Kind of like he wanted to be invisible. A fly on the wall. The guy in the chair just tried to blend in with the decor. Like he was just another instrument a barber might use. The kind of instrument that might be used to take down some high-hat's chops a bit.

The barber, who was about 5'6", looked up at Satch. "What did they get you for?"

"Speeding, Your Honor."

"Guilty?"

"Yup."

"How fast were you going?"

"Fifty in a thirty-mile-per-hour zone, wrong way on a one-way street," said the cop, whose perks apparently did not include trims. Red hair spiked out from under his cap.

"That's a double whammy. You boys in a hurry?"

"Got a ball game to pitch."

"A ball game? Where you playing?"

"Fenway."

The barber laughed. "That's the most insulting excuse I ever heard. There's no games in Fenway in October. And there's no lights. I've seen your teams. The Zulus and the Clowns might *be* dark, but none of them *play ball* in the dark."

"They're bringing in lights."

"That so? Where from?"

"Kansas City."

Satch felt how stupid the whole story must have sounded. He just wanted to pay his fine and get the hell out. He felt trapped in the barber shop, where a red-and-white pole kept spiraling up and going nowhere, where the man in the chair stared at the newspaper in his lap via the mirror. The white hairs around the circumference of the barber's head looked like grass around the fringe of a pitcher's mound. The mound had a raised red lump in the center of it. A Band-Aid on the top of the dirt-colored area cleared of all growth looked like a rubber on the mound of his head. Satch thought to tell him so, but thought better of it.

"Kansas City . . . you don't say. That's a long way to be schlepping lights, isn't it?"

"Three trucks full. The Monarchs got the onliest portable lights."

The barber went back to his work, lips curled like a worm on a hook, his head nodding slowly. He clipped while he spoke. "Night game at Fenway . . . in October." He looked at Satch in the mirror, then at the man's neck again. "So, who's playing—Babe Ruth?"

"Reckon so."

The barber laughed. "Well, you tell the Bambino to come back to Boston. We haven't won shit since Harry Frazee sold him."

"Curse of the Bambino," said the cop, looking under the stack of papers and magazines for one with Joan Crawford on the cover.

"I haven't heard a whopper like this in the twenty years I've been J.P. Are you boys smoking a little opium?"

"We just chew tobacco," said Josh.

"And we ain't lyin'."

"You're a pitcher?"

"Yup."

"See that gumball machine?"

"Yup."

"Put a penny in there and get one."

"I chew tobacco. Don't like gum."

"You're not going to chew it. You're going to throw it."

Satch picked up the red gumball, half the size of a ping-pong ball.

"I don't like speeders. And I don't like liars. No more than I like cutting Negroes' hair. Don't have anything against your race, but what really burns my ass is a couple of you slickers from Kansas City telling tall tales like we're rubes in Boston. There's only one rube I know, and that's Waddell, which you fellas ought to know if you're really ballplayers."

"With all respect to your honor, there's Rube Foster, too. Colored man. He got his nickname after he beat the pants off the white Rube."

"Don't interrupt me, boy. You're kind of full of yourself, aren't you? You ought to learn something from your buddy here—keep your mouth shut. Now, ordinarily, I might let you go with a ten-dollar fine, but for you jokers it's going to be a dollar for every mile an hour over the limit. That's twenty. And tag on another twenty for the horseshit you've been shoveling all over my shop with that tongue of yours. That's forty. Unless, of course, you're telling the truth. In which case you'll have no trouble taking that gumball and hitting one of those flies on the wall."

Satch looked at the torn poster of Uncle Sam on the wall over which a half dozen flies were doing their own magic trick, sleeping vertically, as if gravity were the rube. And Satch was being asked to pull off a trick no less difficult.

Satch stared at the wall with bulging eyes and turned to the barber. "Which one?"

The cop saw the tips of the barber's ears go red. He tossed Joan Crawford into a slutty pose on the chair. "You're making him hopping mad."

Put on. One-upped. The barber inadvertently jabbed the neck of the patron with his clippers. The man started to wince, but was clearly determined to remain as silent and invisible as possible.

"Tell you what. Maybe a little time in the tank would do you boys some good, give you a little time to reflect on telling the truth. Maybe after a night in a Southie jail you won't be such a wise ass."

"You mean him, your honor, right? I didn't say nothin'. I wasn't even drivin'," said Josh.

"No, but there's nothing like companionship in times of trouble." The barber gave Satch a lopsided smile. "Any time you're ready."

"You got to hit one, Satch. We can't miss that game."

The man in the chair gave a start when he heard the name, then turned his head slightly so that he could see the back wall in the mirror.

"Don't you worry none, Gibby. Ol' Satch just needs a little pressure to make him throw true."

Holy hat, said the man in the chair to himself. *That's fucking Josh Gibson. I should have guessed, from the size of him.*

"See the fat one next to the yellow spot?" said Satch.

Neither the barber nor the cop saw the yellow spot. The man in the chair very slowly put his glasses on and leaned an inch forward, but all he saw was cream-colored wall.

"What yellow spot?" said the cop.

"That one," said Satch, pointing to the wall. The cop took two steps toward Uncle Sam and still didn't see it.

"You can take one more giant step, buddy," said Satch. "Top right of the hat. Say the hat's the plate. Draw a line up from the inside corner."

The cop bent forward. "Shit, he's right. Little yellow spot next to the fly." He pointed.

"Don't scare him off." Satch turned to Josh. "Gibby, give me a signal."

"Fuck, Satch, you ain't got but one pitch anyway. Just throw it like you know how to."

The cop looked at Satch, then at the wall, then back at Satch. "How'd you see that?"

"Seein' it ain't nothin'. All you need is good eyes. Hittin' it is something else. You got to have the arm."

The cop looked at the lanky man's oversized right arm as he wound up, thinking that by the time he let the gumball loose he'd cut the twenty-foot distance to the wall by a good margin. Now the greatest game ever played depended on a gumball and a fly. The thin-haired gent was as still as a corpse in the chair. Satch motioned Josh back a few feet and moved an ashtray stand and an ancient cuspidor back against the chairs. He kicked some loose hair to the side so he wouldn't slip on it and went into his windup, never taking his eyes off the fly by the yellow spot. No one saw the gumball till it had bounced off the wall then back off the floor and off the CLOSED sign on the inside of the front door.

The cop approached the wall stealthily, like a hunting dog wary that his prey might still be alive and liable to fly off on a busted wing. Then the barber joined him, as if the body of a slain gangster lay at Uncle Sam's feet. The cop inspected a small black smudge next to the yellow spot. He flicked at it with a fingernail, and a minute piece of something flew off.

"I think he did it, Al."

In the mirror the man in the chair framed a still-life: *Barber with Comb and Scissors and Mouth Slightly Agape.* Josh laughed. "Who was that masked man?"

The cop turned to the barber and nodded twice.

"Let's get out of here," said Josh, grabbing Satch by the arm with a grip that denied dissent.

"I got another penny if you've got another forty." Josh dragged Satch to the door but he couldn't stop Satch's mouth. "Tell you what. You give me two-to-one and I'll hit one flying."

"Shut up, Satch. Let's go."

The barber let out a sigh and smiled like a good loser. "I don't know where you got that arm, son, and your mouth's not far behind your arm, but if they ever let Negroes in the Major Leagues, I want you playing for Boston. That arm of yours is the exerciser Boston's been waiting for. You boys get out of town before I change my mind."

Satch smiled as Josh pulled him out the door.

"Who *was* that masked man, anyway?" jested the barber, looking at the man in the mirror, and echoing Josh.

"That," said the man loudly, "was Satchel Paige, the greatest Negro pitcher alive."

"You could have said something, Walt. That cost me forty bills."

"And miss that? Satchel Paige hitting a fly on the wall with a gumball? This'll be the best column I've written all year, except no one's going to believe it. Where is that gumball? Might be worth something someday."

The masked man and his trusty companion with the steel grip were back in Satch's Packard. "How'd you do that?" said Josh.

"Ball that big? Nothin' to it. When I was a kid . . ."

"Don't give me that kid shit again."

Satch crossed his heart. "When I was a kid back in Mobile I'd throw marbles at the flies for hours. All's I had was marbles and flies, and a lot of time to kill when I shoulda been in school. I got me more flies in a day than Billy the Kid got gunslingers his whole life."

If it weren't for the lights on Commonwealth Avenue, Satch would have hit sixty. Josh had his hands, then his knees, up against the dashboard. But this time he wasn't telling Satch to slow down.

The man in the chair suddenly threw off the apron and got up like Superman getting out of a phone booth. "Something's up, Al. I'm getting over to Fenway."

"I guess I'll read about it, Walter."

PART THREE

☆

THE GREATEST
GAME EVER PLAYED

19

THE FENS

Captain Hapgood Keyes had a desk that spanned half the rear wall of his office on Berkeley Street. Hap Keyes was Irish on his mother's side. Moon-faced, with a pleasant smile, he had a mustache that covered his upper lip the way his desk spanned his office. He kept a mirror on his desk and meticulously snipped at errant hairs throughout the day. He also kept a straight razor on his desk. With the fingertips of his left hand he would explore the contours of his face and neck. With his tongue he would push out his cheeks to expose any hairs that might be hiding in wrinkles or gullies. When he found any stump of a whisker, he'd flick open the straight razor and cut it off.

Hap Keyes had been a shipmate of Harry Bennett. Before Harry entered the office and called out "Hap," the captain's German Shepherd, head on his paws on a throw-rug in front of the desk, perked up, raising his ears, twitching his whiskers, showing a formidable set of teeth, and emitting a long, low growl that he saved for inauspicious events. Keyes had already put down the razor and was staring at the doorway when Harry appeared, followed by a well-dressed, thin old man. Keyes stood up and shook Harry's hand. "Harry Bennett! What brings you to Boston?"

"Hap, let me introduce you to Henry Ford."

Agape, Keyes shook Ford's hand. Harry circumlocuted, "This is a very peculiar situation . . ."

Uncomfortable with the task at hand, Ford interrupted, tilting his head toward the captain. "Harry, pay the man."

Harry handed Keyes a C-note. "We want every Sam, Dick, and Harry Spade who goes near Fenway Park picked up and kept in the cooler for twelve hours. Can you do that?"

Keyes nodded and stuffed the bill in his pocket. "I'll get right on it. But, if you don't mind, what's so special in Fenway Park?"

"My grandson's birthday present," said Ford. "I told him he could have anything he wanted, and what he wanted was to play baseball with some Major Leaguers."

The captain furrowed his brow. "You don't mean . . ."

Ford nodded, smiling. "Yup. Ruth, Gehrig. But I don't want anyone to know. Catch? I don't want the press finding out I'm spending a fortune on a kid's whimsical birthday request. Bad publicity."

The captain smiled. "How much is this costing you?"

Ford snapped his fingers and held out his hand. Harry unrolled another C-note. Ford opened the screen and let the hundred-dollar bill drift down to the sidewalk. "Pick that up on your way out."

The captain hurried out the door. Two hours later, Louella's private eyes were in the cooler and Louella stomped into the station house. Dried ring-stains from Keyes's coffee mug combined with blotches of ink to create the contours of a grotesque smiling face on the blotter, made more human by the snippets of mustache hair. Raising his eyes from the blotter, Captain Keyes could not help imposing the grotesque smiling face onto that of the woman standing before him, hands on hips, and introducing herself as "Louella Parsons. I imagine you've heard of me."

Keyes stared at her hair that ended in a big, perfect curl that, when she shook her head in anger, seemed to him like the flapping wings of a bird determined to flee. He imagined her hair as a wig that would fly off, and in his mind's eye he was staring at a naked skull with brightly painted, horizontal, red labia that parted and closed over teeth.

"Are you listening to anything I've said?"

Captain Keyes came out of his visual trance and said, "No. Would you mind repeating it?"

"I hired three private investigators to check out what's happening at Fenway Park, and all three of them are in your jail. Why?"

"Illegal activity, common miscreancy, or just being a public nuisance are my best guesses."

"Well, I want them out. I'm posting bail." Louella took a stack of bills from her purse.

As Keyes smiled, all that was visible below the enormous mustache was the bottom of his lower lip. He raised his hand in a "stop" gesture. "Bail comes later. Right now, there is nothing you can do for the unfortunate gentlemen."

"I demand to see them."

"Keep your shirt on, lady."

"Lady?" Louella's eyes dilated. "I am Louella Parsons, and I've got the most widely read column in the nation after Walter Winchell. I can smear you so bad you'll even smell like dog poop. On the other hand," she said, taking twenty dollars out of her purse and throwing it on the captain's desk, "I am willing to pay for information."

Keyes stuffed the twenty back into her purse and shook his head. "Lady, you have no idea who you're up against. You've got thirty seconds to get out of here or you'll be in the can, too."

Louella pivoted and walked noisily out, pondering her next move.

"Wait a minute," called Keyes. "Sergeant Collins will drive you. Where are you staying?"

"The Ritz. But I'll take a ride to the Parker House."

Sergeant Collins screwed the top onto his fountain pen, put it on his desk, and picked up his car keys. "Parker House it is."

As soon as they left, Keyes was on the phone to his benefactor.

Louella stopped dead in the lobby of the Parker House, watching a red-haired black man a few inches over six feet and a few sliding weights east of a scale's limit holding the check-in clerk by the throat with one hand and squeezing a steel-handled bell in the other. Louella's kind of man. She approached close enough to hear the clerk squeak, "Fenway Park," then grasp his released throat with both hands.

"Excuse me . . ."

"No time, lady," said Gus, brushing past her in a long black leather coat.

"You're looking for the same game I am."

Gus stopped short and pivoted. "What do you know about a game?"

"I know that anyone who asks questions about it ends up in the can. And I know that Satchel Paige is at Fenway Park. Would you like to share a cab?" Louella asked graciously, smiling like she was kicking off a cotillion and offering her arm to her escort. Gus didn't know what to do. Louella did. She locked her arm around his and promenaded him out the revolving door.

Louella attributed the bellboy's pop-eyed look, whistling for a cab, to the oddity of a mixed couple exiting the Parker House. He opened the cab door for them.

"Fenway Park."

"You bet. Kind of late for a ball game."

"Shut up and drive."

Louella thought it peculiar that the cabbie wore a white shirt and a bow tie, but she had other things on her mind. The cabbie turned left onto Mass. Ave., then right onto Huntington. "You know why they call it Fenway Park?"

"No. Why?"

"It's in the Fens—lowlands with a lot of reeds and marshes. They drained half of it to make this part of Boston. Say, you feel like driving?"

Louella and Gus were startled when the cabbie parked, got out, and opened the rear door. When Gus saw a pistol inches from his face he raised his hands and swung his legs out.

"What's going on?" asked Louella in a high voice caused by the involuntary constriction of her chest.

Harry looked at her. "You too. In front. You drive," he ordered Gus. He directed them the last few blocks to Fenway Park and told Gus to drive slowly past the police car. Harry lowered the rear window as far as it would go and aimed at the two cops, who ducked out of sight. Harry plugged Fenway in the cement gut and ordered Gus to floor it.

"Where to?"

"Back where we came. Take a right here."

The cruiser pursued, siren blaring. When they approached the fens, Harry ordered, "Left here."

"There's no road."

"Right. Jump the curb."

Gus felt the steel barrel of the pistol by his ear and heard the pistol cock. He jumped the curb and headed for the fens. Harry looked at Louella, who clutched her purse with both hands. "This is the part where the good guy jumps out and the bad guys go for a swim."

Harry opened the door and rolled out. The cab crashed through a copse of tall reeds, hit a granite block and went airborne with enough velocity that all four wheels landed in water. Louella's head hit the windshield hard enough to crack it, but not hard enough to knock her out. The water was just four feet deep. The cops pulled them out, and Gus and Lollipops spent the rest of the night in jail.

That left just me. I had watched Louella's hired dicks get rounded up when they approached the Park and heard her screaming in the front seat when the shot went off and Gus sped away. I saw Harry's demonic eyes flash and imagined the laugh coming from the open mouth. You had to admire his work. He knew he couldn't keep Louella Parsons in jail on some trumped-up charge like he could some local private eyes. She had too much clout, too high a profile.

I still had no plan. Twenty minutes later I saw Harry limp through the gate, pointing at his watch, followed by Knowledge Clapp, who appeared out of the shadows. I saw James Atwood Gray, the gatekeeper, looking at his watch. But I had no plan. A few minutes later James Atwood checked his watch again, looked left and right, then reached for the door. I knew I had to act. I only hoped that years of Hollywood had rubbed off, with improv.

"James Atwood Gray!"

The young man squinted at me as if that would help him place the man he did not recognize. Fortunately, I recognized him as one of Carole Lombard's bodyguards. I had a near-photographic memory of names and faces, and I had checked him and his buddy out.

"You're wanted in three states. Kansas, Wisconsin, and Illinois."

He looked at my physique and at the portable typewriter in my hand and snickered. "You ain't no G-man."

"No, but I know quite a few, including J. Edgar Hoover."

"So what do you want?"

"Just want to see a ball game."

"Any particular ball game?"

"The one that's going on in there, wise guy." I pointed at the park. James Atwood needlessly turned to where I was pointing.

"Sorry, but everyone that was on the list is already in the park. Who the hell are you, anyway?"

"Walter Winchell. And I can make you famous."

James Atwood perked up. "I don't want to be famous, 'less it's like Clyde Barrow or John Dillinger," he said, unable to repress a small smile at the mention of his heroes.

"You want to play hardball? I can have the FBI down here in thirty minutes."

James Atwood grinned. "Harry Bennett will take care of you like he took care of those other guys poking around."

"Harry's watching a ball game. Besides, he may have the local constabulary in his pocket, but he doesn't own the FBI."

James Atwood looked around him, then down the tunnel inside the gate. He looked back at me as if I might dissolve under a strong glare. "All right. I want three things in return."

"Name 'em."

"First, you won't turn me in. Second, you won't write nothing about the game. Third, you'll tell the FBI that John Henry Seadlund is in Weston, at Carole Lombard's place. He's wanted in the same three states I am, plus Minnesota, Alabama, and Tennessee."

"You got it." I started through the gate but ran into James Atwood's outstretched arm.

"No. You gotta say it. Say what you're gonna do, then vow it, on something sacred."

I raised my hand, palm outward. "I won't turn you in. I'll turn in

John Henry, and I won't write about the game as long as I live. On the grave of my mother, so vow I."

You have to give the kid credit. He had me. In my business, promises mean nothing. So there has to be something else, some way to ensure integrity, at least to myself. For me, that's a vow. If I vow something, I never break it. And I never did.

20

DELIRIUM

Mussolini's in love with Shirley Temple, but if he knew there was a rookie dago in center field, he'd have sent the kid carfare and saved Henry Ford a few bucks.

Dizzy Dean? Let me tell you a thing or two. He was human, Dizzy Dean. But if I had a horse named Dizzy Dean I'd bet the farm on him. I'd ride him into the sunset. That horse would be a thoroughbred and you'd know him for the three-hundred-and-sixty-degree windup swish with his tail, and there'd be no flies on him. He'd fan 'em all with that tail.

I talked to Diz before the great game, and he was wondering what it was about the gap between his big toe and the second toe that possessed a horsefly to bite. "I ain't a horse," he protested. But don't expect the bite to have much effect on the way he pitches tonight. It's not like that shot that Earl Averill hit off his left foot a couple of years later. That's the one that did it for Diz, made him put too much pressure on his arm and throw it out.

"God gave me the ol' flipper," he said of his right arm, while we'd all like to believe that God was a little more fair in doling out the endowments. Or would we? Suppose we all had whipsaw arms. What the hell would baseball be then? Better to believe that God gives us all gifts. Different ones, to amuse Himself. Some mysterious, no doubt. Surely God has the best seat in the *ballpark, being, as He is, everywhere. Quick that He is, He might be riding in on a Dean fastball, able to adjust His vision to the many revolutions the ball is making, then hop off as Gibson smites one or maybe just hop around to the other side for the round-trip ride out. If I were God I'd do something like that. I'd invent baseball just for something like that. A kind of "el" ride that you and I will never take, and I'm wondering—if baseball had a patron saint, would he be a lefty or a righty?*

And I'm wondering what in God's eyes would be a perfect game. One where no hitter ever touches the ball? Or one that's called on account of darkness or the dawning of the seventh day because ball after ball has been smacked over the fence, out of the park, even by Durocher? In effect I was wondering if God was a pitcher or a hitter, but that's the kind of dualism that got Marx, not Groucho, off the mark. Look at Babe Ruth. He was both. If you're looking for a model of God, look no further than the pudgy Sultan of Swat, who could match fastballs with the Big Train, Walter Johnson. The Yankees took a page out of Nietzsche's book, the "God is dead" thing, and let the Babe take a walk. But he'll be here, tonight, will make his entrance on two feet, like everybody else—Dasher, Prancer, Ducky, Lippy, Pepper, Flash, Schnoz—then the guy we've been waiting for, the one with the red nose. George Herman Ruth.

We have to wonder also, while we ride out this theological streak, why Diz got his right arm from God, while the myth of a black man with the same magic, in his fingers, is that he got it from the devil, that Robert Johnson sold his soul for the blues. No one ever suggested that Satchel Paige got his right arm from God, though Satch probably would have said that Man o' War was ahead of him in line and chose the feet . . .

Meanwhile, hitters are always exculpated from such deals with power above and below. Their notion of power is right at the belt buckle. They're good ol' boys who chop wood and just turn that stroke horizontal and aim it at a chip headed at them at ninety-eight miles an hour.

Those are the thoughts buzzing through the neWWsboy's portable typewriter, high under the eaves of Fenway Park, just settling into my wooden box seat to watch the greatest game ever played, under GE and the Monarchs' lights. Harry had the Monarchs drivers bring their three trucks, each with one set of lights, to Fenway. The system was so noisy that the outfielders couldn't hear the infielders, and they would occasionally trip over wires, running for fly balls. Catchers had a hard time with foul pops, staring into the lights. Harry had an engineer work on the noise problem, with some success, and he deployed the entire system in the outfield, where the noise was less bothersome, while the GE system was distributed mainly behind first, third, and home. Following the Monarchs' lead, Harry had white canvas draped over the new thirty-seven-foot left-field wall to augment the reflection of light. The Monarchs' lights and dynamo took two guys to handle. Harry recruited John Henry Seadlund and James Atwood Gray for the job and paid them handsomely, especially with the side deal that each kept secret from the other, on Harry's orders. This was his insurance policy, with the white-out clause, the one that would keep him blissfully anemic, that is, minus two thousand pounds of iron in his diet.

This is, think the squirrels and mice of Fenway Park, indeed unusual. The October void left by Babe's moving to New York being filled by something other than our droppings (those little fan notes for Harry Frazee). From September to March, the kingdom of Fenway has been ours, since the Red Sox last won the World Series in 1918. Until today. When Babe returned. Now the eighteen-man cotillion is under way, disturbing our rest with all those miniature suns. Nature turned on her head. The moon and the multiplying suns sharing the same sky. Unnatural spectacle mirrored on terra Fenway. And once in a while one of the stars fell, among the fungoes, out of everyone's grasp. Seen from up there, somewhere an excited God might abide, Fenway was illuminated more than any other diamond on the planet's dark side. The shooting star disappeared, like a gold fob into a pocket, a ball into His mitt, as He bellowed in that celestial voice of His, "Play ball." Not a peanut vendor in sight. Nothing to be scavenged but the condiment leftovers on Ruth's hot-dog wrappers. And those without sauerkraut stragglers.

Now a *light* touch—not the pressure of bat bunting a ball or the catch and throw of Durocher—but the touch of interstellar light on a particular player. It came in packets, little star satchels that scientists and laymen alike assume to be evenly distributed, as if randomness meant justice, as if the makers of stars and their light didn't throw spitters, emery balls of light, making some players shine more brightly. Touching whom, tonight?

It had to do with the open-air cathedral, pagan constellations shining down notwithstanding. Landis found himself walking down the aisle parallel to the one Darrow took, one section over, both of them headed for seats in the middle. Even their descending steps mirrored each other's, Landis in a black suit looking already like an umpire, and Darrow in an off-white linen suit. Landis in a top hat, Darrow a high-crown fedora.

It was the marriage of convenience and of opposites. The two men entered the front row and there seemed no alternative to sitting next to each other. The somehow hallowed neutral territory spurred a smile and a handshake, their individual differences and even animosity checked at the pew's entrance, both men eager to share the excitement of the greatest game ever played. As the game got on, the old enemies were swapping baseball anecdotes. Darrow had both suit-jacket pockets filled with peanuts. He would pull out a handful and Landis would pick one, then another, till both pockets were empty and shards of the feast crunched under their feet.

They were joined by Lombard and Raft.

Henry Ford took a seat next to Landis, who offered him some peanuts. Ford cupped his hands to catch them. When one fell to the ground he voiced a soft "Shit" and retrieved it.

Landis laughed. "You hate losing even a peanut. What'll you do if your team loses the game?"

Ford turned and glared at him. "I got that peanut, didn't I?" The corners of his mouth turned ever so slightly into a grin, leaving Landis to ponder Ford's allusion.

"I just love this game, don't you?" Landis smiled.

"I'll like it more when Harry brings the beer. To tell the truth, before this year I hadn't seen a game in years, and if we don't win this one, it'll be my last."

Landis marveled at the lights. "I see a great future in night games, especially during the week."

"We lost a few hundred man-hours in September. Grown men choosing a game over work." Ford shook his head.

"I see you brought your hat," Darrow joked about his wager with Ford.

"I see you brought yours," said Henry, pulling the boater tighter as the drizzle recommenced and while Bostonians were at home thinking of football, thinking about getting the storm windows in, or thinking about next year—for the Red Sox. Most were not yet thinking about the Bambino's curse. They were glad that the mosquitoes were gone, and the flies, save some stragglers. Bees had already gone past their fall frenzy for failing light and warmth. The moths were all born-again, to the candlepower gods of Fenway, whose penumbra was visible in Brookline, where rumors were flying about other gods, gods in pinstripes. And gods who had to be of the underworld, black gods.

Harry escorted Knowledge Clapp to the row behind Henry and the others. Knowledge was in black, as usual. Black shoes, socks, suit, and hat. The shirt was white and collarless. He might have been taken for a preacher, but the book he carried was not a Bible. Its blank pages were filled with coded references, formulas, and esoteric data as well as the scouting report on the black team. His guilt over selling out his race was assuaged with white powder and by the fact that he'd held something back. He'd pleaded ignorance about Martin Dihigo. But he knew about the Cuban's disdain for walks and that second base was his best position after pitcher, and that nobody ever dared to run on him on a relay.

Satchel had won a coin toss with Diz and chose to bat last. He called the team together in the clubhouse. "I don't have nothin' special to say to y'all. It's just a game. Let's go out and kick their ass."

The players added their individual affirmations and broke for the field to shag flies, play shadow-ball, and limber up. All except Josh. He was hunkered down, trying to get a grip on his anger, the anger of the invisible. His response had always been to take it out on the ball. He would grit his teeth and pound it, send it packing, scuffed, dented, send its stitched mouth to the orthodontist for some heavy repair, send it out of play.

How far could he hit it? How far would he have to hit one for them to notice? And if he hit it too far, would that keep him invisible even longer? If white poets jumped from ships, what should a black ballplayer do? Josh measured himself against Ruth, literally—walking off his home runs with a near-perfect three-foot stride. He didn't come up short.

Think of Joe Jackson, hounded by Landis for fixing games and banned by Comiskey fourteen years earlier. Think of Joe in his moth-eaten, cracker-barrel suit, at the restaurant of the Miles Standish, because the check-in clerk told him that all players had their meals paid for. Think of Joe holding the menu upside down, closing it and saying to the waiter, "I'll have a salad."

"Cobb salad?"

And Joe looking at him suspiciously, thinking—Ty never grazed on green stuff. He'd eat meat, rare, maybe raw. They brought Joe coffee in a china cup so broad it looked like a bowl with a handle that might be a trick for a country boy. In any case, it looked unwieldy, and so he brought his stubbly chin to it and tilted it up, seeing his reflection on the black brew's shiny surface and saying to himself, "I don't belong here in this coffee cup." He poured in the cream.

Umpire Bill Klem came down to dinner smoking his signature calabash pipe, fat as a bishop and dressed in black. Black pants, black shoes, and a loose black sweater drooping over his belly, covered by a Norfolk jacket. The counterman said something to make the ump laugh, and it galled Joe—the off-key laugh—it curdled the regular coffee in his mouth. Anyone who represented the rulers of the game galled Joe these days. The laugh had three descending notes, from mezzo-trombone to mid-range, the same three notes, twice. Joe wanted to bend back three tines of his fork and use the fourth to perform a tracheotomy on the man, just to change the sound of the laugh. Klem seemed to have a prejudice for a sequence of three, which represented to Joe a strikeout, and it didn't sit right with Joe. He mumbled, "Why does ump rhyme with chump?"

Klem turned to the counterman and wheeled off an order a yard long, with no intonation and with a velocity that said that if his stomach were a pitcher it'd be a fireballer, for sure. Joe asked the waiter for the bill, then remembered it was paid for. He asked which way was Fenway Park, and he took off on foot to find the game.

It took his breath away again to be in a Major League ballpark, the way it did when he first set eyes on that promised land. It seemed sacrilegious to tread on it, plant spikes in the halo of groomed infield dirt. So different from the *skin parks* he played on, coming up. So called because the dominant substance was not rock, pebbles, roots, or sand, but skin—from hands and legs left by thousands of slides and tumbles on the iniquitous dirt and gravel that passed for a ball field. Fenway in contrast looked like a vast coloring book filled with green. He felt privileged, chosen, to see the coloring book both open and closed. Closed—when it was completely covered in shadow, in the evening, when the crowds had left. Open—when he trotted out to fifty thousand cheering voices. Unimaginable, the roar of it. Every at-bat was righteous. *He maketh me to stand in a rectangular box facing an elevated mound with the odds always against me.* It had to be.

He had a glove on one hand, supporting himself with the other hand on the knob of a black bat, surveying the park. Pepper stared at the man. "Is that Joe Jackson?"

"Yeah, that's him," said Babe.

"He's uglier than a sheared sheep."

It became one of those moments before the orchestra starts playing when the whole audience goes silent. Everyone's attention seemed diverted to the specter in the shadow of the gate.

"Is that Jackson?" said Leo.

"Reckon so," said Diz. "Don't know who else it could be."

"Jesus, he's ugly."

Frankie shook his head. "Get a load of that uniform. Could've done with a few more mothballs. Well, you're the skipper. Get up there."

"What do you say to Joe Jackson?"

"I see you got some shoes?" Frankie jested.

Leo slapped him on the back of the head. "Wiseass. I mean, really?"

"How about, 'Joe, how the fuck are ya? How's Ty Cobb?' "

Leo frowned and walked over to Shoeless Joe Jackson. He looked on the one hand lost and on the other like he owned the place, some god of the underworld coming back up to reclaim his turf. What was going through his head? The shots he hit? The roar of the crowd? All the years he could have prowled right field? Maybe it was the lights that made him look like a refugee from the underworld. He was a lot heftier than in his playing prime, which worried Leo. His teeth were bad and he hadn't shaved in two days. But his grip on Leo's hand when they shook was reassuring. Despite his appearance, it was kind of like shaking hands with the president, if Roosevelt could crush your hand with his.

Joe introduced Leo to his bat. "This is Betsey. Put her away after Landis banned me in '21. Always thought maybe he would let me back in. Didn't want to break her in case he did."

Leo got anxious again. Was it sentimentality? Senility? Then Joe's bright eyes sparkled. "What do you know about this Paige? Is he as fast as Walter?"

" 'Fraid so."

Jackson smiled. "That's okay. I like a fastball pitcher. You know what he's gonna throw when he's in trouble. When I'm up, he'll be in trouble."

Leo smiled out of camaraderie rather than conviction. Joe saw the man he most wanted to see and made his way over to him.

"Hello, Commissioner. Remember me?"

Landis rose to his feet, shaking a finger at Jackson. "I banished you!"

Jackson smiled, showing his tobacco-stained buck teeth. Landis gulped air like a carp out of water. Darrow put a hand on Landis's shoulder, the commissioner's apoplexy reminding him of Ebenezer Scrooge's encounter with the ghost of Christmas past.

"I didn't say he could play!" shouted Landis.

"You didn't say he couldn't."

"The man is banned permanently from baseball."

"No. The Major Leagues. This is not a Major League game."

Landis saw the futility of pursuing the argument. He fumbled though his pocket for a tin of snuff and put a wad in his cheek.

The rookie, DiMaggio, had the feeling he was being watched. There was a presence in the park he'd never felt before. The kind of presence that made him think "moss" when he saw grass. Something lusher, older. It was as if the something inside him recognized the unseen stranger, as if sixth sense was nothing but the invisible handshake of two blood brothers, meeting for the first time. Then he saw him. A tall specter with a lubbed-up belly like a house that had poorly settled, and crooked teeth stained with decades of tobacco juice. The Natural. The one who broke molds with a full, powerful, fluid swing that sent balls with stunning frequency off and over stadium walls. Line drives you could hang your wash on. "Self, meet self."

"Hiya doin', Joe?"

"Hiya doin', Joe?"

Leo walked Jackson to the dugout, then sidled up to Frankie. He lifted the brim of his cap and wiped his forehead. "He's drunk."

"Who? Ruth?"

Durocher nodded.

"That fat fuck," said Frankie. "Biggest game of his life and he gets drunk."

"That's probably why he got drunk. Remember what Gehrig said—they're coming to collect."

Frankie nodded. He'd faced Satchel Paige, and he knew it would be no picnic. Babe couldn't bunt or choke up and punch a hit like Frankie could. He had only one way to hit—the big cut that sent him sometimes sprawling in the dirt when he missed, and missing against Paige was a stone, mail-in guarantee. Frankie went into the dugout to confront Babe, who was biting on the first of three hot dogs covered with mustard, ketchup, and relish. "A little *heimgemach?*" Frankie knew that

George Herman would understand the German for home-brew. Babe looked up at him with his mouth full.

"You're in the bag."

Babe chomped a few times. "So what?"

"So, get sober, or you're not playing. Maybe that's what you want to do, ride the bench."

"I'll be okay. Played drunk plenty. Old Pete played drunk. Waner, Mungo. Lots of guys."

"Waner always gets sober. You know how?"

"Beats me," Babe said, still chewing.

"Does three back flips and he's sober as a judge."

Frankie took a few steps toward the exit.

Babe laughed. "You ain't suggesting I do back flips?"

Frankie gave what looked to Babe's blurry eyes to be a nod, then walked out.

"So?" said Leo.

"So cross out 'Ruth.' Jackson's in right."

Leo took the lineup card and did as Frankie told him. Then he went into the dugout to tell Babe, who rolled up the wrapper for the first dog and threw it on the floor.

"What the hell's that?" said Leo.

"Couple of hot dogs."

"How many d'you already eat?"

"One."

Leo pointed to a bottle on the bench. "What's that?"

"Bicarbonate of soda."

"Your stomach bad?"

"Hot dogs don't always agree with me."

"Then why do you eat them?"

"I always have. If it works, don't fix it, right? Moe Berg says it's yin and yang."

Babe took a big bite of the second hot dog.

"Gin and what?"

Babe snorted. "Yin. Yin and yang. They balance each other out. Opposites. It's some Chinese thing. Mystical."

"Mystical fucking hot dogs? I don't see any Chinks on the All-Star team."

"I don't see you there, either." Babe took another bite.

"I think you had more gin than yin. And you don't have to be a pencil whiz to know why."

Babe looked at him pie-eyed and at the same time with a little of the deer caught in the headlights.

"You're afraid. All that scallion shit you gave me and Diz . . ." Leo shook his head. "That was grandstanding. You're just afraid you don't have it anymore. Afraid Paige will make a monkey out of you."

"I ain't afraid of Paige or nothin'."

"When you come down to it, you're a big fucking coward."

Babe swung a backhand fist at Leo and smashed it into a locker. He winced. "I get ahold of you, you little monkey . . ."

Leo was already walking up the stairs. He joined Lombardi on a box seat next to the dugout, put his foot up on the fence, and looked out onto the first-time floodlighting of Fenway Park.

"I've been thinking—how we're gonna win this game. Thinking a lot. And it comes down to *slumber and lumber*," said Leo.

"What the hey's that?" said Ernie.

Leo spread his hands against the sky, framing the partially occluded moon, as if his thoughts issued directly from above. "The way things are is already past, catch? If it *is*, it had to be, see? That's what Rickey means when he talks about *inevitability*. It's all a crapshoot in the future, but my whole life is about nothing if it ain't about loading the dice. That's what we do in St. Louis. It's the Gashouse thing—fly in the face of inevitability, and what you do is make your own inevitability, like you're playing a game and making the rules at the same time. That's what Pepper does when he steals a base. What Frankie does when he gets in an umpire's face and we get a make-up call. A strike becomes a ball, and the opponent can't believe it. What looks inevitable gets turned on its head, and you've got an edge, see? Same thing when I get on a guy like Cobb. Jaw at him. Just push him a little bit—up here." Leo tapped his head. "Get him off balance, mentally, just a hair. And that's the difference between a pop-up and a blooper that falls in. That's why I always want a Pepper and a Frankie and a Diz on my team. *Intangibles*—that's another Rickey word. That's the Gashouse. You put that together with the tangibles, like you and Ducky, and you've got *lumber*. Now Gehrig—his presence just changes everything. It's a level playing field till Lou steps up to bat. Then suddenly everyone feels like they're on a slope and Lou is looking down at them, like the batter's box suddenly turned into a mound. Like they're in a bad dream. Or like they're in someone else's dream. That's the *slumber* part. Tangible and intangible—lumber and slumber. I like our chances." Leo slapped him on the knee.

Lombardi turned and looked at him. "You think that all up just now?"

"Nah. Took like a week. I laid in bed every night, thinking about it."

Ernie nodded. "No wonder you guys won the pennant."

And Leo thought—the slumber part was a stretch. *Lumber*, he said to himself, revising his thesis, realizing that it described both Ernie's bat and the way he ran.

The afternoon rain had turned to drizzle at around seven, and was in full retreat by game time, at eight, but the field was soaked. Harry saw some stars poking through the clouds. He felt his heels digging into the base paths as he walked them, anxiously. The grass hadn't been cut in a week and the infield was soggy. Harry tossed a ball across it. The ball bounced but seemed to be held for a fraction of a second with the first impact, losing much of its speed. Harry envisioned the Negroes' slap hits tunneling into the turf. He imagined bunts that would stop dead on the grass with Lombardi waddling futilely after them. Oscar Charleston saw the same thing, and he knew what Harry was saying to Leo and Frankie. He could tell by Harry's body language and gestures that the game was in danger of being postponed or even cancelled. The conditions favored the Negro style of play. He interrupted the cabal. "Conditions ain't the best."

"That's what we're thinking. Might have to call it off."

Harry was thinking of the logistic difficulty of getting the lights back in place and the loss of secrecy that would be entailed by a postpone-ment. But Henry Ford's ultimatum—that Dean's team could not lose—foregrounded his thought.

Oscar rubbed his hand across the grass, then squeezed a handful of dirt through his fingers. "What we do when it's like this, we take about ten gallons of gas, spread it on the infield and the base baths, then light it."

Frankie smiled incredulously. "You what?"

"Burn it off. Ain't perfect, but it helps."

"You'll fry the grass."

Oscar shook his head. "Don't do much to the grass. Mainly, the gas just burns itself up. The heat dries up the field."

"You think that will work?" asked Harry.

"Worth a try. You got some gas to spare, from those generators?"

Harry called and waved to John Henry and James Atwood, who were tending to the whole lighting system and making sure the Mon-archs' dicey system functioned. The two men trotted in from the pen where the generators were set up, a small rectangle cordoned off in the right-field corner with twenty-five feet of chain-link fencing. In 1934, Fenway Park had no bullpens.

"How much gas you got?" Harry asked.

"Three twenty-gallon drums."

"How much do you need for the generators?"

John Henry shrugged. "Maybe forty, fifty gallons, unless it goes extra innings."

Harry read the players' faces. They wanted to give it a shot. "Okay, let's take ten gallons. Oscar, you've done this before. You're in charge. Just don't set the park on fire. We don't want the Boston fire department busting in."

Satch pulled a waterlogged ball out of the soggy turf against the right-field wall. He hefted it. Joe Jackson took the ball from Satch's hand. "What I'd call a dead ball. Like what we used to play with."

"It's dead, Joe, but it's still white," said Oscar, smiling. Jackson was puzzled. He pondered Oscar's meaning as he picked up one of the two five-gallon jerricans. Turkey and Mule rolled a gas barrel into shallow right field. Joe and Oscar each filled a jerrican and spread the gas. Harry dropped a match.

How perfect was it—Willie Wells—*el Diablo,* with a bat in his hand and covering part of his face, with flames leaping in front of him? Something scary about it, too. Frankie and Leo looked at him, thinking of the disfigured, scarred legs he displayed like trophies.

The grass was on fire but not really burning. It was as unreal as a Black-White All-Star game. Steam rose up off the grass and the dirt, like Oscar said it would. The image of hell appeared to everyone's mind at some point. But where hell's fires encircled, here it was the players who encircled the flames. Hell was a diamond, contained, as if it were paying for sins against the players. Still, it was funny seeing Joe Jackson's face lit up by the fire, standing shoulder to shoulder with the greats, outside the flaming diamond, where whites and blacks intermingled in a way that somehow would not have occurred without the intervention of the fire. Lou Gehrig found himself chatting with Josh Gibson and Mule Suttles. Oscar Charleston shared some chew with Frankie Frisch. Cool Papa Bell and Satchel Paige compared kangaroo-hide baseball shoes with Leo Durocher.

"Hey, Dizzy Dean, you got the marshmallows?" said Willie Wells.

Diz asked Willie if he had heard the latest episode of *Amos and Andy.* Josh joked with Gehrig about what it would be like playing ball against the Japanese, never imagining the seventeen-year-old kid who would blank them a week later and duplicate Hubbell's feat of striking out Ruth and Gehrig back to back.

The fire's warmth reminded them of a chill they'd come to take for granted. It was, after all, an October night. Satch stood closest to the fire, leading with his right shoulder, his pitching arm. Looking through the smoke at the white canvas over the Lifebuoy ad on the left-field wall, Satch thought of the scalding shower he had just taken in the locker room and the scalding one he would take after it, as if baseball was just something he did between showers. Cool Papa Bell checked the sponges around the wounds on his shins. John Henry looked at the cloudy sky, with an occasional break, a hole big enough for starlight, big enough for an angel to fall through. He thought of them all falling, like parachutists, through space, with no hint of conspiracy. These angels were just a bunch of good ol' boys, standing by the fire, reminiscing about the good old days, exchanging theories on how far back the center-field wall could be on the head of a pin, how baseball got segregated and the chance that it might integrate.

John Henry and James Atwood blended with the players, who were different in that they wore uniforms that itched, and were closer to the gods in their ability to play the game of baseball, doing their baroque eighteen-man version of a dance on a diamond instead of on the head of a pin.

Diz walked over to Satch and put an arm around his shoulders. "You come on down to St. Louis and we'll wrap up the pennant by the Fourth of July and we'll all go fishin.' I mean it, Satch. Between us, we'll win sixty games."

Satch looked Diz in the eye and deadpanned, "Heck, I'd win sixty myself."

"Ain't but one man stopping you," said Frankie, pointing to Commissioner Landis, who sat with his chin on his fist like a gavel, on the bar around the box, staring at the men who stared at him.

"He's a religious nut, right?" Satch asked Diz.

"Yup. A Holy Roller."

"Suppose there is a heaven and you can't get in 'cuz you're not that religion. And you say you'll convert but they say they don't take no converts. How'd you feel?"

Why they stared at each other—Landis, cold and baleful, Satch transmitting in return resentment—was unclear. Perhaps because at this distance a showdown was safe. They were both out of range, and they knew it, as the moon came out winking—sliver moon, the emblem of every outhouse in America, now in the dark sky over Fenway Park.

Landis munched on a couple of peanuts from Darrow's stash. Harry leaned over. "You got any Cracker Jack?"

The fault lines of a smile appeared on the crag of Landis's face. He ate only peanuts at a ball game and fancied himself a purist. First were peanuts, which begat popcorn, which begat Cracker Jack. That was the evolution of it. There was no value-added element in a goober, just the personal, manual labor of popping the shell and removing the chemise. The Cracker Jack and its prize in the box were a decadent fabrication. Something for nothing. Not to Landis's taste. Sometimes Landis would pop a peanut and there was nothing in it. The Burgess shale was littered with such fossils. In 1934, Cracker Jack was in ascendance. What would they think of seventy years hence? Raw fish wrapped in seaweed?

"Bring me Paige," Landis ordered, and Harry obeyed. Satch shook his hand. He was surprised that the old man was as short as he was, and surprised at the sparkle in his eyes, sparkle that was not saying "Let's be friends."

Landis stared at him, trying to take his measure. "What are you after?"

For a moment Satch felt like the kid carrying bags at the Union Railroad Station in Mobile, where he got his name. Then he grinned. Landis grew mildly irritated. "What is it? Money? Fame? Quim?"

Satch saw in Landis's white collar then a flag of surrender. And that was in part what he was after—the Major Leagues surrendering to integration. But that was not the whole story. That wasn't it, exactly.

"Delirium."

Landis was taken aback. He repeated Satch's answer in his head. *Delirium.* "I've got a fastball I call 'Long Tom.' You know where that comes from, hmm?"

Landis stared at him, motionless.

"Uncle Tom. I throw it fast enough that it ain't nothin' but a white blur. You can't really see it so you can't really say what it is. That ball is delirious. And that's what I'm after."

Landis had stared down the movers and shakers of America. He prided himself on knowing when a man, or woman, was telling the truth. He knew that Satchel's strange answer was the truth, but all he understood of *delirium* till that moment was that *it* was everything a Tin Lizzie wasn't. And he began to fear for the first time that Dizzy Dean and his All-Stars could not beat this man.

Then the fire burnt itself out. Steam stopped rising off the infield, and Harry shouted, "Let's play ball."

* * *

Dean's team took batting practice. Joe Jackson was captivated by DiMaggio. The kid caught everyone's eye. It was impossible not to watch. The kid had that big, fluid swing and walloped everything off or over the wall. It was uncanny, too, the way the air seemed to become concentrated in a rectangle where Joe stood and everyone's head was pulled by the low pressure created by his aggrandizement of even the air. Cy Slapnicka was right—he did look like a statue. But if he had the Statue of Liberty in mind, he was misguided. Joe was pure anarchy. As if every pitch were a rule and he was allowed to break it, hit the cowhide off of it, send it unraveling into the nickel seats. "Grace," said St. Augustine, was "that which was almost unseen." There it was, nonetheless—grace, first cousin of feral—in everything DiMaggio did.

Old Joe watched young Joe with a nostalgia as big as a grapefruit. When DiMaggio walked away from the plate, old Joe shook his head, smiling. He looked at old Betsey. "Look what you started, honey."

Old Joe stepped in to take his turn. He rested Betsey against his closed legs and grabbed a handful of dirt, letting it fall through his fingers as he rubbed it. Then he pulled his cap down and stepped to the plate.

"Joe Jackson, why don't you get a new cap," said Dandy. "You look like a Civil War veteran."

"Honey, I feel like one."

Dihigo didn't understand the term of endearment. Was that the way players talked twenty years ago? Or guys from South Carolina? Or was Joe just weird, one of *those* guys.

Willie walked up. "Ain't that the Natural? Shoeless Joe?"

"Damn, I think it is."

"He was a hell of a hitter, but he couldn't write 'fuck' on a shithouse wall."

The black players laughed, and Joe stepped out nervously. He spat and got some tobacco juice on his sleeve. No one but Joe himself noticed.

Babe came forward with a bat on his shoulder. "Don't get smoked up over it, Joe."

"I ain't smoked, honey. I'm fucking heartsick, is what I am. Them colored boys is right. I been thinking for years now about what kind of man I coulda been if I'd gone to school. All the things I might know that I don't know. And I never will, damn it, I never will. I fucked up with baseball, and I can't fucking read. I'm fucking sorry I lived. That should be my epitaph—'Here lies Shoeless Joe. He couldn't write "fuck" on a shithouse wall.' "

Joe felt a little of how his Irish forebears felt, flushed out of Ireland—not piped—the whole tribe descended from a pair that was said to have sneaked aboard the ark. Where Joe lived, selling dry goods and playing ball on weekends, in South Carolina, they didn't believe in species. They believed in the Jackson mythology. "Did you see the one Joe hit in . . . ?" He felt he should have stayed there, in the mythology.

Satch could see that Joe was pretty steamed up, but he couldn't clearly hear the conversation. "Hey, Joe, how do you spell 'hit'?" Satch just meant to tease him, good-naturedly, one Southern boy to another, the way he well knew Joe had been teased, or hazed, for his illiteracy from the day he came to the Majors and he was caught studying a menu upside down. He was innumerate, too. Couldn't tell time, so you couldn't expect Joe to be on time for anything. One spring training everyone had to write down how many eggs he wanted. The manager came by and saw a half-dozen uneaten eggs on his plate and asked why. Joe confessed he didn't know how to make a "2," so he wrote down two ones.

Remorse now magnified Joe's emotions and reactions to everything on a ball field, especially slights. In the old days, insults used to roll right off Joe's back, but it bothered him that Negroes would make fun of him. He felt like taking Betsey back to the hotel and heading back to Greenville. He stepped away from the plate. Leo saw that it had gotten under his skin. He walked over to Joe.

"Don't let that razzing get to you, Joe."

"That boy got my rabbit up."

Leo turned to the hecklers and smiled. "You want to know how to spell 'hit,' Satch? Just take your mother's name and drop the 's.' Then you've got 'hit.' "

Oscar started for Leo, but Satch held him back. "It's okay, man. I've heard a lot worse. I can take care of business myself. I got the apple."

The players watched Oscar walk truculently away. They didn't immediately notice that Joe was headed for the door with Betsey on his shoulder.

"Where's he goin'?" said Leo.

"Home," said Frankie.

"Like hell he is," said Babe, throwing down his bat and jogging after Joe. He caught him at the end of the tunnel.

"Joe, wait up."

Joe turned and waited, with a glum look on his face.

"Come on back, Joe. We need you."

Joe shook his head. "You don't need me."

Joe started to walk again, and Babe grabbed him by the shoulder. "They threw you out once. Now you're back. You can't just walk out."

"I don't have it anymore, Babe. And those guys got my rabbit up. They can read, and I can't. They're colored, and I'm white. I can't go out there, let them laugh at me."

"Fuck reading. Reading's overrated. Does reading make you money? Does reading get anybody laid? I can read, but if I had a choice between being able to read like Einstein or hit like Joe Jackson, I know what I'd take. I've seen 'em all. I've seen Cobb, and I've seen Hornsby, and I've seen Gehrig, but I ain't never seen a man hit a ball as clean as you. When I was a kid I watched you play. I saw you hit, and I *heard* it. I can close my eyes and hear it now. The ball made a different sound when you hit it. It was clean."

Joe lowered his head. "That wasn't Joe. That was Betsey."

Babe stared at Joe, hoping Joe would meet his eyes. "I've seen Black Betsey, and I've seen Yellow Betsey, and I wouldn't be surprised if I'd seen Blue Betsey. I ain't much at math, but it's what Branch Rickey calls the common denominator. It's you, Joe. This team needs you. I know what you're going through. Why do you think my head's bigger than Mae West's titties? This is the biggest fucking game in the history of baseball, and I don't want to be the goat any more than you do. I don't belong on this team any more than you do. Foxx, Waner, Greenberg, Simmons—those guys belong here, not us. But Landis made the rules, and we're the best these guys have got. You've got to play till I get sober. Give me six innings, Joe. I can't play like this. They'll laugh at me."

"They're laughin' at me."

"They're just trying to spook you. Get under your skin. I saw you taking batting practice. You didn't miss one ball. Okay, you didn't put any over the fence, but you made good contact with every pitch."

"It's practice. He ain't throwin' hard."

"You hit Walter. Paige ain't any faster than Walter."

"That was twenty years ago."

Babe was frustrated. Joe seemed as stubborn as Ducky and as paranoid as Frankie. He started to walk away. "Tell me the truth, Joe. Do you still get it up?"

"Yeah, I get it up."

Babe just looked at him with those big, aggie eyes. He wasn't sure why he asked that question; he just went on his nerve. Joe looked back at the baby-faced man at the end of his career. Joe didn't entirely get the analogy, the only kind Babe could make, but he sort of intuited it. Babe walked back to the field. Joe watched him exit, then stared at the tunnel wall. He took Betsey off his shoulder and commenced to make an *F*. Then a *U*. Followed by a *C*, and a backwards *K*. He couldn't prove it, but he knew it was *fuck*. He'd seen it a thousand times on shithouse walls. No one had ever read it to him, but he knew it. He wasn't, for nothing, the Natural.

Babe hit a Dean warm-up ball over the fence, foul, then took a practice swing, waiting for the next pitch, when he was shoved from behind.

"Get out of there, yannigan. I ain't finished."

No one ever pushed Babe Ruth out of the batter's box, as Babe did with hundreds of guys, whenever he felt like hitting, even as a rookie. Joe had that intense gaze and the weird smile of a kid who'd just bagged a squirrel with a slingshot. Babe backed off without a word, smile, or gesture of any kind. Joe hit five balls, two of them the kind of line drive he was known for, then stepped out and let Babe finish his turn. Half in the bag, he hit one halfway to Alston.

21

THE GAME

Bill Klem flipped a quarter that glittered in the Monarchs' lights and was correctly called tails by Satchel Paige before it hit the ground. Satch called his players to the field and Frankie trotted to the dugout, pointing at Leo.

"Let's go over the signals one more time, okay?" Leo said. "Anything red I touch is hit and run. If I touch something red then rub hands on pants, it's off. Okay? Stealing—it's the way I stand. If my legs are far apart, you go. If I stand normal, you hold. Clear? This ain't a bunting team, but if we need a bunt, my arms will be crossed. Got it?"

"What if someone else is coaching and he don't have nothin' red on?" said Joe Jackson, who had nothing red on.

Babe laughed. "Just touch your neck, Joe."

"Red" seemed like a nonissue to the other players, who laughed as Ducky jokingly said, "Just fucking bleed," while Pepper walked to the plate and Frankie moved to the on-deck circle.

Turkey Stearnes scowled at the noise the Monarchs' generator made in the right-field pen. Turkey had a pointed nose and high cheekbones. He looked like an Indian, but not enough to play in the Major Leagues. He seldom spoke, except to himself, and his constant monologue in the outfield bothered a lot of players. If the noise of the Monarchs' generator hadn't drowned him out, Cool Papa Bell would have heard him warn about the wires that snaked through the outfield grass.

Josh deliberately made a spectacle of putting a thin piece of raw steak on home plate and slamming it with his fist, then putting it in his glove. Leo, on his way to the coaching box, stared at him with lines of revulsion wrinkling his brow and the corners of his mouth.

Josh smiled. "Protection. Catch Satch without it for nine innings, and your hand will have to be amputated."

Savages, Leo thought. He'd never understand them.

The first batter, Pepper Martin, was careful not to step on any lines as he entered the batter's box. That would bring him bad luck. He also wore no jock or underwear, ostensibly believing that God loves not only a drunk but a third baseman. Frankie was careful not to step on foul lines when he ran out to the field. He also counted cracks in the sidewalk, but that was neurosis, not superstition. Superstitions were rife. Ruth always touched second base running in from the field. Hubbell had a red ball only he could touch. He always wore the same necktie to the ballpark. Medwick wore his sweatshirt backward for good luck.

Luck was in such demand it had to be tired out. So many people calling on its services so much of the time, and for such small potatoes. But they had it all wrong—luck as a lady. Women, in general, could be counted on to stick by you. It was a man who would dump you and leave you crying, walking back to the dugout with your head hanging at the same angle as the useless bat in your hand. But "man" didn't alliterate with "luck." That was man's dumb luck. If you want caprice, bet on the three-letter guys. The priests of luck, walking down the church aisle of a base path, like Pepper Martin now, making the sign of the cross over his heart.

Satch wrinkled his brow and shook as if in fear. "Is you Mr. Martin? Is you?"

Pepper whipped his bat around and nodded.

"They tells me you kin hit."

Pepper grinned.

"Well, hit this."

Satch fired what he called a "trouble ball" for a called strike one.

"Next one's gonna be a pea at your knee, and the last one's gonna be smoke at your yoke."

"Luck," said Wesley Branch Rickey, "is the residue of design." Satch had the greater design. Three fastballs on three corners of the imaginary rectangle that was the design of the strike zone. Pepper liked to take a few, to get used to a pitcher. He took three too many.

"What's he throwing?" said Frankie as Pepper walked by.

"I don't know. Didn't see any."

"Tell 'em about Frisch, when *dey* in *dare* rockin' chair. Tell 'em about Frisch!" Satchel taunted, good-naturedly, referring to Damon Runyon's famous ditty to posterity. Frankie was near ready for the rocking chair, and everyone knew it. Ruth was already in it. As for Joe Jackson, the black guys could hardly believe he was still alive. Ruth had been a good runner in his youth, stole his share of bases, and Jackson had been no slouch. Frisch still could run when he had to. He still stole bases, though he was not the same player who stole forty-nine in a single season. The skill that had not diminished was making contact with the ball. Satch knew he wouldn't get Frankie the same way he got Pepper, and he didn't try. His first pitch was a curve, and Frankie fouled it off. The bench breathed a sigh of relief. Paige was hittable, at least for foul balls. Frankie wagged his bat constantly, which distracted some pitchers. He fouled off a few more, took a few, and found himself on first with a walk, which brought up Ducky.

"Tell 'em about Frisch." Ducky laughed, psyching himself up to face Satch. Willie and Dandy woofed on Medwick, making duck calls.

Ducky swung and missed the first fastball, then hit a long foul ball on the second. Satch threw a changeup and Ducky whiffed.

"That's three strikes, Mr. Medwick. You can sit down now," Josh said with a smile.

That brought up Gehrig. He took a ball, then a strike. Leo got on Klem right away. "That wasn't even in the vicinity of the strike zone."

Gehrig took another ball and another strike. Leo started whistling

"Three Blind Mice." Klem turned and Leo stopped. Gehrig popped the next ball foul.

"That all you can do, man?" said Josh. "I can spit that far into a headwind."

With the count two and two, Satch figured Lou would be taking, and he drilled one in Lou's comfort zone. For a batter, a good pitch was a paradox—it was where you wanted it while threatening your status as safe, a pitch that asked "Am I your type?" when the answer was in the bat already swinging.

There was a very loud crack as the ball was propelled into the right-center-field seats. Babe watched with wistful eyes and followed his teammates onto the grass to shake Lou's hand. This time Babe could not ignore him.

"Tell 'em about Gehrig," woofed Ducky.

Ernie Lombardi stepped up.

"Hey, Ernie," Wells called, "we got good news and bad news. The good news is there's room for you in heaven. And the bad news is there's not enough room for your nose."

Haw. Haw. Haw.

Willie looked right and left. "I mean, seriously, guys, Lombardi is so ugly his wife makes him wear that mask in bed."

Ernie took it all in stride, then tapped a roller back to Satch, who fielded it nonchalantly, put down the ball and glove, picked up the rosin bag, straightened up and rubbed his hand as the Lombardi express lumbered toward first. Satch put down the rosin bag, picked up the ball and glove, and threw a hundred-mile-an-hour strike to Buck to catch Ernie by a hair.

"There's showboatin' and there's showboatin'," said Pepper, shaking his head.

Dizzy Dean walked regally to the mound. He felt like he owned it. Still, it was eerie to pitch in the silence of thirty-thousand empty seats as spectators, all with their bottoms folded up, like knees against their chests. It was a source of continual surprise, renewal even, how the pop of the thing out of his hand, arm in a catapult, the buzz off his fingertips, the spin on the thing—he knew instantly the ball fled in self-determination, fit of independence, exactly where it was going and the path it would take to get there. Throw, toss, hurl, pitch, chuck, fling—what he lived for. With a man in front of him, sixty feet away. A man with a stick, with the vanity of a fan blade.

Switch-hitting Cool Papa Bell stepped up to the plate batting lefty. He looked out at the right-field grandstand, and Diz shook his head. "Cool, the day you hit a homer off me will be a day that don't end in a 'y.' "

Harry Bennett took a swig from a pocket flask and leaned forward, speaking to Landis. "They say he doesn't drink, doesn't curse, and out-runs the word of God."

"That's blasphemy!"

"That's the truth."

Pepper and Gehrig were both in on the grass. On a count of one and two, Cool pushed a pretty bunt down the third-base line that had Ernie and Pepper both trying to make the play. Cool beat the throw by a full step.

Cool took a big lead, and Diz checked him back. His first pitch was a strike, as Wells feigned bunt and pulled away. Diz looked over at Cool, who had a normal lead. When he hitched up his pants, Frankie gave Ernie the pitchout sign, and Ernie gave it to Diz. Cool took off for second, and Ernie's throw to Leo was a little high.

"Safe!" yelled Klem.

"Safe?" Ernie protested. "The bastard's out!"

"The bastard's safe."

With a man on second, Pepper and Gehrig pulled back, expecting Wells to hit away. On Diz's next pitch, Wells pushed a bunt down the third-base line. Diz was able to field it and got Wells by a step. Cool slid into third and popped up almost magically as soon as his foot hit the bag.

With left-handed Turkey Stearnes up, Gehrig played deep, but Pepper had to stay close enough to third to keep Cool from taking an outrageous lead. Stealing home was always an option with Cool, who rattled Diz by jumping down the line, faking steal and razzing him,

"Can't a Negro get away with nothin'? Steal something in Georgia, they lynch him. Steal home on Dizzy Dean in Boston, he bean you the next time up. No, sir. I'm playin' it safe. Second and third is the onliest bases I be stealin' on Dizzy Dean."

Turkey walked. Ernie looked at Cool, who retreated toward third, while Turkey ran to first as if he was running out an infield hit. Ernie tossed the ball back to Diz as Turkey touched first and made the turn toward second. He was in high gear now, and Diz was looking desultorily at Cool, who hadn't retreated all the way to third, and was inviting a throw to Pepper, who was on the bag.

"He's going!" hollered Frankie, who had never seen the play, and Diz at first thought he meant Cool.

"Second!" Frankie shouted.

Diz turned, with plenty of time to get Turkey, then eyed Cool making a motion toward home. He faked a throw to third to hold Cool, then threw to Leo at second. Turkey stopped dead and Cool put on the brakes. Frankie covered behind Turkey, who moved slightly toward second. Leo felt he had a good chance to get Cool, who took a step back toward third, so he fired to Pepper, as Cool expected he would, and he broke for home. Pepper threw to Ernie. Klem hesitated, then called, "Safe!"

Ernie was hopping mad, but he threw the ball to Pepper before giving Klem a piece of his mind. "The bastard's out!"

"The bastard's safe. Again."

Frankie shook his head, watching Turkey take his lead off second, thinking on how outrageous it was to steal second on a walk. One out, now, with a runner on second. Gibson up. Josh was a private man. His sense of privacy extended to the strike zone. He guarded it, with a bat, crouching to make his privacy more private, as a small, hard white world intruded from less than sixty feet. Sometimes it came at his head. It came at him red-veined, spitting or buzzing, but always some version of white. And often as not it would be sent packing, sent spanked, clouted, deformed even, off his bat. With a perfect swing and a forty-six-ounce bat, he could alter the world for as long as it took to run the bases, could make it disappear entirely, so the breathtaking moment of perfect power was, in effect, an afterlife. Each time his foot touched the plate after a ball had been driven out, he felt himself waiting for praise that was as impossible as playing in the Major Leagues, found himself saying, "Was that one good enough, Dad? Was that one far enough to reach you?"

The infield pulled back completely off the dirt.

"He's bunting," shouted Babe.

"How do you know?" asked Nittols.

"Satch just wiped his hand across his face."

"Probably just chasin' a fly off his nose."

Leo was even more convinced that Babe was pie-eyed. The black Babe Ruth bunt? Josh took a ball, then a strike, then laid one down. Pepper didn't even try for it. He covered third, letting Diz and Ernie vie for it. Diz got it, but it never should have been his ball. Josh beat the throw easily, and Turkey took third. Diz shook his head. He was in trouble, and no ball had been hit past the infield. If Gibson bunted, what about the two-hundred-and-forty-pound Mule Suttles?

Mule took his practice cuts with the pinky on his left hand flying like a debutante picking up a teacup. Leo cupped his hands over his mouth. "Hey, there, Mule! Hey, there, Turkey! Hey, where's 'Chicken'?"

The Gashouse guys laughed. "Is this a ball field or a barnyard?" shouted Pepper.

On the first pitch, Josh took off for second and Mule put down a suicide squeeze. Pepper was a step late, and though it was not a great bunt, Turkey slid in safe under the tag.

Dihigo was up with only one out. The first pitch was a fastball, belt-level. Dihigo swung and missed. The next two pitches were wide. Dihigo fouled off the first and struck out on the next.

Diz laughed. "So that's the big bad Dihigo."

Satch cornered Dihigo in the dugout. "I know what they say about walks in the DR—'you can't walk off an island,' but this is America, man. You can't get away with that *macho* shit with Dizzy Dean. He'll pick up on it. He ain't no *Roads* Scholar, but he know his baseball. He's probably figured you out already. You won't get nothin' over the plate no more."

Dihigo stared at his bat, as if he could find in the grain the reason for his strikeout. He turned away from Satch without looking him in the eye, but he nodded, and that was good enough for Satch.

With left-handed Buck Leonard up, Gehrig was on the bag to hold Mule. Babe looked back and forth from Gehrig to Leonard with a kind of cognitive dissonance, seeing the black first baseman with the white first baseman's number "4" on his pin-striped back. Then it dawned on him—the black teams always scavenged the uniforms the Major League teams threw out every year, at rag prices. Buck played for the Brooklyn Royal Dodgers in '33. Obviously, he got Gehrig's old uniform. Babe leapt off the bench. "Hey, Lou, that Negro's wearing your uniform, hand-me-down!"

Buck was embarrassed. He'd asked for number four. Gehrig was his idol. The Gashouse crew laughed, which pissed Willie off. "Yeah, that's Gehrig's uniform all right. Bucky reached down to scratch his balls and he couldn't find 'em. I guess the Iron Horse ain't the Iron Stallion. Guess it's the old gray iron mare."

Dandridge slapped his thighs, laughing. Josh said, "I don't see nobody wearing no pinstripe number three. Is that on account of how much you stink, Babe?"

The black team laughed. Everybody knew that Babe used to put on the same underwear after he showered, and got so much flak for it that he stopped wearing underwear altogether. Babe knew he'd been one-upped, and he had no animosity toward the black team. He just wanted to get their goat. He laughed at the joke on himself as Klem said, "Let's play ball."

Buck took a called strike. On the next pitch he bunted up the first-base line. Gehrig was back on his heels, but he had to field it. He flipped the ball to Diz, but not on time. Two outs and the bases loaded, but Pepper knew that anything was possible, even another suicide squeeze. He played in close on the right-handed Dandridge. Dandy was a slap hitter with a very long bat. He wore a red kerchief around his neck and, like Wells, was bowlegged. Diz nipped the high inside corner three out of four times, getting himself out of a jam the way he needed to, so he could come down off the mound like a lion tamer, even though Paige's team had scored two runs without hitting a ball past the pitcher's mound.

SECOND INNING

Leo watched Paige walk sleepily to the mound. "What I like about Diz—he doesn't take all day. Show me a guy who takes his time on the mound and I'll show you a loser." When you're 6'4" and standing on an eighteen-inch mound, you're on top of a small, green world, the greater part of whose denizens sit in wooden-backed chairs, eating and drinking, roughly in a circle around you, some small contingent of them understanding that a base on balls is the curse of nations.

Pitcher's mound. Why did they build it in the center? Why did they heap dirt onto this emerging sphere, like the sun coming up right in the middle, if the one who trod on it were not the god of the game? In Egypt it was pyramids. In America it was a mound. Diz rubbed the front cleats of his left shoe in a short arc in front of the rubber. He felt the same way about this piece of earthen real estate as Ruth did when he said, "As soon as I got out there I felt a strange relationship with the pitcher's mound. It was as if I'd been born out there."

DiMaggio stepped into the batter's box to lead off the second. Josh stood behind him, tossing the last warm-up back to Satch, and tried to rattle the rookie. "Basically, kid, he's only got twelve pitches—be-ball, midnight creeper, bat-dodger, four-day rider, hurry-up ball, wobbly ball, Long Tom, nothing ball, trouble ball, curve, changeup, and one he calls 'thoughtful stuff.' But he throws 'em all overhand, sidearm, or underhand, so I don't know, how many's that?"

Satch gripped the sweat-soaked brim of his cap and felt the various grooves made by his thumb. Twelve of them, the commandments Satch brought down. Joe DiMaggio just looked at Josh. You could see the touch of fear, but mostly there was a look of disdain from a kid who had smacked Leon Day around and who knew that names didn't matter, that the ball would sail up there and the bat would come around and, if you were good enough, there would be contact. And he knew he was good enough. He'd never played against anyone better than himself. Till now.

"Come on," said Satch, listening to Josh's prattle, "you're a schoolboy. Three times twelve—what's that?"

"Thirty-six."

Josh threw the ball into his mitt twice. "Then it's with the hesitation or without it, so multiply by two."

Joe felt compelled to answer, thinking that these guys really didn't know the answer to simple multiplication. "Seventy-two."

Josh nodded to Satch. "Seventy-two. Sounds about right. So, if you're gonna hit my man here, you gotta guess which one it is, then you got about one in four chances of hitting it. And if you hit it fair, it's gotta get by my boys out there, so what are we up to now? You calculating?"

Joe looked down and hit some dirt off his cleats. He wasn't used to this kind of razzing. "So don't even bother. Take that stick of yours and go sit down. Save yourself the . . . what do you call it?"

"Humiliation," said Satch from the mound.

"Yeah, humiliation. He's gonna make you look silly up there."

DiMaggio looked at Satch. "Throw the ball."

"Here come the wobbly, kid."

Satch's arms shot backward and forward like a piston on a Ford V12 engine. His curve was two inches off the plate. DiMaggio swung and missed.

"Woo-o. Lot of air," said Josh. "Okay, now here's Long Tom."

DiMaggio took a called strike on the inside corner. Satch was grinning, and Joe was starting to feel the heat.

"Gonna put you out of your misery now. Hurry-up ball, right down the middle."

Satch went into his big windup, put his foot down, hesitated, and threw the nothing ball. Joe almost hit it with a second swing as the bat wrapped around him following through. Cool fell down laughing, kicking his feet. Joe took his bat back to the dugout, head hung low.

"You oughtn't have done that," said Jackson from the dugout.

"You ain't gonna do any better, old man," said Satch.

"You can *bet* on that," said Willie, with a double entendre meant to embarrass Jackson, who took his turn in the on-deck circle as Leo came up with one out.

Frankie encouraged him. "He ain't got nothin' on the ball. Sally Rand's got more on her ass than he's got on the ball."

With the count three and two, Leo leaned over the plate, daring Satch to come inside. He did. The ball audibly brushed Leo's uniform. Leo threw down the bat and started for first. "Strike three," yelled Klem.

"What do you mean? He hit me."

Klem nodded. "He did. But it was a strike. You're out,"

Leo threw down the bat and squared off with Klem. "Listen, I didn't go to school just to eat my lunch. He hit me."

"Out!" yelled Klem.

Leo kicked the dirt and mumbled, "Catfish bastard."

"That's a warning," said Klem.

Leo sat down. Satchel had felt Jackson's eyes on him, from the on-deck circle. Nothing cocky about the way he walked, but there was an air of dignity to the old guy. He still played, semipro, in Greenville, South Carolina, for five bucks a game. He could still hit, in Greenville. In his prime, he was 6'1", 200 pounds. He was at least thirty pounds over that now, with a paunch. Josh wrote "curve" in the sand near Joe's rear foot, then tapped him on the leg and pointed to the writing.

"That's what you're gettin'."

Jackson ignored the taunt. Joe DiMaggio blinked and shook his head, in almost disbelief and muttered to himself, "Fucking Joe Jackson, at bat! Fucking Joe Jackson! Shoeless, I mean."

Satchel leaned on the glove over his left knee, as if covering a signal he might be sending with the leading knee, which was curious, because Satch always said he read batters' knees. But Satch had never seen anything like this, in black or white ball—Joe Jackson, posed like an adolescent girl. The Natural? Satch shook his head. This was the most unnatural stance he'd ever seen. Even wilder than Heinie Groh's aboutface stance and chop for a swing. It was effeminate, especially with his expanded fanny. His feet were only four inches apart. No bend at the knees. A slight bend at the waist, and the bat dipped over his shoulder like a parasol. He turned his right shoulder in, and the bat, when not pointing at the ground, pointed at the pitcher. The stance fooled a pitcher into complacency. The man was a master of disguise. The knees of Joe Jackson gave nothing away. Joe Jackson. Fucking Joe Jackson.

There was time for a collective deep breath before it might be taken away by one of his archetypal, minimal trajectory shots that would bounce off the wall. Joe's bat was thirty-six inches and forty-eight ounces, an immense club that in various incarnations was "White Betsey," "Yellow Betsey," and "Black Betsey." But black was what he preferred.

Satch took the sign from Gibson, then straightened up and put his glove against his waist. "Joe, are you hitting or scratching your back with that thing?" Satch asked.

Joe spat some tobacco juice from a great wad in his stubble-bearded cheek. "Just chuck it, honey."

Satch did not know what to expect from the aged Jackson. Would he have flashes of the great natural hitter who taught Ruth how to swing? Or would he be a pathetic fanner far past his prime? He knew that Jackson was the original power hitter, that he hit line drives rather than the arcing shots Ruth hit. He knew he had broken a pitcher's leg with a shot, and hit one so hard to the outfield that it went through Tris Speaker's glove and hit him in the neck. The one that broke the pitcher's shin bounced all the way to third and Joe got thrown out at first.

Satch didn't want to test Jackson's power, and he knew that in the old days, like Frisch and DiMaggio, he almost never struck out. You could get him out, but he'd make contact. Joe watched the curve break over the outside corner for strike one. Then Satch threw him a fastball down and over the corner for called strike two. Joe just watched, unfazed. Satch tried to get him to bite on three balls out of the zone—a curve outside, followed by a fastball high and another one low. But Joe never lifted the bat off his shoulder, which led Satch to suspect that the old man was just trying to bluff his way on base. Satch went right at him with the pay-off pitch, a be-ball that *be-ed* knee high on the outside corner. Strike three.

Joe walked nonchalantly to the bench. The sentimentalists among the spectators, like Raft and Darrow, were disappointed. But joy in baseball, like sadness and tobacco, was a constant quantity, and for every cheek that was emptied with a spate, another plug of it got stuffed into someone else's. Joe sat down. He had more at-bats coming. As for Joe, it was part of the script he had written. Redemption is all that batting is—it's just a shot away.

Satch led off the bottom of the second. Diz smiled at him. "You can put down the wood, Satchel. The only way you're gonna hit is if I throw the ball at your bat."

Satch tried to bunt on the first two pitches. He had nothing to lose by bunting on the third, and Pepper threw him out easily. Satch's team had gone through the lineup with every man who made contact bunting, so when Cool came up again, Pepper and Gehrig both played way in. Cool showed bunt on three consecutive pitches and pulled back, taking them for balls. Frankie ran in and told Diz to remember what Harry had said—the last thing you want to do is to walk Bell. Diz fired a fastball down the middle and Cool slashed a weak grounder that Gehrig would have had easily if he wasn't in so far, but the ball kicked past him. Jackson charged the ball and Cool made the turn toward second. With Joe holding the ball, he stopped. He might have paid more attention to how effortlessly Joe snapped a strike to Frankie at second.

Bell took a normal lead, but he didn't hitch his pants, so Frankie didn't call a pitchout. Meanwhile, Cool had noticed that if Diz looked hard at a runner he would not look back a second time, so when Diz stared at him for five seconds, he was off with the start of the windup. Diz threw a curve and Willie laid down a beauty. Pepper, Diz, and Ernie all converged on it, each slowing a fraction of a second, unsure who would get it. Ordinarily, it was the catcher's ball, but Pepper knew how slow Ernie was, so he made a play for it, picking up the slow-rolling ball bare-handed. He didn't even look at second, knowing he had no play. He threw to first, but not in time to get Willie. Cool, meanwhile, saw that third was uncovered and he never contemplated sliding in at second. He kept going at full throttle. Ernie saw him and heard Frankie yelling, "Third." Diz thought he could beat Ernie to third, so he ran for it, too, but he saw that Cool would beat them both, and he pulled up, not wanting to interfere with the throw. Cool saw that he had third easy and that now no one was covering home. Pepper, who never covered home, just stood there, frozen, and he never expected the runner to keep going, but he did. He was several steps down the line when Ernie caught the ball at third. Frankie was yelling, "Home, Pepper!" and Pepper was saying to himself, "John Brown!" his version of "Holy shit!' Pepper was the fastest man on the team, and he had to cover half the distance that Cool did, but Cool had a full head of steam. Ernie's throw was waist-high. Pepper swung his glove back and felt it hit Cool's cap, which he had lost a split-second earlier, sliding. Klem spread his arms in a safe signal, then switched to out.

Oscar came storming out of the dugout. Diz laughed. "Pigs don't get no corncobs if they don't make it to the trough."

Cool jumped up, incredulous. "He missed me by a mile!"

Klem put his mask back on and stepped toward Cool. "You're out because you can't do that against Major Leaguers. You can't score from first on a bunt."

"Well, I did it."

"And you're out."

Ernie looked at Klem and shook his head. Klem had a reputation for honesty, and he was already starting to regret his call. Wells ended up on second. Turkey stepped into the box and Klem leaned over Ernie's shoulder. "I've got to make that up," he said.

Leo and Pepper watched Josh warm up with five bats.

"What the fuck's he doin'?" said Leo.

"Warmin' up."

"With five bats? You're shittin' me."

"He looks like a catcher. Got that broad back."

"Catcher? He looks like a backstop."

Turkey, who got his nickname from the way he flapped his arms when he ran, hit a hard grounder that kicked up and hit Pepper in the chest, then bounced toward the pitcher's mound. Pepper pounced on it, but his throw was not in time, and Willie took third. Now Josh was up with two outs.

Dean versus Gibson. Two opposing worldviews, as if the bathtub water swirled in opposite directions on the mound and in the batter's box. For Dean, beauty was velocity. Freedom consisted in a fastball jumping and eluding bats. Freedom was the extension of his arm's simple truth that had to be taught over and over, three times to each batter, till the thumbs-up signal of a strike erased the challenge.

For Gibson, the soft-spoken empiricist carrying the big stick, the idea of truth was a tyranny imposed. His duty was to send it packing, air-freight, and stamped with a forty-six-ounce bat, "lie, lie, lie." Truth was not a thing eternal. It was to be constantly tested, contested.

Josh rolled up his left sleeve, looked at Pepper, and smiled. Pepper had never been scared of any hitter, and Josh had bunted on him his last time up. The rest of the infield was back on the grass, but he had to play a normal third. Josh dug in, which was a no-no for Diz. After his third practice swing, Gibson backed off and sneezed.

"What the fuck did you do that for?" Diz hollered.

"Do what?"

"Go ahead and sneeze on me when I'm getting just mad enough to send you headfirst into the dirt. I don't even know what to throw you now."

"Don't matter. All goin' the same place."

Diz spat and turned the ball in his glove, as if all those revolutions put a twist on the ball that would unwind inscrutably on the way to the plate.

After the obligatory brushback, Diz threw a curve and Josh got a big batful of air. On the next pitch he hit a liner that was in Pepper's glove almost as soon as it left the bat. Pepper could hardly believe it himself. He literally felt a tremble when he released the ball onto the mound and trotted to the dugout. Josh went to the bench pointing at him and smiling. Pepper would play back and pray for him to bunt the next time up.

THIRD INNING

Water collected in depressions left by the feet of all the men working on the lights in the pen. Stepping into one, James Atwood felt water come up through the hole in the sole, making its way past the empty Chesterfield pack he had placed between his perforated sock and the hole in his shoe. Finding a discarded glove with broken webbing and a hole through the pocket, James Atwood sliced off the entire thumb and fitted the leather inside his left shoe. It felt right.

John Henry hung over the chain-link fence, scanning the stands for Carole. When he saw her, he waved. For a moment there was no response, then a wave. And . . . wasn't there a smile, too? A recognition, an affirmation, hewing away at John Henry, all knot at the heart.

With the game tied at two apiece, Diz led off.

"Hey, Dean, you still wipe your ass with corn silk?" Willie taunted.

Diz ignored him and hit the first pitch on the ground to Dihigo, who threw him out easily. That brought Pepper Martin up for the second time.

"Make him throw a strike," Leo hollered from the third-base coaching box.

The pitch came straight across the plate. "Strike one," said Klem. Pepper looked at Leo.

"Make him throw another."

Klem called the fastball "strike two."

"I did what you told me."

"Now hit this one."

Pepper swung and missed the fastball at the letters. He looked at Leo. "Sit down now."

Pepper went to the bench. Babe came out of the bathroom. "That was fast."

"Fast is what he is," Pepper said, pointing at Satch.

"What did you do, pop up?"

Pepper shook his head. "Leo told me to make him throw a strike. I did better—made him throw three."

Frankie ran the count to three and two, then fouled off a few. Satch shook off all the signs. Josh ran out. "You done shook off everything."

"I got the stomach miseries again, and Jewbaby ain't here to help."

Josh yelled to Mule to bring out Floyd's bag. Nobody knew why Floyd, who was black, was called "Jewbaby."

"What's he usually give you?"

"Something white."

Josh ransacked the bag and some green pills spilled. He gave one to Satch, who swallowed it.

"Hey, play ball!" yelled Frisch. "Quit stallin'."

"It's okay," Satch told Josh. "Next few are comin' in underhand. Then sidearm. It's over the top hurts most."

Dandy followed Josh back toward the plate. "What did you give him?" Mule asked.

"One of them things Floyd takes for high blood pressure."

"How's that gonna help his stomach?"

Josh looked at Dandy. "How's he gonna know it don't?"

Satch threw a hesitation pitch.

"Ball four!" Klem exclaimed. Willie started in, to give Klem a piece of his mind, and Satch looked him off, walking in himself.

"Time!" called Klem. Then the preemptive "You got something to say to me?"

Satch nodded, calmly. "It's okay, man. I understand that you don't respect the black man. And I just want you to know it's okay."

Satch turned and ambled back to the mound. Klem's mouth froze in the open position. He was not a racist. No more than the next man. But Satch took advantage of that residue, however small, in Klem, who now had to prove to an ostensibly disbelieving team, and its leader, that he wasn't a racist. After Ducky singled to left and Frankie went to third, Satch got Gehrig to end the inning with a fly ball to Mule against the right-field wall.

Diz walked quickly to the mound. He had a version of the grace DiMaggio had. He made it look so easy. His work was the ordinary wonder of a gingerbread man, cut out of paper with many folds, so that when you pulled on both ends simultaneously, the same guy with the same hole in his stomach was delivered twenty-seven times—that for Diz was the democracy of the diamond. And if Augustine was right that grace was "almost unseen," wasn't it there in the small white offering that came in at ninety-eight miles an hour, was deformed and sent back invisibly fast for at least the first ten feet with only a sound, a crack, as a sign of its existence?

Leo trotted in as Diz was taking Frankie's sign, relayed via Lombardi. "This guy, Mule, he's a long-ball hitter. Just don't throw him your fastball. He'll kill it."

"I'm a fastballer, Leo. You just go sit down and watch me strike him out."

Leo nodded and ran back to short. He did not sit. Diz kicked the dirt on the back slope of the mound and spat on the ground.

"What'd you say to him?" Frankie asked Leo.

"I said he kills a fastball."

"He's a curveball hitter."

Leo smiled. "I know. Now he's gotta prove he can throw his fastball past Mule. Psychology, Frankie."

Diz threw a hard fastball that tailed up and away, just nipping the strike zone, in Klem's opinion.

"That was a ball," said Mule matter-of-factly, not looking back at Klem.

"Bray a little less and hit a little more," said Ernie, who gave Diz the same sign and location for the next pitch.

"Kick, Mule, kick!" shouted Satch. Mule came around on the pitch and pulled it out of the park, foul. A lot of hearts were in throats.

Leo ran to the mound. "How come you let him dig in on you like that?"

"He's digging in?"

"Sure he's digging in."

"That son of a bitch. Hey, Mule, you don't dig in on me!"

Diz fired at Mule's head, but not one hundred percent. Mule dropped on his ass.

"You didn't tell Diz to bean him?" Frankie asked.

"Not in so many words."

"Just takes two."

Leo slapped his glove. "Nice guys don't win ball games."

"They don't start race riots, either."

Diz put the next fastball over the outside corner, with Mule leaning back. Strike three. Diz smiled and looked at Leo. "Told you."

Leo smacked his fist in his glove. Frankie shook his head. He hated gloating.

Dihigo walked on a three-two count and smiled at Satch as Buck Leonard stepped in. "Bucko," said Diz, "you think you can hit me with that hickory stick? You're dreaming."

Buck was one of the few players who didn't use an ash bat. He grounded out to Frisch. Dandy slapped a single to right. Dihigo made the turn at third, but decided not to challenge Jackson, even though Satchel was up next with two down. Diz smiled at the black team's bench three times, once after each called strike. Lombardi rolled the ball back to the mound.

Fourth Inning

A stew kettle on the head was adequate protection against the falling of the sky, but not against the smile of a woman even three hundred and fifty feet away. James Atwood rotated his gaze to the white canvas sheets over the great wall in left field, covering most of the ad for Vimms, leaving only the *V* visible. He subconsciously gritted his teeth, looking back at Carole. He gripped the fence so tightly that the tips of his fingers went white. He snickered loud enough for John Henry to hear, then said, "Told you so, John Henry. She doesn't even like you. She was just slumming. Got bored and you happened to be in the right place at the right time."

John Henry grinned sarcastically. "You think she would have gone for you if it was me out getting the paper instead of you? You're a nutcase, James Atwood. Everyone thinks so. Even Carole."

James Atwood picked up a wrench and approached John Henry. "She never said that about me," he protested, cocking his arm. He was stopped short by the loud crack of a bat, Ernie Lombardi taking out on the ball the aggression James Atwood had planned for John Henry's skull. He cheered loudly and managed to transfer much of his hostility to the game. He became as invested in the white team as Henry Ford and Harry Bennett were.

With the count three and two, Lombardi had fouled off three fastballs and a changeup. Joe Jackson was watching intently from the coaching box. Satch shook his head in irritation at Ernie. "Cheese, Nebraska! Can't you hit it straight, Ernie? My arm's gettin' tired." He pointed to fair territory. "Out here. Not back there. The upper deck don't count back there."

Satch came out of a sidearm windup and just missed the outside corner.

"Ball four."

As soon as Klem spoke, Jackson waved to the dugout for relief from the third-base coaching box, like he had to urgently pee. He trotted gingerly back to the dugout, smiling through the gaps in his teeth. Frankie waited to hear what he had to say before taking his place. Leo was getting his bat.

"Dadgum it, I got 'em!"

"Got what?"

"His signals."

"You can't see Gibson's signals," said Frankie. "I tried. His thighs are as big as that glove."

"That's 'cuz he don't flash no signals. Paige has got two pitches—fast and slow. When he slaps his mitt with his fist it's a changeup. When he slaps it twice, it's a pitchout. Everything else you just look for the fastball."

"He's got a curve, too."

"A dozen a game. Forget about it. Don't let all those names he's got for pitches fool you. They're just variations of the two basic pitches."

Satch intercepted Ernie halfway up the line and ran backward to first. "Can't you move your fanny any faster than that? Come on, I'll race you backward. You beat me to first and I'll serve you up a meatball next time up."

"Don't like you making fun like that, Paige," said Jackson.

"Old man, the only way you're getting on base is if you take one on that potbelly of yours."

Pepper approached Babe with a mischievous mien. "Got any of that cheese you eat?"

"Limburger?"

"Yeah."

"Why?"

"Maybe I want to eat some. What do you mean, 'Why?' "

"Okay. Keep your shirt on. I'll get you some."

Babe got him the cheese. Pepper smiled. "Watch this."

Pepper picked up Ernie's mitt when he wasn't looking and carried it back to the end of the bench, where Babe was sitting. He forced the cheese up into the finger holes of the mitt. Babe laughed. Pepper redeposited the mitt and nobody noticed.

DiMaggio managed to hit two solid foul balls before Satch struck him out for the first out. In Leo's philosophy of hitting, all you could ever do was go downhill. You would start batting 1.000 and never go higher. For most, the fall was dramatic, the company spectacular. You were at the top of your game before your first at-bat, and pitchers mercilessly whittled you, while for them—pitchers—there was at least temporary perfection—a no-hitter, a perfect game. What kind of rapture must Johnny Vander Meer have been in when he threw two no-hitters back to back and was well into a third when the spell broke off?

Darrow elbowed Landis. "Judge, you know why baseball is so popular?" Landis threw him a beady-eyed glance and waited for the answer. "Because it mimics sex. Look at all those guys in pajamas with that stick in their hands. The fair and the foul. The home run, the strikeout. The lovers and the voyeurs—that's us, the voyeurs."

Landis looked at him again. "Is it true what they say about you . . . the monkey-gland thing?"

Darrow laughed and ate a peanut. Landis took his silence for a yes. "How, uh, how does it work?"

Darrow was taken off the hook by Leo's bat meeting the ball. It trickled to Wells, who threw him out, which brought up Jackson. Despite striking him out the first time up, Satch still felt a little bit awed. He started him with a high fastball, then a fastball that Joe took for a strike. He threw a curve that Klem called a ball. Satch shook his head.

"Joe, ain't no free lunch. You wanna hit, you got to swing." Satch mimicked swinging. "Swing. This next one's gonna be down the middle."

The fastball was called a strike, down the middle, waist high. Then Satchel wasted a nickel curve inside for a full count. He got the ball back from Josh and motioned for the catcher to come out to the mound. Josh ran out. Satch looked perplexed.

"I throwed this guy eleven pitches and he ain't got his bat off his shoulder yet. I run out of pitches."

"Just get it over. He can't hit anymore. Just don't walk him. Fastball, down the middle."

When Josh crouched, Satch shook his head. Josh went through a number of phony signs, then smacked his glove once and Satch nodded. Cool Papa Bell had started at his normal shallow center-field position, but gradually moved in, convinced that Jackson couldn't hit anymore. Stearnes and Charleston shaded a bit toward center to cover for him. Satch threw the only pitch he had that Jackson hadn't seen, the hesitation pitch, which many thought was his hardest to hit. It didn't have much velocity, but the timing differential was near impossible to deal with. Jackson teed off on it, a line drive to deep center that Bell wouldn't have been able to snare even at Lou Gehrig depth. It was a rifle shot. Mule and Oscar both ran after it. Jackson had lost all of his speed, but managed to get to second standing up and even made the turn, giving third a look. Frisch, coaching third, gave him the sign to hold up. Dihigo took the relay at second and threw a bullet to Josh, but Ernie just beat the throw and scored.

"He cowtailed that one," Pepper remarked.

Satch looked at Joe with disbelief, taken deep to center by a potbellied squirrel-hunter on holiday, who looked like he might stumble over the cracker barrel. Joe smiled. "I knowed you was gonna throw that one."

James Atwood jumped. Either his aggressivity had transformed to excitement or he just got carried away. John Henry found himself rooting for the black team. He didn't admit it to himself until James

Atwood went berserk over Shoeless Joe's line drive. Then it all made perfect sense, his identification with the outcasts.

Satch shook his head. He'd been outsmarted. Dean's team's dugout clapped and cheered the old timer, who got an RBI. John Henry kicked the fence. "That was the only pitch slow enough for Jackson to hit," he moaned.

Jackson took his lead off second. "That was one sweet shot," said Willie Wells. "How's that feel?"

"Like old times, honey. Like old times."

Diz struck out, but he carried a one-run lead into the bottom of the fourth. Paige had made the third out, and for the second time Diz faced Cool Papa Bell as lead-off batter. After Diz took his warm-ups, Ernie's mitt started to stink. Bell took his practice swings. He looked at Ernie with a scowl. "Man, you Italians stink."

Ernie didn't know what to say. He thought he stunk, too. Pepper looked at Babe, who nearly fell off the bench laughing. Meanwhile, Gehrig had come way in, challenging Bell to bunt, knowing it would be hard for him to pull Dean's fastball down the line. Martin too was way in. The count went to two and two. Gehrig and Martin stepped back, but Diz called them in again.

Josh jumped out of the dugout and waved at Oscar to call time. Josh ran over to Oscar. "I think I got their signals. Watch Frisch. If he moves a step toward second, it's a curve."

"Lombardi gives the signals."

"He relays 'em. Frisch calls 'em."

Bell was batting lefty again. Frisch took a short step toward second and Oscar shouted, "Hoopy-doopy," which Cool understood as "curve." He slapped at the curve on the outside corner and Martin didn't have a chance. The ball scooted past him. Durocher anticipated the hit and fielded the ball deep behind Martin. If he'd had a cannon he might have gotten Bell. John Henry shook his fist as Klem shouted, "Safe."

Willie Wells threw down his warm-up bat and stepped in. Leo woofed on Willie, whose nickname was "the Devil." He kicked the dirt around second base and swept something out of the sand with his foot. "What the hell is this? Looks like cloven-hoof marks."

Willie paid him no mind. He bunted again down the third-base line. Pepper didn't even think of checking Bell. He threw Willie out, and on the first pitch to Stearnes, Cool stole third.

Bell took his lead off third and Satchel mirrored him in the coaching box, down to the hands hanging at the waist. Martin dashed to the bag and took the pickoff throw from Dean, but Bell made it back without sliding. Satchel moved back up to the end of the coaching box and again mirrored Bell's stealing stance. Diz looked over at Satch and made a monkey gesture with his free hand and his glove, which Satchel mirrored, too. In the pen, James Atwood mimicked Diz scratching his sides and making monkey sounds. John Henry shoved him on the shoulder. Diz got a little rattled when Bell faked the steal of home on the next pitch, which Turkey fouled off, and when Diz walked him, Durocher came in onto the grass and began screaming. "You're fucking blind!"

"Shut up, you applehead!" said Klem.

Leo turned and kicked the dirt on every step back to his position, a little closer to second, and deep. Gibson was up.

Bell took a good lead off third and Martin inched back, remembering Gibson's last at-bat. If Bell wanted to steal home, that was Dean's worry. Martin kept inching back, and Bell inched forward, then mysteriously walked back to the bag.

Something fishy going on here, Diz said to himself. He checked first. Turkey took a step closer to second, but Bell was standing on the bag. Diz turned toward first again and in the corner of his eye he saw motion heading for the plate. Diz stepped off the rubber, thinking he was going to nail Cool on a delayed steal of home, but it was Satch in the coaching box. That was why he was mirroring Cool. *Something fishy.* Now Cool actually danced several steps back toward second, all of which was an effective diversion for Turkey making a delayed steal of second.

Diz heard Frisch calling, "Throw the ball!" He started to turn and Bell was now back around third, heading for home. Pepper knew he was going, so he grabbed him by the belt, a trick he often used with runners tagging up. With only one umpire, he knew he could get away with it. What he got away with was Cool's belt. Cool had unloosened the buckle, knowing about Pepper's tricks. Pepper was holding the belt and Cool was two steps toward home, and Diz knew he was on the horns of a delayed double steal. He had to make a decision, instantly—getting Stearnes now was not even a sure thing, and if he did throw to second, Bell would have a good shot at stealing home. In the end, having been burned by Bell weighed heavier. Cool stopped and pushed off his right foot to get back to third, but he slid in the still-wet dirt. Pepper thought he had him, but Klem called, "Safe."

Leo was furious. He threw down his glove and stormed over to Klem, who shook a finger at him. "I'll toss you."

"Go ahead, you catfish bastard! You're giving them the game anyway. What does it matter?"

"It was close," said Klem in a voice that meant, to everyone but Leo, that he owed them one.

Ernie nodded. "We're even now. Let's win this fair and square."

"You call this fair?" Leo could see that he had no support. He was smart enough to know when to lay off. He shook his head and went back to short. Oscar, who was coaching third, wasn't going to take the high road. He needled Diz, "There goes your double play."

Diz spat. "Don't matter. Your big monkey ain't gonna see the ball."

"There's another big monkey after him. One of 'em's gonna catch that fastball of yours."

"See about that."

Frankie spat from the huge wad of tobacco in his cheek. "You can do it, Diz. You're the chalk horse."

Never mind, Frankie, that you can imagine the earth shaking as the man walks to the plate. Never mind that he was swinging five bats and even the one he still held looked scary. Never mind that your third baseman, who wore no jock or underwear and fielded balls off his chest, now risked having his ribs broken, and that your shortstop was so far back that he could not throw the man out on any slow-hit ball, and never mind that the batter looked like a fireplug and your pitcher with his leg way up and raining down curveballs had as much chance as any mutt's spate of pee putting a hole in a hydrant.

"The rookie's in center field?" Josh asked Oscar, leaving the on-deck circle.

"Yeah. He can play, though. Best minor leaguer in the country."

Gibson rolled up his left sleeve, dug in, and Diz was fuming. "Doggone it, Josh, whatchu gone done that for? You know nobody digs in on me. Now I gotta knock you down. Don't like to do it, but I gotta. Least I warned ya."

Diz let go a curve that started behind Gibson's head, and Josh was paralyzed. He didn't know which way to duck. At the last minute he ducked back and the ball whizzed past his nose. Diz laughed. "Thought I had you. They said you was a curveball hitter. Now I know you ain't."

John Henry kicked the fence. "Son of a bitch," he said, referring to Dean, but part of him knew that the object of his wrath was George Raft.

If Gibson was distressed, he didn't show it. It was part of the job—diving into the dirt and getting back up. John Henry walked back to the noisy generator and kicked it. There was a momentary dimming of the outfield lights, and eyes did turn to John Henry, but they shifted back to Gibson and Dean as soon as the lights came back to full strength. With the exception of Carole's. Her eyes had been fixed on John Henry, but the distance was as great as the candlepower was poor.

For a moment, John Henry felt a rush of power like he'd never felt before, as if a thousand kilowatts had been diverted from the lights to his toes. He was making the whole thing happen, or not happen. He and James Atwood had all the power in the world, the small version of it in the open-topped dome in Boston. He looked across the green field to Harry and Henry, then snickered at himself, realizing his role as a cog in the machinery greased by the man in the straw hat. Now he was walking the pen like a caged animal, only to regrip the fence and stare in Carole's direction, which was also the direction of the drama at the plate. The ruffian, stretched out as if on a chain-link cross, couldn't tell what she was feeling or if she was feeling anything at all. This miniature world, with its artificial sun that James Atwood and John Henry were the caretakers of, seemed to be powered fundamentally by tensions, the electricity that kept the lights going.

George Raft was standing and cheering for Dean to put one in his ear, while the commissioner joined him—standing—to honor the confrontation, to see the black man put in his place. John Henry felt at that moment more black than white, more animal than human, in the pen with James Atwood laughing at him and needling him.

Josh moved his feet around, but just a little more gingerly. A kind of compromise that Diz accepted. He turned and looked at center field, looked back at Gibson, then stepped back off the mound and waved DiMaggio back. Joe took his hands off his knees and retreated three steps and socked his fist in his glove. Diz took a few steps toward second and waved him back again. Joe looked at Medwick, who nodded, and he took three more steps back. Diz had his hands on his hips, staring at DiMaggio. He looked at the umpire, called time, and threw down his glove and the ball. He strode out to center field, and Babe got up, wondering if Diz was taking himself out of the game.

"Damn you, boy, I said move back. You know who's hitting?"

"Gibson."

"That boy hits a ball farther than Ruth. They say he hit one out of Yankee Stadium, and he's hit more out of Griffith than anyone, including that old man over there." Diz pointed at Jackson with his right hand. "So, when I say 'back,' I mean back. You ever play olly-olly-oxen-free?"

"Sure."

"Well, go back to the fence, put your forearm against it and press your eyes to your forearm, then count to ten."

"Mr. Dean, I'm here to play baseball, not a kid's game."

"Kid, go to the fence, like I told ya. Turn around and count to ten."

DiMaggio gave him that prescient, hog-castrating look.

"You want Babe to take your place?"

DiMaggio walked to the outfield fence, planted his forearm against it, counted, while Jackson and Medwick were laughing hard at what a rookie had to take.

"Okay, now, turn around and stay there."

"Against the wall?"

"Sonny, that's the only chance you got if Josh tags one. He hits 'em low. Line drives. And if you're lucky, and you time it right, you just might snag one."

When the pitch finally came, Josh teed off on it, sending it deep to center. DiMaggio jumped, but the ball thundered off the wall two feet above his glove. Jackson guessed where the ball would hit the wall and he ran to cut off the carom. Ducky hardly moved, and when the ball kicked slightly to left field, Joe was still much closer, but Ducky gave chase anyway. Josh had second easy, and when Satch saw the slow-running Jackson chasing the ball, he gave Josh the "go" sign. Babe was on the dugout steps, shaking his head, then smiling. He'd seen a younger Jackson stand behind home and throw the ball over the right-center-field fence, fifteen years earlier. Now the ball came out of Jackson's hand almost effortlessly, but looked like a cannon-shot. Pepper was as surprised as Josh was when the ball beat him to third on one bounce.

"Out!"

Pepper hopped toward Leo and tossed him the ball. "Do you believe that?"

Leo smiled and threw the ball to Frankie. Around the horn. Out of breath, Joe walked, then trotted back to his position.

Fucking Joe Jackson.

Two runs were in, but John Henry bit his lip and frowned. He wanted Gibson to stretch it, right in front of Carole. Now Mule Suttles was up. Remembering how he had psyched out Fatty Fothergill in the '27 pennant race, Leo came rushing up to home plate, stopped ten feet from Suttles and said, "Is that a Mule or is it a Turkey? Mr. Landis, check that batting card. Got a head like a turkey and an ass like a mule. I'm confused."

Diz was laughing. He didn't understand why Paige was splitting his sides in the third-base coach's box. "It's Mule, Mr. Leo! You ever see a mule kick? You get back out there and say a prayer the Mule don't get on first, 'cuz he'll show ya."

Dean's first pitch was over the outside corner. Mule crowded the plate. Dean shook his head. "Hm-hm, Mule, you oughtn't do that."

Mule just stared and took a practice swing. When the fastball came predictably inside he leaned in, then back, taking the pitch on the back of his massive biceps. He looked at Leo and tossed his bat back. You could see the Adam's apple in Leo's throat go up, then down, as he swallowed. He could hardly believe Dean's fastball could bounce so harmlessly off flesh, or that Mule deliberately invited the pain of a Dizzy Dean fastball. Mule's arm hurt like hell, but he didn't show it. He trotted to first, and when he got there it still smarted. Mule was looking for payback, and everyone knew it. Leo had trouble focusing on the pitch, self-preservation drawing his eyes toward the big man who had him clearly in his sights.

Diz thrived on pressure. As long as he was in control, he didn't worry. The game was in his hands. But now he knew what was coming and he was powerless to do anything about it.

"He's coming down, Leo!" hollered Satch.

"Come on down, then. I'm ready." But Durocher's voice betrayed him. His "ready" whistled. Not a lot, but enough to bring snickers to the faces in the dugout. And now the whole infield was nervous. Mule took his lead. Diz fired to Gehrig, who slapped his glove on Mule's thigh, but Mule was easily back.

Satch looked up at the sky and held his palms up. "Lord, please throw down some more rain and save your little Leo Durocher . . . Sorry, Leo, don't think the Lord is watching baseball tonight."

John Henry was. He was smiling, too. One of those rare moments. James Atwood whittled at the handle of a broken bat and John Henry wondered if Mule was one of those guys who sharpened his spikes. As if in answer, Mule cleaned the clogged toe spikes of one foot, then the other. And Leo was asking himself the same question John Henry was.

Diz glanced at first, took a short windup and threw a pitchout. Lombardi cocked his arm but held it. Mule was back on first.

"Knew that was coming," said Satch from the third-base coach's box. "Stay of execution."

Diz took the sign, and a chant went up. One voice, then two, then the whole dugout in chorus, in unison with stomping of the feet, "Kick, Mule, kick!"

Mule raised a leg like a sumo wrestler and planted it at the end of his lead. Lombardi called for another pitchout. But again Mule stayed put. Lombardi shook his head and threw disgustedly back to Diz.

"He's coming on this one, Leo. Hey, I hear you go to church every Sunday. You want to call in your priest for last rites?"

"Hey, shut the hell up, Satchel. We got a ball game to play," said Diz.

Mule took a good lead. Diz was tired of the gamesmanship. 2 and 0. He knew this was it, but let it be. He couldn't afford to waste another and give Dihigo a 3 and 0 count. He threw a fastball down the middle that he knew Dihigo would swing late at, and miss, deliberately, giving Mule a moment's cover.

"Kick, Mule, kick!" went the chorus.

He was on his way. For a big man, Mule was fast. A virtual storm of dirt blurred the outcome, so both teams were out on the grass to get a better look. The storm in the cloud was human, and horizontal, two hundred and forty pounds three feet off the ground. Legs tucked back into the body. Then the kick. The dirt blanketing it all. Both teams watching it settle on Durocher's coffin. Both men were down. Tangled. Lombardi had thought about throwing wide, to the left of the bag, but Mule had gotten a good lead. *If you talk the talk . . .* Lombardi thought, finally. The ball came in like an arrow, belt high. The man in black ran toward second, and when the cloud cleared his arms flew out in a "safe" signal, but he quickly reversed himself with a double cock of the arm, seeing Leo's glove held up with the ball still in it, and Leo's mouth shut and bloody. *Out.* Mule got up, looked down at Leo, smiled, and trotted off. The infield held its collective breath, then Leo got up. Tried to hop up, but limped. His uniform from thigh to below the knee was in shreds and he was bleeding.

"Walk it off," said Frankie.

"S'what I'm doing."

Satch hollered, "Guess you're not confused anymore about who it was. Got your ani*mules* straightened out, huh?"

Diz glared at him. "You better cut off the motormouth or I'm gonna stuff it with this here apple." Diz dropped the ball on the grass with his team down four to three.

FIFTH INNING

The Monarchs' lights had been dimming occasionally since the start of the game. When they dimmed at the start of the fifth inning, Landis turned to Bennett, sitting behind him. "Henry Ford owns half the cars in this nation. Can't he afford a few gallons of gas?"

After Ford laughed, Harry did. "I've got them timed to dim when Dean fires the fastball." Harry put a hand on Darrow's shoulder. "What do you think, Darrow?"

Darrow leaned back while continuing to watch Diz take his warm-ups. "The effect is . . . absolutely Stygian."

"What did he say?" Harry asked Landis.

"He said it's just like daytime," Landis lied.

From behind, it looked like someone had left a bushel on a bench, a chubby, broad bushel, with pinstripes imitating slats, and with something like an upside-down head of celery cropping out on top. Someone left the number "3" on the bushel, to identify it, to come back later and pick it up. Goods in the bushel. And something rotten at the bottom. An egg, maybe, stinking the place out. And maybe no one was picking it up after all. Maybe it had been left there, benched, to rot some more.

Perched up on one haunch, Babe rolled his butt back down onto the bench like a boat dropping its keel. Ducky Medwick waved his hand before his face and echoed Mrs. Ford's commentary at the dinner before the seventh game with the Tigers, "That was Ruthian."

"Augean," said Frankie.

"What's that?"

Frankie didn't answer. It wasn't worth the effort. He had other things to worry about. Player by player, they all got up off the bench to get air and gathered as if in ovation for the batter, Pepper Martin, who looked over and did a double take. Babe sat by himself, proving that familiarity breeds contempt, even of a flatus. Babe was a more complex character than he let on. Part of him was a self-conscious kid from St. Mary's who felt more of a loner, deserted, first for being benched, and now because, as Diz would say, "My insides are disputin' me." And another part of

Babe, the pure swagger, was saying, "Take that, you motherfuckers. And take this one, too."

"He always like that?" Lombardi asked Gehrig.

"Nope. Sometimes it stinks."

Lombardi's eyebrows rose. He didn't know that Lou Gehrig had a dry sense of humor. Lou looked at Leo. "Come on. You guys are the *Gas*house gang, right?"

"Let him pinch-hit, Leo. When Gibson gets a face full of that, he'll give him an intentional pass."

Ducky waved his hand again. "How does he do that? He's twenty feet away."

"It's physics," said Frankie. "Every force has an equal and opposite reaction. The way he hits 'em out, they blow back."

Knowing nothing of physics but a lot about apparel, Leo said, "Now I know why he doesn't wear underwear. No drawers I know could take a day of that."

On the top step of the dugout Leo razzed Satch. "You gonna call the outfield in when Gehrig's up?"

"No, Leo. I'm gonna call 'em in when you're up. And I'm gonna sit the infield down. All except Buck, in case Josh drops the third strike."

Pepper pushed a bunt halfway between Josh and Satch. Each thought the other would get it. Finally, Josh picked it up, pivoted, and threw to Buck, but Pepper beat it out. Then he beat his chest. In the pen James Atwood aped him. Pepper enjoyed giving the Negroes a taste of their own medicine. For the same reason, he was eager to run on Paige. If Satch had a weakness, it was arrogance. He was so confident that his fastball would not allow a runner to steal that he paid him little attention.

Landis for the first time showed some excitement. Pepper Martin was his favorite player. He elbowed Darrow. "Now you'll see some baserunning."

Pepper danced off the bag, inviting a throw, and Satch had to check him with a throw that Pepper beat without diving. He tried to plant his spikes in Leonard's foot, which Buck lifted just in time. Didn't even look down. He smiled. "What you tryin' to do, Pepper? That Gashouse jive don't mean jack to me. You might have gotten into the heads of those Tigers, but we been playing that way since the game started. I been stepped on, spiked, throwed at by crackers in twenty states. Same goes for every feller on this team. Every nigger in this league sharpens his spikes. We all Ty Cobbs."

Pepper got a good lead and took off on the next pitch. He slid in safe under Willie's tag. Frankie hit what would have been a double-play ball to Willie and was thrown out, and Pepper had to hold at second. Ducky was up, with a black bat, like Jackson's. He swung three times and missed three times. Gehrig grounded to Dihigo to end the inning, stranding Pepper.

Dihigo was the first batter in the bottom of the fifth. Diz threw three curves at the corners and ran the count to 3 and 0. The next pitch was a fastball in the high end of the strike zone. For the infield, it was the crack of the bat that spelled trouble. The outfield could not hear it so clearly, but they could read trouble in the trajectory and the speed of the ball. It was not a high, Ruthian shot. It was a mirror-image of a Joe Jackson poke two decades earlier. A kind of high line drive, with just enough arc to take it to the bleachers in straight-away center field. The ball got out in a hurry. DiMaggio had time to take only three or four steps backward before the ball was hopelessly over his head.

Frankie walked to the mound as Dihigo touched second. "What the hell's so hot about Dihigo?" he yelled, sarcastically echoing Diz's words of a few days earlier.

"Shit-fire, Frankie. You're even up with him. Harry said so. Now you go and hit one for me," Diz said earnestly.

Diz settled down and took care of business, striking out Leonard, Dandridge, and Paige on nine pitches.

SIXTH INNING

Leo would be the third man up. He sent Frankie to coach third and slipped quietly into the clubhouse, remembering how he and Boney Pradella had conspired to steal Babe's watch. The clubhouse was as empty as the hit column of Leo's scoresheet. He was 0 for 2, and Satch was laughing at him.

He found Babe's locker and opened the simple lock with the pick that he kept lodged inside his belt to scratch up balls for pitchers. On the shelf were cigars, after-shave, a razor, a watch, a wallet, and a brown paper bag. Leo pushed the wallet out of the way and took out the bag. He took out the pint of whiskey and examined the bag. Nothing. He put back the whiskey and the bag and looked at the bottom of the locker. There were Babe's shoes and some rolled-up clothing that looked like undershorts. Nothing. He started to slam the locker, then remembered that Babe never wore undershorts. He pulled back the locker door and picked up the carefully rolled, clean shorts. He unrolled them. Bingo. Babe's own stash. Six perfect scallions. He took two, then put one back. One was all he could take, raw. He spat the plug of tobacco from his mouth, bit off the very bottom of the root end, and spat it out. Then he chewed on the bulb, gradually feeding the entire scallion into his mouth, grimacing, and swallowing. He rerolled the scallions, put back the shorts, and shut the locker door. He found the water fountain and washed down the sharp taste of the scallions, then put a fresh plug of tobacco in his cheek. He was ready to face Satchel Paige.

Ernie was first up. He lugged a bat that looked like a tree trunk. *Fastball,* thought Satch. *He'll never get that around on me.*

"It's the Molasses Mauler," said Josh, playing on Ernie's legendary slowness and Jack Dempsey's nickname, "the Manassas Mauler."

Cool kept edging in. Ernie noticed him playing only about fifty feet behind second base and nodding to Leonard. He realized that if Cool fielded the ball he was going to try to throw him out at first. Ernie squeezed the bat handle even harder and took a second fastball for strike two. Another fastball, and this time he fouled it off past first base. Ernie worried that he was being set up for a curve, and sure enough the next ball curved out wide. He waited on a fastball now and got it. He was determined to pull the ball but plugged a line drive over second. Cool considered diving for it, but the ball was coming so fast he decided, instantly, to take it on the hop. *Thrown out at first base,* thought Ernie—

from center field. He'd never live that down. And so he put the logging truck in gear and ran his heart out.

"John Brown!" exclaimed Pepper.

"Holy shit!" said Diz. "Did you see that?"

Diz looked at the stunned faces in the dugout. Lombardi had dived into first like Pepper and Frankie. Klem thrust his hands out wide in a "safe" sign. Ernie got up, wiped the dust off, looked at the dugout, and smiled. Even Henry Ford lifted his forearm and shook his fist. "Slow and steady," said Henry.

"We're in a ball game," said Frankie, with the solemnity of a Fordham Jesuit.

Pepper cupped his hands around his mouth. "Welcome to the Gashouse, Ernie."

Ernie grasped the bill of his cap, which he'd creased like Leo's and Pepper's, and gave a slight nod.

Old-timers say there was no sound quite like the ball meeting Josh Gibson's bat. Just as distinctive might be a crate of twenty-four beer bottles dropping a few inches onto cement and ringing for a second. George knew before he turned to see Harry squatting like a catcher and smiling like he'd called a pitchout that beer had arrived, and he guessed before he looked who had delivered it.

The man's hands must have been deadly in a fight, thought George, or even deadlier in the days of duels in Dodge City, for in the blink of an eye he'd pulled two bottles from their slats, held them by their necks, then flipped both of them a half revolution and proffered them neckend first to the Hollywood couple. He passed bottles to Darrow, Ford, and Clapp. He reached into his pocket for an opener, but George had his own and he popped the cap off of everyone's beer.

"Hits the spot," said Carole.

"Where's the crackerjacks?" asked Darrow.

"Save your appetite," said Harry. "Steak and eggs at the Ritz after the game."

In the pen James Atwood licked his lips. "I could do with one of them."

John Henry watched them, thinking how far the world had turned on its axis since the afternoon when he felt so tangled with Carole's legs and sheets that he might never get free. It wasn't that a different set of stars were overhead; it was just a gentle turning away, the earth rolling over, that let one see them from a different perspective, twinkles coming all that black way.

John Henry was as thirsty and envious as James Atwood, but accepted thirst as his lot. That was just the way it was, he reflected. The high-hat spectators got the beer. He was just a working stiff, doing his best to manufacture daylight. He looked at Henry Ford, on the other side of Carole. He could not see the white head rising through the beer bottle's neck and dripping onto Ford's pant leg. *What,* John Henry wondered, *was the old man thinking, sitting next to a goddess?* John Henry remembered the summer he'd sweated through at a Cadillac plant, after being denied a higher-paying job at Ford. He remembered being fired and getting a job that paid even less, a drill-press operator at American Steel and Wire, watching the sex act of drill and metal all day, with the constant drip of white lubricating fluid down the drill bit. It was more than John Henry could take—being mocked eight hours a day by a machine.

DiMaggio managed three foul balls, then hit a one hopper right at Wells, forcing Ernie at second, but beating out the double play. Carole clapped as Klem gave the "safe" signal.

Leo stepped into the batter's box.

"Who you foolin' with that stick, Leo?" jibed Oscar. "You all glove, no stick."

Leo spat tobacco juice in Oscar's direction and took his practice swings. Satchel started his windup and Josh stood up, shouting, "Time out, Mr. Klem." He turned to the umpire. "This here man done made a mistake. Brought a stick instead of a glove. He better off hittin' with his glove."

Klem shook his head. "Play ball, wise guy."

Josh squatted. "You'd best put that thing aside, Mr. Leo, before you hurt yourself. You got no intentions of hitting that ball."

Leo swung and missed a fastball. Satch laughed. "Best hit you ever got was a out—off Alexander, '28 World Series. Remember?" Satch called Turkey in from left field. "Now all you got to do is pull it and you've got your homer. Only thing is, Satch ain't Alexander."

A home run was the impossible translated to the improbable. Yet we saw with our own eyes sixty balls fly out, from the bat of a single player. Then the Durochers—dogs after an old bone, wagging, turning around three times, as if missing with each revolution some mysterious, imagined ball, before curling up on a version of the dugout bench. This too we saw, and marveled at. And thought that the zodiac of baseball should be emended from Leo the lion to Leo the dog. When Leo did hit one out, he saw his blast as equal to Gehrig's—"Hey, they don't move the fence in for Biscuit Pants," he said. Every dog was thrown a bone, now and then. Gopher ball, they called it. What was the difference between Leo and Lou? Just a couple of vowels juxtaposed. Redemption was available to every man. *It's just a shot away . . .* But they don't move the dugout bench in, either. Leo could reach it in ten strides. Struck out looking. Scallions with the aftertaste of crow. Leo never did buy the *baseball as religion* crap. Who'd be its patron saint? Saint George? Herman? Saint Tyrus? Saint Joseph D., gone berserk at the photo of his wife years later with her skirt blown up?

The white canvas over the green left-field wall reminded Henry Ford that his greenbacks that made the game happen could not buy the result that had to obtain if his worldview were not to shrink to the size of a straw boater on a platter. The dame next to him tempted him to contemplate exchanging all of those greenbacks for the youth of George Raft, the balls to wear a yellow suit and matching wide-brimmed tando, or even to trade places with the blue-collar, knot-hole lads in the pen.

Carole touched Henry on the knee. "Could you pass me another beer, please?"

He nodded and handed her one, enthralled by the pump of her crossed leg, with a white and dangling high-heel shoe lacking a heel cup he might drink fermented hops and barley from. She smiled and said, "Thank you." He again nodded, at a loss for words however trivial, and feeling invisible save for the clink, as he crossed his own legs, of loose change in his pocket.

* * *

Batter's *box?* A true box needs three dimensions. Walls and confines and ceiling. The batter's box is defined by lime on reddish dirt, lines the width of large gauze strips. Length: six feet. Width: four feet. Height: not even the sky's the limit. Not even the vaults of heaven. A whole cracker-barrel full of angels could party on the flat plane box where humans trod, including the guardian angel of batters. Call him "Louisville." Tobacco-chewing angel, hard-drinking, cussing. No helmet necessary when you wear a batting crown. And when the game is done, the box is as lonely as Grace Durocher. But come closer. See one pigeon, then another, alight like biblical doves among the ants who are already building pyramids with knuckleball-inspired tunnels, inured to the daily cataclysm of cleats. *Build it . . .* and they'll trample it.

Jackson stepped into the box. Tobacco juice running down his chin, he still had the gangly look of a windblown Georgia pine in sap-running season, all with a rough-hewn dignity that wore thin when he took that girlish stance with the bat tilted down at an absurd angle. He still looked like a Greenville, South Carolina sharecropper stumbling out of a cornfield he'd gotten lost in.

"Say it ain't so, Joe."

" 'Fraid it is. Me again."

"Joe Jackson, you fooled me once. Shame on you, Joe. Fool me twice, shame on me. Joe, you ain't foolin' me twice. You got nothin' in that bat."

Joe gave him a wrinkled smile and said nothing. He spat some tobacco juice and swung the bat slowly.

"You a guess hitter, Joe. Now, I know. I'm gonna make it easy for you. This one's a fastball down the middle."

Joe guessed that Satch was telling the truth. He took a big cut and missed the mid-nineties fastball at the knees.

"Don't need to guess, Joe. Fastball down the pike."

Joe choked up an inch and took a smaller cut at the ball on which Satch put everything he had. The sidearm fastball popped in Josh's mitt. He pulled his hand out and shook it. "You gonna kill me, Satch."

"That's two right guesses. I'm gonna have to make it tougher on you. The next one is a fastball on the corner, but I ain't tellin' you which one."

Satch gave him a three-quarter overhand fastball on the outside corner. It was the pitch that hurt, that was putting the most stress on his sore arm, but he had something to prove to the Natural. Joe guessed right. He shortened his swing to a Cobb-like slash, but missed.

"Show's over, Joe. That's all you get."

The white dugout shook its collective head. Satch had Joe's number, and they knew it. Seeing Joe go down like that sat badly with Babe. He felt his lips pull back and his teeth grit. There was even an involuntary tightening of the girth beneath his belt. He slammed the dugout floor with his bat, thinking of Sudbury and chopping at a knot with his axe, the determination of chopping through it rather than splitting the log in an easier spot. He threw down the bat. He stood up and put his hands up at thirty degrees, then bent his knees. Then he resumed a normal posture and repeated the process. He shook his head, then stepped onto the bench.

"Hey, Nittols, come here."

"What are you doing, hanging yourself? Want some help?"

Babe raised the back of his hand at the midget. "You little shit."

Nittols turned away.

"Hey, wait. Come here. I'm doing a back flip. Like Waner."

"He doesn't stand on a bench."

Babe stood on the end of the bench. There was room, lengthwise, to do a flip.

"I ain't Waner. Need a little leverage. I've done this with kids, in a pool. When I flip back, you pull up as hard as you can on the back of my knees. Put your arm out there. No, get a bat."

"You're gonna kill yourself."

"Who's gonna miss me? You?"

"You got a point."

Babe feigned slapping him again with the back of his hand, then put both arms out at ninety degrees from the shoulders.

"Ready?"

"You sure you want to do this?"

Babe looked around, then at the landing zone. "Put some shit there. That chest protector, my glove, your glove."

Nittols rounded up the stuff and put it behind Babe.

"You got a will?"

"Nothing's going to you, so don't fuck around. Lift when I flip. Ready?"

"Holy Hanna, nobody's gonna believe this."

"I can do it in a pool."

"Bet there's a big fucking splash."

"No reason I can't do it here."

"Keep talking to yourself."

"Ready?"

Nittols put the bat behind Babe's knees. Babe's head went back and his eyes widened but saw nothing. He looked like something on the Sistine Chapel ceiling, something deliberately distorted so that people far below could make out the features. He told himself, *There's a pool behind me.* He felt Nittols' bat snap on the back of his knees. He made the revolution, barely, and sprawled onto the stuff Nittols had spread onto the floor. His right knee hit the cement floor painfully. He rolled up his pants leg. It was bleeding. Nittols came over with a half-pint of whiskey.

"This'll make you as good as new."

Babe pushed him away. "I gotta be better than new," said Babe. "You know who's pitching."

"You didn't think I was giving it to you to drink?"

Babe's expression told him yes. Nittols poured the whiskey over the wound.

"They'll smell that and think I was nipping."

"You were."

"But I'm sober. Waner's trick works. I gotta tell Leo."

Diz struck out Bell to start the bottom of the sixth. Wells flied out to DiMaggio, which brought up Turkey Stearnes with two out. He hit a fastball deep to center, over DiMaggio's head. The ball hit the wall and kicked thirty feet toward left field. Joe chased after it, but Ducky called him off. He charged the ball that hit a wire for the lights and took a bad hop past him. He scurried after it, with Turkey well past second. Leo took the cutoff and saw that Turkey was not stopping at third. He made a perfect throw. Turkey heard the surprising pop of the ball in Lombardi's mitt, saw the catcher turn toward him, completely blocking the plate, and he knew his only chance was to knock the ball loose. Lombardi saw Turkey's eyes on his thighs, saw him lift into a late slide, spikes high. He gripped the ball like a nut in his right hand and took Turkey's spikes on the mitt, sweeping the left foot away. He fell on top of Turkey and slammed the ball into his chest. The dirt flew, and in a moment Turkey was on his back, rolling back and forth, clutching his leg and groaning.

"Out!" yelled Klem.

Oscar was livid. He jumped off the bench and blindsided Ernie, knocking him down. Back on his feet, Ernie saw Oscar coming at him and cocked his arm. Oscar knew he'd have to take the ball off his body, and he knew that with chest protector, shin guards, and mitt, Lombardi was well protected. Only the big schnozz was open. He knew too that his first punch was unlikely to land and that Lombardi would then be on top of him. He wanted to fistfight him, not wrestle the big sonofabitch.

He jumped forward and turned sideways, with a hand up to protect his face from the ball. Suddenly he was in a bear hug. He recognized the arms crushing his ribs as Josh's, and he knew there was no getting out of it. He was off his feet and being lugged toward the dugout.

"Put me down. I won't go after him."

Josh released him. Oscar turned and gave Lombardi a look of disgust. By this time, Ducky had already stepped in front of Lombardi, and it was quiet enough for them all to notice Turkey still groaning.

Klem asked, "Are you okay?"

"I think my leg's broken."

Turkey's teammates surrounded him.

"Get Jewbaby's bag," Josh ordered.

Turkey writhed and groaned. "What's he got in the bag?"

"I don't know."

"Oh, shit." Josh looked at Turkey's leg. It was swollen and bent at an unnatural angle, but not bleeding, and no bones were sticking out. Josh didn't know what to do. Turkey sat up, holding his leg. He looked at Josh. "Don't just stand there, knock me out."

Turkey turned his jaw up, with his eyes and lips closed hard. "Wait. Take this." Turkey handed him his wallet. "I want to know who's got it." Turkey turned up his jaw again. "Okay. Now."

Josh's punch was like his swing, compact, but to the temple, not the jaw. Turkey fell forward and out like a light. Josh and Mule carried him to the bench.

Oscar looked at the white guys. "Next?"

Josh didn't like it. He looked coldly at Oscar.

"Looks like I'm in," said Oscar. He took right field, and Mule moved over to left.

SEVENTH INNING

George Raft made a beeline for the men's room, thinking about the lay of the land. About getting it, having been declared *it* by Louella. About how irritating it was to have his penis serve two masters, having to wait for it to subside to where the pee got the green light at that subtle switching station with the funny Latin name, *vas deferens. Vive la différence,* said the kidneys. *Amen,* said George.

Staring at the wall above the Fenway Park urinal, he reflected on how the mind was similarly bifurcated between savant and idiot, genius and pretension. *Take* Immaculata Frangipane—beneath the bleachers at Ebbets Field in 1919, when Arnold Rothstein and Teddy Horne were conspiring to fix the World Series, which got Shoeless Joe booted from the Major Leagues. George and Immaculata had taken off for the seventh-inning stretch, and while the crowd was on its feet George was on his back and Immaculata was on her knees. Olive-skinned, gap-toothed, at seventeen she was already a pioneer of the next decade's sensuality. *Take* her words, for instance, "I've always wanted to do that"—the adverb of time at that age incomprehensible. *Take* her father, who made submarine sandwiches on Delanccy Street. He had a hand like a catcher's mitt and a forearm the size and color of a hanging prosciutto hock, in other words, a hand like Lombardi's and a forearm like Foxx's. He was always sawing things. He seemed to like the sound. *Take* George himself—"Yo, ho, ho," he'd say, shaking Franco's huge hand, his roistering words unintelligible beneath the buzz of the saw that spat out time like dust.

Carole, meanwhile, was thinking about the dream she'd had the previous night—a vast field of flowers that she watched rise, opening their lazy heads to the sun, then transform into a field of penises, every one with a funny little hat, straining toward a dark triangle, a vast, floral-spiked bed that did not require the secret knowledge of a yogi-man to lie on.

Carole surveyed the huddle outside the dugout. DiMaggio was nonchalantly gripping a bat and listening to Durocher without making eye contact. She saw DiMaggio as her find and silently cheered for him to emerge as the game's unlikely hero. George felt much the same way, but he was pulling even more for his old buddy Durocher. It felt funny to him to be watching a ball game that he had no money riding on, but he felt lucky to be here, not only for the game but for the special bond he imagined it created with Carole. He was thinking "threesome"—Raft, Lombard, Baseball. It satisfied something in him.

In a moment of silence, Carole thought she could hear the rustle of the few leaves clinging to the trees out on Landsdowne Street. Then the noise of beer bottles on cement and the noise of the spectators chatting brought her back to the world of artifice. She looked at the stage that measured three hundred and twelve feet to left, with the canvas curtains that turned the green wall white. The empty seats didn't matter. This was a private screening for an audience huddled between third and home, with the exception of the perpetual loner with his typewriter and the two roughnecks in the pen.

Knowledge Clapp was comforted by having Harry Bennett at his side, but his paranoia was so encompassing that he kept turning to check his back, afraid that Gus had bought his way into the stadium and had seen him sitting with representatives of the white team. Any question of loyalty could set off a rage in Gus, and Knowledge knew well the consequences of Gus's temper. He imagined Gus sneaking up behind him and whispering, "What are the odds that I could have you buried six feet under third base tonight and no one would ever know?"

After Diz struck out, Pepper Martin hit a ground ball through the middle, then stole second and was singled to third by Frisch. He scored on Ducky's sacrifice fly. Gehrig singled, Lombardi walked, and with the bases loaded DiMaggio lined out to Bell.

Josh was first up for Paige's All-Stars in the bottom of the seventh. *The thing is not to feed Gibson curves, and don't give him anything low when he's crouching,* Diz remembered. But Diz didn't listen. The first pitch to the crouching Gibson was a low curve that dropped sharply and came in very fast. Gibson got ahold of it and sent it high and long down the first-base line, where it took a sharp break to the right and ended its flight fifty feet to the right of the foul pole.

"Bet you can't throw that one again!" Satch shouted to Diz.

The next pitch was a fastball high and inside, just catching the corner. Gibson dug in with his rear foot and Dean snarled. "You all done? Send for the groundskeeper and get a shovel, 'cuz that's where they're gonna bury you."

Diz fired a high brushback. Gibson backpedaled out of the batter's box, and leaned back exaggeratedly on the next inside fastball, which Klem called a ball.

"Put the glasses back on!" shouted Durocher.

Josh turned his cap bill around and crouched, as he usually did when he felt a confrontation. He dug in and wagged his bat.

Damn Negroes, don't they ever learn? Diz said to himself, then snarled, took a full windup and let a fast one go at Josh's beezer. Josh hit the sand fast. As he was getting up, Ray Dandridge walked slowly out of the dugout, surprising everyone, including his own bench. He looked like a manager about to remove his pitcher. He didn't look threatening, but Leo loped in to defend Diz if necessary. After a couple of steps, Frisch decided he wasn't needed, and his legs didn't feel like moving any more than necessary. Klem could have stopped Dandridge, but he was just as fed up with Diz's beanballs as Squatty was. He let him have his say.

"That's too many, Dean. That one was for no reason."

"Well, that had plenty of reason on it, including the fact that I didn't like the way he was lookin' at me."

Squatty turned toward his dugout, then looked back at Diz. "Maybe you don't like the way they're lookin' at you, either."

Diz saw two leashed German Shepherds straining toward him. The ordinary drool at their mouths looked to Diz like froth.

"The first one's trained to go for the throat. The second one waits till you're fending off the first, then goes for the privates. Got 'em down in Mexico, from an old manager. He never had no trouble with beanballs. That's all I'm gonna say."

Squatty never raised his voice. He turned and started walking back, then looked at Leo. "Got a third one just dying to sink his teeth into you. Name's Oscar. Saw him bite a guy's ear off once, in Mexico City. He'll take your nose, too."

Squatty had made his point. Diz continued to brush guys back, but there were no more overt beanballs, no diving for cover in the anthills. Mule, on deck, swung his bat, which suddenly felt as light as Satch's. Dean got the ball back, stepped off the rubber and turned, keeping his eyes on Bell, and rubbing the ball.

"He's cutting it!" shouted Satch.

"I'm watching him," said Klem.

Frisch called time and ran in, followed by Durocher and Lombardi.

"Y'all playing football? Huddling up?" hooted Charleston, from the dugout.

"Get out there and watch 'em," Satch shouted to Klem, who walked slowly toward the mound. He could see Diz throwing the ball into his glove, and was satisfied that he wasn't cutting it. He called time-in and walked back to the plate.

Leo had his belt buckle filed to a sharp edge and had the pick lodged in the inside of his belt. He asked Diz for the ball, nicked it, and handed it back to Diz. "It's on the bottom, buddy."

Oscar didn't see it all, but he had his suspicions, as did Josh.

"Time out! Time out!" Oscar walked out of the dugout. Klem and Lombardi turned toward the manager.

"Time out! I've got to get to the hardware store and get Dean some more sandpaper."

"Get back in the dugout," said Klem.

"Gimme that ball!" Oscar ordered.

"You'll get it when it's your turn up," Ernie said.

Oscar kicked the grass and pivoted. "You see the way Durocher walks? That's 'cuz he's got a blacksmith's file up his ass. Check it out."

Oscar walked back to the dugout, sat down, and spat.

"Play ball," hollered Klem.

Josh stepped out of the batter's box and asked Klem to look at the ball. Klem gave in. He called time and asked for the ball. He noticed the nick and tossed it out. He threw Diz a new ball. Now Frankie came rushing in. "Let me see that."

Frankie chewed tobacco. He'd already spat on his hand and grabbed some dirt, while attention was focused on Diz. He took the ball, in plain view, and rubbed around it, then pronounced it good. There was enough mud in the seam to make the ball sail. Diz had no idea where it would go, so he aimed it right down the pike.

"Ball," hollered Klem.

Diz walked toward the plate. "That was a strike."

"Get back on the mound."

Diz mumbled something that Klem thought might be "Catfish bastard." Klem followed Diz back to the mound. "What did you say?"

"Mr. Klem, you been guessin' all night. Now you'll just have to guess what I said."

Ernie had followed Klem. He conferred with Diz as Klem walked back to the plate.

"Three and two now, Ernie," said Diz. "What would Hubbell do?"

"Screwball."

"Well, then, that's what I'm throwing."

Ernie knew Diz well enough not to challenge him outright. "Sure, Diz, but . . . you don't have a screwball." Frankie and Leo ran in to powwow.

"I've tried a few. Nothing to it. If he's expecting a fastball, which he probably is since I'm the premier fastball pitcher in the game, he'll be early. And if he's expecting a curve, he'll miss it 'cuz it's coming in at him."

"Carl's deformed. He's a deformed man. That's how he throws the screwball. You seen his arm? It's like this." Frisch turned his right arm in ninety degrees.

"Yeah," said Leo. "You don't want your arm to look like that."

"Thanks for worrying about my arm, fellas, but this one time ain't gonna hurt me none."

Lombardi, Frisch, and Durocher all realized it was senseless to try to talk him out of it. They nodded.

"Sure, Diz."

"Screwgie, yeah. That's the one."

"Time-in. Play ball," hollered Klem.

Lombardi walked lugubriously back to the plate, followed by Klem in black. They looked to Gibson like a funeral procession. He was puzzled.

"You boys got a surprise for me?" he said, grinning. He tapped his spikes and dug in. He knew Dean was not going to waste one at him now. Diz didn't feel any pain till the pitch was halfway to the plate. Then it was clear the screwball was for King Carl. It was *not* for Gibson, who chased futilely after it with his powerful wrists. Not in time. He struck out. But Diz's arm now hurt as much as Satch's.

Mule crowded the plate and took a fastball outside. He was waiting on an inside fastball, and when he got it he hit it over the wall in left field. That was the only run they got, as Dihigo grounded to third and Leonard flied to right.

Eighth Inning

Down two runs, Leo led off the eighth with a trickler just to the left of the mound. Satch picked it up nonchalantly, hopped, and inadvertently found himself on the uphill part of the mound as he let the ball go. It sailed over Leonard's head, and Leo headed for second, spikes high, taking out Willie Wells, who fell over him in a heap, swiping him across the cheek with a hard tag. What endured more than the pain was the otherworldly gleam in *el Diablo*'s eyes, big as baseballs, upon being spiked, followed by a stream of drooled tobacco juice. Klem had run past the pitcher's mound to get a closer view, but it was clear that Leo was safe, whatever that meant under the circumstances.

Wells called time out and pulled up his leggings to inspect the damage. His shins were pockmarked. They looked like a connect-the-dots puzzle where the dots are dashes, a constellation of dashes, scars marking the orbit of a sharpened spike. He smiled at Leo and pointed. "This one is from Cobb. Put him out twice in one game, stealing. Since then he never played against Negroes. These two are from Oscar. This one is Hornsby."

Durocher was repulsed by Wells's treating his shins like the baseball version of Grauman's Chinese, where the Hollywood stars left their footprints. "You're one sick bastard, Willie."

"El Diablo, hombre," said Dihigo, coming over to listen.

Satch smiled. "He's got my autograph on both legs." Satch looked at Willie. "You want to show him the stitches in your uniform?" Satch looked back at Leo. "I don't know how that thing holds together. Every time we play, Willie's on the bus sewing up the legs again. He's got stitches going all the way up to the groin."

Satch and Dihigo went back to their positions as Frankie ran out to second. He patted Leo on the shoulder. "Heads-up play. Now, listen. Jackson's just going to take, so you're going to steal third. Paige won't pay you much mind. Let Joe take a few, then run. You understand me? Run like you stole something."

With the count 0 and 2 to Jackson, Leo couldn't wait any longer. He lit out for third like Babe was after him with a fifty-six-ounce bat and dived safely into third. Jackson struck out looking, bringing up Diz.

Durocher was dancing off the bag, making false starts to rattle Satchel. Dandridge gave a whistle, signaling Gibson that their play was on. "Wake up, Leroy, the man is gonna steal the shirt off your back," Dandridge said, feigning irritation. Then, sotto voce, to Leo, "He's fast, but he ain't too smart. Don't pay attention to runners."

Dandridge set up just in front of third. Satch ignored him com-

pletely and fired Long Tom with a lot on it over the inside corner for
a strike. Josh threw to third at three-quarters speed and Leo dived
in safely. Now Satch took a sign from Josh, without even a look at
Leo. Josh caught the low-and-away ball and threw to Dandridge, again
at the same speed. Leo dived in with time to spare. It was Gashouse
Gang baseball, and the team loved it. They urged Leo on. Henry and
Harry were both on their feet, cheering. Knowledge tugged at Harry's
arm, making a face that warned Harry that Leo was being set up.
Satch let Leo go farther down the line, not even looking at him.
The next pitch was a fastball high and outside. Josh gunned it as
fast as he could to Dandridge, who this time was set up one stride down
the third-base line. Leo knew this one would be close. He dived at
Dandy's feet, expecting the bag to be right behind him. He reached
around and felt nothing but the third baseman's glove knocking his
cap off.

"Out," yelled Klem. It was a play Josh learned from Biz Mackey, the
best catcher in the business. He'd used it time and again, barnstorming.

Leo was livid, and embarrassed. He'd missed the base by inches, and
he didn't see how Klem could possibly notice that his reach had been
short. He got up and dusted himself off. Dandy immediately gave it to
him. "You should wear them creased trousers of yours on the field. Nobody would block a base. They'd be afraid the crease would cut 'em too
bad."

Willie Wells and Buck Leonard laughed. Leo stalked toward Klem
and threw his cap down. "You're no better than a two-dollar whore!"

"Sit down, you applehead!"

Leo put his face up against Klem's chin, which protruded like a cow-
catcher on a steam locomotive. "You know what I'm gonna say to you,
don't you, Catfish?"

"I hope you like hot water, 'cuz you'll be heading for the showers any
minute."

"That was a rotten, fucking call! I was safe by a mile!"

"You were out then, you're out now, and you're gonna be out of the
game if you don't sit down."

Leo pulled on Klem's mask and let it snap back on his face. "You know, I'd let you have it on the chin but I don't know which one to hit."

"Hit me and I'll bite your head off."

Leo got right in Klem's face. "You do, and you'll have more brains in your stomach than in your head."

"That's it. You're out!"

"Oh, yeah?" Leo skimmed a handful of lime off the sand in the batter's box and threw it in Klem's face. Klem hollered in pain.

"Now *you're* out, you Catfish bastard!"

Klem turned away and bent at the waist, then snapped his torso upright twice, as if that would shake the lime from his eyes. "I'm blind!"

"Yeah, so what's new?"

Klem wheeled off and weaved vaguely away from the diamond. No one went directly to his aid because no one knew exactly what to do. And Klem kept screaming, "I'm blind!" He was seeing not stars but suns, red and yellow. He tried opening his eyes and it didn't seem to matter. He put the base of his palms back over his eyes.

Cool Papa Bell and Gehrig approached him from either side. "I'll get him an ambulance," said Gehrig.

"There's cops outside," said Frankie. "They can take him."

There were already cabbies on Landsdowne Street, curious about the lights from Fenway Park.

"Did you see that?" said one cabbie.

"See what?"

"The guy in pinstripes. That's Lou Gehrig. There's a game in there."

The second cabbie got a real kick out of it. "Baseball's over, knucklehead. Must be a fight. They just carried that guy out."

Inside the park, Leo kicked the dirt with one foot, then the other. He just looked at the ground and kicked it.

Diz threw his cap on the ground. "There goes the umpire."

Both teams had formed a circle around home plate. Ducky stepped between Oscar and Leo in case trouble was coming.

"Gotta be one of them," said Mule.

The players scanned the stands.

"Yeah, which one."

Pickings were slim. "Clapp is a cokehead," said Josh, who got his dope from some of the same guys Knowledge got his coke from.

"Ford doesn't know baseball from badminton," offered Diz.

"I don't trust George Raft or Harry Bennett," said Satch.

Babe turned and looked at Josh, who was already looking at him. Babe nodded.

"Where are they going?" said Pepper.

Babe and Josh walked in stride, almost sleeve to sleeve, like two hinged parts of an immense barn door.

"The judge," said Oscar.

Frankie looked at Satch, who looked at his teammates. Some nodded.

"Gotta be," said Satch.

Kenesaw Mountain Landis perched like the gargoyle of Box 27B, a shock of white hair blown into a meringue. He saw what was coming, and he sat more forward in his box, as if in some counterattack. He stared at them, parchment-like skin split by a crack for a mouth; the face of Andrew Jackson three years dead, in a black suit with a four-in-hand tie and a black sweater with a cigar-ash burn hole just below the neck.

"You gotta umpire."

"Son, I already am an umpire. I umpire the big boys. I put the likes of Rockefeller out. I don't do ball games. I'm the commissioner."

"Yeah, but you gotta umpire. It's you or that old man," said Josh, nodding toward the man on Landis's left.

"Dadblast it! You can't have Darrow umpire. He'll take the fifth on a close play, and he's no friend of the Negro."

"Clarence Darrow?" said Josh.

"Clarence Darrow," said Landis, derisively.

"At your service." Darrow tipped his hat, smiling at Landis's dilemma.

Josh kicked aside the squashed black Cuban cigar and sat down in the aisle next to Landis, putting himself below the commissioner's level, so as not to appear intimidating, putting the white-haired head between himself and the moon that momentarily was half obfuscated by the temple created by the commissioner's fingertips, as if he were holding half of the crescent of moon in his fingers, as if the crescent moon were the remnant of a cookie that some divinity had granted him permission to bite off.

"Darrow saved Ossian Sweet's ass," said Josh. "Oscar and Turkey helped collect for him. He'd be okay."

Landis was beside himself. "Okay if you paid him. He's a hired gun. The man doesn't believe in anything. He's not even a Christian. He's an atheist. How can you trust his judgment? He's probably an anarchist. He . . . he, probably doesn't even believe in baseball, for criminy's sake!"

Darrow slapped his knee and belly-laughed.

"The thing is," said Josh, shaking his head, "the players already decided. You the umpire."

Josh looked at Babe and Babe nodded. Landis sensed it coming. He leaned forward with all the menace he could muster. He gave them the Andrew Jackson top-knot scalping look, the Abe Lincoln trouble-in-my-yard look, the John Brown fire-and-brimstone look. But the sluggers had endured worse looks from bigots and shell-shocked pitchers. And Babe had a score to settle from when Landis fined him for barnstorming and made him come back begging. So now the Squire was soaring, like a buzzard, tails flapping in the Fenway fall breeze, feet pedaling air like a magic bicycle, as the players' features became clearer. Over the dugout roof, with a jolt to his armpits as the sluggers leapt with their judicial cargo onto the field.

"Shit, Judge, you ain't no heavier than a mascot," Babe said. Mule was mentally comparing the commissioner to Bullet Rogan. A brown Florsheim fell onto home plate as the Squire alighted off-kilter on the hard rubber. Some other part of Kennesaw Mountain Landis was strangely tickled by the deus-ex-machina manner of his transport.

"Safe!"

"Get my dad-blasted shoe."

Cool Papa Bell picked it up and tossed it to Satch, standing beside home plate.

"Out."

"You can manhandle me all you want, but I am not umpiring this game. It shouldn't even be taking place. I don't know why I agreed in the first place."

Satch looked at Raft and Lombard. He figured they'd gotten in as guests of either Ruth or Durocher.

"Look, Judge," said Satch. "We don't want to put you on the spot, but we ain't got many choices. There's Carole Lombard up there. Guess she'd know what balls is, but I don't know about strikes. And we also got George Raft."

Frankie stepped forward. "And I heard that Greenlee is at the Parker House, looking for Satch. I guess we could call him."

"Gangsters. Both of them." Landis sneered.

"There's one more guy," said Babe, "way back there in the eaves."

Only Babe had the eyes to pick out the man with the straw boater out of season, but Landis had seen the neWWsboy, the man with double consonants in his nickname and his last name, come in. He had a personal grudge against the columnist for something he'd written years before. He shook his head. "This game is canceled." Landis stepped toward the catcher's box and Oscar blocked his way, staring at him. "No. You're canceled."

Landis stared back with the steely blue-pellet eyes that had made Rockefeller and his houseful of attorneys blink. He'd stared down the one eye of Big Bill Haywood and hundreds of criminals. But this showdown was a mismatch. He was Billy Bonney to Oscar's Pat Garrett, ironically. This was a man with mayhem in his eyes, a man with racial scars and scores to settle, who felt Landis was personally responsible for his being kept out of the Major Leagues, a man with bottomless anger, a psychopath in pinstripes.

The Squire backed off. There was only one place to go. Josh held out the chest protector and the face mask, which the Squire promptly put on to hide his confused feelings, his embarrassment at being keelhauled to the field, but also his childlike joy in participating in what he knew was the greatest game ever played. The mask was loose, but not impossibly so. He objected more to the smell of it, the new perspiration. But he felt at home in it, behind something, making calls that counted. God's true emissary to the playing field. Behind the mask, he was smiling.

"So, I'm the umpire now?"

Each of the players was afraid to be the first to speak, as if that would

expose his team to the first judgment call of a hostile ump. Frankie nodded, eventually, as did Satch.

"I take that as 'yes.' Are you gentlemen ready to play ball?"

The response was immediate. Nine men reeled off toward their positions amid a few yips. They didn't get far.

"One more thing . . ."

They all stopped and turned.

"Durocher's out of the game."

Leo protested, "What?"

Landis took a step backward in case Leo had more lime. "Any further
incidents or unrestrained bellyaching and Dean's team will be immediately disqualified. Mr. Ruth, do you understand me?"

Babe nodded, hoisted Leo up over his shoulder and carried him to
the dugout.

"Put me down, you fucking ape! I can walk."

Frankie took off his cap and scratched his head. "We've only got
eight . . ."

Landis turned toward the third-base stands and waved. Frankie
halted his speech as Harry Bennett stood up in the dark recesses far behind third base. Next to him was a man in a jacket over a uniform, unrecognizable. Landis waved. Harry slapped the broad-shouldered player
on the back and he walked down the stairs. Was it the gait that gave him
away? The physique? Or did the Babe just have better night vision than
anyone on the field?

"It's the Beast," Babe said.

"Foxxie all right," confirmed Leo. "You can tell by the arms. He's got
the same problem putting on a shirt as I do putting on a rubber."

Babe smirked. "Leo, you wouldn't know which end of a rubber goes
on first."

Frankie looked at Landis. "You said . . ."

"I changed my mind. Under extenuating circumstances, special dis-
pensation can always be made. We have extenuating circumstances. You
only have eight eligible men."

"Three fifty seven minus one," said Diz. "Remember? Wasn't Gehringer. It was Foxxie."

The physique was now unmistakable. Jimmy Foxx had a leg for an arm. The muscles just popped all over him. His strength was as legendary as his home runs. His favorite trick was to pick up Bill Werber by the ankles, just one hand on each ankle. Raise him vertically off the ground. Werber went one seventy-eight. Foxx was the right man for the game, respected by the blacks. He played a lot of interracial ball.

"He can't play short," said Pepper.

"He can play third," Frankie retorted, jokingly throwing a scare into Pepper. He looked at Diz. "He can pitch, too." Then Frankie smiled. "DiMaggio's a shortstop. We'll put Foxxie in center."

"Mr. Dean, you're still up," said Landis. "Play will resume from its status when Durocher was called out."

Leo kept his distance from Landis, so as not to appear threatening. "It's all on one condition."

"You're not in the position to name any conditions," said Landis, feeling more vulnerable without the circle of peacemaking behemoths to defend him. Leo threw up his hands in a gesture of surrender. "I'm out of the game, okay. But I'm still the manager."

Landis saw no reason to quarrel. "You may manage, Mr. Durocher."

Leo walked back to the dugout. Landis called to Martin, "Pepper Martin, come here. I want to show you something."

Martin turned and trotted back, wondering what the hey the commissioner would want with him. Landis pushed back the mask and looked at home plate, issuing a spate of tobacco juice onto it from between his teeth. Pepper smiled and let fly his own spate onto the plate. The commissioner smiled. "I always admired the way you did that. I'd been trying for years to duplicate it, and it wasn't till the sixth game of the Series this year that I learned how. In my head, I was shouting, 'Hey, Pepper Martin, look!' "

Pepper put his hands on his hips and shook his head, eyes downcast. "Mr. Landis, you spit like Ol' Diz pitches."

"I miss once in a while, too. You go and warm up now. And none of that spit on the ball."

The game was on. Diz struck out but reached first when the ball got away from Josh. Pepper grounded to Wells to end the first half of the inning. In the last half of the eighth, Dandridge and Paige went down on strikes, bringing up Cool Papa Bell. Pepper and Gehrig were in close, even with two outs, and Diz was resolved to throw strikes and not let Cool on with a walk. Cool took two strikes down the middle and let a curve dip low and outside. He guessed that the next pitch would be a strike again down the middle, and put good wood to it.

The moment the ball left the bat, just by the sound of it, Jackson knew he was in trouble. The ball was going over his head, between him and Foxx. He put his two hundred and thirty pounds into motion. He had lost a little in every department except weight and smarts, but his arm had deserted him least. He then glanced over his left shoulder and saw the ball's trajectory. He'd been right. It was heading for the fence and would get there before he could. The only chance he had, he figured, was if the ball hit the top of the fence and he could play the carom. He also figured the most likely angle of the carom and headed for the spot, and looked up to see the ball pass over his head, and Foxx at full speed after it. Foxx noticed Jackson in his peripheral vision and wondered if Jackson was actually trying to beat him to the ball. Then he heard, "Yours, Foxxie!"

They knew Bell would be past second by now with no thought of stopping at third, with the old man running after the ball. But maybe Cool Papa would be too confident, and maybe he'd let up just a fraction of a step, and that fraction would make the difference, what Leo kept calling *intangible*, echoing Branch Rickey. Foxx got the ball on the second hop off the wall, almost diving, and ended up sliding on his right knee.

"Throw me the ball!" Jackson shouted. Foxx's instinct was to get up, turn, and throw, but Jackson was insistent. "Throw me the ball!" Foxx realized he could backhand the ball to Jackson, ten feet in front of him, already turned and poised to throw. He also knew that Jackson in his prime had a cannon. He flipped the ball forward. Jackson hopped once and never considered relaying the ball to Frankie, who was waving his hands on the grass. He knew he had about two-eighty to the plate, and he knew that fifteen years ago he could have hit it on the fly. Bell knew it, too. Jackson had had that kind of arm. Now he couldn't, and Frisch knew it, too. Frankie was on the grass, waiting for the relay, while Jackson saw Bell approaching third and had to make an instant decision—overthrow Frankie and get Bell on one hop, if he was lucky, or play it safe—go to the relay man, whom he could hit with a bullet. A lifetime of plays went through Jackson's head, all processed in a fraction of a second as the ball took its arc, a message from the Natural, from far right field. Frankie saw the ball coming high, higher, and he was back on the infield, backpedaling to get it, with Jackson hollering for him to let it go, but Frankie heard nothing. What he saw was the ball over his outstretched glove, and now Diz realized what Jackson was doing and he too made an instant decision. He saw Lombardi moving five feet up the line and he figured that Jackson's beautiful throw was going to be off that fraction of a degree—what would have been a perfect strike at sixty feet was five feet off at two hundred and eighty.

Ernie was a sitting duck. The way the Negroes played, Diz figured he was about to lose his only catcher. Either that or Bell would scoot right by him. So Diz intercepted the ball at knee level, knowing he was going to be approximately sixty feet from the plate and that the motion he had perfected could put a ninety-eight-mile-an-hour bullet at Lombardi's knees if everything went perfectly, if all the *intangibles* were in alignment. And it did—go perfectly. Bell hesitated a fraction of a step again, seeing Lombardi move back toward home and setting up to catch a pitch, and it dawned on him that Dean was going to take the cutoff and try to gun him down. He dropped into his slide. His foot pushed through the big man's mitt and across home plate, but the ball was already in it. Landis's heart was pounding as he made the closest call in his judicial career. He hoisted his arm and screamed, unequivocally, "Yer out!"

No one was more thrilled than Frankie. His long shot and his money-player had brought down the fastest man alive.

NINTH INNING

The sky was now magically clear, as if the stars above had come fully out to see the ones below. Satch's team was counting on his arm with a two-run lead. Three more outs was all it would take. The players were all business. No more horsing around. No taunts from Willie or Oscar. There was just a job to do, and each man knew his role in it. Eighteen men were jockeying for supremacy in baseball, the only game that counted in a country where almost everything could be "fixed."

Satchel's arm was saying, "Enough." The bones said it to the ligaments, who said it to the tendons, who said it to the muscles, who shrieked. The protest turned into a synchrony of throbbing. The moment the arm was at rest, the chorus of complaint recommenced. It felt best when the muscle fibers were busy carrying out their commands, so Satch was in constant motion, his arm swinging by his side when not in a windup or a delivery. Satch was saying to his arm that it could all be over in as few as three pitches. Give me three on the corners, three they will bite at, and eight other boys will take care of it.

Satch knew that Dihigo was watching him, and that he could relieve him. But maybe pride could call on luck, as if luck owed it something. Maybe the line drive would be hit right at Dandy or Buck. Maybe the Monarchs' lights would dim just as the pitch left his hand. Maybe he could throw "wobbly" after "wobbly" and the batter would be saying, *This one has to be a fastball. This is Satchel Paige.*

As if the arm had some back-door access to Satch's mind, he was saying to himself, *You don't need the Major Leagues. Winning is no ticket to St. Louis. You're making more money barnstorming than Dizzy Dean makes with the Cardinals. Don't throw out your arm on account of one game. It's your meal ticket for the rest of your life.*

In the end, arms are the good soldiers that do what they're told. Until they can't.

Down six to four in their last at-bat, Dean's team too was all business. Ten men all with the mien of Lou Gehrig. It was different for Carole Lombard, a welter of emotions in the last inning. John Henry would be at her rented house, and George Raft was at her side. She could throw up a bat between them and let them grasp it in turns, hand over hand, the way kids chose up, allowing, of course, for the final *V* of the fingers just below the knobbed end.

Babe paced around, itchy and penitent. No one paid any mind to his stomach disputin' him. He approached Leo, who hardly noticed him, staring at the field. Babe held his bat in front of him like a scepter, inspecting the grain.

"I'm feeling hitterish, Leo."

Leo smelled something like booze. He stepped away. "You drinking again?"

"No."

Leo gestured at Babe's knee. "Did you fall down?"

"No. I just came over to tell you that I'm ready. We're down two runs in a game we can't lose. Joe don't have a prayer. Let me hit for him."

Leo huffed. "Sit down, you big drunken galoot. You get up there and you'll windup like a top and fall down. Fucking embarrass yourself."

Babe didn't respond. Maybe he didn't hear him. He had that faraway look in his eyes, focused up over the wall behind the right-field bleachers. If a ball could be "looked" out of the park, Babe could do it. Leo stared at him. He still had that baby face, coupled with the contained ferocity of a motionless cat watching its prey. Babe walked away and sat down.

Satch tried to be inconspicuous about rubbing his arm between warm-up pitches. Josh noticed and trotted out to the mound. Knowledge Clapp might have told Josh that the laws of optics were such that if he looked hard enough at the large glass-blown bubbles of sweat that hung from Satch's cap, he'd see some inverted, convex image of a dark brown eye. Josh was distracted because by rights the sweat drop should have fallen long before, but it was showing the same persistence as Frankie Frisch's famous at-bat in the seventh game of the Series, the same stubbornness Satch had when it was time to come out.

"What are you looking at?" said Satch.

Josh was relieved when the laws of physics came through in the clutch and the drop fell, and he could honestly say to Satch, "Nothing." To which he added, "You sore?"

Satch nodded his head. "Hasn't felt right all night. Must have been that thump I took in the boat."

"It's up to you, horse, but Dihigo can pitch."

Satch shook his head. "I've got to finish. This is my game. Me against Diz. No one else. I only got three outs to go."

That was good enough for Josh. He jogged back to the plate and put on his mask, mumbling to himself, "Fucking coconut."

"Batter up!"

"Two walks and a hit. Tell 'em about Frisch!" Leo taunted.

Throwing marbles at flies on a wall, Satch learned humility—that it was necessary to have it even if you didn't like it. You could pick at it, like a scab. These thoughts Satch had as he picked the ball from his glove and gripped it across the seams and fired it at the imaginary fly knee-high on the outside corner.

And Landis called, "Ball one."

Satch alternated sidearm, underhand, and overhand, but his control was off. He ran the count to three and one, and Frankie hit a rope to left.

"You're due, Ducky," Leo encouraged Medwick. Ducky didn't waste any time, clouting the first pitch to left center for a line-drive single, as Frankie threatened to take third but held up.

Josh called time and walked to the mound. "You've got to bear down, Satch. This is your game, but it's ours, too."

Satch pushed sand with his shoe and adjusted his cap. He got Gehrig on a line drive to right. Both runners tagged up but didn't run.

Ernie swung and missed Satch's first two pitches. The third was a fastball on the outside corner that he took a full cut at, sending a slow roller down the first-base line that was a little too fast to be a perfect bunt, but Buck and Satch were indecisive. Satch started for it, but Buck called him off and Satch ran to cover first.

Seeing Satch go for the ball, Dihigo also ran to cover first. Buck fielded it fairly but hesitated just a moment, seeing two of his teammates converging at first. Satch got there first and took the throw, but collided with Dihigo, and the ball was knocked loose. Frankie was already around third when he saw the ball rolling toward second. Satch and Dihigo were both on the ground, and Frankie decided to go for it even before Leo shouted, "Go! Go!"

Dihigo was closer to the ball. He lunged for it, sprawling, and grabbed it with his bare hand. Ernie lumbered for second, shouting, "Get me! Get me!" Dihigo paid him no attention. From his knees he fired a strike to Josh. Ernie had time to look over his shoulder, as Wells's body language told him he was being ceded second base. He saw the ball come in knee-high at about eighty miles an hour.

"Out!" yelled Landis.

"Out?" Leo yelled from the dugout. "He was safer than a light switch in the Rebbi's house on Saturday."

"What the hell is that?" said Ernie, incredulous at the speed and accuracy of the peg.

"He does that all the time," said Willie, smiling. Knowledge Clapp couldn't help stamping his feet at the result of the knowledge he did not impart to Harry, who was now giving him a strange look, which fueled Clapp's paranoia even more.

Josh walked to the mound again before Joe DiMaggio got to the plate with two outs to go. Josh made it look like a general talk, not one that dealt with the rookie who approached not with a swagger but with only a modicum of the intimidation that most rookies would feel in a game this big, facing Satchel Paige. The 0 for 3 DiMaggio looked almost eager for the slaughter.

"Be careful with this kid," Josh said. "First time up he fanned on nothing but air. Then he grounded out and lined out. Every time up he's getting better."

Josh walked back to the plate and put his mask on. Satch wiped his brow. Frisch leaned forward to see if Satch was putting anything on the ball. DiMaggio took his practice cuts.

"That's it, kid. Look lively. Don't matter if you don't hit nothin'." DiMaggio swung and missed a fastball just outside the strike zone.

"Swing that old lumber. I need a little fan after Satch's heat."

DiMaggio took an off-speed pitch for a ball. "Shoulda bit on that one, kid. That's the slowest ball you'll see all day. Hey, Satch. Fastball at the knees. Eyes closed."

Satch went into a full windup where DiMaggio could see his eyes closed. It worked. DiMaggio froze up and took a nasty sidearm fastball low on the outside corner.

"Strike."

Josh could tell by the way Satch worked through the practiced antic that his pitcher wasn't into it, that he didn't want to fool around, even with a rookie. Not in the ninth inning. Joe shook his head and took a practice swing. Josh razzed him. "I thought you was a lively one, lively bat and all. Gotta swing the stick if you're gonna hit one. Okay, Leroy, sit this boy down." Josh then spoke to Joe. "Guess you know what's comin'."

Joe looked at Josh and spoke for the first time. "I know what's coming. And I know where it's going."

Josh didn't bother to give a signal. Satch knew what to throw. Josh set the target right in the middle of the plate. Satch knew he had to blow this one by the kid. Long Tom time. Cool as usual was playing shallow. Mule too was playing shallow for a play at the plate, and he was shaded toward center, thinking the kid couldn't pull a three-and-two fastball. It was a smart move.

DiMaggio had swung on and missed a lot of Paige's pitches, but all eyes were on him nonetheless, the bat whipping through the zone, fully extended and pulling the shoulders and arms around, twisting the torso and dropping the right knee to a baseball's diameter from the ground, then the green ironwood of his arms, twisted and knotted. Almost a genuflection. Josh was bluffing when he said to DiMaggio, "Son, you haven't got a *prayer*"—not with that swing that was the game's imprint of that *act*. If prayer was efficacious, the yannigan was already a holy man. In the dim light conditions that favored the pitcher, Long Tom was equivalent to one hundred plus. The quondam altar boy who loved the finality of the priest's concluding words—*Ita missa est*—which sounded ironically to him like "It was a miss," when he connected, was heard to utter one mundane, two-syllable word, "Bingo."

What sounded like a line drive was driven by topspin into a Texas-leaguer. Either Willie would make a phenomenal grab, going backward, or . . . here was Cool Papa Bell running, and running, covering an impossible amount of ground in seconds, and calling Willie off, but Willie thought that if any outfielder had a play it would be Mule, and Mule wasn't calling him off. Willie couldn't imagine Cool having a play on it. He backpedaled into a diving Cool and toppled over him, the ball bouncing off the fingers of his glove. Mule picked up the ball on one hop. Ducky should have scored easily, but he was a poor baserunner. He reacted late but slid in past Josh's tag.

"Safe!" yelled Landis.

Josh was irate. "Safe?"

"You missed him."

"Missed him? If I'd tagged him any harder he'd have a new asshole!"

Landis turned away. Lombardi had taken third, and DiMaggio was on first with Jimmy Foxx up. Leo looked at Joe Jackson on deck, then at Ruth staring intently at the field with one foot on the top dugout step and one arm across his bent knee, leaning on a bat in his right hand.

"Good hit, kid," Buck said to DiMaggio. "But everyone on this team woulda taken second."

Ahead now by one run, and with two outs, Satch called the outfield in closer, even with Foxx up. Satch was cautious, mixing up his pitches and deliveries. Foxx worked the count to three and two, then drilled an overhand fastball to center. Cool took it on one bounce. Lombardi took off, but Leo called him back. With two outs, he was not going to risk the ball game on Lombardi's legs. He already had a better plan in mind. Jackson was on deck. He got halfway to the plate when Leo called out to Landis, "Pinch hitter." Babe squeezed the bat, then did a double take when Leo looked at Nittols and wagged his finger, summoning the little guy. He whipped around and saw the midget picking up a sawed-off bat.

Oscar ran in screaming. "That's illegal. He's illegal. Bat's illegal!"

Landis ruled immediately. "The player is eligible. The bat is not regulation. Mr. Durocher, give him a real bat."

Leo rummaged through the stack and handed Nittols the lightest bat he could find, his own thirty-three-ouncer.

"Leo, what are you doing?" Babe asked.

Leo didn't respond. Nittols slowly made his way up the steps.

"You're not gonna let that little midget hit? . . . Leo!"

Leo stood with his hands on his hips, waiting for Nittols.

"Leo, I did it," Babe said plaintively.

"Did what?"

"Backflip. Ask Nittols."

Leo looked at Nittols, who gave him a look that he took as confirmation, and he pondered a moment. Only a moment. He looked indirectly at Babe. "The midget's up. I already put him in."

Babe cut menacingly at the air with his bat, scowled and headed toward Leo. "That little fuck is not batting in front of me!"

"Sit down, Babe. All we need is one to tie. You're the greatest, but the greatest ain't a sure thing. Nittols is."

Frankie shook his head. He didn't like it, but he'd given up the captaincy to Leo. He knew there was little chance of changing Leo's mind, but he had to give it a shot. He ran in and put his arm across Leo's shoulders. "Let's do it right, Leo. Put Babe up."

"There's two outs." Leo gestured toward Paige's dugout, where Bebop was sitting. "Look at that bench. You see what I see?"

"Yeah, I see."

"You think the coloreds would hesitate to use him in the same situation?"

"Yeah, I do."

"Yeah? Then why'd they bring him?"

Frankie had no convincing answer. Babe butted in. "That ain't no way to win, specially against the coloreds."

"You're right. It ain't no way to win, but it's better than losing, ain't it?" Leo said, using Babe's vernacular to sway and assuage him. "This way, we get one for sure. Then the bases are loaded and we still could win big. I might even let you hit for Diz and pitch it out."

Babe spat. "You can stick that logic up your skinny ass. I ain't sittin' for a midget." He strode toward the plate.

"Make up your mind, Mr. Durocher. Who's up?" said Landis.

"The midget."

Landis looked up at Ruth. "Step in that box and you're out."

"You can't call me out unless I make an out."

"I just about did. And I will."

Babe shook his head and turned toward the dugout. "Who else you got in the clubhouse—Lola the shimmy dancer?"

Babe looked back at the midget, who was dragging his bat out toward the batter's box. Babe remembered when Landis suspended him for barnstorming. He looked at the steely-eyed judge and knew he wasn't bluffing. He threw his bat against the wall and stomped toward the dugout.

Henry Ford had a grin as wide as the grille on a Tin Lizzie. He turned to Darrow with just Landis's vacant seat between them, and caught his eye, then bit into his boater, reminding Darrow of their bet. Ford then turned to the row behind him and gleefully asked Knowledge Clapp, "What do you figure the odds are that that man will walk?"

Clapp looked at Ford malevolently. "There's one thing in baseball you never bet against. That's Satchel Paige."

Chastened, Ford turned his attention to the field, with the remnants of a smile on his face. Josh walked to the mound, reassuring Satch that he could handle the midget.

"How do you strike out a guy whose strike zone is smaller than a baseball?"

"You can do it, Satch. Same way you cut the corners of a matchbook."

"This is a matchbook vertically."

"You just gotta cut 'em both ways, like when you're playing X and O's. You always put your X in the middle."

Satch shook his head and nodded toward Nittols. "You can put an X in there. Ain't no room for a K."

"You can do it, Satch. Sidearm sinker."

Satch stared at Nittols, who stopped outside the batter's box to check out the situation. "Maybe I can, and maybe I can't. I just don't like the odds. I got a better idea."

Satch uncorked his quick pitch and the midget didn't see the ball till it was nearly on him. Then it was a blur and all he could do was turn his head. Satch knew he had to keep it low in case Nittols ducked. Even a dirt ball might do the trick. But it didn't hit dirt. It hit Nittols square on the knee and knocked him down.

Gibson ran up the third-base line in foul territory to cover the ball. Martin was already twenty feet down the line toward home, and Satch was only a step ahead of him. But Pepper didn't like the odds of beating Gibson back. He pulled up. In the back of his head was the thought that the midget would still get to bat, and the game might be won. He headed quickly back to third. Gibson cocked his arm, but held the ball. He had no chance to get the swift Martin.

"Hit batter!" shouted Leo. "Put him on!"

Landis turned and glowered. He disliked the tactic as much as he disliked Durocher.

"Batter is not in the box. The ruling is no pitch."

"Then he balked. Run scores."

"No balk without a batter in the box. The throw is ruled a pickoff attempt."

"Pickoff? He hit the darn midget, ninety feet from any base!" shouted Leo.

Meanwhile Nittols was screaming in agony, writhing like a torched worm, holding his knee. "My leg's broken. Get me a doctor."

Leo ran up. "Why are you holding your knee if your leg's broken? Your leg's okay. Get up and hit."

"I can't stand up."

"Suck it up. This is what you're getting paid for. You don't get up there, and you don't get a dime."

Leo helped him up, but when he put weight on his leg, he collapsed again, grimacing.

"Use the bat," said Leo, "like a cane. Hop up there."

Leo helped him up again and he was able to hop, holding the bat as a cane.

"He can't bat like that. Gotta put the bat on his shoulders," said Satch.

"He can hold the bat any way he likes," said Landis immediately.

Nittols got into the batter's box, and Leo headed back to the bench.

Gibson was head to head with the midget, on his haunches. "Now, listen here, little man, most likely that knee is busted in about ten places. You gonna be in a cast for six weeks. Satch ain't gonna pitch to you and walk a run in. No, sir, he's gonna pitch *at* you, and when Long Tom comes in, even good hitters say it ain't nothin' but a zuzu biscuit. With that leg busted, and holding onto the bat like that, you can't duck, so it'll hit you in the head. Or maybe Satch'll take out your other knee, leave you crippled for life. So, is it worth it?"

Gibson punched his glove with his fist, then made a target right behind the midget's head.

"Can't do that," said Landis.

"I'm gonna tell you the God's truth, now," Josh told Nittols. "Satch
has never thrown deliberately at a man's head. He don't believe in caving
a man's skull to win a ball game. He did hit a guy in the head once, by
accident. They had to throw the ball out. It was flat."

Nittols looked at Josh. "What about the guy?"

Josh just smiled, and when Nittols turned to face Satch, Josh put his
mitt behind the midget's good knee and brushed it. "One more thing—
ol' Satch never liked midgets. Says they're bad luck. There's one he ain't
gonna have to worry about no more."

Nittols called, "Time out." He hopped back out of the box, looked
at Paige glowering at him, then at Gibson—smiling murderously, he
thought—and that did it. He was getting a hundred bucks, but it wasn't
worth it, not for a concussion or another broken knee. And if the sick,
quivering feeling in his gut was not enough, the wetness in the thighs of
his pants was an adequate reminder of what he was feeling. *Not for a
hundred,* he thought. *Not for two hundred. Nope. Not a chance.* He hobbled
back toward the dugout.

"Looks like I'm up after all," Babe said to Leo, picking up his cap
and pulling it tight down on his forehead. He had a vision of the piano
he'd pushed onto the ice in Sudbury, himself playing it as the ice melted
and it sank. He shook it off and sucked in his belly.

Leo looked straight ahead. "Hit one out, Babe."

Babe replaced Nittols in the batter's box. Someone mumbled, "Shul-
tan of Shot." Babe wondered what was meant by "shot." Was it a shot
glass, or did he mean that he was shot as a player? He shook off the ambiguity and went back into the thing he became when he was hitting, a
kind of ghost inhabiting a batting machine, in the same trance as when
chopping wood, bringing the axe down exactly on the spot he was aiming at. A study in concentration, a gull riding the currents, dipping a
left wing feather here, a tail feather there, testing the strength and direction of air currents. Undistractable. All irrelevant sensory input filtered
out. That which was too gross to be filtered was shunted to some wait-

ing room of consciousness, as he took his practice swings and stared out to right-center field. On its face, something silly, preposterous—this appropriation of the future path of a ball by will. But the practitioner was deadly serious. Wizard in his four-by-six chamber. Alchemist, mystagogue baptized George Herman, in his lime-traced mandala.

Tapping home plate with his bat, Babe felt like he was back at St. Mary's, with Brother Matthias saying to him, "What do you want to do with your life?" and Babe replying in the language of baseball, with its one phoneme, in different registers, as the ball left the bat.

Babe stepped back and hunched over his bat, adjusting his grip. Satch was struck by the broadness of the man. *Mano a mano* again with the great one.

"You the great Bambino?"

Babe looked at Satch, then at his bat, which he lifted as if to judge its straightness, like a pool cue, but Satch felt like he was looking down the sights of a rifle. Babe twirled the thin-handled, forty-four-ounce bat like a gunslinger. With no malevolence. More of an intent curiosity. An alertness. Funny, to Satch, that a man that big, that old, would have that cat-sense to him, a big-eyed alertness that belied his age. The man who thought nothing of striking out three times in a row, nearly falling down with his cuts, then coming up the fourth time, waiting for you to be careless just once, leave one curve hanging, throw one changeup that he would be sitting on, and it was gone. Then that bandy-legged trot around the bases. Game over.

Frankie looked out at Satchel and recognized the thumpless signal of a fastball, what Babe had preyed on for nearly twenty years. He took the big cut he was famous for. Satch was relieved to hear the pop in Josh's mitt. It seemed to him as if baseball had a heart and this was its beat.

"Strike!"

Josh tossed the ball back to Satch, who shook his head. "A man that can't hit his weight ain't no great hitter."

Babe said nothing. Pepper spoke up, "You hit your weight, Satch. What's that make you?"

"Makes me a pitcher. That's what it makes me," Satch said matter-of-factly. Babe was sizing him up, too. The tone. The walk. The body language. It all computed and came out as a weight. The lanky one was off the scales.

Willie Wells called time and ran to the mound. "Satch, I just remembered what Willie Powell said about Ruth. He likes to hit low balls, drop balls."

Satch nodded. "He say anything else?"

"He sticks his tongue out when he throws a curve."

Satch sneered and picked up the rosin bag. Landis called time-in. Babe refused to bite at Satch's offerings just out of the strike zone and worked the count to three and two. Satch picked up the plangency of the Monarchs' generator in the right-field pen. He heard the descant, the single pound of Josh's hand in his mitt. So did Babe. Changeup.

Babe's eyes were on the trajectory of the struck ball, and Satch could tell by the turtle-ish tilt of Babe's head that it was high. He could tell by the sound that it would be long. But he couldn't turn to look. His eyes were enthralled by Ruth's. It seemed in retrospect that the eyes in the baby face were fixed to the ball, and that Satch had no chance with anything in the strike zone.

It was gone, almost. The ball hit the top of the thirty-seven-foot wall in left field. It was not clear if it was bouncing out or back in. Mule was in front of the subtle rise, which was all that was left of Duffy's embankment, hoping to catch the carom. The ball fell past his outstretched glove. If not a home run, it was a double, by definition, a ball hit that hard, that far. In fact, the ball had traveled only three hundred and twelve horizontal feet when interrupted by the wall. Mule played the carom well. He had the ball and he had an arm. The runners were off with the pitch, and Mule thought he had little chance of getting Foxx at the plate. But Babe looked gettable. He had been watching his shot, ambling toward first, the lard in his belly and arse borne by scallion-like legs. He looked like a misfiring V8, sputtering into second, dropping into an ungainly, earth-punishing slide, his foot driving into the glove of Martin Dihigo, who had taken Mule's perfect peg.

"Out!" shouted Landis.

Foxx managed to score. Babe had driven in three runs. His team went into the bottom of the ninth two runs up. The rest of the team was already on the field when Babe picked up his glove and grabbed Leo by the arm so hard that Leo winced. "Dean is done. Let me pitch."

"This isn't 1918. You're a hitter, not a pitcher."

Babe was adamant. "I can pitch."

Leo scoffed. "When was the last time you pitched?"

"October, a year ago. I went nine innings against the Red Sox and beat them. I can beat these guys, too. They ain't seen a lefty."

Leo was torn. Diz was wearing down, and Babe made a good case. But this was Dean's team. He made the game. It was his showdown with Paige.

"You're in right field. They're waiting for you."

There was little chatter now, and no razzing, except from Leo, who was in the dugout. Pepper walked toward second and kicked the dirt, unconsciously staking out the border of his territory and communicating it to DiMaggio, who had never played with him. Joe moved up, then back, calibrating just where he wanted to play Willie Wells. Oscar was in the dugout. In front of him was an array of bats he hefted and dropped.

"Hey, look. There's a nigger in the woodpile," shouted Leo, and everyone was relieved when Oscar ignored him. A couple of innings earlier, Oscar would have gone after him, but this was one of those times you had to take it. Down two runs in their last at-bat. Oscar couldn't get tossed, which was what Leo was up to. Oscar lived for these moments. He was the money-man. He knew he'd never play in the Majors. This was his last chance to play against this caliber of opposition, to show the world who Oscar Charleston was.

After Wells dropped a perfect bunt that died just before Pepper could field it, Oscar came up, all barrel chest and spindly legs, like Ruth. He took two strikes on the outside corner, then inched closer to the plate and dug in deep. He wanted to go Ruth one better, put it over the wall, and he couldn't afford to take another strike on the outside.

"You'd best not do that, Oscar. You're digging your grave."

Oscar spat and continued digging. It didn't matter to Diz that this game was a one-shot deal, and putting a man on base was serious. He'd forgotten about Dandy's dogs. He threw him a Gillette. Oscar ducked and took a glancing blow off the top of his head. He went down and for a few moments didn't move. Then he scrambled to his feet and rushed in a crooked line at Pepper Martin, who panicked, shouting, "It wasn't me. It was him."

Pepper pointed at Diz, and Oscar stopped, confused. Dandy didn't loose the dogs. He knew that Oscar was just as bad. Landis rushed after him and put a restraining arm around his shoulder. "Can you see first?"

"Yeah."

"Then get on it."

Oscar on unsteady legs made his way to first, and kept one foot on the bag, shaking out the cobwebs.

"Pepper Martin, you chickenshit!" said Diz.

"Hey, I didn't hit him. You did. Take your medicine."

With no outs, the winning run was at the plate in Josh Gibson. Tough medicine.

22
THE SHOT

The curveball, some physicists said, was an illusion. The world itself, some philosophers said, was an illusion. Both of these camps surely were inspired by trying to hit against Dizzy Dean in the late innings of a doubleheader with no lights, or at night with lights as they were in 1934. It got the metaphysicians thinking: What if a ball was struck perfectly, but no one saw it after it cleared the third baseman's head—did the ball fly ineluctably out of the park?

Josh was thinking that the game itself was his foot in the door to the Major Leagues. If he hit one out, his whole wide body would sashay over the threshold. There would be no denying him. Satch kept turning the *caprelata* around his neck that Dihigo had given him, a version of *He-loves-me-He-loves-me-not*, "He" being some African deity Satch was as out of touch with as he was with the man on the cross, the House of David guy.

Josh tapped home with his bat. It looked like a two-dimensional version of the simple white schoolhouse in Buena Vista, Georgia, where the blackboard with all of its rules came tumbling down decades ago. If Diz at that moment had called him a Humpty Dumpty, that slang for a nothing ballplayer, he would have come undone. What he heard was

Satch shouting, "Over that big wall." Josh looked at it. It was, he thought, the closest left-field wall he had ever seen.

Harry Bennett was standing with his arms folded, a signal to the pen to get ready. He looked down and found it almost comical that all of the spectators in front of him had slid forward and were literally on the edges of their seats. Here, he was thinking, were the essential ingredients of a blues song—the coldhearted man, himself, and the woman torn between two men, one of them with an axe. In his heart Harry was a jazzman. *How I love,* he thought, *improvisation.* As long as it was played the way he liked it, improv on a score that he provided. Arms folded, the leader of his own band had given the nod to two solo players. *Take it,* James Atwood. *Take it,* John Henry.

Darrow noticed the sudden activity in the pen. What he thought he saw in John Henry and James Atwood was a queer version of Adam and Eve, exiled to a barren corner of the garden of Fenway. He imagined what he would do if he were God. He would let infinite variations of the game play out—time being meaningless—including the one where the girl falls in love with the old man, for a night, maybe, that infinity. Then maybe He would allow Himself to answer a few prayers. Maybe he would come down as a starling to brush over Gibson's shoulder and whisper, "Curveball." Oh, the fairy dust he could sprinkle into a rosin bag. Maybe He did. Maybe a little sprinkle on Gibson's shoulder in his last at-bat . . . Darrow's fantasy went out like a light as James Atwood quietly, quickly opened a duffel bag of light-generator tools, the same kind of bag that was used to carry the Cardinals' bats, and took from it a razor-edged axe. What caught his eye and struck him as blasphemous was the scribbling on the outside of the much-stained and used bag: *EAT ME,* done apparently with a stick dipped in the sludge of oil and grease. *EAT ME*—it was so foreign to the solemn task at hand. James Atwood Gray was so far from an obscene act, so empowered with solipsistic righteousness, he could easily, he thought, have struck down the obscene scrivener with the axe if at that moment he showed his face. Should Gibson clout one, James Atwood Gray would counter it with one of his own, bringing darkness down over Fenway Park, and no one would know for sure if the shot was fair or foul, in the park or out of it. Bennett's brainstorm. Ford's insurance policy.

But *why?* He'd already forgotten, when he asked himself the question. He seemed to be running on destructive instinct, a bizarre sense of righteousness, a distorted sense of social justice. *Why?* James Atwood Gray was as taken by the game of the century as any of the spectators. These were his heroes, and now he was prepared to end the great game. *Why?* he asked himself again. It was perhaps less an issue of black vs. white than of green. *Money* was the reason that came to him consciously as he watched Gibson take his practice cuts. But not money as Harry Bennett knew it. It was, in James Atwood's mind, booty. He could feel the doubloons and pieces of eight rain through his fingers and clink their middlin' clink—neither solid nor tinny. Money as a paycheck, as it came to the lumpen masses of America, did not interest him. His lucre needed to give off the sheen of violence. He needed to blunder into a coal hole and come up with a diamond. He needed to plunder. He needed to jack off into the face of everyone in Osage in broad daylight and make his escape in a Ford that had as many cylinders as a sow had teats.

In a similar showdown, Satch had psyched Josh out, walking two batters just to get to him for the crucial out. That time Josh struck out, on a fastball. Now Josh was thinking curveball and Diz was, too.

Once upon a time there was . . . and, *once upon a time there was . . .* John Henry could not finish his own story. It seemed to have gotten stuck. He recalled rubbing shoulders with the stars of the Negro Leagues, watching with them the steam and smoke rising from the gas burning on the infield grass and dirt, enraptured as they were, by fire, what fire could do.

Once upon a bed—was it possible?—John Henry reminisced of lying with Carole Lombard, so lightly it seemed he was floating. He had the looks and the background to become another Raft, he'd been told. As for technique—Carole laughed—just look at Gable.

Once upon a time, James Atwood slipped his axe from a duffel bag, and John Henry's dilemma dissipated. Harry hadn't double-crossed him, exactly. James Atwood was his double indemnity. Harry always had a backup plan. But John Henry was struck by Harry's duplicity. *Once upon a time* John Henry had crossed swords, metaphorically, with Gable and Raft, and now as he felt the heft of his own axe in his hand he knew he had to bring down James Atwood, if it came to that, if the crack of Gibson's bat started the arc of James Atwood's axe up over his shoulders. Then it came again to John Henry—that flash that represented to him Armageddon, but only the briefest intensity of orange and flame—his focus this time was on the fissure down the middle of it, the zigzag lightning stroke of black that expanded to snuff out the flame. It made sudden and perfect sense that Armageddon would be blackness—what there was before the beginning and after the end. Armageddon was here in the hands of James Atwood Gray. John Henry hefted his axe as if it were his turn at bat, Josh Gibson's long shot an eephus pitch coming down at him.

Diz let it fly, and Josh sent it back toward the left-field foul pole, a rising liner that hugged the foul line indeterminately. Thus began the contest of two mortals who never imagined a constellation named after them, this long after the patterns of the stars had been determined by the acts of heroes. The direction of history was from swords to ploughshares. The "drinking gourd" would never be configured into "John Henry's Axe," or James Atwood's.

The contest was as swift as the mating of a black widow and her mate. John Henry's blade clicked off James Atwood's with sparks that were seen by no one else—not only because they were small and fleeting, but because all other eyes were on left field, so that even the mayhem of men with axes went unnoticed. After the spark came the disfigurement, the realignment, of the arc of James Atwood's axe, from circle to ellipse, the path of a Dean curveball. The axe did not strike the cord artery where James Atwood had aimed it. It forced John Henry's axe down, as he tried to blunt James Atwood's stroke. It was John Henry's axe that severed the cord completely. Darkness came upon the stadium. It seemed at first complete. All eyes watching Gibson's ball saw nothing, and then, moments later, their eyes adjusted and they saw the familiar stars that were always there, just overwhelmed by the transitory intensity of the artificial light. The drinking gourd was what, and where, it had always been.

Star-crossed—Josh Gibson? The path of light past objects dense and dark and hidden was said to be crooked. *Black crook,* thought Diz, shaking his head.

Hours after the players and the seven spectators had left Fenway, the pigeons returned and the moon reached its zenith. In its dim, reflected light, the grass continued to grow. Slower. Ford would keep his money, and Bennett his job. In the morning, the Monarchs would collect their lights. The long flatbed trucks from GE Lynn, that very night, would surreptitiously be loaded. It would be years before artificial light would again fall on Fenway.

And the ball?

The ball is the story that escaped telling, yarn still unraveling.

23

THE BALL

It was a beautiful October morning, with a few slow-pitched, soft-ball-sized clouds in the sky. I was still in a daze from the game, and had nothing to do but take a stroll after ham and eggs at a greasy spoon on Boylston Street where I read the *Herald*, which had nothing about the game, and that made me chuckle. I could have been reading my own column, maybe the biggest individual scoop in sports history, but by *fide* I had to keep my big mouth shut. Of course I made sure to check Louella's column, but she was spinning the same tiresome gossip, from the same keyhole in the locker room. You've seen one you've seen them all, unlike a ball game. Anyway, I found myself out walking, and found myself drawn to the Fenway. There before me was the park, where a couple of guys were apparently being paid to pick up trash left from the previous night's proceedings. I gave the crew chief five bucks to let me in, and I combed the left foul line seats for an hour, looking for Gibson's ball.

"Something went on here last night," said the crew chief.

"Yeah. Something did."

I told the guys I'd pay them ten bucks for any ball they found. All we found were gumballs. I even walked the field itself. Finally, I gave up. It started to seem more possible that the ball had traveled out of the park. I gave the crew boss my number, in case he found the ball, and I prowled Landsdowne Street, outside left field at Fenway Park, looking for the one piece of evidence that might exist of Gibson's shot. This I realized was a long shot in itself, but on a nice sunny day, what else did I have to do but get in a constitutional?

I walked the street up and down, twice, and was ready to pack it in when two black kids, about eight and ten, were tossing a ball. The older kid, whose name was Pete, had no glove at all, and the younger one, Joey, sported a relic of the Cap Anson era. Shreds of leather hung off the thing, and the strap that should cover the back of the hand flapped in the breeze, as did the two pieces of webbing. The kid loved the glove nevertheless, and they were both enjoying tossing the shiny white ball with bright red seams.

I asked if I could see the ball, and they were reluctant, until I gave each kid a nickel to let me inspect it. I think they figured if they didn't take the nickels I'd twist their ears till they gave it to me anyway. The ball was scratched and cut on two sides, but had every other sign of being a brand-new Major League ball.

"Where'd you get that ball?" I asked.

Pete shrugged. "Just got it. You done with it?"

"How'd it get cut?"

"Don't know."

"You know this is a Major League ball?"

"We always get Major League balls. Sneak into the park and get the home runs. Ain't too many get hit out."

"You get this one in the park?"

"No. My dad gave it to me."

"Last night?"

"Don't remember when he gave it to me."

"Where do you guys live?"

The older kid, Pete, pointed to an apartment building two doors down. Joey pointed to a dilapidated brick building behind him, so it was no surprise, but still a heart-pounder, to look up at the second floor and see a busted window.

"When did that happen?"

"Don't remember."

"Last night?"

"Nope."

"Tell me the truth. That ball was hit through that window last night, right?"

Pete laughed. "Wasn't no game last night. Never play no night games here. Besides, no one hits 'em that far. My daddy measured it. Said it was around five hundred feet. Nobody hits that far, except Babe Ruth, maybe."

Pete was proud of his knowledge.

"If no one hits 'em that far, why did your dad measure it?"

"Don't know. Just in case, maybe."

"Did either of you see lights last night, in the park?"

"Yup," said Joey.

"What do you think they were doing?"

"Don't know. But it wasn't baseball. They never play night games. Besides, the Red Sox never play in October. And wasn't no noise like in a real game."

"I heard George Raft is in town," said Pete. "Maybe he's making a movie in there."

"Suppose I told you Babe Ruth was playing in that park, last night."

"I ain't no fool," Pete scoffed.

"Ever heard of Josh Gibson?"

"Sure I heard of Josh Gibson," Pete said. "My daddy says he hits 'em farther than Babe Ruth."

I smiled. "Who do you think hit the ball that broke Joey's window last night?"

Pete looked at Joey. "That's my ball," said Joey, pouting. "Had it a long time."

He couldn't look me in the eye, but then he had hardly made eye contact throughout our conversation. I could have kept up the interrogation, à la Darrow. I could have paid the kids a buck for the ball and another buck to tell the truth, but what kind of truth would it be—

bought? As for the ball, if it was Gibson's shot, the idea of it, for Joey, would be worth far more than I could have paid him for it.

But, Joey, if you're alive today and somehow you're reading this, I have just four words to say to you:

Say it's so, Joe.

HISTORICAL AND OTHER NOTES

A book I just read to my son was dedicated to those who seek truth. I would offer this novel to those who would settle for fiction or would see truth as a product of our imagination, which is to say that this novel works from a framework of facticity that gets stretched, but never so much that it is unrecognizable. So, for instance, while I originally had Carole Lombard playing tennis with Alice Marble, Sarah Palfrey filled in when I discovered that Alice was recuperating from a serious injury in the fall of 1934, when the game was to have taken place. Historicity seems to matter, but not so much so that I cannot countenance words factually spoken by one character being transposed to the mouth of another character, or to the same character but at a different time. These seem to me demands of an interesting fiction, but one that walks a tightrope, since historical fiction loses its punch when it strays too far from our collective, but neither unanimous nor conclusive, consensus of historical fact. So it becomes important that "the greatest game ever played" take place before Ruth and Gehrig leave with Moe Berg's squad to play in Japan and that all of the players who took part in the game actually could have, to the best of my knowledge. Virtually all of the major characters in this novel, and most of the minor ones, are veridical personages. The exceptions that come to mind are Ginger, Hap Keyes, Flerida, Immaculata, the pool-hall characters, and the handful of kids. Knowledge Clapp is based on an associate of Gus Greenlee who shared that nickname.

This novel was born of an itch in the groove of my middle finger, created by decades of scrivening. A few years of casting for ideas finally landed Dizzy Dean, the madeleine that brought back my father's stories of the old-timers: Satchel Paige, Heinie Groh, Iron Man McGinnity, Three Finger Brown, Shoeless Joe Jackson, Wee Willie Keeler, Wahoo Sam Crawford, the Iron Horse, Big Poison, Little Poison, et al. While they seemed larger and more enthralling than life, it was as much as anything else the poetry of the names that captivated me. In the fifties I traded a rare Mickey Mantle baseball card for an antiquated Red Ruffing and, I think, a Gabby Street. (I would have traded my glove for an Urban Shocker or a Van Lingle Mungo.) Rediscovering Dizzy Dean coincided with a growing fascination with the Negro Leagues, most of whose players I confess I had never heard of. Hard to believe that I'd gone nearly five decades without having heard of Josh Gibson, as if the Negro Leagues had been a parallel universe to the southern Connecticut one I'd grown up in. The novel coalesced when I discovered that there actually *was* a plot to kidnap Dizzy Dean, hatched by protagonists John Henry Seadlund and James Atwood Gray, who were executed for kidnapping someone else in 1937.

ACKNOWLEDGMENTS

I wish to thank my wife, Ellen, for her patience and support and my son, Aidan, for the long naps that allowed much of this story to be written. A tip o' the pen to Gene Wolff for his storehouse of baseball facts and anecdotes. I am indebted to both my editor, Brian Tart, for his clear vision and keen eye for the missing and the supererogatory and my agent, Mark Chelius, who has fessed up to being a Mets fan in Brooklyn. Thanks to Frank O'Hara for one riffed-on image and to William Empson for an egregious one. The gratefully borrowed, twenty-one-word description of Judge Landis ("parchment-like . . . suit") on page 384 was written by journalist John Reed, c. 1918. The following constitute a short list of works helpful for the historical research I did: Robert Gregory's *Diz*; Vince Staten's *Ol' Diz*; Gerald Eskenazi's *The Lip: A Biography of Leo Durocher*; James A. Riley's *Buck Leonard, the Black Lou Gehrig*; Robert Peterson's *Only the Ball Was White*; Murray Polner's *Branch Rickey*; John Holway's *Josh and Satch*; Lewis Yablonsky's *George Raft*; Larry Swindell's *Screwball: The Life of Carole Lombard*; David Pietrusza's *Lights On!*; and Irving Stone's *Clarence Darrow for the Defense, a Biography*.